PENGUIN STUDENT EDITIO

FRANKENSTEIN

Mary Shelley was born in London in 1797, daughter of William Godwin and Mary Wollstonecraft, famous radical writers of the day. Mary's mother died ten days after her birth and Mary was brought up by her father. In 1814 she met and soon fell in love with the poet Percy Bysshe Shelley, and in July they eloped to the Continent. In 1816, after Shelley's first wife Harriet committed suicide, Mary and Percy married. Of the four children she bore him, only Percy Florence survived. The couple lived in Italy from 1818 until 1822, when Shelley drowned in a boating accident. Mary returned with her son to London, where she continued to live as a professional writer until her death in 1851.

The idea for *Frankenstein* came to Mary Shelley during a summer in 1816 with her husband on the shores of Lake Geneva, where Lord Byron was also staying. She began her unique tale after Byron suggested a ghost story competition. Mary completed her story back in England and it was published as *Frankenstein, or, The Modern Prometheus* in 1818. Among her other novels are *The Last Man*, a story set in the twenty-first century (1826), *Perkin Warbeck* (1830), *Lodore* (1835) and *Falkner* (1837). She also wrote many stories and essays, and a book based on Continental travels with her son Percy Florence and his friends, *Rambles in Germany and Italy* (1844).

Hilary Jenkins studied English Literature at Oxford University and completed her M.Litt. on the history of children's literature. She has taught Literature and English as a Foreign Language in Oxford, India, China and Saudi Arabia. She joined the British Council in 1988 and since 1996 has been Literature Education Manager, with responsibility for the annual Oxford Conference on the Teaching of Literature, and editor of *Literature Matters*. She has also edited Jean Rhys's *Wide Sargasso Sea* for Penguin Student Editions.

Ronald Carter is Professor of Modern English Language in the School of English Studies, University of Nottingham. He has published widely in the field of language and literature studies, applied linguistics and English teaching. He is the co-author with John McRae of *The Penguin Guide to English Literature* (1996) and *The Routledge History of Literature in English: Britain and Ireland* (second edition, 2001).

John McRae is Special Professor of Language in Literature Studies in the School of English Studies at the University of Nottingham. He is author and editor of more than forty books, including, with Ronald Carter, *The Penguin Guide to English Literature*. He has lectured in over forty countries worldwide.

Penguin Student Editions
Series editors: Ronald Carter and John McRae

Other titles in this series:
Animal Farm by George Orwell
The Beach by Alex Garland
Cal by Bernard Mac Laverty
The Call of the Wild by Jack London
A Christmas Carol by Charles Dickens
Dubliners by James Joyce
Emma by Jane Austen
The Fox and Other Stories by D. H. Lawrence
The Garden Party and Other Stories by Katherine Mansfield
A Good Man in Africa by William Boyd
Great Expectations by Charles Dickens
The Hound of the Baskervilles by Arthur Conan Doyle
The Importance of Being Earnest by Oscar Wilde
Jane Eyre by Charlotte Brontë
Lord Arthur Savile's Crime and Other Stories by Oscar Wilde
Nineteen Eighty-Four by George Orwell
A Passage to India by E. M. Forster
Pride and Prejudice by Jane Austen
Sons and Lovers by D. H. Lawrence
The Strange Case of Dr Jekyll and Mr Hyde by Robert Louis Stevenson
Ten Short Stories by Roald Dahl
Tess of the D'Urbervilles by Thomas Hardy
The Time Machine by H. G. Wells
The Turn of the Screw by Henry James
Wide Sargasso Sea by Jean Rhys

Mary Shelley

Frankenstein

or, The Modern Prometheus

Edited by Hilary Jenkins

PENGUIN BOOKS

PENGUIN BOOKS

Published by the Penguin Group
Penguin Books Ltd, 80 Strand, London WC2R ORL, England
Penguin Putnam Inc., 375 Hudson Street, New York, New York 10014, USA
Penguin Books Australia Ltd, Ringwood, Victoria, Australia
Penguin Books Canada Ltd, 10 Alcorn Avenue, Toronto, Ontario, Canada M4V 3B2
Penguin Books India (P) Ltd, 11, Community Centre, Panchsheel Park, New Delhi – 110 017, India
Penguin Books (NZ) Ltd, Cnr Rosedale and Airborne Roads, Albany, Auckland, New Zealand
Penguin Books (South Africa) (Pty) Ltd, 24 Sturdee Avenue, Rosebank 2196, South Africa

Penguin Books Ltd, Registered Offices: 80 Strand, London WC2R ORL, England

Frankenstein first published 1818
Published in Penguin Student Editions 2002
1

Editorial matter copyright © Hilary Jenkins, 2002
All rights reserved

The moral right of the editor has been asserted

Set in 9.75/12.5 pt Monotype Plantin
Typeset by Rowland Phototypesetting Ltd, Bury St Edmunds, Suffolk
Printed in England by Clays Ltd, St Ives plc

Contents

Introduction

'And now, once again, I bid my hideous progeny go forth and prosper'
— Mary Shelley, 1831 Introduction to *Frankenstein*

The monstrous image of Frankenstein, of the mad scientist who is destroyed by his own creation, is one of our most popular and enduring myths. Most people feel they know the man and his creature well through films and images on television, and figures of speech, so it might come as a shock to find that the original novel is far more complex than the general image of it.

One of the most surprising things is the fact that Frankenstein is the name of the man, the creator, and not the monster. Another is that the monster is not nearly as terrifying as he is in the films. In fact for most of the book the reader sympathizes with him. Moreover, the man and the monster are not so different from each other, and it is quite difficult to decide which is more the 'hero' of the story.

Another surprise might be the realization that there is so much serious material in the novel. It includes discussions on science and education, lengthy descriptions of travel and landscape, and there are many literary references: all of which contribute to a moral debate which is not present in the popular cultural myth.

It is much more than a story about a monster. *Frankenstein* raises questions about the future and about the ethics of science, and about the responsibility of the individual. In many ways it was the first science fiction novel.

Frankenstein has always been popular with a wide range of

readers, rather than only admired by a literary elite. It quickly became successful when it was published, anonymously, as was normal practice at the time, in 1818. Even more popular was the simplified stage play, *Presumption, or the Fate of Frankenstein*, by Richard Brinsley Peake, the first re-writing of this much re-written text, which appeared almost immediately after the book's publication. Like all of the many versions of the story in popular culture, this first version foregrounded the 'other', the monster, by taking it out of context.

That it is still a popular myth is evident from the numerous film versions, from Universal's 1931 *Frankenstein*, starring Boris Karloff, through *Bride of Frankenstein* (1935) and *Son of Frankenstein* (1939), right up to recent versions by Ken Russell and Kenneth Branagh. Not to mention other similar or derivative stories such as *The Rocky Horror Show*, *Dr Strangelove*, *Blade Runner*, *The Terminator* and *Rocky IV*.

Why is it such a powerful myth and why is it so enduring? And what does the metaphor mean? The answer lies both in the context of the original text, and in the many critical books and cultural re-writings inspired by it.

Frankenstein is the most famous Gothic novel still read. In 1818 Jane Austen's *Northanger Abbey* and Thomas Love Peacock's *Nightmare Abbey*, the first parodies of the Gothic novel, a form that had been immensely popular over the preceding sixty years, were also published. *Frankenstein* is unashamedly in the Gothic tradition, and has outlived both of these parodies of the form. Like most Gothic novels it is set in dramatic scenery (largely in Switzerland, which is also where it was conceived). It contains horror, despair, suspense, murder, death, dreams and fantastic events. In its form, too, the novel is typical of its time, designed like a set of Chinese boxes, or Russian dolls. The monster's story is inside Frankenstein's story, and the whole text is enclosed by a series of letters by Robert Walton (on an Arctic expedition) to his sister (safely at home, and whom we never meet).

In several other ways it is a very unusual literary phenomenon. It was written by a teenager, and an exceptional one: she was the daughter of William Godwin, the radical thinker and novelist, author of *Political Justice* and *Caleb Williams*, and Mary Wollstonecraft, author of *A Vindication of the Rights of Woman*, which was considered equally radical, if not more so, in its day. She was also the lover and then the wife of Percy Bysshe Shelley, the Romantic poet, and a close friend of many other Romantic writers, including Lord Byron, and his doctor Polidori, who wrote the first vampire novel in the same summer as *Frankenstein*.

Into *Frankenstein* Mary Shelley put many of the key themes and issues of her day, questioning everything: the latest ideas on justice, education, the role of the family, the rights of women, as well as the Romantic themes of creation, ambition and responsibility to society. What was unusual was that she also added her own feelings and experiences. To create a story about a monstrous birth she drew on her guilty feelings about her mother, who had died giving birth to her; her own experiences of being a mother and of losing her first baby, and of being married. A close reading of *Frankenstein* shows how, far from being simply an adoring and obedient admirer of P. B. Shelley, as early critics suggested, she questioned everything he held most dear, including the rights of Romantic heroes, and poets, to pursue their obsessions.

The story of how *Frankenstein* came to be written has almost become a myth in itself. P. B. Shelley wrote the original preface in 1817, giving the impression that he had written the novel himself, and in fact all the early reviewers assumed he was the author. He describes the famous evening at the Villa Diodati in the summer of 1816 when the Shelleys, and Mary's stepsister Claire, joined Lord Byron and Dr Polidori for talk about science, politics and literature. 'The season was cold and rainy, and in the evenings we crowded around a blazing wood fire, and occasionally amused ourselves with some German stories of ghosts which happened to fall into our hands. These tales excited in us a playful desire of imitation. Two other friends . . . and myself agreed to write each a story, founded on some super-natural occurrence . . . The following tale is the only one which has been completed' (12.15).

Mary Shelley's own introduction was written much later, when she revised the novel in 1831 (and it is this revised edition which is printed here). She describes how after Byron announced that 'We will each write a ghost story', the three men all produced something. Byron wrote a fragment he later printed at the end of *Mazeppa*, P. B. Shelley wrote a poem 'on the experiences of his early life', and Polidori wrote part of *The Vampyre* (published 1819). Mary herself tried to think of a story that 'would speak to the mysterious fears of our nature and awaken thrilling horror – one to make the reader dread to look round, to curdle the blood, and quicken the beatings of the heart'.

Several days went by until she was listening one evening to Shelley and Byron talk about galvanism. This proved the inspiration, and that night 'my imagination, unbidden, possessed and guided me . . . I saw the pale student of unhallowed arts kneeling beside the thing he had put together. I saw the hideous phantasm of a man stretched out, and then, on the working of some powerful engine, show signs of life . . .'

Mary's introduction is of course yet another interpretation of the myth of her 'hideous progeny'. She distances herself from the tale, almost as if disclaiming responsibility, while at the same time comparing her story to a child. While in the past critics have emphasised the parallels between Mary Shelley's life and the themes of the novel, contemporary critics have explored the role of *Frankenstein* as a metaphor for our time. The themes it raises, of birth and creation, of parenthood and masculinity, of alienation and society, sexuality and the double, and of the natural versus the unnatural, are just as important today. The role of science in society, at a time when the issues of cloning, BSE and global warming are raising fundamental fears about the survival of the individual and the planet, is even more relevant today than it was in Shelley's time. A quick search on the internet reveals numerous examples of links between scientific fears and Mary Shelley's monster. For example a press release from the Friends of the Earth in August 1998 was headed: 'Stop Frankenstein Experiments! Challenge to Government on Genetic Engineering.' Genetically modified food is often referred to in the press as 'Frankenstein

Foods'. Frankenstein is a handy monster for bureaucracy too. 'The Medicare bureaucracy is a Frankenstein Monster that is destroying American medicine,' declared a headline in *Capitalism Magazine* in December 2000.

But *Frankenstein* is not only about science. The main themes of the novel revolve around the act of creation itself and the ironic fact that what Frankenstein creates is a monster. When Frankenstein announces the wonderful implications of his discovery of the secret of life he says:

Life and death appeared to me ideal bounds that I should first break through, and pour a torrent of light into our dark world. A new species would bless me as its creator and source; many happy and excellent natures would owe their being to me. No father could claim the gratitude of his child so completely as I should deserve theirs. (54.4)

Here he uses the philosophical language of the eighteenth century Enlightenment (light versus darkness) as well as the scientific language of discovering a new species. It is also the language of revolution, of Romanticism, and of paternalism. As Fred Botting points out, whereas *Frankenstein* projects 'an absolute and Romantic ideal of human unity',[1] this ideal has monstrous results. Frankenstein's creature refuses to submit to his creator's assumed power and authority. Indeed he even calls Frankenstein his slave, and in so doing he shows the irreconcilability of the creator and the created. Botting believes that this also refers to the role of contemporary fiction because the behaviour of the monster shows 'literature's refusal to be subordinated to moral uses and categories, a diabolical power that "cannot be made to serve a master" '.[2]

The role of the monster is also a political one. He is a kind of Noble Savage, born good as Rousseau and Godwin believed, but corrupted by his experiences in society. His 'father', Frankenstein, rejects him from the moment of 'birth' because of his monstrous

1. Fred Botting (ed.), *New Casebooks. Frankenstein. Mary Shelley*, page 8. Macmillan, 1995.
2. ibid. page 9.

appearance (for which of course his 'father' was responsible). The fact that no one will accept him as a human being then forces him in the end to become the monster. He is capable of love and affection because he falls in love with the De Lacey family. He is also educable: he teaches himself to speak, read and write, and he can appreciate literature, history and politics. In fact he is driven into monstrous behaviour only when he gives up hope of ever living a normal life, and, unable to forgive Frankenstein for his callous irresponsibility, swears revenge. He has been corrupted by the behaviour meted out to him, and his monstrousness therefore reflects society. What then is a monster? Not something that comes from outside society, but from within. It is the product of Frankenstein's ideals and ambitions.

The novel is subtitled 'The Modern Prometheus' and this foregrounds Mary Shelley's interest in the mythology of self and the act of creation. We know that she was reading Aeschylus' play *Prometheus Bound* during 1816, and that P. B. Shelley was writing *Prometheus Unbound* on the same theme. According to the myth, Prometheus created the world and human life, and was punished for ever by the gods for his presumption. Mary Shelley also draws on Coleridge's *The Ancient Mariner*, which has a similar theme, as well as the more Christian interpretations of Milton's *Paradise Lost* and Goethe's *Faust*. Harold Bloom thinks that it was precisely this image of the Romantic self that made *Frankenstein* so popular:

I am suggesting that what makes *Frankenstein* an important book is that it vividly projects a version of the Romantic mythology of self, found, among other places, in Blake's *Book of Urizen*, Shelley's *Prometheus Unbound* and Byron's *Manfred*. It lacks the sophistication and imaginative complexity of such works but precisely because of that *Frankenstein* affords a unique introduction to the archetypal world of Romantics.[1]

The narrative structure of the novel is constructed around the voices of three romantic heroes: Walton, Frankenstein and the

1. Fred Botting (ed.), *New Casebooks*, Frankenstein, *Mary Shelley*, page 13. Macmillan, 1995.

monster. Each talks in the first person and the point of view shifts accordingly. First of all, in his letters we hear about Walton's quest to discover a sea passage through the Arctic Ocean. The narrative voice then shifts to Frankenstein, who describes to Walton his own quest to discover the secret of life and the horror it brings him. Then we hear the monster's own voice as he describes his story to Frankenstein. He catalogues his corruption from innocence through to experience, ending with a plea for a mate.

The narrative voice then shifts back to Frankenstein, who at first agrees to create a mate, but then decides that this would be irresponsible. He thinks that a female monster would wish to procreate and the world would be doomed. When the monster realizes that Frankenstein will not help him, he kills first Clerval and then Elizabeth on their wedding night. Then he sets off for the north pole, chased by Frankenstein. The final words are Walton's after Frankenstein has taken refuge on his ship. But although Walton admires Frankenstein, the reader is not quite convinced. The subtle play of points of view throughout the novel leads the reader to the conclusion that such a pursuit of ambition combined with irresponsibility is equivalent to a parent's abandoning their child. This judgement is reinforced by the fact that Walton abandons his own quest: he listens to the wishes of his crew and returns home.

Although the novel is written by a woman, women's roles within the novel are passive and seemingly marginal. However, their points of view are clear. Walton has to justify himself to his sister, and she clearly disapproves of his recklessness. The whole novel is in fact written in the face of her silent criticism. Elizabeth Lavenza plays a similar role. Frankenstein cannot bring himself to tell her about his ambitions and what happens as a result. She is aware of his suffering and offers to release him from their engagement. She is right, of course, but he is too cowardly to release her. Frankenstein's fear of the havoc a female monster would create is ironic. He has caused the most damage by trying to subvert nature and create a child by unnatural means. None of the women in the novel would have been capable of such arrogance. And yet

Introduction

ultimately the monster came from Mary Shelley's imagination. In trying to demonstrate the dangers of science, of political unrest, or male creative ambition, she unleashed a monster that still stalks the world, and shows no sign of becoming tamed.

Chronology

Mary Shelley's Life

1797 William Godwin and Mary Wollstonecraft (who already has a daughter, Fanny Imlay) marry on 29 March. Mary Shelley (née Godwin) born 30 August. Her mother dies on 10 September.
1801 William Godwin marries Mrs Mary Jane Clairmont on 21 December. She brings with her Charles (7) and Jane (4), later called Claire.

1807 Godwin family move to Skinner Street, Holborn.

1812 On 3 January P. B. Shelley (recently married to Harriet Westbrook) writes to Godwin, whose ideas he admires, and becomes a regular visitor. Mary is away visiting friends in Dundee but meets Shelley briefly on 11 November.
1814 Mary returns home in May. Begins relationship with Shelley. On 28 July they elope to the Continent taking Claire with them. They return in September. On 30 November Harriet Westbrook gives birth to Charles, her second child.
1815 In February Mary gives birth to her first child, a daughter who dies prematurely. By August Percy and Mary are settled at

Mary Shelley's Times

1798   Coleridge's *Rime of the Ancient Mariner*.
1800   Alessandro Volta creates prototype electric battery. Maria Edgeworth's *Castle Rackrent* published.

1802   Humphrey Davy publishes *A Discourse, Introductory to a Course of Lectures on Chemistry*.
1803   Britain at war with France.
1804   Napoleon becomes Emperor.
1805   Battle of Trafalgar.
1806   Death of William Pitt.
1807   Slave trade abolished in the British Empire.
1808   Goethe publishes *Faust* (Part One).
1811–17   Luddite riots. Jane Austen publishes *Sense and Sensibility*; P. B. Shelley publishes *The Necessity of Atheism*.
1812   Napoleon's retreat from Moscow.
1813   Jane Austen publishes *Pride and Prejudice*.

Bishops Gate, Windsor. Claire meets Byron.

1816 In January Mary gives birth to a son, William. Percy, Mary and Claire go to Geneva in early May and set up home near Byron at the Villa Diodati. Mary begins to write *Frankenstein* in June. They return to England in September. On 9 October Fanny Imlay commits suicide. In December Harriet is found drowned. Mary and Percy marry on 30 December.

1817 In March the Shelleys, with Claire and her daughter by Byron, Allegra, move to Marlow. On 14 May *Frankenstein* is completed. In September Mary gives birth to Clara. *History of a Six Weeks' Tour* is published in November.

1818 *Frankenstein* is published anonymously at beginning of January. The Shelleys and Claire leave for Italy on 11 March. Baby Clara dies in Venice in September. The Shelleys spend winter in Rome and Naples.

1819 In March they return to Rome. William dies in June. Mary writes *Matilda*. In Florence in November Mary gives birth to Percy Florence.

1821 In April the Shelleys move to Bagni di San Giuliano, and in October they go to Pisa, with Edward and Jane Williams. Byron is nearby. Mary sends *Castruccio* (later *Valperga*) to publishers.

1822 In April Allegra dies. In May they settle near Lerici at Casa Magni, where, in June, Mary nearly dies from a miscarriage. In early July Percy and Edward Williams sail to Leghorn to meet Leigh Hunt, but they are lost at sea on the return journey. In September Mary joins the Hunts and Byron at Geneva.

1823 *Valperga* published in February. Second edition of *Frankenstein*. In August Mary returns to London with Percy Florence.

1824 Mary starts to write *The Last Man*. Byron dies in Greece.

1826 In February *The Last Man* is published.

1830 *Perkin Warbeck* published.

1835 *Lodore* published.

1835–7 Volumes 1–3 *Lives of the Most Eminent Literary and*

1816 Jane Austen publishes *Emma*. Invention of wooden stethoscope.

1817 Byron publishes *Manfred*.

1818 Jane Austen publishes *Northanger Abbey* and Thomas Love Peacock publishes *Nightmare Abbey*. First (unsuccessful) blood transfusion at Guy's Hospital, London.

1820 Death of George III.

1821 Death of Napoleon.

1827 Death of Beethoven.

Scientific Men of Italy, Spain and Portugal for Lardner's *Cabinet Cyclopedia* published. Most of the essays are attributed to Mary.

1837   *Falkner* published.

1838–9   Numerous essays for *Lives of the Most Eminent Literary and Scientific Men of France* for Lardner.

1839   Mary prepares and publishes an edition of P. B. Shelley's *The Poetical Works*.

1844   Rambles in Germany and Italy.

1851   Mary dies on 1 February at Chester Square, London. Buried in St Peter's Churchyard, Bournemouth, between the remains of her mother and father.

Frankenstein;

or, The Modern Prometheus.

> Did I request thee, Maker, from my clay
> To mould me man? Did I solicit thee
> From darkness to promote me?—
> Paradise Lost

Author's Introduction
to the Standard Novels Edition
(1831)

The publishers of the Standard Novels, in selecting *Frankenstein*
for one of their series, expressed a wish that I should furnish them
with some account of the origin of the story. I am the more
willing to comply, because I shall thus give a general answer to the
question, so very frequently asked me. 'How I, then a young girl,   5
came to think of and to dilate upon so very hideous an idea?' It is
true that I am very averse to bringing myself forward in print; but
as my account will only appear as an appendage to a former
production, and as it will be confined to such topics as have
connexion with my authorship alone, I can scarcely accuse myself   10
of a personal intrusion.

It is not singular that, as the daughter of two persons of distinguished literary celebrity, I should very early in life have thought
of writing. As a child I scribbled; and my favourite pastime during
the hours given me for recreation was to 'write stories'. Still, I had   15
a dearer pleasure than this, which was the formation of castles in
the air – the indulging in waking dreams – the following up trains
of thought, which had for their subject the formation of a succession
of imaginary incidents. My dreams were at once more fantastic
and agreeable than my writings. In the latter I was a close imitator   20
– rather doing as others had done than putting down the suggestions of my own mind. What I wrote was intended at least for one
other eye – my childhood's companion and friend; but my dreams
were all my own; I accounted for them to nobody; they were my
refuge when annoyed – my dearest pleasure when free.   25

I lived principally in the country as a girl, and passed a considerable time in Scotland. I made occasional visits to the more

que parts; but my habitual residence was on the blank and northern shores of the Tay, near Dundee. Blank and dreary prospection I call them; they were not so to me then. They the eyry of freedom, and the pleasant region where unheeded ould commune with the creatures of my fancy. I wrote then – ut in a most common-place style. It was beneath the trees of the grounds belonging to our house, or on the bleak sides of the woodless mountains near, that my true compositions, the airy flights of my imagination, were born and fostered. I did not make
10 myself the heroine of my tales. Life appeared to me too common-place an affair as regarded myself. I could not figure to myself that romantic woes or wonderful events would ever be my lot; but I was not confined to my own identity, and I could people the hours with creations far more interesting to me at that age than my own
15 sensations.

After this my life became busier, and reality stood in place of fiction. My husband, however, was from the first, very anxious that I should prove myself worthy of my parentage, and enrol myself on the page of fame. He was for ever inciting me to obtain literary
20 reputation, which even on my own part I cared for then, though since I have become infinitely indifferent to it. At this time he desired that I should write, not so much with the idea that I could produce any thing worthy of notice, but that he might himself judge how far I possessed the promise of better things hereafter.
25 Still I did nothing. Travelling, and the cares of a family, occupied my time; and study, in the way of reading or improving my ideas in communication with his far more cultivated mind, was all of literary employment that engaged my attention.

In the summer of 1816, we visited Switzerland and became the
30 neighbours of Lord Byron. At first we spent our pleasant hours on the lake, or wandering on its shores; and Lord Byron, who was writing the third canto of *Childe Harold*, was the only one among us who put his thoughts upon paper. These, as he brought them successively to us, clothed in all the light and harmony of poetry,
35 seemed to stamp as divine the glories of heaven and earth, whose influences we partook with him.

But it proved a wet, ungenial summer, and incessant ⸱
confined us for days to the house. Some volumes of ghos⸱
translated from the German into French, fell into our hands.
was the *History of the Inconstant Lover*, who, when he thoug⸱
clasp the bride to whom he had pledged his vows, found him.
in the arms of the pale ghost of her whom he had deserted. The
was the tale of the sinful founder of his race whose miserable doon⸱
it was to bestow the kiss of death on all the younger sons of his fated
house, just when they reached the age of promise. His gigantic,
shadowy form, clothed like the ghost in *Hamlet*, in complete 10
armour, but with the beaver up, was seen at midnight, by the
moon's fitful beams, to advance slowly along the gloomy avenue.
The shape was lost beneath the shadow of the castle walls; but
soon a gate swung back, a step was heard, the door of the chamber
opened, and he advanced to the couch of the blooming youths, 15
cradled in healthy sleep. Eternal sorrow sat upon his face as he
bent down and kissed the forehead of the boys, who from that hour
withered like flowers snapt upon the stalk. I have not seen these
stories since then; but their incidents are as fresh in my mind as if
I had read them yesterday. 20

'We will each write a ghost story', said Lord Byron; and his
proposition was acceded to. There were four of us. The noble
author began a tale, a fragment of which he printed at the end of
his poem of *Mazeppa*. Shelley, more apt to embody ideas and
sentiments in the radiance of brilliant imagery, and in the music of 25
the most melodious verse that adorns our language, than to invent
the machinery of a story, commenced one founded on the experiences of his early life. Poor Polidori had some terrible idea about a
skull-headed lady who was so punished for peeping through a
keyhole – what to see I forget – something very shocking and wrong 30
of course; but when she was reduced to a worse condition than the
renowned Tom of Coventry, he did not know what to do with her
and was obliged to dispatch her to the tomb of the Capulets, the
only place for which she was fitted. The illustrious poets also,
annoyed by the platitude of prose, speedily relinquished their 35
uncongenial task.

myself *to think of a story,* – a story to rival those which
ed us to this task. One which would speak to the mysteri-
rs of our nature and awaken thrilling horror – one to make
ader dread to look round, to curdle the blood, and quicken
beatings of the heart. If I did not accomplish these things, my
ost story would be unworthy of its name. I thought and pondered
vainly. I felt that blank incapability of invention which is the
greatest misery of authorship, when dull Nothing replies to our
anxious invocations. 'Have you thought of a story?' I was asked
each morning, and each morning I was forced to reply with a
mortifying negative.

Every thing must have a beginning, to speak in Sanchean
phrase; and that beginning must be linked to something that went
before. The Hindoos give the world an elephant to support it, but
they make the elephant stand upon a tortoise. Invention, it
must be humbly admitted, does not consist in creating out of void,
but out of chaos; the materials must, in the first place, be afforded:
it can give form to dark, shapeless substances, but cannot bring
into being the substance itself. In all matters of discovery and
invention, even of those that appertain to the imagination, we
are continually reminded of the story of Columbus and his egg.
Invention consists in the capacity of seizing on the capabilities of a
subject: and in the power of moulding and fashioning ideas suggested to it.

Many and long were the conversations between Lord Byron and
Shelley, to which I was a devout but nearly silent listener. During
one of these, various philosophical doctrines were discussed, and
among others the nature of the principle of life, and whether there
was any probability of its ever being discovered and communicated.
They talked of the experiments of Dr Darwin (I speak not of what
the Doctor really did, or said that he did, but, as more to my
purpose, of what was then spoken of as having been done by him),
who preserved a piece of vermicelli in a glass case, till by some
extraordinary means it began to move with voluntary motion. Not
thus, after all, would life be given. Perhaps a corpse would be
re-animated; galvanism had given token of such things: perhaps

8

the component parts of a creature might be manufactured, brought together, and endued with vital warmth.

Night waned upon this talk, and even the witching hour had gone by, before we retired to rest. When I placed my head on my pillow, I did not sleep, nor could I be said to think. My imagination, unbidden, possessed and guided me, gifting the successive images that arose in my mind with a vividness far beyond the usual bounds of reverie. I saw – with shut eyes, but acute mental vision – I saw the pale student of unhallowed arts kneeling beside the thing he had put together. I saw the hideous phantasm of a man stretched out, and then, on the working of some powerful engine, show signs of life, and stir with an uneasy, half-vital motion. Frightful must it be; for supremely frightful would be the effect of any human endeavour to mock the stupendous mechanism of the Creator of the world. His success would terrify the artist; he would rush away from his odious handywork, horror-stricken. He would hope that, left to itself, the slight spark of life which he had communicated would fade; that this thing, which had received such imperfect animation would subside into dead matter; and he might sleep in the belief that the silence of the grave would quench forever the transient existence of the hideous corpse which he had looked upon as the cradle of life. He sleeps; but he is awakened; he opens his eyes; behold, the horrid thing stands at his bedside, opening his curtains and looking on him with yellow, watery, but speculative eyes.

I opened mine in terror. The idea so possessed my mind, that a thrill of fear ran through me, and I wished to exchange the ghastly image of my fancy for the realities around. I see them still; the very room, the dark *parquet*, the closed shutters, with the moonlight struggling through, and the sense I had that the glassy lake and white high Alps were beyond. I could not so easily get rid of my hideous phantom; still it haunted me. I must try to think of something else. I recurred to my ghost story – my tiresome, unlucky ghost story! O! if I could only contrive one which would frighten my reader as I myself had been frightened that night!

Swift as light and as cheering was the idea that broke in upon

me. 'I have found it! What terrified me will terrify others; and I
need only describe the spectre which had haunted my midnight
pillow.' On the morrow I announced that I had *thought of a story*. I
began that day with the words 'It was on a dreary night of Novem-
5 ber,' making only a transcript of the grim terrors of my waking
dream.

At first I thought but a few pages – of a short tale; but Shelley
urged me to develope the idea at greater length. I certainly did not
owe the suggestion of one incident, nor scarcely of one train of
10 feeling, to my husband, and yet but for his incitement it would
never have taken the form in which it was presented to the world.
From this declaration I must except the preface. As far as I can
recollect, it was entirely written by him.

And now, once again, I bid my hideous progeny go forth and
15 prosper. I have an affection for it, for it was the offspring of happy
days, when death and grief were but words, which found no true
echo in my heart. Its several pages speak of many a walk, many a
drive, and many a conversation, when I was not alone; and my
companion was one who, in this world, I shall never see more.
20 But this is for myself; my readers have nothing to do with these
associations.

I will add but one word as to the alterations I have made. They
are principally those of style. I have changed no portion of the story
nor introduced any new ideas or circumstances. I have mended
25 the language where it was so bald as to interfere with the interest
of the narrative; and these changes occur almost exclusively in
the beginning of the first volume. Throughout they are entirely
confined to such parts as are mere adjuncts to the story, leaving
the core and substance of it untouched.

30   M.W.S.

London, October 15th, 1831.

Preface
(by P. B. SHELLEY, 1818)

The event on which this fiction is founded, has been supposed, by
Dr Darwin, and some of the physiological writers of Germany, as
not of impossible occurrence. I shall not be supposed as according
the remotest degree of serious faith to such an imagination; yet, in
assuming it has the basis of a work of fancy, I have not considered   5
myself as merely weaving a series of supernatural terrors. The event
on which the interest of the story depends is exempt from the
disadvantages of a mere tale of spectres or enchantment. It was
recommended by the novelty of the situations which it develops,
and, however impossible as a physical fact, affords a point of view   10
to the imagination for the delineating of human passions more
comprehensive and commanding than any which the ordinary
relations of existing events can yield.

I have thus endeavoured to preserve the truth of the elementary
principles of human nature, while I have not scrupled to innovate   15
upon their combinations. The *Iliad*, the tragic poetry of Greece, –
Shakespeare in *The Tempest* and *Midsummer Night's Dream*, – and
most especially Milton, in *Paradise Lost*, conform to this rule;
and the most humble novelist, who seeks to confer or receive
amusement from his labours, may, without presumption, apply to   20
prose fictions a licence, or rather a rule, from the adoption of which
so many exquisite combinations of human feeling have resulted in
the highest specimens of poetry.

The circumstance on which my story rests was suggested in
casual conversation. It was commenced partly as a source of amuse-   25
ment, and partly as an expedient for exercising any untried
resources of mind. Other motives were mingled with these as the

work proceeded. I am by no means indifferent to the manner in which whatever moral tendencies exist in the sentiments or characters it contains shall affect the reader; yet my chief concern in this respect has been limited to the avoiding the enervating
5 effects of the novels of the present day, and, to the exhibition of the amiableness of domestic affection, and the excellence of universal virtue. The opinions which naturally spring from the character and situation of the hero are by no means to be conceived as existing always in my own conviction; nor is any inference
10 justly to be drawn from the following pages as prejudicing any philosophical doctrine of whatever kind.

It is a subject also of additional interest to the author, that this story was begun in the majestic region where the scene is principally laid, and in society which cannot cease to be regretted. I passed
15 the summer of 1816 in the environs of Geneva. The season was cold and rainy, and in the evenings we crowded around a blazing wood fire, and occasionally amused ourselves with some German stories of ghosts which happened to fall into our hands. These tales excited in us a playful desire of imitation. Two other friends (a tale
20 from the pen of one of whom would be far more acceptable to the public than any thing I can ever hope to produce) and myself agreed to write each a story, founded on some super-natural occurrence.

The weather, however, suddenly became serene; and my two friends left me on a journey among the Alps and lost, in the
25 magnificent scenes which they present, all memory of their ghostly visions. The following tale is the only one which has been completed.

MARLOW
September 1817

Volume One

Letter I

To Mrs Saville, England

St Petersburgh, Dec. 11th, 17–

You will rejoice to hear that no disaster has accompanied the commencement of an enterprise which you have regarded with such evil forebodings. I arrived here yesterday; and my first task is 5 to assure my dear sister of my welfare, and increasing confidence in the success of my undertaking.

I am already far north of London; and as I walk in the streets of Petersburgh, I feel a cold northern breeze play upon my cheeks, which braces my nerves, and fills me with delight. Do you under- 10 stand this feeling? This breeze, which has travelled from the regions towards which I am advancing, gives me a foretaste of those icy climes. Inspirited by this wind of promise, my day dreams become more fervent and vivid. I try in vain to be persuaded that the pole is the seat of frost and desolation; it ever presents itself to my 15 imagination as the region of beauty and delight. There, Margaret, the sun is for ever visible, its broad disk just skirting the horizon, and diffusing a perpetual splendour. There – for with your leave, my sister, I will put some trust in preceding navigators – there snow and frost are banished; and, sailing over a calm sea, we may be 20 wafted to a land surpassing in wonders and in beauty every region hitherto discovered on the habitable globe. Its productions and features may be without example, as the phenomena of the heavenly bodies undoubtedly are in those undiscovered solitudes.

What may not be expected in a country of eternal light? I may there
discover the wondrous power which attracts the needle; and may
regulate a thousand celestial observations, that require only this
voyage to render their seeming eccentricities consistent for ever. I
5 shall satiate my ardent curiosity with the sight of a part of the world
never before visited, and may tread a land never before imprinted
by the foot of man. These are my enticements, and they are
sufficient to conquer all fear of danger or death, and to induce me
to commence this laborious voyage with the joy a child feels when
10 he embarks in a little boat, with his holiday mates, on an expedition
of discovery up his native river. But, supposing all these conjectures
to be false, you cannot contest the inestimable benefit which I shall
confer on all mankind to the last generation, by discovering a
passage near the pole to those countries, to reach which at present
15 so many months are requisite; or by ascertaining the secret of
the magnet, which, if at all possible, can only be effected by an
undertaking such as mine.

These reflections have dispelled the agitation with which I began
my letter, and I feel my heart glow with an enthusiasm which
20 elevates me to heaven; for nothing contributes so much to tran-
quillize the mind as a steady purpose – a point on which the soul
may fix its intellectual eye. This expedition has been the favourite
dream of my early years. I have read with ardour the accounts of
the various voyages which have been made in the prospect of
25 arriving at the North Pacific Ocean through the seas which surround the pole. You may remember that a history of all the voyages
made for purposes of discovery composed the whole of our good
uncle Thomas's library. My education was neglected, yet I was
passionately fond of reading. These volumes were my study day
30 and night, and my familiarity with them increased that regret
which I had felt, as a child, on learning that my father's dying
injunction had forbidden my uncle to allow me to embark in a
seafaring life.

These visions faded when I perused, for the first time, those
35 poets whose effusions, entranced my soul, and lifted it to heaven.
I also became a poet, and for one year lived in a Paradise of my

own creation; I imagined that I also might obtain a niche in the temple where the names of Homer and Shakespeare are consecrated. You are well acquainted with my failure, and how heavily I bore the disappointment. But just at that time I inherited the fortune of my cousin, and my thoughts were turned into the channel   5
of their earlier bent.

Six years have passed since I resolved on my present undertaking. I can, even now, remember the hour from which I dedicated myself to this great enterprise. I commenced by inuring my body to hardship. I accompanied the whale-fishers on several expeditions   10
to the North Sea; I voluntarily endured cold, famine, thirst, and want of sleep; I often worked harder than the common sailors during the day, and devoted my nights to the study of mathematics, the theory of medicine, and those branches of physical science from which a naval adventure might derive the greatest practical   15
advantage. Twice I actually hired myself as an under-mate in a Greenland whaler, and acquitted myself to admiration. I must own I felt a little proud, when my captain offered me the second dignity in the vessel and intreated me to remain with the greatest earnestness so valuable did he consider my services.   20

And now, dear Margaret, do I not deserve to accomplish some great purpose? My life might have been passed in ease and luxury; but I preferred glory to every enticement that wealth placed in my path. Oh, that some encouraging voice would answer in the affirmative! My courage and my resolution is firm; but my hopes   25
fluctuate, and my spirits are often depressed. I am about to proceed on a long and difficult voyage, the emergencies of which will demand all my fortitude: I am required not only to raise the spirits of others, but sometimes to sustain my own, when theirs are failing.

This is the most favourable period for travelling in Russia. They   30
fly quickly over the snow in their sledges; the motion is pleasant, and, in my opinion, far more agreeable than that of an English stage-coach. The cold is not excessive, if you are wrapped in furs – a dress which I have already adopted; for there is a great difference between walking the deck and remaining seated motionless for   35
hours, when no exercise prevents the blood from actually freezing

in your veins. I have no ambition to lose my life on the post-road between St Petersburgh and Archangel.

I shall depart for the latter town in a fortnight or three weeks; and my intention is to hire a ship there, which can easily be done
5 by paying the insurance for the owner, and to engage as many sailors as I think necessary among those who are accustomed to the whale-fishing. I do not intend to sail until the month of June; and when shall I return? Ah, dear sister, how can I answer this question? If I succeed, many, many months, perhaps years, will
10 pass before you and I may meet. If I fail, you will see me again soon, or never.

Farewell, my dear, excellent Margaret. Heaven shower down blessings on you, and save me, that I may again and again testify my gratitude for all your love and kindness.
15   Your affectionate brother,
                                                R. WALTON

Letter II

How slowly the time passes here, encompassed as I am by frost
and snow! yet a second step is taken towards my enterprise. I have
hired a vessel, and am occupied in collecting my sailors; those
whom I have already engaged, appear to be men on whom I can
depend and are certainly possessed of dauntless courage.   5

But I have one want which I have never yet been able to satisfy;
and the absence of the object of which I now feel as a most severe
evil. I have no friend, Margaret: when I am glowing with the
enthusiasm of success, there will be none to participate my joy; if
I am assailed by disappointment, no one will endeavour to sustain   10
me in dejection. I shall commit my thoughts to paper, it is true;
but that is a poor medium for the communication of feeling. I
desire the company of a man who could sympathise with me; whose
eyes would reply to mine. You may deem me romantic, my dear
sister, but I bitterly feel the want of a friend. I have no one near   15
me, gentle yet courageous, possessed of a cultivated as well as of a
capacious mind, whose tastes are like my own, to approve or amend
my plans. How would such a friend repair the faults of your
poor brother! I am too ardent in execution, and too impatient of
difficulties. But it is a still greater evil to me that I am self-educated: 20
for the first fourteen years of my life I ran wild on a common, and
read nothing but our uncle Thomas's books of voyages. At that
age I became acquainted with the celebrated poets of our own
country; but it was only when it had ceased to be in my power to

derive its most important benefits from such a conviction, that I perceived the necessity of becoming acquainted with more languages than that of my native country. Now I am twenty-eight and am in reality more illiterate than many schoolboys of fifteen. It is
5 true that I have thought more, and that my day dreams are more extended and magnificent, but they want (as the painters call it) *keeping*; and I greatly need a friend who would have sense enough not to despise me as romantic, and affection enough for me to endeavour to regulate my mind.

10   Well, these are useless complaints; I shall certainly find no friend on the wide ocean, nor even here in Archangel, among merchants and seamen. Yet some feelings, unallied to the dross of human nature, beat even in these rugged bosoms. My lieutenant, for instance, is a man of wonderful courage and enterprise; he is madly
15 desirous of glory: or rather, to word my phrase more characteristically, of advancement in his profession. He is an Englishman, and in the midst of national and professional prejudices, unsoftened by cultivation, retains some of the noblest endowments of humanity. I first became acquainted with him on board a whale vessel: finding
20 that he was unemployed in this city, I easily engaged him to assist in my enterprise.

The master is a person of an excellent disposition, and is remarkable in the ship for his gentleness and the mildness of his discipline. This circumstance, added to his well-known integrity and dauntless
25 courage, made me very desirous to engage him. A youth passed in solitude, my best years spent under your gentle and feminine fosterage, has so refined the groundwork of my character that I cannot overcome an intense distaste to the usual brutality exercised on board ship: I have never believed it to be necessary, and when
30 I heard of a mariner equally noted for his kindliness of heart and the respect and obedience paid to him by his crew, I felt myself peculiarly fortunate in being able to secure his services. I heard of him first in rather a romantic manner, from a lady who owes to him the happiness of her life. This, briefly, is his story. Some years
35 ago he loved a young Russian lady of moderate fortune; and having amassed a considerable sum in prize-money, the father of the girl

consented to the match. He saw his mistress once before the destined ceremony; but she was bathed in tears, and, throwing herself at his feet, intreated him to spare her, confessing at the time that she loved another, but that he was poor, and that her father would never consent to the union. My generous friend reassured 5 the supplicant, and on being informed of the name of her lover, instantly abandoned his pursuit. He had already bought a farm with his money, on which he had designed to pass the remainder of his life; but he bestowed the whole on his rival, together with the remains of his prize-money to purchase stock, and then himself 10 solicited the young woman's father to consent to her marriage with her lover. But the old man decidedly refused, thinking himself bound in honour to my friend; who, when he found the father inexorable, quitted his country, nor returned until he heard that his former mistress was married according to her inclinations. 15 'What a noble fellow!' you will exclaim. He is so; but then he is wholly uneducated: he is as silent as a Turk, and a kind of ignorant carelessness attends him, which, while it renders his conduct the more astonishing, detracts from the interest and sympathy which otherwise he would command. 20

Yet do not suppose, because I complain a little, or because I can conceive a consolation for my toils which I may never know, that I am wavering in my resolutions. Those are as fixed as fate, and my voyage is only now delayed until the weather shall permit my embarkation. The winter has been dreadfully severe, but the spring 25 promises well, and it is considered as a remarkably early season; so that perhaps I may sail sooner than I expected. I shall do nothing rashly: you know me sufficiently to confide in my prudence and considerateness whenever the safety of others is committed to my care. 30

I cannot describe to you my sensations on the near prospect of my undertaking. It is impossible to communicate to you a conception of the trembling sensation, half pleasurable and half fearful, with which I am preparing to depart. I am going to unexplored regions to 'the land of mist and snow'; but I shall kill no albatross, 35 therefore do not be alarmed for my safety, or if I should come back

to you as worn and woeful as the 'Ancient Mariner'. You will smile
at my allusion; but I will disclose a secret. I have often attributed
my attachment to, my passionate enthusiasm for, the dangerous
mysteries of ocean, to that production of the most imaginative of
5 modern poets. There is something at work in my soul, which I
do not understand. I am practically industrious – painstaking; a
workman to execute with perseverance and labour: – but besides
this, there is a love for the marvellous, a belief in the marvellous,
intertwined in all my projects, which hurries me out of the common
10 pathways of men, even to the wild sea and unvisited regions I am
about to explore.

But to return to dearer considerations. Shall I meet you again,
after having traversed immense seas, and returned by the most
southern cape of Africa or America? I dare not expect such success,
15 yet I cannot bear to look on the reverse of the picture. Continue
for the present to write to me by every opportunity: I may receive
your letters on some occasions when I need them most to support
my spirits. I love you very tenderly. Remember me with affection,
should you never hear from me again.

20   Your affectionate brother,
                                        ROBERT WALTON

Letter III

July 7th, 17–

MY DEAR SISTER,

I write a few lines in haste to say that I am safe – and well advanced on my voyage. This letter will reach England by a merchantman now on its homeward voyage from Archangel; more fortunate than I, who may not see my native land, perhaps, for many years. I am, however, in good spirits: my men are bold, and 5 apparently firm of purpose, nor do the floating sheets of ice that continually pass us, indicating the dangers of the region towards which we are advancing, appear to dismay them. We have already reached a very high latitude; but it is the height of summer, and although not so warm as in England, the southern gales, which 10 blow us speedily towards those shores which I so ardently desire to attain, breathe a degree of renovating warmth which I had not expected.

No incidents have hitherto befallen us that would make a figure in a letter. One or two stiff gales, and the springing of a leak, 15 are accidents which experienced navigators scarcely remember to record; and I shall be well content if nothing worse happen to us during our voyage.

Adieu, my dear Margaret. Be assured, that for my own sake, as well as yours, I will not rashly encounter danger. I will be cool, 20 persevering and prudent.

But success *shall* crown my endeavours. Wherefore not? Thus far I have gone, tracing a secure way over the pathless seas: the very stars themselves being witnesses and testimonies of my triumph. Why not still proceed over the untamed yet obedient element? What can stop the determined heart and resolved will of man?

5   My swelling heart involuntarily pours itself out thus. But I must finish. Heaven bless my beloved sister!

R.W.

Letter IV

To Mrs Saville, England

August 5th, 17–

So strange an accident has happened to us that I cannot forbear recording it, although it is very probable that you will see me before these papers can come into your possession.

Last Monday (July 31st) we were nearly surrounded by ice, which closed in the ship on all sides, scarcely leaving her the 5 sea-room in which she floated. Our situation was somewhat dangerous, especially as we were compassed round by a very thick fog. We accordingly lay to, hoping that some change would take place in the atmosphere and weather.

About two o'clock the mist cleared away, and we beheld, 10 stretched out in every direction, vast and irregular plains of ice, which seemed to have no end. Some of my comrades groaned, and my own mind began to grow watchful with anxious thoughts, when a strange sight suddenly attracted our attention, and diverted our solicitude from our own situations. We perceived a low carriage, 15 fixed on a sledge and drawn by dogs, pass on towards the north, at the distance of half a mile; a being which had the shape of a man, but apparently of gigantic stature, sat in the sledge, and guided the dogs. We watched the rapid progress of the traveller with our telescopes until he was lost among the distant inequalities of the 20 ice.

This appearance excited our unqualified wonder. We were, as we believed, many hundred miles from any land; but this apparition seemed to denote that it was not, in reality, so distant as we had supposed. Shut in, however, by ice, it was impossible to follow his track, which we had observed with the greatest attention.

About two hours after this occurrence we heard the ground sea; and before night the ice broke, and freed our ship. We, however, 5 lay to until the morning, fearing to encounter in the dark those large loose masses which float about after the breaking up of the ice. I profited of this time to rest for a few hours.

In the morning, however, as soon as it was light, I went upon deck and found all the sailors busy on one side of the vessel, 10 apparently talking to some one in the sea. It was, in fact, a sledge, like that we had seen before, which had drifted towards us in the night on a large fragment of ice. Only one dog remained alive; but there was a human being within it, whom the sailors were persuading to enter the vessel. He was not as the other traveller 15 seemed to be, a savage inhabitant of some undiscovered island, but an European. When I appeared on deck, the master said, 'Here is our captain, and he will not allow you to perish on the open sea.'

On perceiving me, the stranger addressed me in English, although with a foreign accent. 'Before I come on board your 20 vessel,' said he, 'will you have the kindness to inform me whither you are bound?'

You may conceive my astonishment on hearing such a question addressed to me from a man on the brink of destruction and to whom I should have supposed that my vessel would have been a 25 resource which he would not have exchanged for the most precious wealth the earth can afford. I replied, however, that we were on a voyage of discovery towards the northern pole.

Upon hearing this he appeared satisfied, and consented to come on board. Good God! Margaret, if you had seen the man who thus 30 capitulated for his safety, your surprise would have been boundless. His limbs were nearly frozen, and his body dreadfully emaciated by fatigue and suffering. I never saw a man in so wretched a condition. We attempted to carry him into the cabin; but as soon as he had quitted the fresh air, he fainted. We accordingly brought 35 him back to the deck, and restored him to animation by rubbing him with brandy and forcing him to swallow a small quantity. As soon as he showed signs of life, we wrapped him up in blankets and placed him near the chimney of the kitchen stove. By slow degrees he recovered, and ate a little soup which restored him wonderfully.

Two days passed in this manner before he was able to speak; 5 and I often feared that his sufferings had deprived him of understanding. When he had in some measure recovered, I removed him to my own cabin, and attended on him as much as my duty would permit. I never saw a more interesting creature; his eyes have generally an expression of wildness, and even madness, but there 10 are moments when, if any one performs an act of kindness towards him or does him any the most trifling service, his whole countenance is lighted up, as it were, with a beam of benevolence and sweetness that I never saw equalled. But he is generally melancholy and despairing; and sometimes he gnashes his teeth; as if impatient 15 of the weight of woes that oppresses him.

When my guest was a little recovered, I had great trouble to keep off the men, who wished to ask him a thousand questions; but I would not allow him to be tormented by their idle curiosity, in a state of body and mind whose restoration evidently depended upon 20 entire repose. Once, however, the lieutenant asked why he had come so far upon the ice in so strange a vehicle?

His countenance instantly assumed an aspect of the deepest gloom; and he replied, 'To seek one who fled from me.'

'And did the man whom you pursued travel in the same fashion?' 25 'Yes.'

'Then I fancy we have seen him, for the day before we picked you up, we saw some dogs drawing a sledge, with a man in it, across the ice.'

This aroused the stranger's attention, and he asked a multitude 30 of questions concerning the route which the daemon, as he called him, had pursued. Soon after, when he was alone with me, he said, 'I have, doubtless, excited your curiosity, as well as that of these good people; but you are too considerate to make enquiries.'

'Certainly; it would indeed be very impertinent and inhuman in 35 me to trouble you with any inquisitiveness of mine.'

'And yet you rescued me from a strange and perilous situation: you have benevolently restored me to life.'

Soon after this he enquired if I thought that the breaking up of the ice had destroyed the other sledge? I replied, that I could not
5 answer with any degree of certainty, for the ice had not broken until near midnight, and the traveller might have arrived at a place of safety before that time; but of this I could not judge.

From this time a new spirit of life animated the decaying frame of the stranger. He manifested the greatest eagerness to be upon
10 deck, to watch for the sledge which had before appeared; but I have persuaded him to remain in the cabin, for he is far too weak to sustain the rawness of the atmosphere. I have promised that some one should watch for him and give him instant notice if any new object should appear in sight.

15 Such is my journal of what relates to this strange occurrence up to the present day. The stranger has gradually improved in health, but is very silent, and appears uneasy when anyone except myself enters the cabin. Yet his manners are so conciliating and gentle, that the sailors are all interested in him, although they have had
20 very little communication with him. For my own part, I begin to love him as a brother; and his constant and deep grief fills me with sympathy and compassion. He must have been a noble creature in his better days, being even now in wreck so attractive and amiable.

I said in one of my letters, my dear Margaret, that I should find
25 no friend on the wide ocean; yet I have found a man who, before his spirit had been broken by misery, I should have been happy to have possessed as the brother of my heart.

I shall continue my journal concerning the stranger at intervals, should I have any fresh incidents to record.

August 13th, 17–
30 My affection for my guest increases every day. He excites at once my admiration and my pity to an astonishing degree. How can I see so noble a creature destroyed by misery, without feeling the most poignant grief? He is so gentle, yet so wise; his mind is so cultivated, and when he speaks, although his words are culled

with the choicest art, yet they flow with rapidity and unparalleled eloquence.

He is now much recovered from his illness, and is continually on the deck, apparently watching for the sledge that preceded his own. Yet, although unhappy, he is not so utterly occupied by his own misery but that he interests himself deeply in the projects of others. He has frequently conversed with me on mine, which I have communicated to him without disguise. He entered attentively into all my arguments in favour of my eventual success, and into every minute detail of the measures I had taken to secure it. I was easily led by the sympathy which he evinced, to use the language of my heart, to give utterance to the burning ardour of my soul; and to say, with all the fervour that warmed me, how gladly I would sacrifice my fortune, my existence, my every hope, to the furtherance of my enterprise. One man's life or death were but a small price to pay for the acquirement of the knowledge which I sought for the dominion I should acquire and transmit over the elemental foes of our race. As I spoke, a dark gloom spread over my listener's countenance. At first I perceived that he tried to suppress his emotion; he placed his hands before his eyes, and my voice quivered and failed me as I beheld tears trickle fast from between his fingers – a groan burst from his heaving breast. I paused; at length he spoke, in broken accents – 'Unhappy man! Do you share my madness? Have you drunk also of the intoxicating draught? Hear me – let me reveal my tale, and you will dash the cup from your lips!'

Such words, you may imagine, strongly excited my curiosity; but the paroxysm of grief that had seized the stranger overcame his weakened powers, and many hours of repose and tranquil conversation were necessary to restore his composure.

Having conquered the violence of his feelings, he appeared to despise himself for being the slave of passion; and quelling the dark tyranny of despair, he led me again to converse concerning myself personally. He asked me the history of my earlier years. The tale was quickly told: but it awakened various trains of reflection. I spoke of my desire of finding a friend – of my thirst for a more intimate sympathy with a fellow mind than had ever fallen to my lot; and expressed my conviction that a man could boast of little happiness, who did not enjoy this blessing.

'I agree with you,' replied the stranger; 'we are unfashioned
5 creatures, but half made up, if one wiser, better, dearer than ourselves – such a friend ought to be – do not lend his aid to perfectionate our weak and faulty natures. I once had a friend, the most noble of human creatures, and am entitled, therefore, to judge respecting friendship. You have hope, and the world before you, and have no cause for despair. But I – I have lost every thing
10 and cannot begin life anew.'

As he said this his countenance became expressive of a calm, settled grief, that touched me to the heart. But he was silent, and presently retired to his cabin.

15 Even broken in spirit as he is, no one can feel more deeply than he does the beauties of nature. The starry sky, the sea, and every sight afforded by these wonderful regions, seems still to have the power of elevating his soul from earth. Such a man has a double existence: he may suffer misery and be overwhelmed by disappoint-
20 ments, yet, when he has retired into himself, he will be like a celestial spirit, that has a halo around him, within whose circle no grief or folly ventures.

Will you smile at the enthusiasm I express concerning this divine wanderer? You would not, if you saw him. You have been tutored
25 and refined by books and retirement from the world, and you are therefore somewhat fastidious; but this only renders you the more fit to appreciate the extraordinary merits of this wonderful man. Sometimes I have endeavoured to discover what quality it is which he possesses, that elevates him so immeasurably above any other
30 person I ever knew. I believe it to be an intuitive discernment; a quick but never-failing power of judgment; a penetration into the causes of things, unequalled for clearness and precision; add to this a facility of expression, and a voice whose varied intonations are soul-subduing music.

August 19th, 17–

Yesterday the stranger said to me, 'You may easily perceive, Captain Walton, that I have suffered great and unparalled misfortunes. I had determined, at one time, that the memory of these evils should die with me, but you have won me to alter my determination. You seek for knowledge and wisdom, as I once did; and I ardently hope that the gratification of your wishes may not be a serpent to sting you, as mine has been. I do not know that the relation of my disasters will be useful to you; yet, when I reflect that you are pursuing the same course, exposing yourself to the same dangers which have rendered me what I am, I imagine that you may deduce an apt moral from my tale; one that may direct you if you succeed in your undertaking, and console you in case of failure. Prepare to hear of occurrences which are usually deemed marvellous. Were we among the tamer scenes of nature, I might fear to encounter your unbelief, perhaps your ridicule; but many things will appear possible in these wild and mysterious regions, which would provoke the laughter of those unacquainted with the ever-varied powers of nature; – nor can I doubt but that my tale conveys in its series internal evidence of the truth of the events of which it is composed.'

You may easily imagine that I was much gratified by the offered communication, yet I could not endure that he should renew his grief by a recital of his misfortunes. I felt the greatest eagerness to hear the promised narrative, partly from curiosity, and partly from a strong desire to ameliorate his fate, if it were in my power. I expressed these feelings in my answer.

'I thank you,' he replied, 'for your sympathy, but it is useless; my fate is nearly fulfilled. I wait but for one event, and then I shall repose in peace. I understand your feeling,' continued he, perceiving that I wished to interrupt him: 'but you are mistaken, my friend, if thus you will allow me to name you; nothing can alter my destiny; listen to my history, and you will perceive how irrevocably it is determined.'

He then told me, that he would commence his narrative the next day, when I should be at leisure. This promise drew from me the warmest thanks. I have resolved every night, when I am not

imperatively occupied by my duties, to record, as nearly as possible in his own words, what he has related during the day. If I should be engaged, I will at least make notes. This manuscript will doubtless afford you the greatest pleasure: but to me, who know him and
5 who hear it from his own lips – with what interest and sympathy shall I read it in some future day! Even now, as I commence my task, his full-toned voice swells in my ears; his lustrous eyes dwell on me with all their melancholy sweetness; I see his thin hand raised in animation, while the lineaments of his face are irradiated
10 by the soul within. Strange and harrowing must be his story, frightful the storm which embraced the gallant vessel on its course and wrecked it – thus!

Chapter I

I am by birth a Genevese, and my family is one of the most distinguished of that republic. My ancestors had been for many years counsellors and syndics; and my father had filled several public situations with honour and reputation. He was respected by all who knew him, for his integrity and indefatigable attention to public business. He passed his younger days perpetually occupied by the affairs of his country; a variety of circumstances had prevented his marrying early, nor was it until the decline of life that he became a husband and the father of a family. 5

As the circumstances of his marriage illustrate his character, I cannot refrain from relating them. One of his most intimate friends was a merchant who, from a flourishing state, fell, through numerous mischances, into poverty. This man, whose name was Beaufort, was of a proud and unbending disposition and could not bear to live in poverty and oblivion in the same country where he had formerly been distinguished for his rank and magnificence. Having paid his debts, therefore, in the most honourable manner, he retreated with his daughter to the town of Lucerne, where he lived unknown and in wretchedness. My father loved Beaufort with the truest friendship, and was deeply grieved by his retreat in these unfortunate circumstances. He bitterly deplored the false pride which led his friend to a conduct so little worthy of the affection that united them. He lost no time in endeavouring to seek him out, with the hope of persuading him to begin the world again through his credit and assistance. 10

15

20

25

Beaufort had taken effectual measures to conceal himself; and it was ten months before my father discovered his abode. Overjoyed at this discovery, he hastened to the house, which was situated in a mean street near the Reuss. But when he entered, misery and despair alone welcomed him. Beaufort had saved but a very small sum of money from the wreck of his fortunes, but it was sufficient

5   to provide him with sustenance for some months, and in the mean time he hoped to procure some respectable employment in a merchant's house. The interval was, consequently, spent in inaction; his grief only became more deep and rankling, when he had leisure for reflection; and at length it took so fast hold of his

10 mind, that at the end of three months he lay on a bed of sickness, incapable of any exertion.

His daughter attended him with the greatest tenderness; but she saw with despair that their little fund was rapidly decreasing, and that there was no other prospect of support. But Caroline Beaufort

15 possessed a mind of an uncommon mould, and her courage rose to support her in her adversity. She procured plain work; she plaited straw; and by various means contrived to earn a pittance scarcely sufficient to support life.

Several months passed in this manner. Her father grew worse;

20 her time was more entirely occupied in attending him; her means of subsistence decreased; and in the tenth month her father died in her arms, leaving her an orphan and a beggar. This last blow overcame her, and she knelt by Beaufort's coffin, weeping bitterly, when my father entered the chamber. He came like a protecting

25 spirit to the poor girl, who committed herself to his care; and after the interment of his friend he conducted her to Geneva, and placed her under the protection of a relation. Two years after this event Caroline became his wife.

There was a considerable difference between the ages of my

30 parents, but this circumstance seemed to unite them only closer in bonds of devoted affection. There was a sense of justice in my father's upright mind, which rendered it necessary that he should approve highly to love strongly. Perhaps during former years he had suffered from the late-discovered unworthiness of one beloved,

35 and so was disposed to set a greater value on tried worth. There was a show of gratitude and worship in his attachment to my

mother, differing wholly from the doating fondness of age, for it was inspired by reverence for her virtues and a desire to be the means of, in some degree, recompensing her for the sorrows she had endured, but which gave inexpressible grace to his behaviour to her. Every thing was made to yield to her wishes and her convenience. He strove to shelter her, as a fair exotic is sheltered by the gardener, from every rougher wind, and to surround her with all that could tend to excite pleasurable emotion in her soft and benevolent mind. Her health, and even the tranquillity of her hitherto constant spirit, had been shaken by what she had gone through. During the two years that had elapsed previous to their marriage my father had gradually relinquished all his public functions; and immediately after their union they sought the pleasant climate of Italy, and the change of scene and interest attendant on a tour through that land of wonders, as a restorative for her weakened frame.

From Italy they visited Germany and France. I, their eldest child, was born at Naples, and as an infant accompanied them in their rambles. I remained for several years their only child. Much as they were attached to each other, they seemed to draw inexhaustible stores of affection from a very mine of love to bestow them upon me. My mother's tender caresses and my father's smile of benevolent pleasure while regarding me, are my first recollections. I was their plaything and their idol, and something better – their child, the innocent and helpless creature bestowed on them by Heaven, whom to bring up to good, and whose future lot it was in their hands to direct to happiness or misery, according as they fulfilled their duties towards me. With this deep consciousness of what they owed towards the being to which they had given life, added to the active spirit of tenderness that animated both, it may be imagined that while during every hour of my infant life I received a lesson of patience, of charity, and of self-control, I was so guided by a silken cord that all seemed but one train of enjoyment to me.

For a long time I was their only care. My mother had much desire to have a daughter, but I continued their single offspring.

When I was about five years old, while making an excursion beyond the frontiers of Italy, they passed a week on the shores of the Lake of Como. Their benevolent disposition often made them enter the cottages of the poor. This, to my mother, was more than a duty; it
5 was a necessity, a passion – remembering what she had suffered, and how she had been relieved, – for her to act in her turn the guardian angel to the afflicted. During one of their walks a poor cot in the foldings of a vale attracted their notice as being singularly disconsolate, while the number of half-clothed children gathered
10 about it spoke of penury in its worst shape. One day, when my father had gone by himself to Milan, my mother, accompanied by me, visited this abode. She found a peasant and his wife, hard working, bent down by care and labour, distributing a scanty meal to five hungry babes. Among these there was one which attracted
15 my mother far above all the rest. She appeared of a different stock. The four others were dark-eyed, hardy little vagrants; this child was thin, and very fair. Her hair was the brightest living gold, and despite the poverty of her clothing, seemed to set a crown of distinction on her head. Her brow was clear and ample, her blue
20 eyes cloudless, and her lips and the moulding of her face so express- ive of sensibility and sweetness that none could behold her without looking on her as of a distinct species, a being heaven-sent, and bearing a celestial stamp in all her features.

The peasant woman, perceiving that my mother fixed eyes of
25 wonder and admiration on this lovely girl, eagerly communicated her history. She was not her child, but the daughter of a Milanese nobleman. Her mother was a German, and had died on giving her birth. The infant had been placed with these good people to nurse: they were better off then. They had not been long married, and
30 their eldest child was but just born. The father of their charge was one of those Italians nursed in the memory of the antique glory of Italy – one among the *schiavi ognor frementi*, who exerted himself to obtain the liberty of his country. He became the victim of its weakness. Whether he had died, or still lingered in the dungeons
35 of Austria, was not known. His property was confiscated; his child became an orphan and a beggar. She continued with her foster

parents, and bloomed in their rude abode, fairer than a garden rose among dark-leaved brambles.

When my father returned from Milan, he found playing with me in the hall of our villa a child fairer than a pictured cherub – a creature who seemed to shed radiance from her looks and whose form and motions were lighter than the chamois of the hills. The apparition was soon explained. With his permission my mother prevailed on her rustic guardians to yield their charge to her. They were fond of the sweet orphan. Her presence had seemed a blessing to them, but it would be unfair to her to keep her in poverty and want, when Providence afforded her such powerful protection. They consulted their village priest, and the result was that Elizabeth Lavenza became the inmate of my parents' house – my more than sister – the beautiful and adored companion of all my occupations and my pleasures.

Everyone loved Elizabeth. The passionate and most reverential attachment with which all regarded her became, while I shared it, my pride and my delight. On the evening previous to her being brought to my home, my mother had said playfully, 'I have a pretty present for my Victor – tomorrow he shall have it.' And when, on the morrow, she presented Elizabeth to me as her promised gift, I, with childish seriousness, interpreted her words literally and looked upon Elizabeth as mine – mine to protect, love, and cherish. All praises bestowed on her I received as made to a possession of my own. We called each other familiarly by the name of cousin. No word, no expression could body forth the kind of relation in which she stood to me – my more than sister, since till death she was to be mine only.

Chapter II

We were brought up together; there was not quite a year difference in our ages. I need not say that we were strangers to any species of disunion or dispute. Harmony was the soul of our companionship, and the diversity and contrast that subsisted in our characters
5   drew us nearer together. Elizabeth was of a calmer and more concentrated disposition; but, with all my ardour, I was capable of a more intense application, and was more deeply smitten with the thirst for knowledge. She busied herself with following the aerial creations of the poets; and in the majestic and wondrous scenes
10   which surrounded our Swiss home – the sublime shapes of the mountains; the changes of the seasons; tempest and calm; the silence of winter, and the life and turbulence of our Alpine summers – she found ample scope for admiration and delight. While my companion contemplated with a serious and satisfied spirit the
15   magnificent appearances of things, I delighted in investigating their causes. The world was to me a secret which I desired to divine. Curiosity, earnest research to learn the hidden laws of nature, gladness akin to rapture, as they were unfolded to me, are among the earliest sensations I can remember.
20   On the birth of a second son, my junior by seven years, my parents gave up entirely their wandering life, and fixed themselves in their native country. We possessed a house in Geneva, and a *campagne* on Belrive, the eastern shore of the lake, at the distance of rather more than a league from the city. We resided principally
25   in the latter, and the lives of my parents were passed in considerable seclusion. It was my temper to avoid a crowd, and to attach myself fervently to a few. I was indifferent, therefore, to my schoolfellows

36

in general; but I united myself in the bonds of the closest friendship to one among them. Henry Clerval was the son of a merchant of Geneva. He was a boy of singular talent and fancy. He loved enterprise, hardship, and even danger for its own sake. He was deeply read in books of chivalry and romance. He composed heroic songs, and began to write many a tale of enchantment and knightly adventure. He tried to make us act plays and to enter into masquerades, in which the characters were drawn from the heroes of Roncesvalles, of the Round Table of King Arthur, and the chivalrous train who shed their blood to redeem the holy sepulchre from the hands of the infidels.

No human being could have passed a happier childhood than myself. My parents were possessed by the very spirit of kindness and indulgence. We felt that they were not the tyrants to rule our lot according to their caprice, but the agents and creators of all the many delights which we enjoyed. When I mingled with other families, I distinctly discerned how peculiarly fortunate my lot was, and gratitude assisted the development of filial love.

My temper was sometimes violent, and my passions vehement; but by some law in my temperature they were turned not towards childish pursuits but to an eager desire to learn, and not to learn all things indiscriminately. I confess that neither the structure of languages, nor the code of governments, nor the politics of various states possessed attractions for me. It was the secrets of heaven and earth that I desired to learn; and whether it was the outward substance of things, or the inner spirit of nature and the mysterious soul of man that occupied me, still my enquiries were directed to the metaphysical, or in its highest sense, the physical secrets of the world.

Meanwhile Clerval occupied himself, so to speak, with the moral relations of things. The busy stage of life, the virtues of heroes, and the actions of men were his theme; and his hope and his dream was to become one among those whose names are recorded in story, as the gallant and adventurous benefactors of our species. The saintly soul of Elizabeth shone like a shrine-dedicated lamp in our peaceful home. Her sympathy was ours; her smile, her soft

voice, the sweet glance of her celestial eyes, were ever there to bless and animate us. She was the living spirit of love to soften and attract: I might have become sullen in my study, rough through the ardour of my nature, but that she was there to subdue me to a
5 semblance of her own gentleness. And Clerval – could aught ill entrench on the noble spirit of Clerval – yet he might not have been so perfectly humane, so thoughtful in his generosity – so full of kindness and tenderness amidst his passion for adventurous exploit, had she not unfolded to him the real loveliness of benefi-
10 cence, and made the doing good the end and aim of his soaring ambition.

I feel exquisite pleasure in dwelling on the recollections of child-hood, before misfortune had tainted my mind, and changed its bright visions of extensive usefulness into gloomy and narrow
15 reflections upon self. Besides, in drawing the picture of my early days, I also record those events which led, by insensible steps, to my after tale of misery: for when I would account to myself for the birth of that passion, which afterwards ruled my destiny, I find it arise, like a mountain river, from ignoble and almost forgotten
20 sources; but, swelling as it proceeded, it became the torrent which, in its course, has swept away all my hopes and joys.

Natural philosophy is the genius that has regulated my fate; I desire, therefore, in this narration, to state those facts which led to my predilection for that science. When I was thirteen years of age
25 we all went on a party of pleasure to the baths near Thonon: the inclemency of the weather obliged us to remain a day confined to the inn. In this house I chanced to find a volume of the works of Cornelius Agrippa. I opened it with apathy; the theory which he attempts to demonstrate, and the wonderful facts which he relates
30 soon changed this feeling into enthusiasm. A new light seemed to dawn upon my mind, and, bounding with joy, I communicated my discovery to my father. My father looked carelessly at the titlepage of my book and said, 'Ah! Cornelius Agrippa! My dear Victor, do not waste your time upon this; it is sad trash.'
35 If, instead of this remark, my father had taken the pains to explain to me that the principles of Agrippa had been entirely

exploded, and that a modern system of science had been introduced, which possessed much greater powers than the ancient,
because the powers of the latter were chimerical, while those of the
former were real and practical; under such circumstances I should
certainly have thrown Agrippa aside and have contented my   5
imagination, warmed as it was, by returning with greater ardour to
my former studies. It is even possible that the train of my ideas
would never have received the fatal impulse that led to my ruin.
But the cursory glance my father had taken of my volume by no
means assured me that he was acquainted with its contents; and I   10
continued to read with the greatest avidity.

When I returned home my first care was to procure the whole
works of this author, and afterwards of Paracelsus and Albertus
Magnus. I read and studied the wild fancies of these writers with
delight; they appeared to me treasures known to few besides myself.   15
I have described myself as always having been imbued with a
fervent longing to penetrate the secrets of nature. In spite of the
intense labour and wonderful discoveries of modern philosophers,
I always came from my studies discontented and unsatisfied. Sir
Isaac Newton is said to have avowed that he felt like a child picking   20
up shells beside the great and unexplored ocean of truth. Those of
his successors in each branch of natural philosophy with whom I
was acquainted, appeared even to my boy's apprehensions, as tyros
engaged in the same pursuit.

The untaught peasant beheld the elements around him, and was   25
acquainted with their practical uses. The most learned philosopher
knew little more. He had partially unveiled the face of Nature, but
her immortal lineaments were still a wonder and a mystery. He
might dissect, anatomise, and give names; but, not to speak of a
final cause, causes in their secondary and tertiary grades were   30
utterly unknown to him. I had gazed upon the fortifications and
impediments that seemed to keep human beings from entering the
citadel of nature, and rashly and ignorantly I had repined.

But here were books, and here were men who had penetrated
deeper and knew more. I took their word for all that they averred,   35
and I became their disciple. It may appear strange that such should

arise in the eighteenth century; but while I followed the routine of education in the schools of Geneva, I was, to a great degree, self-taught with regard to my favourite studies. My father was not scientific, and I was left to struggle with a child's blindness, added
5 to a student's thirst for knowledge. Under the guidance of my new preceptors, I entered with the greatest diligence into the search of the philosopher's stone and the elixir of life; but the latter soon obtained my undivided attention. Wealth was an inferior object; but what glory would attend the discovery, if I could banish disease
10 from the human frame and render man invulnerable to any but a violent death!

Nor were these my only visions. The raising of ghosts or devils was a promise liberally accorded by my favourite authors, the fulfilment of which I most eagerly sought; and if my incantations
15 were always unsuccessful, I attributed the failure rather to my own inexperience and mistake, than to a want of skill or fidelity in my instructors. And thus for a time I was occupied by exploded systems, mingling, like an unadept, a thousand contradictory theories, and floundering desperately in a very slough of multi-
20 farious knowledge, guided by an ardent imagination and childish reasoning, till an accident again changed the current of my ideas.

When I was about fifteen years old we had retired to our house near Belrive, when we witnessed a most violent and terrible thunder-storm. It advanced from behind the mountains of Jura; and the
25 thunder burst at once with frightful loudness from various quarters of the heavens. I remained, while the storm lasted, watching its progress with curiosity and delight. As I stood at the door, on a sudden I beheld a stream of fire issue from an old and beautiful oak, which stood about twenty yards from our house; and so soon
30 as the dazzling light vanished, the oak had disappeared, and nothing remained but a blasted stump. When we visited it the next morning, we found the tree shattered in a singular manner. It was not splintered by the shock, but entirely reduced to thin ribbons of wood. I never beheld anything so utterly destroyed.

35 Before this I was not unacquainted with the more obvious laws of electricity. On this occasion a man of great research in natural

philosophy was with us, and, excited by this catastrophe, he entered on the explanation of a theory which he had formed on the subject of electricity and galvanism, which was at once new and astonishing to me. All that he said threw greatly into the shade Cornelius Agrippa, Albertus Magnus, and Paracelsus, the lords of my imagin-   5
ation; but by some fatality the overthrow of these men disinclined me to pursue my accustomed studies. It seemed to me as if nothing would or could ever be known. All that had so long engaged my attention suddenly grew despicable. By one of those caprices of the mind, which we are perhaps most subject to in early youth, I   10
at once gave up my former occupations, set down natural history and all its progeny as a deformed and abortive creation, and enter-
tained the greatest disdain for a would-be science which could never even step within the threshold of real knowledge. In this mood of mind I betook myself to the mathematics, and the   15
branches of study appertaining to that science, as being built upon secure foundations, and so worthy of my consideration.

Thus strangely are our souls constructed, and by such slight ligaments are we bound to prosperity or ruin. When I look back, it seems to me as if this almost miraculous change of inclination and   20
will was the immediate suggestion of the guardian angel of my life – the last effort made by the spirit of preservation to avert the storm that was even then hanging in the stars, and ready to envelope me. Her victory was announced by an unusual tranquillity and gladness of soul, which followed the relinquishing of my ancient and latterly   25
tormenting studies. It was thus that I was to be taught to associate evil with their prosecution, happiness with their disregard.

It was a strong effort of the spirit of good; but it was ineffectual. Destiny was too potent, and her immutable laws had decreed my utter and terrible destruction.   30

Chapter III

When I had attained the age of seventeen, my parents resolved, that I should become a student at the university of Ingolstadt. I had hitherto attended the schools of Geneva; but my father thought it necessary, for the completion of my education, that
5 I should be made acquainted with other customs than those of my native country. My departure was therefore fixed at an early date; but, before the day resolved upon could arrive, the first misfortune of my life occurred – an omen, as it were, of my future misery.

10 Elizabeth had caught the scarlet fever; her illness was severe, and she was in the greatest danger. During her illness, many arguments had been urged to persuade my mother to refrain from attending upon her. She had, at first, yielded to our intreaties, but when she heard that the life of her favourite was menaced, she could no
15 longer control her anxiety. She attended her sickbed; – her watchful attentions triumphed over the malignity of the distemper, – Elizabeth was saved, but the consequences of this imprudence were fatal to her preserver. On the third day my mother sickened; her fever was accompanied by the most alarming symptoms, and the
20 looks of her medical attendants prognosticated the worst event. On her death-bed the fortitude and benignity of this best of women did not desert her. She joined the hands of Elizabeth and myself: – 'My children,' she said, 'my firmest hopes of future happiness were placed on the prospect of your union. This expectation will
25 now be the consolation of your father. Elizabeth, my love, you must supply my place to my younger children. Alas! I regret that I am taken from you; and, happy and beloved as I have been, is it

not hard to quit you all? But these are not thoughts befitting me; I will endeavour to resign myself cheerfully to death, and will indulge a hope of meeting you in another world.'

She died calmly; and her countenance expressed affection even in death. I need not describe the feelings of those whose dearest ties are rent by that most irreparable evil; the void that presents itself to the soul; and the despair that is exhibited on the countenance. It is so long before the mind can persuade itself that she, whom we saw every day, and whose very existence appeared a part of our own, can have departed forever – that the brightness of a beloved eye can have been extinguished, and the sound of a voice so familiar and dear to the ear can be hushed, never more to be heard. These are the reflections of the first days; but when the lapse of time proves the reality of the evil, then the actual bitterness of grief commences. Yet from whom has not that rude hand rent away some dear connexion? and why should I describe a sorrow which all have felt, and must feel? The time at length arrives when grief is rather an indulgence than a necessity; and the smile that plays upon the lips, although it may be deemed a sacrilege, is not banished. My mother was dead, but we had still duties which we ought to perform; we must continue our course with the rest, and learn to think ourselves fortunate, whilst one remains whom the spoiler had not seized.

My departure for Ingolstadt, which had been deferred by these events, was now again determined upon. I obtained from my father a respite of some weeks. It appeared to me sacrilege so soon to leave the repose, akin to death, of the house of mourning and to rush into the thick of life. I was new to sorrow, but it did not the less alarm me. I was unwilling to quit the sight of those that remained to me; and above all, I desired to see my sweet Elizabeth in some degree consoled.

She indeed veiled her grief, and strove to act the comforter to us all. She looked steadily on life, and assumed its duties with courage and zeal. She devoted herself to those whom she had been taught to call her uncle and cousins. Never was she so enchanting as at this time, when she recalled the sunshine of her smiles and spent

them upon us. She forgot even her own regret in her endeavours
to make us forget.

The day of my departure at length arrived. Clerval spent the last
evening with us. He had endeavoured to persuade his father to
permit him to accompany me and to become my fellow student;
but in vain. His father was a narrow-minded trader, and saw
idleness and ruin in the aspirations and ambition of his son. Henry
deeply felt the misfortune of being debarred from a liberal education. He said little; but when he spoke, I read in his kindling eye
and in his animated glance a restrained but firm resolve, not to be
chained to the miserable details of commerce.

We sat late. We could not tear ourselves away from each other,
nor persuade ourselves to say the word 'Farewell!' It was said; and
we retired under the pretence of seeking repose, each fancying that
the other was deceived: but when at morning's dawn I descended
to the carriage which was to convey me away, they were all there –
my father again to bless me, Clerval to press my hand once more,
my Elizabeth to renew her intreaties that I would write often, and
to bestow the last feminine attentions on her playmate and friend.

I threw myself into the chaise that was to convey me away and
indulged in the most melancholy reflections. I, who had ever
been surrounded by amiable companions, continually engaged in
endeavouring to bestow mutual pleasure, I was now alone. In the
university, whither I was going, I must form my own friends and
be my own protector. My life had hitherto been remarkably
secluded and domestic; and this had given me invincible repugnance to new countenances. I loved my brothers, Elizabeth, and
Clerval; these were 'old familiar faces,' but I believed myself totally
unfitted for the company of strangers. Such were my reflections as
I commenced my journey; but as I proceeded, my spirits and hopes
rose. I ardently desired the acquisition of knowledge. I had often,
when at home, thought it hard to remain during my youth cooped
up in one place, and had longed to enter the world, and take my
station among other human beings. Now my desires were complied
with, and it would, indeed, have been folly to repent.

I had sufficient leisure for these and many other reflections during my journey to Ingolstadt, which was long and fatiguing. At length the high white steeple of the town met my eyes. I alighted, and was conducted to my solitary apartment, to spend the evening as I pleased.

The next morning I delivered my letters of introduction, and 5 paid a visit to some of the principal professors. Chance – or rather the evil influence, the Angel of Destruction, which asserted omnipotent sway over me from the moment I turned my reluctant steps from my father's door – led me first to M. Krempe, professor of natural philosophy. He was an uncouth man, but deeply imbued 10 in the secrets of his science. He asked me several questions concerning my progress in the different branches of science appertaining to natural philosophy. I replied carelessly; and, partly in contempt, mentioned the names of my alchymists as the principal authors I had studied. The professor stared. 'Have you,' he said, 'really spent 15 your time in studying such nonsense?'

I replied in the affirmative. 'Every minute,' continued M. Krempe with warmth, 'every instant that you have wasted on those books is utterly and entirely lost. You have burdened your memory with exploded systems and useless names. Good God! In what 20 desert land have you lived, where no one was kind enough to inform you that these fancies which you have so greedily imbibed are a thousand years old and as musty as they are ancient? I little expected, in this enlightened and scientific age, to find a disciple of Albertus Magnus and Paracelsus. My dear sir, you must begin 25 your studies entirely anew.'

So saying, he stept aside, and wrote down a list of several books treating of natural philosophy, which he desired me to procure; and dismissed me after mentioning that in the beginning of the following week he intended to commence a course of lectures upon 30 natural philosophy in its general relations, and that M. Waldman, a fellow-professor, would lecture upon chemistry the alternate days that he omitted.

I returned home, not disappointed, for I have said that I had long considered those authors useless whom the professor repro- 35 bated; but I returned, not at all the more inclined to recur to these

studies in any shape. M. Krempe was a little squat man, with a gruff voice and a repulsive countenance; the teacher, therefore, did not prepossess me in favour of his pursuits. In rather a too philosophical and connected a strain, perhaps, I have given an
5 account of the conclusions I had come to concerning them in my early years. As a child, I had not been content with the results promised by the modern professors of natural science. With a confusion of ideas only to be accounted for by my extreme youth, and my want of a guide on such matters, I had retrod the steps of
10 knowledge along the paths of time, and exchanged the discoveries of recent enquirers for the dreams of forgotten alchymists. Besides, I had a contempt for the uses of modern natural philosophy. It was very different, when the masters of the science sought immortality and power; such views, although futile, were grand; but now the
15 scene was changed. The ambition of the enquirer seemed to limit itself to the annihilation of those visions on which my interest in science was chiefly founded. I was required to exchange chimeras of boundless grandeur for realities of little worth.

Such were my reflections during the first two or three days of
20 my residence at Ingolstadt, which were chiefly spent in becoming acquainted with the localities, and the principal residents in my new abode. But as the ensuing week commenced, I thought of the information which M. Krempe had given me concerning the lectures. And although I could not consent to go and hear that
25 little conceited fellow deliver sentences out of a pulpit, I recollected what he had said of M. Waldman, whom I had never seen, as he had hitherto been out of town.

Partly from curiosity, and partly from idleness, I went into the lecturing room, which M. Waldman entered shortly after. This
30 professor was very unlike his colleague. He appeared about fifty years of age, but with an aspect expressive of the greatest benevolence; a few grey hairs covered his temples, but those at the back of his head were nearly black. His person was short, but remarkably erect; and his voice the sweetest I had ever heard. He began his
35 lecture by a recapitulation of the history of chemistry and the various improvements made by different men of learning, pro-

nouncing with fervour the names of the most distinguished dis-
coverers. He then took a cursory view of the present state of the
science, and explained many of its elementary terms. After having
made a few preparatory experiments, he concluded with a panegyric upon modern chemistry, the terms of which I shall never   5
forget: –

'The ancient teachers of this science,' said he, 'promised impossi-
bilities, and performed nothing. The modern masters promise very
little; they know that metals cannot be transmuted, and that the
elixir of life is a chimera. But these philosophers, whose hands   10
seem only made to dabble in dirt, and their eyes to pore over the
microscope or crucible, have indeed performed miracles. They
penetrate into the recesses of nature, and show how she works
in her hiding-places. They ascend into the heavens: they have
discovered how the blood circulates, and the nature of the air we   15
breathe. They have acquired new and almost unlimited powers;
they can command the thunders of heaven, mimic the earthquake,
and even mock the invisible world with its own shadows.'

Such were the professor's words – rather let me say such the
words of the fate – enounced to destroy me. As he went on I felt as   20
if my soul were grappling with a palpable enemy; one by one the
various keys were touched which formed the mechanism of my
being: chord after chord was sounded, and soon my mind was
filled with one thought, one conception, one purpose. So much
has been done, exclaimed the soul of Frankenstein, – more, far   25
more, will I achieve: treading in the steps already marked, I will
pioneer a new way, explore unknown powers, and unfold to the
world the deepest mysteries of creation.

I closed not my eyes that night. My internal being was in a state
of insurrection and turmoil; I felt that order would thence arise,   30
but I had no power to produce it. By degrees, after the morning's
dawn, sleep came. I awoke, and my yesternight's thoughts were as
a dream. There only remained a resolution to return to my ancient
studies and to devote myself to a science for which I believed myself
to possess a natural talent. On the same day, I paid M. Waldman   35
a visit. His manners in private were even more mild and attractive

than in public; for there was a certain dignity in his mien during
his lecture, which in his own house was replaced by the greatest
affability and kindness. I gave him pretty nearly the same account
of my former pursuits as I had given to his fellow-professor. He
5 heard with attention the little narration concerning my studies,
and smiled at the names of Cornelius Agrippa and Paracelsus, but
without the contempt that M. Krempe had exhibited. He said that
'these were men to whose indefatigable zeal modern philosophers
were indebted for most of the foundations of their knowledge.
10 They had left to us, as an easier task to give new names, and arrange
in connected classifications the facts which they in a great degree
had been the instruments of bringing to light. The labours of
men of genius, however erroneously directed, scarcely ever fail in
ultimately turning to the solid advantage of mankind.' I listened to
15 his statement, which was delivered without any presumption or
affectation; and then added that his lecture had removed any
prejudices against modern chemists; I expressed myself in
measured terms, with the modesty and deference due from a youth
to his instructor, without letting escape (inexperience in life would
20 have made me ashamed) any of the enthusiasm which stimulated
my intended labours. I requested his advice concerning the books
I ought to procure.

'I am happy,' said M. Waldman, 'to have gained a disciple; and
if your application equals your ability, I have no doubt of your
25 success. Chemistry is that branch of natural philosophy in which
the greatest improvements have been and may be made: it is on
that account that I have made it my peculiar study; but at the same
time, I have not neglected the other branches of science. A man
would make but a very sorry chemist if he attended to that depart-
30 ment of human knowledge alone. If your wish is to become really
a man of science, and not merely a petty experimentalist, I should
advise you to apply to every branch of natural philosophy, including
mathematics.'

He then took me into his laboratory and explained to me the
35 uses of his various machines; instructing me as to what I ought to
procure, and promising me the use of his own when I should have

advanced far enough in the science not to derange their mechanism. He also gave me the list of books which I had requested; and I took my leave.

Thus ended a day memorable to me: it decided my future destiny.   5

Chapter IV

From this day natural philosophy, and particularly chemistry, in
the most comprehensive sense of the term, became nearly my sole
occupation. I read with ardour those works, so full of genius and
discrimination, which modern enquirers have written on these
5 subjects. I attended the lectures, and cultivated the acquaintance,
of the men of science of the university; and I found even in M.
Krempe a great deal of sound sense and real information, combined, it is true, with a repulsive physiognomy and manners, but
not on that account the less valuable. In M. Waldman I found a
10 true friend. His gentleness was never tinged by dogmatism, and
his instructions were given with an air of frankness and good
nature, that banished every idea of pedantry. In a thousand ways
he smoothed for me the path of knowledge, and made the most
abstruse enquiries clear and facile to my apprehension. My applica-
15 tion was at first fluctuating and uncertain; it gained strength as I
proceeded, and soon became so ardent and eager, that the stars
often disappeared in the light of morning whilst I was yet engaged
in my laboratory.

As I applied so closely, it may be easily conceived that my
20 progress was rapid. My ardour was indeed the astonishment of the
students, and my proficiency that of the masters. Professor Krempe
often asked me, with a sly smile, how Cornelius Agrippa went on?
whilst M. Waldman expressed the most heartfelt exultation in my
progress. Two years passed in this manner, during which I paid no
25 visit to Geneva, but was engaged, heart and soul, in the pursuit of
some discoveries which I hoped to make. None but those who have
experienced them can conceive of the enticements of science. In

other studies you go as far as others have gone before you, and there is nothing more to know; but in a scientific pursuit there is continual food for discovery and wonder. A mind of moderate capacity, which closely pursued one study must infallibly arrive at great proficiency in that study; and I, who continually sought the attainment of one object of pursuit and was solely wrapt up in this, improved so rapidly, that, at the end of two years, I made some discoveries in the improvement of some chemical instruments, which procured me great esteem and admiration at the university. When I had arrived at this point and had become as well acquainted with the theory and practice of natural philosophy as depended on the lessons of any of the professors at Ingolstadt, my residence there being no longer conducive to my improvements, I thought of returning to my friends and my native town, when an incident happened that protracted my stay.

One of the phenomena which had peculiarly attracted my attention was the structure of the human frame, and, indeed, any animal endued with life. Whence, I often asked myself, did the principle of life proceed? It was a bold question, and one which has ever been considered as a mystery; yet with how many things are we upon the brink of becoming acquainted, if cowardice or carelessness did not restrain our enquiries. I revolved these circumstances in my mind, and determined thenceforth to apply myself more particularly to those branches of natural philosophy which relate to physiology. Unless I had been animated by an almost supernatural enthusiasm, my application to this study would have been irksome, and almost intolerable. To examine the causes of life, we must first have recourse to death. I became acquainted with the science of anatomy: but this was not sufficient; I must also observe the natural decay and corruption of the human body. In my education my father had taken the greatest precautions that my mind should be impressed with no supernatural horrors. I do not ever remember to have trembled at a tale of superstition, or to have feared the apparition of a spirit. Darkness had no effect upon my fancy; and a churchyard was to me merely the receptacle of bodies deprived of life, which, from being the seat of beauty and strength, had

become food for the worm. Now I was led to examine the cause and progress of this decay, and forced to spend days and nights in vaults and charnel-houses. My attention was fixed upon every object the most insupportable to the delicacy of the human feelings.
5 I saw how the fine form of man was degraded and wasted; I beheld the corruption of death succeed to the blooming cheek of life; I saw how the worm inherited the wonders of the eye and brain. I paused, examining and analysing all the minutiae of causation, as exemplified in the change from life to death, and death to life, until
10 from the midst of this darkness a sudden light broke in upon me – a light so brilliant and wondrous, yet so simple, that while I became dizzy with the immensity of the prospect which it illustrated, I was surprised, that among so many men of genius who had directed their enquiries towards the same science, that I alone should be
15 reserved to discover so astonishing a secret.

Remember, I am not recording the vision of a madman. The sun does not more certainly shine in the heavens, than that which I now affirm is true. Some miracle might have produced it, yet the stages of the discovery were distinct and probable. After days and
20 nights of incredible labour and fatigue, I succeeded in discovering the cause of generation and life; nay, more, I became myself capable of bestowing animation upon lifeless matter.

The astonishment which I had at first experienced on this discovery soon gave place to delight and rapture. After so much time
25 spent in painful labour, to arrive at once at the summit of my desires, was the most gratifying consummation of my toils. But this discovery was so great and overwhelming, that all the steps by which I had been progressively led to it were obliterated, and I beheld only the result. What had been the study and desire of the
30 wisest men since the creation of the world was now within my grasp. Not that, like a magic scene, it all opened upon me at once: the information I had obtained was of a nature rather to direct my endeavours so soon as I should point them towards the object of my search, than to exhibit that object already accomplished. I was
35 like the Arabian who had been buried with the dead and found

a passage to life, aided only by one glimmering and seemingly ineffectual light.

I see by your eagerness and the wonder and hope which your eyes express, my friend, that you expect to be informed of the secret with which I am acquainted; that cannot be: listen patiently until the end of my story, and you will easily perceive why I am reserved upon that subject. I will not lead you on, unguarded and ardent as I then was, to your destruction and infallible misery. Learn from me, if not by my precepts, at least by my example, how dangerous is the acquirement of knowledge and how much happier that man is who believes his native town to be the world, than he who aspires to become greater than his nature will allow.

When I found so astonishing a power placed within my hands, I hesitated a long time concerning the manner in which I should employ it. Although I possessed the capacity of bestowing animation, yet to prepare a frame for the reception of it, with all its intricacies of fibres, muscles, and veins, still remained a work of inconceivable difficulty and labour. I doubted at first whether I should attempt the creation of a being like myself, or one of simpler organisation; but my imagination was too much exalted by my first success to permit me to doubt of my ability to give life to an animal as complex and wonderful as man. The materials at present within my command hardly appeared adequate to so arduous an undertaking; but I doubted not that I should ultimately succeed. I prepared myself for a multitude of reverses; my operations might be incessantly baffled, and at last my work be imperfect: yet, when I considered the improvement which every day takes place in science and mechanics, I was encouraged to hope my present attempts would at least lay the foundations of future success. Nor could I consider the magnitude and complexity of my plan as any argument of its impracticability. It was with these feelings that I began the creation of a human being. As the minuteness of the parts formed a great hindrance to my speed, I resolved, contrary to my first intention, to make the being of a gigantic stature; that is to say, about eight feet in height, and proportionably large. After having formed this determination and having spent some months in successfully collecting and arranging my materials, I began.

No one can conceive the variety of feelings which bore me onwards, like a hurricane, in the first enthusiasm of success. Life
5 and death appeared to me ideal bounds, which I should first break through, and pour a torrent of light into our dark world. A new species would bless me as its creator and source; many happy and excellent natures would owe their being to me. No father could claim the gratitude of his child so completely as I should deserve
10 theirs. Pursuing these reflections, I thought, that if I could bestow animation upon lifeless matter, I might in process of time (although I now found it impossible) renew life where death had apparently devoted the body to corruption.

These thoughts supported my spirits, while I pursued my under-
15 taking with unremitting ardour. My cheek had grown pale with study, and my person had become emaciated with confinement. Sometimes, on the very brink of certainty, I failed; yet still I clung to the hope which the next day or the next hour might realise. One secret which I alone possessed was the hope to which I had
20 dedicated myself; and the moon gazed on my midnight labours, while, with unrelaxed and breathless eagerness, I pursued nature to her hiding-places. Who shall conceive the horrors of my secret toil as I dabbled among the unhallowed damps of the grave or tortured the living animal to animate the lifeless clay? My limbs
25 now tremble, and my eyes swim with the remembrance; but then a resistless, and almost frantic impulse, urged me forward; I seemed to have lost all soul or sensation but for this one pursuit. It was indeed but a passing trance, that only made me feel with renewed acuteness so soon as, the unnatural stimulus ceasing to operate, I
30 had returned to my old habits. I collected bones from charnel-houses and disturbed, with profane fingers, the tremendous secrets of the human frame. In a solitary chamber, or rather cell, at the top of the house, and separated from all the other apartments by a gallery and staircase, I kept my workshop of filthy creation: my
35 eyeballs were starting from their sockets in attending to the details of my employment. The dissecting room and the slaughter-house

furnished many of my materials; and often did my human nature turn with loathing from my occupation, whilst, still urged on by an eagerness which perpetually increased, I brought my work near to a conclusion.

The summer months passed while I was thus engaged, heart and soul, in one pursuit. It was a most beautiful season; never did the fields bestow a more plentiful harvest, or the vines yield a more luxuriant vintage: but my eyes were insensible to the charms of nature. And the same feelings which made me neglect the scenes around me caused me also to forget those friends who were so many miles absent, and whom I had not seen for so long a time. I knew my silence disquieted them; and I well remembered the words of my father: 'I know that while you are pleased with yourself, you will think of us with affection, and we shall hear regularly from you. You must pardon me if I regard any interruption in your correspondence as a proof that your other duties are equally neglected.'

I knew well therefore what would be my father's feelings; but I could not tear my thoughts from my employment, loathsome in itself, but which had taken an irresistible hold of my imagination. I wished, as it were, to procrastinate all that related to my feelings of affection until the great object, which swallowed up every habit of my nature, should be completed.

I then thought that my father would be unjust if he ascribed my neglect to vice, or faultiness on my part, but I am now convinced that he was justified in conceiving that I should not be altogether free from blame. A human being in perfection ought always to preserve a calm and peaceful mind, and never to allow passion or a transitory desire to disturb his tranquillity. I do not think that the pursuit of knowledge is an exception to this rule. If the study to which you apply yourself has a tendency to weaken your affections, and to destroy your taste for those simple pleasures in which no alloy can possibly mix, then that study is certainly unlawful, that is to say, not befitting the human mind. If this rule were always observed; if no man allowed any pursuit whatsoever to interfere with the tranquillity of his domestic affections, Greece had not been enslaved; Caesar would have spared his country; America would have been discovered more gradually; and the empires of Mexico and Peru had not been destroyed.

But I forget that I am moralising in the most interesting part of
5 my tale, and your looks remind me to proceed.

My father made no reproach in his letters, and only took notice of my silence by enquiring into my occupations more particularly than before. Winter, spring, and summer passed away during my labours; but I did not watch the blossom or the expanding leaves
10 – sights which before always yielded me supreme delight – so deeply was I engrossed in my occupation. The leaves of that year had withered before my work drew to a close; and now every day showed me more plainly how well I had succeeded. But my enthusiasm was checked by my anxiety, and I appeared rather like one doomed by
15 slavery to toil in the mines, or any other unwholesome trade than an artist occupied by his favourite employment. Every night I was oppressed by a slow fever, and I became nervous to a most painful degree; the fall of a leaf startled me, and I shunned my fellow-creatures as if I had been guilty of a crime. Sometimes I grew
20 alarmed at the wreck I perceived that I had become; the energy of my purpose alone sustained me: my labours would soon end, and I believed that exercise and amusement would then drive away incipient disease; and I promised myself both of these when my creation should be complete.

Chapter V

It was on a dreary night of November, that I beheld the accomplish-
ment of my toils. With an anxiety that almost amounted to agony,
I collected the instruments of life around me, that I might infuse a
spark of being into the lifeless thing that lay at my feet. It was
already one in the morning; the rain pattered dismally against the   5
panes, and my candle was nearly burnt out, when, by the glimmer
of the half-extinguished light, I saw the dull yellow eye of the
creature open; it breathed hard, and a convulsive motion agitated
its limbs.

How can I describe my emotions at this catastrophe, or how   10
delineate the wretch whom with such infinite pains and care I had
endeavoured to form? His limbs were in proportion, and I had
selected his features as beautiful. Beautiful! – Great God! His
yellow skin scarcely covered the work of muscles and arteries
beneath; his hair was of a lustrous black, and flowing; his teeth of   15
pearly whiteness; but these luxuriances only formed a more horrid
contrast with his watery eyes, that seemed almost of the same colour
as the dun-white sockets in which they were set, his shrivelled
complexion and straight black lips.

The different accidents of life are not so changeable as the   20
feelings of human nature. I had worked hard for nearly two years,
for the sole purpose of infusing life into an inanimate body. For
this I had deprived myself of rest and health. I had desired it
with an ardour that far exceeded moderation; but now that I had
finished, the beauty of the dream vanished, and breathless horror   25
and disgust filled my heart. Unable to endure the aspect of the
being I had created, I rushed out of the room, and continued a

long time traversing my bedchamber, unable to compose my mind to sleep. At length lassitude succeeded to the tumult I had before endured; and I threw myself on the bed in my clothes, endeavouring to seek a few moments of forgetfulness. But it was in vain: I slept,
5 indeed, but I was disturbed by the wildest dreams. I thought I saw Elizabeth, in the bloom of health, walking in the streets of Ingolstadt. Delighted and surprised, I embraced her, but as I imprinted the first kiss on her lips, they became livid with the hue of death; her features appeared to change, and I thought that I held
10 the corpse of my dead mother in my arms; a shroud enveloped her form, and I saw the grave-worms crawling in the folds of flannel. I started from my sleep with horror; a cold dew covered my forehead, my teeth chattered, and every limb became convulsed: when, by the dim and yellow light of the moon, as it forced its way through
15 the window shutters, I beheld the wretch – the miserable monster whom I had created. He held up the curtain of the bed; and his eyes, if eyes they may be called, were fixed on me. His jaws opened, and he muttered some inarticulate sounds, while a grin wrinkled his cheeks. He might have spoken, but I did not hear; one hand
20 was stretched out, seemingly to detain me, but I escaped, and rushed downstairs. I took refuge in the courtyard belonging to the house which I inhabited; where I remained during the rest of the night, walking up and down in the greatest agitation, listening attentively, catching and fearing each sound as if it were to
25 announce the approach of the demoniacal corpse to which I had so miserably given life.

Oh! no mortal could support the horror of that countenance. A mummy again endued with animation could not be so hideous as that wretch. I had gazed on him while unfinished; he was ugly
30 then; but when those muscles and joints were rendered capable of motion, it became a thing such as even Dante could not have conceived.

I passed the night wretchedly. Sometimes my pulse beat so quickly and hardly that I felt the palpitation of every artery; at
35 others, I nearly sank to the ground through languor and extreme weakness. Mingled with this horror, I felt the bitterness of dis-

appointment; dreams that had been my food and pleasant rest for so long a space were now become a hell to me; and the change was so rapid, the overthrow so complete!

Morning, dismal and wet, at length dawned, and discovered to my sleepless and aching eyes the church of Ingolstadt, its white 5 steeple and clock, which indicated the sixth hour. The porter opened the gates of the court, which had that night been my asylum, and I issued into the streets, pacing them with quick steps, as if I sought to avoid the wretch whom I feared every turning of the street would present to my view. I did not dare return to the 10 apartment which I inhabited, but felt impelled to hurry on, although drenched by the rain which poured from a black and comfortless sky.

I continued walking in this manner for some time, endeavouring by bodily exercise to ease the load that weighed upon my mind. I 15 traversed the streets without any clear conception of where I was or what I was doing. My heart palpitated in the sickness of fear, and I hurried on with irregular steps, not daring to look about me:

> Like one, on a lonesome road who,
>> Doth walk in fear and dread,
> And, having once turned round, walks on,
>> And turns no more his head;
> Because he knows a frightful fiend
>> Doth close behind him tread.[1]

Continuing thus, I came at length opposite to the inn at which the various diligences and carriages usually stopped. Here I paused, 20 I knew not why; but I remained some minutes with my eyes fixed on a coach that was coming towards me from the other end of the street. As it drew nearer I observed that it was the Swiss diligence: it stopped just where I was standing; and, on the door being opened, I perceived Henry Clerval, who, on seeing me, instantly 25 sprung out. 'My dear Frankenstein,' exclaimed he, 'how glad I am

---

1. Coleridge's *Ancient Mariner* [author's footnote].

to see you! how fortunate that you should be here at the very moment of my alighting!'

Nothing could equal my delight on seeing Clerval; his presence brought back to my thoughts my father, Elizabeth, and all those
5 scenes of home so dear to my recollection. I grasped his hand, and in a moment forgot my horror and misfortune; I felt suddenly, and for the first time during many months, calm and serene joy. I welcomed my friend, therefore, in the most cordial manner, and we walked towards my college. Clerval continued talking for some
10 time about our mutual friends and his own good fortune in being permitted to come to Ingolstadt. 'You may easily believe,' said he, 'how great was the difficulty to persuade my father that all necessary knowledge was not comprised in the noble art of book-keeping; and, indeed, I believe I left him incredulous to the last, for his
15 constant answer to my unwearied intreaties was the same as that to the Dutch schoolmaster in *The Vicar of Wakefield*: "I have ten thousand florins a year without Greek, I eat heartily without Greek." But his affection for me at length overcame his dislike of learning, and he has permitted me to undertake a voyage of dis-
20 covery to the land of knowledge.'

'It gives me the greatest delight to see you; but tell me how you left my father, brothers, and Elizabeth.'

'Very well, and very happy, only a little uneasy that they hear from you so seldom. By the by, I mean to lecture you a little upon
25 their account myself – But, my dear Frankenstein,' continued he, stopping short and gazing full in my face, 'I did not before remark how very ill you appear; so thin and pale; and look as if you had been watching for several nights.'

'You have guessed right; I have lately been so deeply engaged in
30 one occupation, that I have not allowed myself sufficient rest, as you see; but I hope, I sincerely hope, that all these employments are now at an end, and that I am at length free.'

I trembled excessively; I could not endure to think of, and far less to allude to, the occurrences of the preceding night. I walked
35 with a quick pace, and we soon arrived at my college. I then reflected, and the thought made me shiver, that the creature whom

I had left in my apartment might still be there, alive and walking about. I dreaded to behold this monster; but I feared still more that Henry should see him. Intreating him, therefore, to remain a few minutes at the bottom of the stairs, I darted up towards my own room. My hand was already on the lock of the door before I 5
recollected myself. I then paused; and a cold shivering came over me. I threw the door forcibly open, as children are accustomed to do when they expect a spectre to stand in waiting for them on the other side; but nothing appeared. I stepped fearfully in: the apartment was empty; and my bedroom was also freed from its 10
hideous guest. I could hardly believe that so great a good fortune could have befallen me; but when I became assured that my enemy had indeed fled, I clapped my hands for joy and ran down to Clerval.

We ascended into my room, and the servant presently brought 15
breakfast; but I was unable to contain myself. It was not joy only that possessed me; I felt my flesh tingle with excess of sensitiveness, and my pulse beat rapidly. I was unable to remain for a single instant in the same place; I jumped over the chairs, clapped my hands, and laughed aloud. Clerval at first attributed my unusual 20
spirits to joy on his arrival, but when he observed me more attentively, he saw a wildness in my eyes for which he could not account; and my loud, unrestrained, heartless laughter frightened and astonished him.

'My dear Victor,' cried he, 'what, for God's sake, is the matter? 25
do not laugh in that manner. How ill you are! What is the cause of all this?'

'Do not ask me,' cried I, putting my hands before my eyes, for I thought I saw the dreaded spectre glide into the room; '*he* can tell. – Oh, save me! save me!' I imagined that the monster seized me; I 30
struggled furiously and fell down in a fit.

Poor Clerval! what must have been his feelings? A meeting, which he anticipated with such joy, so strangely turned to bitterness. But I was not the witness of his grief; for I was lifeless, and did not recover my senses for a long, long time. 35

This was the commencement of a nervous fever, which confined

me for several months. During all that time Henry was my only nurse. I afterwards learned that, knowing my father's advanced age, and unfitness for so long a journey, and how wretched my sickness would make Elizabeth, he spared them this grief by con-
5 cealing the extent of my disorder. He knew that I could not have a more kind and attentive nurse than himself; and, firm in the hope he felt of my recovery, he did not doubt that, instead of doing harm, he performed the kindest action that he could towards them.

10 But I was in reality very ill; and surely nothing but the unbounded and unremitting attentions of my friend could have restored me to life. The form of the monster on whom I had bestowed existence was forever before my eyes, and I raved incessantly concerning him. Doubtless my words surprised Henry; he at first believed
15 them to be the wanderings of my disturbed imagination; but the pertinacity with which I continually recurred to the same subject, persuaded him that my disorder indeed owed its origin to some uncommon and terrible event.

By very slow degrees, and with frequent relapses that alarmed
20 and grieved my friend, I recovered. I remember the first time I became capable of observing outward objects with any kind of pleasure, I perceived that the fallen leaves had disappeared and that the young buds were shooting forth from the trees that shaded my window. It was a divine spring; and the season contributed
25 greatly to my convalescence. I felt also sentiments of joy and affection revive in my bosom; my gloom disappeared, and in a short time I became as cheerful as before I was attacked by the fatal passion.

'Dearest Clerval,' exclaimed I, 'how kind, how very good you
30 are to me. This whole winter, instead of being spent in study, as you promised yourself, has been consumed in my sick room. How shall I ever repay you? I feel the greatest remorse for the disappointment of which I have been the occasion; but you will forgive me.'

'You will repay me entirely, if you do not discompose yourself,
35 but get well as fast as you can; and since you appear in such good spirits, I may speak to you on one subject, may I not?'

I trembled. One subject! What could it be? Could he allude to an object on whom I dared not even think?

'Compose yourself,' said Clerval, who observed my change of colour, 'I will not mention it if it agitates you; but your father and cousin would be very happy if they received a letter from you in 5
your own handwriting. They hardly know how ill you have been, and are uneasy at your long silence.'

'Is that all, my dear Henry? How could you suppose that my first thought would not fly towards those dear, dear friends whom I love, and who are so deserving of my love?' 10

'If this is your present temper, my friend, you will perhaps be glad to see a letter that has been lying here some days for you: it is from your cousin, I believe.'

Chapter VI

Clerval then put the following letter into my hands. It was from my own Elizabeth: –

MY DEAREST COUSIN,

You have been ill, very ill, and even the constant letters of dear
5   kind Henry are not sufficient to reassure me on your account. You are forbidden to write – to hold a pen; yet one word from you, dear Victor, is necessary to calm our apprehensions. For a long time I have thought that each post would bring this line, and my persuasions have restrained my uncle from undertaking a journey to
10 Ingolstadt. I have prevented his encountering the inconveniences and perhaps dangers of so long a journey, yet how often have I regretted not being able to perform it myself! I figure to myself that the task of attending on your sickbed has devolved on some mercenary old nurse, who could never guess your wishes, nor
15 minister to them with the care and affection of your poor cousin. Yet that is over now: Clerval writes that indeed you are getting better. I eagerly hope that you will confirm this intelligence soon in your own handwriting.

Get well – and return to us. You will find a happy, cheerful
20 home, and friends who love you dearly. Your father's health is vigorous, and he asks but to see you, but to be assured that you are well; and not a care will ever cloud his benevolent countenance. How pleased you would be to remark the improvement of our Ernest! He is now sixteen, and full of activity and spirit. He is
25 desirous to be a true Swiss, and to enter into foreign service, but we cannot part with him, at least until his elder brother return to

us. My uncle is not pleased with the idea of a military career in a
distant country, but Ernest never had your powers of application.
He looks upon study as an odious fetter; his time is spent in the
open air, climbing the hills or rowing on the lake. I fear that he will
become an idler, unless we yield the point, and permit him to enter 5
on the profession which he has selected.

Little alteration, except the growth of our dear children, has
taken place since you left us. The blue lake, and snow-clad mountains – they never change; and I think our placid home and our
contented hearts are regulated by the same immutable laws. My 10
trifling occupations take up my time and amuse me, and I am
rewarded for any exertions by seeing none but happy, kind faces
around me. Since you left us, but one change has taken place in
our little household. Do you remember on what occasions Justine
Moritz entered our family? Probably you do not; I will relate her 15
history, therefore, in a few words. Madame Moritz, her mother,
was a widow with four children, of whom Justine was the third.
This girl had always been the favourite of her father; but, through
a strange perversity, her mother could not endure her, and after
the death of M. Moritz, treated her very ill. My aunt observed this, 20
and when Justine was twelve years of age, prevailed on her mother
to allow her to live at our house. The republican institutions of our
country have produced simpler and happier manners than those
which prevail in the great monarchies that surround it. Hence there
is less distinction between the several classes of its inhabitants; and 25
the lower orders, being neither so poor nor so despised, their
manners are more refined and moral. A servant in Geneva does
not mean the same thing as a servant in France and England.
Justine, thus received in our family, learned the duties of a servant;
a condition which, in our fortunate country, does not include the 30
idea of ignorance, and a sacrifice of the dignity of a human being.

Justine, you may remember, was a great favourite of yours; and
I recollect you once remarked that if you were in an ill humour,
one glance from Justine could dissipate it, for the same reason that
Ariosto gives concerning the beauty of Angelica – she looked so 35
frank-hearted and happy. My aunt conceived a great attachment

for her, by which she was induced to give her an education superior to that which she had at first intended. This benefit was fully repaid; Justine was the most grateful little creature in the world: I do not mean that she made any professions; I never heard one pass
5 her lips, but you could see by her eyes that she almost adored her protectress. Although her disposition was gay, and in many respects inconsiderate, yet she paid the greatest attention to every gesture of my aunt. She thought her the model of all excellence and endeavoured to imitate her phraseology and manners, so that even
10 now she often reminds me of her.

When my dearest aunt died, every one was too much occupied in their own grief to notice poor Justine, who had attended her illness with the most anxious affection. Poor Justine was very ill, but other trials were reserved for her.
15 One by one, her brothers and sister died; and her mother, with the exception of her neglected daughter, was left childless. The conscience of the woman was troubled; she began to think that the deaths of her favourites were a judgment from heaven to chastise her partiality. She was a Roman catholic; and I believe her confessor
20 confirmed the idea which she had conceived. Accordingly, a few months after your departure for Ingolstadt, Justine was called home by her repentant mother. Poor girl! she wept when she quitted our house; she was much altered since the death of my aunt; grief had given softness and a winning mildness to her manners which had
25 before been remarkable for vivacity. Nor was her residence at her mother's house of a nature to restore her gaiety. The poor woman was very vacillating in her repentance. She sometimes begged Justine to forgive her unkindness but much oftener accused her of having caused the deaths of her brothers and sister. Perpetual
30 fretting at length threw Madame Moritz into a decline, which at first increased her irritability, but she is now at peace forever. She died on the first approach of cold weather, at the beginning of this last winter. Justine has returned to us, and I assure you I love her tenderly. She is very clever and gentle, and extremely pretty; as I
35 mentioned before, her mien and her expressions continually remind me of my dear aunt.

I must say also a few words to you, my dear cousin, of little darling William. I wish you could see him; he is very tall of his age, with sweet laughing blue eyes, dark eyelashes, and curling hair. When he smiles, two little dimples appear on each cheek, which are rosy with health. He has already had one or two little *wives*, but 5
Louisa Biron is his favourite, a pretty little girl of five years of age.

Now, dear Victor, I dare say you wish to be indulged in a little gossip concerning the good people of Geneva. The pretty Miss Mansfield has already received the congratulatory visits on her approaching marriage with a young Englishman, John Melbourne, 10
Esq. Her ugly sister, Manon, married M. Duvillard, the rich banker, last autumn. Your favourite school-fellow, Louis Manoir, has suffered misfortunes since the departure of Clerval from Geneva. But he has already recovered his spirits and is reported to be on the point of marrying a very lively, pretty Frenchwoman, 15
Madame Tavernier. She is a widow, and much older than Manoir; but she is very much admired and a favourite with every body.

I have written myself into better spirits, dear cousin; but my anxiety returns upon me as I conclude. Write, dearest Victor – one line – one word will be a blessing to us. Ten thousand thanks to 20
Henry for his kindness, his affection, and his many letters: we are sincerely grateful. Adieu! my cousin, take care of yourself; and, I intreat you, write!

ELIZABETH LAVENZA
Geneva, March 18th, 17– 25

'Dear, dear Elizabeth!' I exclaimed, when I had read her letter, 'I will write instantly, and relieve them from the anxiety they must feel.' I wrote, and this exertion greatly fatigued me; but my convalescence had commenced, and proceeded regularly. In another 30
fortnight I was able to leave my chamber.

One of my first duties on my recovery was to introduce Clerval to the several professors of the university. In doing this, I underwent a kind of rough usage, ill befitting the wounds that my mind had sustained. Ever since the fatal night, the end of my labours, and 35
the beginning of my misfortunes, I had conceived a violent

Frankenstein

antipathy even to the name of natural philosophy. When I was otherwise quite restored to health, the sight of a chemical instrument would renew all the agony of my nervous symptoms. Henry saw this and had removed all my apparatus from my view. He had
5 also changed my apartment, for he perceived that I had acquired a dislike for the room which had previously been my laboratory. But these cares of Clerval were made of no avail when I visited the professors. M. Waldman inflicted torture when he praised, with kindness and warmth, the astonishing progress I had made in the
10 sciences. He soon perceived that I disliked the subject; but not guessing the real cause, he attributed my feelings to modesty and changed the subject from my improvement to the science itself, with a desire, as I evidently saw, of drawing me out. What could I do? He meant to please, and he tormented me. I felt as if he had
15 placed carefully, one by one, in my view those instruments which were to be afterwards used in putting me to a slow and cruel death. I writhed under his words, yet dared not exhibit the pain I felt. Clerval, whose eyes and feelings were always quick in discerning the sensations of others, declined the subject, alleging, in excuse,
20 his total ignorance; and the conversation took a more general turn. I thanked my friend from my heart, but I did not speak. I saw plainly that he was surprised, but he never attempted to draw my secret from me; and although I loved him with a mixture of affection and reverence that knew no bounds, yet I could never persuade
25 myself to confide to him that event which was so often present to my recollection, but which I feared the detail to another would only impress more deeply.

M. Krempe was not equally docile; and in my condition at that time, of almost insupportable sensitiveness, his harsh, blunt
30 encomiums gave me even more pain than the benevolent approbation of M. Waldman. 'D–n the fellow!' cried he; 'why, M. Clerval, I assure you he has outstript us all. Ay, stare if you please; but it is nevertheless true. A youngster who, but a few years ago, believed in Cornelius Agrippa as firmly as in the Gospel, has now
35 set himself at the head of the university; and if he is not soon pulled down, we shall all be out of countenance. – Ay, ay,' continued he,

observing my face expressive of suffering, 'M. Frankenstein is modest, an excellent quality in a young man. Young men should be diffident of themselves, you know, M. Clerval: I was myself when young, but that wears out in a very short time.'

M. Krempe had now commenced a eulogy on himself, which 5 happily turned the conversation from a subject that was so annoying to me.

Clerval had never sympathised in my tastes for natural science; and his literary pursuits differed wholly from those which had occupied me. He came to the university with the design of making 10 himself complete master of the Oriental languages, as thus he should open a field for the plan of life he had marked out for himself. Resolved to pursue no inglorious career, he turned his eyes towards the East as affording scope for his spirit of enterprise. The Persian, Arabic, and Sanscrit languages engaged his attention, 15 and I was easily induced to enter on the same studies. Idleness had ever been irksome to me, and now that I wished to fly from reflection and hated my former studies, I felt great relief in being the fellow pupil with my friend, and found not only instruction but consolation in the works of the Orientalists. I did not, like him, 20 attempt a critical knowledge of their dialects, for I did not contemplate making any other use of them than temporary amusement. I read merely to understand their meaning, and they well repaid my labours. Their melancholy is soothing, and their joy elevating, to a degree I never experienced in studying the authors of any other 25 country. When you read their writings, life appears to consist in a warm sun and a garden of roses, in the smiles and frowns of a fair enemy, and the fire that consumes your own heart. How different from the manly and heroical poetry of Greece and Rome!

Summer passed away in these occupations, and my return to 30 Geneva was fixed for the latter end of autumn; but being delayed by several accidents, winter and snow arrived, the roads were deemed impassable, and my journey was retarded until the ensuing spring. I felt this delay very bitterly; for I longed to see my native town and my beloved friends. My return had only been delayed so 35 long from an unwillingness to leave Clerval in a strange place before he had become acquainted with any of its inhabitants. The winter, however, was spent cheerfully, and although the spring was uncommonly late, when it came its beauty compensated for its dilatoriness.

5   The month of May had already commenced, and I expected the letter daily which was to fix the date of my departure, when Henry proposed a pedestrian tour in the environs of Ingolstadt, that I might bid a personal farewell to the country I had so long inhabited. I acceded with pleasure to this proposition: I was fond of exercise,
10 and Clerval had always been my favourite companion in the rambles of this nature that I had taken among the scenes of my native country.

The we passed a fortnight in these perambulations: my health and spirits had long been restored, and they gained additional strength
15 from the salubrious air I breathed, the natural incidents of our progress, and the conversation of my friend. Study had before secluded me from the intercourse of my fellow-creatures, and rendered me unsocial, but Clerval called forth the better feelings of my heart; he again taught me to love the aspect of nature, and
20 the cheerful faces of children. Excellent friend! how sincerely did you love me and endeavour to elevate my mind until it was on a level with your own! A selfish pursuit had cramped and narrowed me, until your gentleness and affection warmed and opened my senses; I became the same happy creature who, a few years ago,
25 loved and beloved by all, had no sorrow or care. When happy, inanimate nature had the power of bestowing on me the most delightful sensations. A serene sky and verdant fields filled me with ecstasy. The present season was indeed divine; the flowers of spring bloomed in the hedges, while those of summer were already in
30 bud. I was undisturbed by thoughts which during the preceding year had pressed upon me, notwithstanding my endeavours to throw them off, with an invincible burden.

Henry rejoiced in my gaiety, and sincerely sympathised in my feelings: he exerted himself to amuse me, while he expressed the
35 sensations that filled his soul. The resources of his mind on this occasion were truly astonishing: his conversation was full of imagin-

ation; and very often, in imitation of the Persian and Arabic writers, he invented tales of wonderful fancy and passion. At other times, he repeated my favourite poems, or drew me out into arguments, which he supported with great ingenuity.

We returned to our college on a Sunday afternoon: the peasants 5 were dancing, and everyone we met appeared gay and happy. My own spirits were high, and I bounded along with feelings of unbridled joy and hilarity.

Chapter VII

On my return, I found the following letter from my father: –

MY DEAR VICTOR,

   You have probably waited impatiently for a letter to fix the date
of your return to us; and I was at first tempted to write only a few
5 lines, merely mentioning the day on which I should expect you.
But that would be a cruel kindness, and I dare not do it. What
would be your surprise, my son, when you expect a happy and glad
welcome, to behold, on the contrary, tears and wretchedness? And
how, Victor, can I relate our misfortune? Absence cannot have
10 rendered you callous to our joys and griefs; and how shall I inflict
pain on my long-absent son? I wish to prepare you for the woeful
news, but I know it is impossible; even now your eye skims over
the page, to seek the words which are to convey to you the horrible
tidings.
15   William is dead! – that sweet child, whose smiles delighted and
warmed my heart, who was so gentle, yet so gay! Victor, he is
murdered!
   I will not attempt to console you; but will simply relate the
circumstances of the transaction.
20   Last Thursday (May 7th) I, my niece, and your two brothers
went to walk in Plainpalais. The evening was warm and serene,
and we prolonged our walk farther than usual. It was already
dusk before we thought of returning; and then we discovered that
William and Ernest, who had gone on before, were not to be found.
25 We accordingly rested on a seat until they should return. Presently
Ernest came, and enquired if we had seen his brother: he said that

he had been playing with him, that William had run away to hide himself, and that he vainly sought for him, and afterwards waited for him a long time, but he did not return.

This account rather alarmed us, and we continued to search for him until night fell, when Elizabeth conjectured that he might have returned to the house. He was not there. We returned again, with torches, for I could not rest when I thought that my sweet boy had lost himself and was exposed to all the damps and dews of night; Elizabeth also suffered extreme anguish. About five in the morning I discovered my lovely boy, whom the night before I had seen blooming and active in health, stretched on the grass livid and motionless: the print of the murderer's finger was on his neck.

He was conveyed home, and the anguish that was visible in my countenance betrayed the secret to Elizabeth. She was very earnest to see the corpse. At first I attempted to prevent her, but she persisted, and entering the room where it lay, hastily examined the neck of the victim, and clasping her hands, exclaimed, 'Oh, God! I have murdered my darling child!'

She fainted, and was restored with extreme difficulty. When she again lived, it was only to weep and sigh. She told me that that same evening William had teased her to let him wear a very valuable miniature that she possessed of your mother. This picture is gone, and was doubtless the temptation which urged the murderer to the deed. We have no trace of him at present, although our exertions to discover him are unremitted; but they will not restore my beloved William!

Come, dearest Victor; you alone can console Elizabeth. She weeps continually and accuses herself unjustly as the cause of his death; her words pierce my heart. We are all unhappy, but will not that be an additional motive for you, my son, to return and be our comforter? Your dear mother! Alas, Victor! I now say, Thank God she did not live to witness the cruel, miserable death of her youngest darling!

Come, Victor; not brooding thoughts of vengeance against the assassin, but with feelings of peace and gentleness, that will heal, instead of festering, the wounds of our minds. Enter the house of mourning, my friend, but with kindness and affection for those who love you, and not with hatred for your enemies.

Your affectionate and afflicted father,
ALPHONSE FRANKENSTEIN
Geneva, May 12th, 17–

5

Clerval, who had watched my countenance as I read this letter, was surprised to observe the despair that succeeded to the joy I at first expressed on receiving news from my friends. I threw the letter on the table, and covered my face with my hands.

10 'My dear Frankenstein,' exclaimed Henry, when he perceived me weep with bitterness, 'are we always to be unhappy? My dear friend, what has happened?'

I motioned to him to take up the letter, while I walked up and down the room in the extremest agitation. Tears also gushed from
15 the eyes of Clerval, as he read the account of my misfortune.

'I can offer you no consolation, my friend,' said he; 'your disaster is irreparable. What do you intend to do?'

'To go instantly to Geneva: come with me, Henry, to order the horses.'

20 During our walk Clerval endeavoured to say a few words of consolation; he could only express his heartfelt sympathy. 'Poor William!' said he. 'Dear lovely child, he now sleeps with his angel mother! Who that had seen him bright and joyous in his young beauty, but must weep over his untimely loss! To die so miserably;
25 to feel the murderer's grasp! How much more a murderer, that could destroy such radiant innocence! Poor little fellow! one only consolation have we; his friends mourn and weep, but he is at rest. The pang is over, his sufferings are at an end forever. A sod covers his gentle form, and he knows no pain. He can no longer be a
30 subject for pity; we must reserve that for his miserable survivors.'

Clerval spoke thus as we hurried through the streets; the words impressed themselves on my mind, and I remembered them afterwards in solitude. But now, as soon as the horses arrived, I hurried into a cabriolet and bade farewell to my friend.

35 My journey was very melancholy. At first I wished to hurry on,

for I longed to console and sympathise with my loved and sorrowing friends; but when I drew near my native town, I slackened my progress. I could hardly sustain the multitude of feelings that crowded into my mind. I passed through scenes familiar to my youth, but which I had not seen for nearly six years. How altered 5 every thing might be during that time! One sudden and desolating change had taken place; but a thousand little circumstances might have by degrees worked other alterations, which, although they were done more tranquilly, might not be the less decisive. Fear overcame me; I dared not advance, dreading a thousand name- 10 less evils that made me tremble, although I was unable to define them.

I remained two days at Lausanne, in this painful state of mind. I contemplated the lake: the waters were placid: all around was calm; and the snowy mountains, 'the palaces of nature', were not 15 changed. By degrees the calm and heavenly scene restored me, and I continued my journey towards Geneva.

The road ran by the side of the lake, which became narrower as I approached my native town. I discovered more distinctly the black sides of Jura, and the bright summit of Mont Blanc. I wept 20 like a child. 'Dear mountains! My own beautiful lake! How do you welcome your wanderer? Your summits are clear; the sky and lake are blue and placid. Is this to prognosticate peace, or to mock at my unhappiness?'

I fear, my friend, that I shall render myself tedious by dwelling on 25 these preliminary circumstances; but they were days of comparative happiness, and I think of them with pleasure. My country, my beloved country! who but a native can tell the delight I took in again beholding thy streams, thy mountains, and, more than all, thy lovely lake! 30

Yet, as I drew nearer home, grief and fear again overcame me. Night also closed around; and when I could hardly see the dark mountains, I felt still more gloomily. The picture appeared a vast and dim scene of evil, and I foresaw obscurely that I was destined to become the most wretched of human beings. Alas! I prophesied 35 truly, and failed only in one single circumstance, that in all the misery I imagined and dreaded, I did not conceive the hundredth part of the anguish I was destined to endure.

It was completely dark when I arrived in the environs of Geneva; the gates of the town were already shut; and I was obliged to pass
5 the night at Secheron, a village at the distance of half a league from the city. The sky was serene; and as I was unable to rest, I resolved to visit the spot where my poor William had been murdered. As I could not pass through the town, I was obliged to cross the lake in a boat to arrive at Plainpalais. During this short voyage I saw the
10 lightnings playing on the summit of Mont Blanc in the most beautiful figures. The storm appeared to approach rapidly; and, on landing, I ascended a low hill, that I might observe its progress. It advanced; the heavens were clouded, and I soon felt the rain coming slowly in large drops, but its violence quickly increased.

15 I quitted my seat and walked on, although the darkness and storm increased every minute and the thunder burst with a terrific crash over my head. It was echoed from Salêve, the Juras, and the Alps of Savoy; vivid flashes of lightning dazzled my eyes, illuminating the lake, making it appear like a vast sheet of fire; then
20 for an instant every thing seemed of a pitchy darkness, until the eye recovered itself from the preceding flash. The storm, as is often the case in Switzerland, appeared at once in various parts of the heavens. The most violent storm hung exactly north of the town, over that part of the lake which lies between the promontory of
25 Belrive and the village of Copêt. Another storm enlightened Jura with faint flashes; and another darkened and sometimes disclosed the Môle, a peaked mountain to the east of the lake.

While I watched the tempest, so beautiful yet terrific, I wandered on with a hasty step. This noble war in the sky elevated my spirits;
30 I clasped my hands and exclaimed aloud, 'William, dear angel! this is thy funeral, this thy dirge!' As I said these words, I perceived in the gloom a figure which stole from behind a clump of trees near me; I stood fixed, gazing intently: I could not be mistaken. A flash of lightning illuminated the object, and discovered its shape plainly
35 to me; its gigantic stature, and the deformity of its aspect, more hideous than belongs to humanity, instantly informed me that it

was the wretch, the filthy daemon to whom I had given life. What did he there? Could he be (I shuddered at the conception) the murderer of my brother? No sooner did that idea cross my imagination, than I became convinced of its truth; my teeth chattered, and I was forced to lean against a tree for support. The figure passed me quickly, and I lost it in the gloom. Nothing in human shape could have destroyed that fair child. *He* was the murderer! I could not doubt it. The mere presence of the idea was an irresistible proof of the fact. I thought of pursuing the devil; but it would have been in vain, for another flash discovered him to me hanging among the rocks of the nearly perpendicular ascent of Mount Salêve, a hill that bound Plainpalais on the south. He soon reached the summit, and disappeared.

I remained motionless. The thunder ceased, but the rain still continued, and the scene was enveloped in an impenetrable darkness. I revolved in my mind the events which I had until now sought to forget: the whole train of my progress towards the creation; the appearance of the work of my own hands alive at my bedside; its departure. Two years had now nearly elapsed since the night on which he first received life; and was this his first crime? Alas! I had turned loose into the world a depraved wretch, whose delight was in carnage and misery; had he not murdered my brother?

No one can conceive the anguish I suffered during the remainder of the night, which I spent, cold and wet, in the open air. But I did not feel the inconvenience of the weather; my imagination was busy in scenes of evil and despair. I considered the being whom I had cast among mankind, and endowed with the will and power to effect purposes of horror, such as the deed which he had now done, nearly in the light of my own vampire, my own spirit let loose from the grave, and forced to destroy all that was dear to me.

Day dawned; and I directed my steps towards the town. The gates were open, and I hastened to my father's house. My first thought was to discover what I knew of the murderer, and cause instant pursuit to be made. But I paused when I reflected on the story that I had to tell. A being whom I myself had formed, and endued with life, had met me at midnight among the precipices of

an inaccessible mountain. I remembered also the nervous fever
with which I had been seized just at the time that I dated my
creation, and which would give an air of delirium to a tale otherwise
so utterly improbable. I well knew that if any other had communi-
5 cated such a relation to me, I should have looked upon it as the
ravings of insanity. Besides, the strange nature of the animal would
elude all pursuit, even if I were so far credited as to persuade my
relatives to commence it. And then of what use would be pursuit?
Who could arrest a creature capable of scaling the overhanging
10 sides of Mont Salêve? These reflections determined me, and I
resolved to remain silent.

It was about five in the morning when I entered my father's
house. I told the servants not to disturb the family, and went into
the library to attend their usual hour of rising.

15 Six years had elapsed, passed as a dream but for one indelible
trace, and I stood in the same place where I had last embraced my
father before my departure for Ingolstadt. Beloved and venerable
parent! He still remained to me. I gazed on the picture of my
mother which stood over the mantel-piece. It was an historical
20 subject, painted at my father's desire, and represented Caroline
Beaufort in an agony of despair, kneeling by the coffin of her dead
father. Her garb was rustic, and her cheek pale; but there was an
air of dignity and beauty, that hardly permitted the sentiment of
pity. Below this picture was a miniature of William; and my tears
25 flowed when I looked upon it. While I was thus engaged, Ernest
entered: he had heard me arrive, and hastened to welcome me. He
expressed a sorrowful delight to see me. 'Welcome, my dearest
Victor,' said he. 'Ah! I wish you had come three months ago, and
then you would have found us all joyous and delighted. You come
30 to us now to share a misery which nothing can alleviate; yet your
presence will, I hope, revive our father, who seems sinking under
his misfortune; and your persuasions will induce poor Elizabeth to
cease her vain and tormenting self-accusations. – Poor William! he
was our darling and our pride!'

35 Tears, unrestrained, fell from my brother's eyes; a sense of
mortal agony crept over my frame. Before, I had only imagined the

wretchedness of my desolated home; the reality came on me as a new and a not less terrible disaster. I tried to calm Ernest; I enquired more minutely concerning my father, and her I named my cousin.

'She most of all,' said Ernest, 'requires consolation; she accused herself of having caused the death of my brother, and that made her very wretched. But since the murderer has been discovered –'

'The murderer discovered! Good God! how can that be? who could attempt to pursue him? It is impossible; one might as well try to overtake the winds or confine a mountain-stream with a straw. I saw him too; he was free last night!'

'I do not know what you mean,' replied my brother, in accents of wonder, 'but to us the discovery we have made completes our misery. No one would believe it at first; and even now Elizabeth will not be convinced, notwithstanding all the evidence. Indeed, who would credit that Justine Moritz, who was so amiable and fond of all the family, could suddenly become capable of so frightful, so appalling a crime?'

'Justine Moritz! Poor, poor girl, is she the accused? But it is wrongfully; every one knows that; no one believes it, surely, Ernest?'

'No one did at first; but several circumstances came out that have almost forced conviction upon us; and her own behaviour has been so confused as to add to the evidence of facts a weight that, I fear, leaves no hope for doubt. But she will be tried today, and you will then hear all.'

He related that, the morning on which the murder of poor William had been discovered, Justine had been taken ill, and confined to her bed for several days. During this interval one of the servants, happening to examine the apparel she had worn on the night of the murder, had discovered in her pocket the picture of my mother, which had been judged to be the temptation of the murderer. The servant instantly showed it to one of the others, who, without saying a word to any of the family, went to a magistrate; and, upon their deposition, Justine was apprehended. On being charged with the fact, the poor girl confirmed the suspicion in a great measure by her extreme confusion of manner.

This was a strange tale, but it did not shake my faith, and I replied earnestly, 'You are all mistaken; I know the murderer. Justine, poor, good Justine, is innocent.'

At that instant my father entered. I saw unhappiness deeply
5 impressed on his countenance, but he endeavoured to welcome me cheerfully; and after we had exchanged our mournful greeting, would have introduced some other topic than that of our disaster, had not Ernest exclaimed, 'Good God, Papa! Victor says that he knows who was the murderer of poor William.'

10 'We do also, unfortunately,' replied my father; 'for indeed I had rather have been forever ignorant than have discovered so much depravity and ingratitude in one I valued so highly.'

'My dear father, you are mistaken; Justine is innocent.'

'If she is, God forbid that she should suffer as guilty. She is to
15 be tried today, and I hope, I sincerely hope, that she will be acquitted.'

This speech calmed me. I was firmly convinced in my own mind that Justine, and indeed every human being, was guiltless of this murder. I had no fear, therefore, that any circumstantial evidence
20 could be brought forward strong enough to convict her. My tale was not one to announce publicly; its astounding horror would be looked upon as madness by the vulgar. Did any one indeed exist, except I, the creator, who would believe, unless his senses convinced him, in the existence of the living monument of presumption
25 and rash ignorance which I had let loose upon the world?

We were soon joined by Elizabeth. Time had altered her since I last beheld her; it had endowed her with loveliness surpassing the beauty of her childish years. There was the same candour, the same vivacity, but it was allied to an expression more full of sensibility
30 and intellect. She welcomed me with the greatest affection. 'Your arrival, my dear cousin,' said she, 'fills me with hope. You perhaps will find some means to justify my poor guiltless Justine. Alas! who is safe, if she be convicted of crime? I rely on her innocence as certainly as I do upon my own. Our misfortune is doubly hard to
35 us; we have not only lost that lovely darling boy, but this poor girl, whom I sincerely love, is to be torn away by even a worse fate. If

she is condemned, I never shall know joy more. But she will not, I am sure she will not; and then I shall be happy again, even after the sad death of my little William.'

'She is innocent, my Elizabeth,' said I, 'and that shall be proved; fear nothing, but let your spirits be cheered by the assurance of her 5 acquittal.'

'How kind and generous you are! every one else believes in her guilt, and that made me wretched, for I knew that it was impossible: and to see every one else prejudiced in so deadly a manner rendered me hopeless and despairing.' She wept. 10

'Dearest niece,' said my father, 'dry your tears. If she is, as you believe, innocent, rely on the justice of our laws, and the activity with which I shall prevent the slightest shadow of partiality.'

Chapter VIII

We passed a few sad hours, until eleven o'clock, when the trial was to commence. My father and the rest of the family being obliged to attend as witnesses, I accompanied them to the court. During the whole of this wretched mockery of justice I suffered living
5 torture. It was to be decided, whether the result of my curiosity and lawless devices would cause the death of my fellow-beings: one a smiling babe full of innocence and joy; the other far more dreadfully murdered, with every aggravation of infamy that could make the murder memorable in horror. Justine also was a girl of
10 merit, and possessed qualities which promised to render her life happy; now all was to be obliterated in an ignominious grave, and I the cause! A thousand times rather would I have confessed myself guilty of the crime ascribed to Justine; but I was absent when it was committed, and such a declaration would have been considered as
15 the ravings of a madman, and would not have exculpated her who suffered through me.

The appearance of Justine was calm. She was dressed in mourning; and her countenance, always engaging, was rendered, by the solemnity of her feelings, exquisitely beautiful. Yet she appeared
20 confident in innocence and did not tremble, although gazed on and execrated by thousands; for all the kindness which her beauty might otherwise have excited was obliterated in the minds of the spectators by the imagination of the enormity she was supposed to have committed. She was tranquil, yet her tranquillity was evidently
25 constrained; and as her confusion had before been adduced as a proof of her guilt, she worked up her mind to an appearance of courage. When she entered the court she threw her eyes round it,

and quickly discovered where we were seated. A tear seemed to dim her eye when she saw us; but she quickly recovered herself, and a look of sorrowful affection seemed to attest her utter guiltlessness.

The trial began; and after the advocate against her had stated the charge, several witnesses were called. Several strange facts combined against her, which might have staggered any one who had not such proof of her innocence as I had. She had been out the whole of the night on which the murder had been committed, and towards morning had been perceived by a market-woman not far from the spot where the body of the murdered child had been afterwards found. The woman asked her what she did there; but she looked very strangely, and only returned a confused and unintelligible answer. She returned to the house about eight o'clock; and when one enquired where she had passed the night, she replied that she had been looking for the child and demanded earnestly if any thing had been heard concerning him. When shown the body, she fell into violent hysterics, and kept her bed for several days. The picture was then produced, which the servant had found in her pocket; and when Elizabeth, in a faltering voice, proved that it was the same which, an hour before the child had been missed, she had placed round his neck, a murmur of horror and indignation filled the court.

Justine was called on for her defence. As the trial proceeded, her countenance had altered. Surprise, horror, and misery were strongly expressed. Sometimes she struggled with her tears; but when she was desired to plead, she collected her powers, and spoke in an audible although variable voice.

'God knows,' she said, 'how entirely I am innocent. But I do not pretend that my protestations should acquit me: I rest my innocence on a plain and simple explanation of the facts which have been adduced against me; and I hope the character I have always borne will incline my judges to a favourable interpretation, where any circumstance appears doubtful or suspicious.'

She then related that, by the permission of Elizabeth, she had passed the evening of the night on which the murder had been

83

committed at the house of an aunt at Chêne, a village situated at
about a league from Geneva. On her return, at about nine o'clock,
she met a man who asked her if she had seen any thing of the child
who was lost. She was alarmed by this account, and passed several
5 hours in looking for him, when the gates of Geneva were shut, and
she was forced to remain several hours of the night in a barn
belonging to a cottage, being unwilling to call up the inhabitants,
to whom she was well known. Most of the night she spent here
watching; towards morning she believed that she slept for a few
10 minutes; some steps disturbed her, and she awoke. It was dawn,
and she quitted her asylum, that she might again endeavour to find
my brother. If she had gone near the spot where his body lay, it
was without her knowledge. That she had been bewildered when
questioned by the market-woman was not surprising, since she had
15 passed a sleepless night and the fate of poor William was yet
uncertain. Concerning the picture she could give no account.

'I know,' continued the unhappy victim, 'how heavily and fatally
this one circumstance weighs against me, but I have no power of
explaining it; and when I have expressed my utter ignorance, I am
20 only left to conjecture concerning the probabilities by which it
might have been placed in my pocket. But here also I am checked.
I believe that I have no enemy on earth, and none surely would
have been so wicked as to destroy me wantonly. Did the murderer
place it there? I know of no opportunity afforded him for so doing;
25 or, if I had, why should he have stolen the jewel, to part with it
again so soon?

'I commit my cause to the justice of my judges, yet I see no room
for hope. I beg permission to have a few witnesses examined
concerning my character; and if their testimony shall not overweigh
30 my supposed guilt, I must be condemned, although I would pledge
my salvation on my innocence.'

Several witnesses were called who had known her for many years,
and they spoke well of her; but fear and hatred of the crime
of which they supposed her guilty rendered them timorous, and
35 unwilling to come forward. Elizabeth saw even this last resource,
her excellent dispositions and irreproachable conduct, about to

fail the accused, when, although violently agitated, she desired permission to address the court.

'I am,' said she, 'the cousin of the unhappy child who was murdered, or rather his sister, for I was educated by and have lived with his parents ever since and even long before, his birth. It may therefore be judged indecent in me to come forward on this occasion; but when I see a fellow creature about to perish through the cowardice of her pretended friends, I wish to be allowed to speak, that I may say what I know of her character. I am well acquainted with the accused. I have lived in the same house with her, at one time for five, and at another for nearly two years. During all that period she appeared to me the most amiable and benevolent of human creatures. She nursed Madame Frankenstein, my aunt, in her last illness, with the greatest affection and care, and afterwards attended her own mother during a tedious illness, in a manner that excited the admiration of all who knew her; after which she again lived in my uncle's house, where she was beloved by all the family. She was warmly attached to the child who is now dead, and acted towards him like a most affectionate mother. For my own part, I do not hesitate to say that, notwithstanding all the evidence produced against her, I believe and rely on her perfect innocence. She had no temptation for such an action: as to the bauble on which the chief proof rests, if she had earnestly desired it, I should have willingly given it to her; so much do I esteem and value her.'

A murmur of approbation followed Elizabeth's simple and powerful appeal; but it was excited by her generous interference, and not in favour of poor Justine, on whom the public indignation was turned with renewed violence, charging her with the blackest ingratitude. She herself wept as Elizabeth spoke, but she did not answer. My own agitation and anguish was extreme during the whole trial. I believed in her innocence; I knew it. Could the daemon who had (I did not for a minute doubt) murdered my brother also in his hellish sport have betrayed the innocent to death and ignominy? I could not sustain the horror of my situation, and when I perceived that the popular voice and the countenances of the judges had already condemned my unhappy victim, I rushed out of the court in agony. The tortures of the accused did not equal mine; she was sustained by innocence, but the fangs of remorse tore my bosom and would not forego their hold.

5 I passed a night of unmingled wretchedness. In the morning I went to the court; my lips and throat were parched. I dared not ask the fatal question; but I was known, and the officer guessed the cause of my visit. The ballots had been thrown; they were all black, and Justine was condemned.

10 I cannot pretend to describe what I then felt. I had before experienced sensations of horror; and I have endeavoured to bestow upon them adequate expressions, but words cannot convey an idea of the heart-sickening despair that I then endured. The person to whom I addressed myself added, that Justine had already

15 confessed her guilt. 'That evidence,' he observed, 'was hardly required in so glaring a case, but I am glad of it; and, indeed, none of our judges like to condemn a criminal upon circumstantial evidence, be it ever so decisive.'

This was strange and unexpected intelligence; what could it

20 mean? Had my eyes deceived me? And was I really as mad as the whole world would believe me to be, if I disclosed the object of my suspicions? I hastened to return home, and Elizabeth eagerly demanded the result.

'My cousin,' replied I, 'it is decided as you may have expected;

25 all judges had rather that ten innocent should suffer than that one guilty should escape. But she has confessed.'

This was a dire blow to poor Elizabeth, who had relied with firmness upon Justine's innocence. 'Alas!' said she. 'How shall I ever again believe in human goodness? Justine, whom I loved and

30 esteemed as my sister, how could she put on those smiles of innocence only to betray? her mild eyes seemed incapable of any severity or guile, and yet she has committed a murder.'

Soon after we heard that the poor victim had expressed a desire to see my cousin. My father wished her not to go, but said that he

35 left it to her own judgment and feelings to decide. 'Yes,' said Elizabeth, 'I will go, although she is guilty; and you, Victor, shall

accompany me: I cannot go alone.' The idea of this visit was torture to me, yet I could not refuse.

We entered the gloomy prison chamber and beheld Justine sitting on some straw at the farther end; her hands were manacled, and her head rested on her knees. She rose on seeing us enter; and when we were left alone with her, she threw herself at the feet of Elizabeth, weeping bitterly. My cousin wept also.

'Oh, Justine!' said she. 'Why did you rob me of my last consolation? I relied on your innocence, and although I was then very wretched, I was not so miserable as I am now.'

'And do you also believe that I am so very, very wicked? Do you also join with my enemies to crush me, to condemn me as a murderer?' Her voice was suffocated with sobs.

'Rise, my poor girl,' said Elizabeth; 'why do you kneel, if you are innocent? I am not one of your enemies; I believed you guiltless, notwithstanding every evidence, until I heard that you had yourself declared your guilt. That report, you say, is false; and be assured, dear Justine, that nothing can shake my confidence in you for a moment, but your own confession.'

'I did confess; but I confessed a lie. I confessed, that I might obtain absolution; but now that falsehood lies heavier at my heart than all my other sins. The God of heaven forgive me! Ever since I was condemned, my confessor has besieged me; he threatened and menaced, until I almost began to think that I was the monster that he said I was. He threatened excommunication and hell fire in my last moments if I continued obdurate. Dear lady, I had none to support me; all looked on me as a wretch doomed to ignominy and perdition. What could I do? In an evil hour I subscribed to a lie; and now only am I truly miserable.'

She paused, weeping, and then continued – 'I thought with horror, my sweet lady, that you should believe your Justine, whom your blessed aunt had so highly honoured and whom you loved, was a creature capable of a crime which none but the devil himself could have perpetrated. Dear William! Dearest blessed child! I soon shall see you again in heaven, where we shall all be happy; and that consoles me, going as I am to suffer ignominy and death.'

'Oh, Justine! Forgive me for having for one moment distrusted you. Why did you confess? But do not mourn, dear girl. Do not fear. I will proclaim, I will prove your innocence. I will melt the stony hearts of your enemies by my tears and prayers. You shall
5 not die! You, my playfellow, my companion, my sister, perish on the scaffold! No! No! I never could survive so horrible a misfortune.'

Justine shook her head mournfully. 'I do not fear to die,' she said; 'that pang is past. God raises my weakness and gives me
10 courage to endure the worst. I leave a sad and bitter world; and if you remember me and think of me as of one unjustly condemned, I am resigned to the fate awaiting me. Learn from me, dear lady, to submit in patience to the will of heaven!'

During this conversation I had retired to the corner of the prison
15 room, where I could conceal the horrid anguish that possessed me. Despair! Who dared talk of that? The poor victim, who on the morrow was to pass the awful boundary between life and death, felt not, as I did, such deep and bitter agony. I gnashed my teeth and ground them together, uttering a groan that came from my
20 inmost soul. Justine started. When she saw who it was, she approached me and said, 'Dear sir, you are very kind to visit me; you, I hope, do not believe that I am guilty?'

I could not answer. 'No, Justine,' said Elizabeth; 'he is more convinced of your innocence than I was; for even when he heard
25 that you had confessed, he did not credit it.'

'I truly thank him. In these last moments I feel the sincerest gratitude towards those who think of me with kindness. How sweet is the affection of others to such a wretch as I am! It removes more than half my misfortune; and I feel as if I could die in peace, now
30 that my innocence is acknowledged by you, dear lady, and your cousin.'

Thus the poor sufferer tried to comfort others and herself. She indeed gained the resignation she desired. But I, the true murderer, felt the never-dying worm alive in my bosom, which allowed of no
35 hope or consolation. Elizabeth also wept and was unhappy; but hers also was the misery of innocence, which, like a cloud that

passes over the fair moon, for a while hides but cannot tarnish its brightness. Anguish and despair had penetrated into the core of my heart; I bore a hell within me which nothing could extinguish. We stayed several hours with Justine; and it was with great difficulty that Elizabeth could tear herself away. 'I wish,' cried she, 'that I were to die with you; I cannot live in this world of misery.'

Justine assumed an air of cheerfulness, while she with difficulty repressed her bitter tears. She embraced Elizabeth and said, in a voice of half-suppressed emotion, 'Farewell, sweet lady, dearest Elizabeth, my beloved and only friend; may Heaven, in its bounty, bless and preserve you; may this be the last misfortune that you will ever suffer! Live, and be happy, and make others so.'

And on the morrow Justine died. Elizabeth's heart-rending eloquence failed to move the judges from their settled conviction in the criminality of the saintly sufferer. My passionate and indignant appeals were lost upon them. And when I received their cold answers and heard the harsh, unfeeling reasoning of these men, my purposed avowal died away on my lips. Thus I might proclaim myself a madman, but not revoke the sentence passed upon my wretched victim. She perished on the scaffold as a murderess!

From the tortures of my own heart, I turned to contemplate the deep and voiceless grief of my Elizabeth. This also was my doing! And my father's woe, and the desolation of that late so smiling home – all was the work of my thrice-accursed hands! Ye weep, unhappy ones; but these are not your last tears! Again shall you raise the funeral wail, and the sound of your lamentations shall again and again be heard! Frankenstein, your son, your kinsman, your early, much-loved friend; he who would spend each vital drop of blood for your sakes – who has no thought nor sense of joy, except as it is mirrored also in your dear countenances – who would fill the air with blessings and spend his life in serving you – he bids you weep – to shed countless tears; happy beyond his hopes, if thus inexorable fate be satisfied, and if the destruction pause before the peace of the grave have succeeded to your sad torments!

Thus spoke my prophetic soul, as, torn by remorse, horror, and despair, I beheld those I loved spend vain sorrow upon the graves of William and Justine, the first hapless victims to my unhallowed arts.

END OF VOLUME ONE

Volume Two

Chapter I

Nothing is more painful to the human mind than, after the feelings have been worked up by a quick succession of events, the dead calmness of inaction and certainty which follows and deprives the soul both of hope and fear. Justine died; she rested; and I was alive. The blood flowed freely in my veins, but a weight of despair and 5 remorse pressed on my heart, which nothing could remove. Sleep fled from my eyes; I wandered like an evil spirit, for I had committed deeds of mischief beyond description horrible, and more, much more (I persuaded myself) was yet behind. Yet my heart overflowed with kindness, and the love of virtue. I had begun life with benevol- 10 ent intentions, and thirsted for the moment when I should put them in practice and make myself useful to my fellow beings. Now all was blasted: instead of that serenity of conscience which allowed me to look back upon the past with self-satisfaction, and from thence to gather promise of new hopes, I was seized by remorse 15 and the sense of guilt, which hurried me away to a hell of intense tortures, such as no language can describe.

This state of mind preyed upon my health, which had perhaps never entirely recovered from the first shock it had sustained. I shunned the face of man; all sound of joy or complacency was 20 torture to me; solitude was my only consolation – deep, dark, deathlike solitude.

My father observed with pain the alteration perceptible in my disposition and habits, and endeavoured by arguments, deduced from the feelings of his serene conscience and guiltless life, to 25

inspire me with fortitude, and awaken in me the courage to dispel the dark cloud which brooded over me. 'Do you think, Victor,' said he, 'that I do not suffer also? No one could love a child more than I loved your brother' – tears came into his eyes as he spoke –
5 'but is it not a duty to the survivors that we should refrain from augmenting their unhappiness by an appearance of immoderate grief? It is also a duty owed to yourself; for excessive sorrow prevents improvement or enjoyment, or even the discharge of daily usefulness, without which no man is fit for society.'
10 This advice, although good, was totally inapplicable to my case; I should have been the first to hide my grief and console my friends, if remorse had not mingled its bitterness, and terror its alarm, with my other sensations. Now I could only answer my father with a look of despair, and endeavour to hide myself from his view.
15 About this time we retired to our house at Belrive. This change was particularly agreeable to me. The shutting of the gates regularly at ten o'clock and the impossibility of remaining on the lake after that hour, had rendered our residence within the walls of Geneva very irksome to me. I was now free. Often, after the rest of the
20 family had retired for the night, I took the boat and passed many hours upon the water. Sometimes, with my sails set, I was carried by the wind; and sometimes, after rowing into the middle of the lake, I left the boat to pursue its own course, and gave way to my own miserable reflections. I was often tempted, when all was at
25 peace around me, and I the only unquiet thing that wandered restless in a scene so beautiful and heavenly – if I except some bat, or the frogs, whose harsh and interrupted croaking was heard only when I approached the shore – often, I say, I was tempted to plunge into the silent lake, that the waters might close over me and my
30 calamities forever. But I was restrained, when I thought of the heroic and suffering Elizabeth, whom I tenderly loved, and whose existence was bound up in mine. I thought also of my father and surviving brother: should I by my base desertion leave them exposed and unprotected to the malice of the fiend whom I had let
35 loose among them?

At these moments I wept bitterly, and wished that peace would revisit my mind only that I might afford them consolation and happiness. But that could not be. Remorse extinguished every hope. I had been the author of unalterable evils, and I lived in daily fear lest the monster whom I had created should perpetrate some new wickedness. I had an obscure feeling that all was not over, and that he would still commit some signal crime, which by its enormity should almost efface the recollection of the past. There was always scope for fear, so long as anything I loved remained behind. My abhorrence of this fiend cannot be conceived. When I thought of him I gnashed my teeth, my eyes became inflamed, and I ardently wished to extinguish that life which I had so thoughtlessly bestowed. When I reflected on his crimes and malice, my hatred and revenge burst all bounds of moderation. I would have made a pilgrimage to the highest peak of the Andes, could I, when there, have precipitated him to their base. I wished to see him again, that I might wreak the utmost extent of abhorrence on his head, and avenge the deaths of William and Justine.

Our house was the house of mourning. My father's health was deeply shaken by the horror of the recent events. Elizabeth was sad and desponding; she no longer took delight in her ordinary occupations; all pleasure seemed to her sacrilege toward the dead; eternal woe and tears she then thought was the just tribute she should pay to innocence so blasted and destroyed. She was no longer that happy creature who in earlier youth wandered with me on the banks of the lake, and talked with ecstasy of our future prospects. The first of these sorrows which are sent to wean us from the earth, had visited her, and its dimming influence quenched her dearest smiles.

'When I reflect, my dear cousin,' said she, 'on the miserable death of Justine Moritz, I no longer see the world and its works as they before appeared to me. Before, I looked upon the accounts of vice and injustice, that I read in books or heard from others as tales of ancient days or imaginary evils; at least they were remote and more familiar to reason than to the imagination; but now misery has come home, and men appear to me as monsters thirsting for each other's blood. Yet I am certainly unjust. Every body believed

that poor girl to be guilty; and if she could have committed the crime for which she suffered, assuredly she would have been the most depraved of human creatures. For the sake of a few jewels, to have murdered the son of her benefactor and friend, a child
5 whom she had nursed from its birth, and appeared to love as if it had been her own! I could not consent to the death of any human being; but certainly I should have thought such a creature unfit to remain in the society of men. But she was innocent. I know, I feel, she was innocent; you are of the same opinion, and that confirms
10 me. Alas! Victor, when falsehood can look so like the truth, who can assure themselves of certain happiness? I feel as if I were walking on the edge of a precipice, towards which thousands are crowding, and endeavouring to plunge me into the abyss. William and Justine were assassinated, and the murderer escapes: he walks
15 about the world free, and perhaps respected. But even if I were condemned to suffer on the scaffold for the same crimes, I would not change places with such a wretch.'

I listened to this discourse with the extremest agony. I, not in deed, but in effect, was the true murderer. Elizabeth read my
20 anguish in my countenance, and kindly taking my hand, said, 'My dearest friend, you must calm yourself. These events have affected me, God knows how deeply; but I am not so wretched as you are. There is an expression of despair, and sometimes of revenge, in your countenance that makes me tremble. Dear Victor, banish
25 these dark passions. Remember the friends around you, who centre all their hopes in you. Have we lost the power of rendering you happy? Ah! while we love – while we are true to each other, here in this land of peace and beauty, your native country, we may reap every tranquil blessing – what can disturb our peace?'

30 And could not such words from her whom I fondly prized before every other gift of fortune, suffice to chase away the fiend that lurked in my heart? Even as she spoke I drew near to her, as if in terror; lest at that very moment the destroyer had been near to rob me of her.

35 Thus not the tenderness of friendship, nor the beauty of earth, nor of heaven, could redeem my soul from woe: the very accents

of love were ineffectual. I was encompassed by a cloud which no beneficial influence could penetrate. The wounded deer dragging its fainting limbs to some untrodden brake, there to gaze upon the arrow which had pierced it, and to die – was but a type of me.

Sometimes I could cope with the sullen despair that over-   5
whelmed me: but sometimes the whirlwind passions of my soul drove me to seek, by bodily exercise and by change of place, some relief from my intolerable sensations. It was during an access of this kind that I suddenly left my home, and bending my steps towards the near Alpine valleys, sought in the magnificence, the   10
eternity of such scenes, to forget myself and my ephemeral, because human, sorrows. My wanderings were directed towards the valley of Chamounix. I had visited it frequently during my boyhood. Six years had passed since then: *I* was a wreck – but nought had changed in those savage and enduring scenes.   15

I performed the first part of my journey on horseback. I after-wards hired a mule, as the more sure-footed and least liable to receive injury on these rugged roads. The weather was fine: it was about the middle of the month of August, nearly two months after the death of Justine; that miserable epoch from which I dated all   20
my woe. The weight upon my spirit was sensibly lightened as I plunged yet deeper in the ravine of Arve. The immense mountains and precipices that overhung me on every side – the sound of the river raging among the rocks, and the dashing of the waterfalls around, spoke of a power mighty as Omnipotence – and I ceased   25
to fear, or to bend before any being less almighty than that which had created and ruled the elements, here displayed in their most terrific guise. Still, as I ascended higher, the valley assumed a more magnificent and astonishing character. Ruined castles hanging on the precipices of piny mountains; the impetuous Arve, and cottages   30
every here and there peeping forth from among the trees, formed a scene of singular beauty. But it was augmented and rendered sublime by the mighty Alps, whose white and shining pyramids and domes towered above all, as belonging to another earth, the habitations of another race of beings.   35

I passed the bridge of Pèlissier, where the ravine, which the river forms, opened before me, and I began to ascend the mountain that overhangs it. Soon after I entered the valley of Chamounix. This valley is more wonderful and sublime, but not so beautiful and picturesque, as that of Servox, through which I had just passed.

5 The high and snowy mountains were its immediate boundaries; but I saw no more ruined castles and fertile fields. Immense glaciers approached the road; I heard the rumbling thunder of the falling avalanche and marked the smoke of its passage. Mont Blanc, the supreme and magnificent Mont Blanc, raised itself from the

10 surrounding *aiguilles*, and its tremendous *dôme* overlooked the valley.

A tingling long-lost sense of pleasure often came across me during this journey. Some turn in the road, some new object suddenly perceived and recognised, reminded me of days gone by,

15 and were associated with the light-hearted gaiety of boyhood. The very winds whispered in soothing accents, and maternal nature bade me weep no more. Then again the kindly influence ceased to act – I found myself fettered again to grief and indulging in all the misery of reflection. Then I spurred on my animal, striving so to

20 forget the world, my fears, and more than all, myself – or, in a more desperate fashion, I alighted and threw myself on the grass, weighed down by horror and despair.

At length I arrived at the village of Chamounix. Exhaustion succeeded to the extreme fatigue both of body and of mind which

25 I had endured. For a short space of time I remained at the window, watching the pallid lightnings that played above Mont Blanc, and listening to the rushing of the Arvet, which pursued its noisy way beneath. The same lulling sounds acted as a lullaby to my too keen sensations: when I placed my head upon my pillow, sleep crept

30 over me; I felt it as it came and blest the giver of oblivion.

Chapter II

I spent the following day roaming through the valley. I stood beside the sources of the Arveiron, which take their rise in a glacier, that with slow pace is advancing down from the summit of the hills, to barricade the valley. The abrupt sides of vast mountains were before me; the icy wall of the glacier overhung me; a few shattered 5 pines were scattered around; and the solemn silence of this glorious presence-chamber of imperial Nature was broken only by the brawling waves or the fall of some vast fragment, the thunder sound of the avalanche or the cracking, reverberated along the mountains, of the accumulated ice, which, through the silent working of 10 immutable laws, was ever and anon rent and torn, as if it had been but a plaything in their hands. These sublime and magnificent scenes afforded me the greatest consolation that I was capable of receiving. They elevated me from all littleness of feeling; and although they did not remove my grief, they subdued and tranquil- 15 lised it. In some degree, also, they diverted my mind from the thoughts over which it had brooded for the last month. I retired to rest at night; my slumbers, as it were, waited on and ministered to by the assemblance of grand shapes which I had contemplated during the day. They congregated round me; the unstained snowy 20 mountain-top, the glittering pinnacle, the pine woods, and ragged bare ravine, the eagle, soaring amidst the clouds – they all gathered round me and bade me be at peace.

Where had they fled when the next morning I awoke? All of soul-inspiring fled with sleep, and dark melancholy clouded every 25 thought. The rain was pouring in torrents, and thick mists hid the summits of the mountains, so that I even saw not the faces of those

mighty friends. Still I would penetrate their misty veil and seek them in their cloudy retreats. What were rain and storm to me? My mule was brought to the door, and I resolved to ascend to the summit of Montanvert. I remembered the effect that the view of
5 the tremendous and ever-moving glacier had produced upon my mind when I first saw it. It had then filled me with a sublime ecstasy, that gave wings to the soul, and allowed it to soar from the obscure world to light and joy. The sight of the awful and majestic in nature had indeed always the effect of solemnising my mind and
10 causing me to forget the passing cares of life. I determined to go without a guide, for I was well acquainted with the path, and the presence of another would destroy the solitary grandeur of the scene.

The ascent is precipitous, but the path is cut into continual and
15 short windings, which enable you to surmount the perpendicularity of the mountain. It is a scene terrifically desolate. In a thousand spots the traces of the winter avalanche may be perceived, where trees lie broken and strewed on the ground; some entirely destroyed, others bent, leaning upon the jutting rocks of the moun-
20 tain or transversely upon other trees. The path, as you ascend higher, is intersected by ravines of snow, down which stones con- tinually roll from above; one of them is particularly dangerous, as the slightest sound, such as even speaking in a loud voice, produces a concussion of air sufficient to draw destruction upon the head of
25 the speaker. The pines are not tall or luxuriant, but they are sombre and add an air of severity to the scene. I looked on the valley beneath; vast mists were rising from the rivers which ran through it and curling in thick wreaths around the opposite mountains, whose summits were hid in the uniform clouds, while rain poured
30 from the dark sky, and added to the melancholy impression I received from the objects around me. Alas! why does man boast of sensibilities superior to those apparent in the brute; it only renders them more necessary beings. If our impulses were confined to hunger, thirst, and desire, we might be nearly free; but now we are
35 moved by every wind that blows and a chance word or scene that that word may convey to us.

We rest; a dream has power to poison sleep.
   We rise; one wand'ring thought pollutes the day.
We feel, conceive, or reason; laugh or weep,
   Embrace fond woe, or cast our cares away;
It is the same: for, be it joy or sorrow,   5
   The path of its departure still is free.
Man's yesterday may ne'er be like his morrow;
   Nought may endure but mutability!

It was nearly noon when I arrived at the top of the ascent. For
some time I sat upon the rock that overlooks the sea of ice. A mist   10
covered both that and the surrounding mountains. Presently a
breeze dissipated the cloud, and I descended upon the glacier. The
surface is very uneven, rising like the waves of a troubled sea,
descending low, and interspersed by rifts that sink deep. The field
of ice is almost a league in width, but I spent nearly two hours in   15
crossing it. The opposite mountain is a bare perpendicular rock.
From the side where I now stood Montanvert was exactly opposite,
at the distance of a league; and above it rose Mont Blanc, in awful
majesty. I remained in a recess of the rock, gazing on this wonderful
and stupendous scene. The sea, or rather the vast river of ice,   20
wound among its dependent mountains, whose aerial summits
hung over its recesses. Their icy and glittering peaks shone in the
sunlight over the clouds. My heart, which was before sorrowful,
now swelled with something like joy; I exclaimed – 'Wandering
spirits, if indeed ye wander, and do not rest in your narrow beds,   25
allow me this faint happiness, or take me, as your companion, away
from the joys of life.'

As I said this, I suddenly beheld the figure of a man, at some
distance, advancing towards me with superhuman speed. He
bounded over the crevices in the ice, among which I had walked   30
with caution; his stature, also, as he approached, seemed to exceed
that of man. I was troubled: a mist came over my eyes, and I felt a
faintness seize me; but I was quickly restored by the cold gale
of the mountains. I perceived, as the shape came nearer (sight
tremendous and abhorred!) that it was the wretch whom I had   35

created. I trembled with rage and horror, resolving to wait his approach, and then close with him in mortal combat. He approached; his countenance bespoke bitter anguish, combined with disdain and malignity, while its unearthly ugliness rendered
5 it almost too horrible for human eyes. But I scarcely observed this; rage and hatred had at first deprived me of utterance, and I recovered only to overwhelm him with words expressive of furious detestation and contempt.

'Devil,' I exclaimed, 'do you dare approach me? and do not you
10 fear the fierce vengeance of my arm wreaked on your miserable head? Begone, vile insect! or rather, stay, that I may trample you to dust! and, oh! that I could, with the extinction of your miserable existence, restore those victims whom you have so diabolically murdered!'

15 'I expected this reception,' said the daemon. 'All men hate the wretched; how, then, must I be hated, who am miserable beyond all living things! Yet you, my creator, detest and spurn me, thy creature, to whom thou art bound by ties only dissoluble by the annihilation of one of us. You purpose to kill me. How dare you
20 sport thus with life? Do your duty towards me, and I will do mine towards you and the rest of mankind. If you will comply with my conditions, I will leave them and you at peace; but if you refuse, I will glut the maw of death, until it be satiated with the blood of your remaining friends.'

25 'Abhorred monster! fiend that thou art! the tortures of hell are too mild a vengeance for thy crimes. Wretched devil! you reproach me with your creation; come on, then, that I may extinguish the spark which I so negligently bestowed.'

My rage was without bounds; I sprang on him, impelled by all
30 the feelings which can arm one being against the existence of another.

He easily eluded me, and said –

'Be calm! I intreat you to hear me, before you give vent to your hatred on my devoted head. Have I not suffered enough, that you
35 seek to increase my misery? Life, although it may only be an accumulation of anguish, is dear to me, and I will defend it.

Remember, thou hast made me more powerful than thyself; my height is superior to thine, my joints more supple. But I will not be tempted to set myself in opposition to thee. I am thy creature, and I will be even mild and docile to my natural lord and king, if thou wilt also perform thy part, the which thou owest me. Oh, Frankenstein, be not equitable to every other and trample upon me alone, to whom thy justice, and even thy clemency and affection, is most due. Remember, that I am thy creature; I ought to be thy Adam, but I am rather the fallen angel, whom thou drivest from joy for no misdeed. Everywhere I see bliss, from which I alone am irrevocably excluded. I was benevolent and good; misery made me a fiend. Make me happy, and I shall again be virtuous.'

'Begone! I will not hear you. There can be no community between you and me; we are enemies. Begone, or let us try our strength in a fight in which one must fall.'

'How can I move thee? Will no intreaties cause thee to turn a favourable eye upon thy creature, who implores thy goodness and compassion? Believe me, Frankenstein: I was benevolent; my soul glowed with love and humanity; but am I not alone, miserably alone? You, my creator, abhor me; what hope can I gather from your fellow-creatures, who owe me nothing? they spurn and hate me. The desert mountains and dreary glaciers are my refuge. I have wandered here many days; the caves of ice, which I only do not fear, are a dwelling to me, and the only one which man does not grudge. These bleak skies I hail, for they are kinder to me than your fellow beings. If the multitude of mankind knew of my existence, they would do as you do, and arm themselves for my destruction. Shall I not then hate them who abhor me? I will keep no terms with my enemies. I am miserable, and they shall share my wretchedness. Yet it is in your power to recompense me, and deliver them from an evil which it only remains for you to make so great, that not only you and your family, but thousands of others, shall be swallowed up in the whirlwinds of its rage. Let your compassion be moved, and do not disdain me. Listen to my tale: when you have heard that, abandon or commiserate me, as you shall judge that I deserve. But hear me. The guilty are allowed, by human laws, bloody as they are, to speak in their own defence before they are condemned. Listen to me, Frankenstein. You accuse me of murder, and yet you would, with a satisfied conscience, destroy your own creature. Oh, praise the eternal justice 5 of man! Yet I ask you not to spare me: listen to me; and then, if you can, and if you will, destroy the work of your hands.'

'Why do you call to my remembrance,' I rejoined, 'circumstances, of which I shudder to reflect, that I have been the miserable origin and author? Cursed be the day, abhorred devil, in which you 10 first saw light! Cursed (although I curse myself) be the hands that formed you! You have made me wretched beyond expression. You have left me no power to consider whether I am just to you, or not. Begone! relieve me from the sight of your detested form.'

'Thus I relieve thee, my creator,' he said, and placed his hated 15 hands before my eyes, which I flung from me with violence; 'thus I take from thee a sight which you abhor. Still thou canst listen to me and grant me thy compassion. By the virtues that I once possessed, I demand this from you. Hear my tale; it is long and strange, and the temperature of this place is not fitting to your fine 20 sensations; come to the hut upon the mountain. The sun is yet high in the heavens; before it descends to hide itself beyond yon snowy precipices, and illuminate another world, you will have heard my story and can decide. On you it rests, whether I quit forever the neighbourhood of man and lead a harmless life, or 25 become the scourge of your fellow creatures, and the author of your own speedy ruin.'

As he said this, he led the way across the ice: I followed. My heart was full, and I did not answer him; but as I proceeded, I weighed the various arguments that he had used, and determined 30 at least to listen to his tale. I was partly urged by curiosity, and compassion confirmed my resolution. I had hitherto supposed him to be the murderer of my brother, and I eagerly sought a confirmation or denial of this opinion. For the first time, also, I felt what the duties of a creator towards his creature were, and that I 35 ought to render him happy before I complained of his wickedness. These motives urged me to comply with his demand. We crossed the ice, therefore, and ascended the opposite rock. The air was cold, and the rain again began to descend: we entered the hut, the fiend with an air of exultation, I with a heavy heart and depressed spirits. But I consented to listen, and seating myself by the fire which my odious companion had lighted, he thus began his tale. 5

Chapter III

'It is with considerable difficulty that I remember the original era of my being: all the events of that period appear confused and indistinct. A strange multiplicity of sensations seized me, and I saw, felt, heard, and smelt at the same time; and it was, indeed, a
5 long time before I learned to distinguish between the operations of my various senses. By degrees, I remember, a stronger light pressed upon my nerves, so that I was obliged to shut my eyes. Darkness then came over me, and troubled me; but hardly had I felt this when, by opening my eyes, as I now suppose, the light poured in
10 upon me again. I walked and, I believe, descended; but I presently found a great alteration in my sensations. Before, dark and opaque bodies had surrounded me, impervious to my touch or sight; but I now found that I could wander on at liberty, with no obstacles which I could not either surmount or avoid. The light became
15 more and more oppressive to me; and the heat wearying me as I walked, I sought a place where I could receive shade. This was the forest near Ingolstadt; and here I lay by the side of a brook resting from my fatigue, until I felt tormented by hunger and thirst. This roused me from my nearly dormant state, and I ate some berries
20 which I found hanging on the trees or lying on the ground. I slaked my thirst at the brook; and then lying down, was overcome by sleep.

'It was dark when I awoke; I felt cold also, and half frightened, as it were, instinctively, finding myself so desolate. Before I had
25 quitted your apartment, on a sensation of cold, I had covered myself with some clothes; but these were insufficient to secure me from the dews of night. I was a poor, helpless, miserable wretch; I

knew, and could distinguish, nothing; but feeling pain invade me on all sides, I sat down and wept.

'Soon a gentle light stole over the heavens, and gave me a sensation of pleasure. I started up and beheld a radiant form rise from among the trees.[1] I gazed with a kind of wonder. It moved slowly, but it enlightened my path, and I again went out in search of berries. I was still cold when under one of the trees I found a huge cloak, with which I covered myself, and sat down upon the ground. No distinct ideas occupied my mind; all was confused. I felt light, and hunger, and thirst, and darkness; innumerable sounds rang in my ears, and on all sides various scents saluted me: the only object that I could distinguish was the bright moon, and I fixed my eyes on that with pleasure.

'Several changes of day and night passed, and the orb of night had greatly lessened, when I began to distinguish my sensations from each other. I gradually saw plainly the clear stream that supplied me with drink, and the trees that shaded me with their foliage. I was delighted when I first discovered that a pleasant sound, which often saluted my ears, proceeded from the throats of the little winged animals who had often intercepted the light from my eyes. I began also to observe, with greater accuracy, the forms that surrounded me, and to perceive the boundaries of the radiant roof of light which canopied me. Sometimes I tried to imitate the pleasant songs of the birds, but was unable. Sometimes I wished to express my sensations in my own mode, but the uncouth and inarticulate sounds which broke from me frightened me into silence again.

'The moon had disappeared from the night, and again, with a lessened form, showed itself, while I still remained in the forest. My sensations had by this time become distinct, and my mind received every day additional ideas. My eyes became accustomed to the light and to perceive objects in their right forms; I distinguished the insect from the herb, and by degrees, one herb from

1. The moon [author's footnote].

another. I found that the sparrow uttered none but harsh notes, whilst those of the blackbird and thrush were sweet and enticing.

'One day, when I was oppressed by cold, I found a fire which had been left by some wandering beggars, and was overcome with
5 delight at the warmth I experienced from it. In my joy I thrust my hand into the live embers, but quickly drew it out again with a cry of pain. How strange, I thought, that the same cause should produce such opposite effects! I examined the materials of the fire, and to my joy found it to be composed of wood. I quickly collected
10 some branches; but they were wet and would not burn. I was pained at this; and sat still watching the operation of the fire. The wet wood which I had placed near the heat dried, and itself became inflamed. I reflected on this; and by touching the various branches, I discovered the cause, and busied myself in collecting a great
15 quantity of wood, that I might dry it and have a plentiful supply of fire. When night came on and brought sleep with it, I was in the greatest fear lest my fire should be extinguished. I covered it carefully with dry wood and leaves, and placed wet branches upon it; and then, spreading my cloak, I lay on the ground, and sunk
20 into sleep.

'It was morning when I awoke, and my first care was to visit the fire. I uncovered it, and a gentle breeze quickly fanned it into a flame. I observed this also and contrived a fan of branches, which roused the embers when they were nearly extinguished. When
25 night came again I found, with pleasure, that the fire gave light as well as heat; and that the discovery of this element was useful to me in my food, for I found some of the offals that the travellers had left had been roasted, and tasted much more savoury than the berries I gathered from the trees. I tried, therefore, to dress my
30 food in the same manner, placing it on the live embers. I found that the berries were spoiled by this operation, and the nuts and roots much improved.

'Food, however, became scarce; and I often spent the whole day searching in vain for a few acorns to assuage the pangs of hunger.
35 When I found this, I resolved to quit the place that I had hitherto inhabited, to seek for one where the few wants I experienced would

be more easily satisfied. In this emigration, I exceedingly lamented the loss of the fire which I had obtained through accident, and knew not how to reproduce it. I gave several hours to the serious consideration of this difficulty; but I was obliged to relinquish all attempts to supply it; and, wrapping myself up in my cloak, I struck 5 across the wood towards the setting sun. I passed three days in these rambles, and at length discovered the open country. A great fall of snow had taken place the night before, and the fields were of one uniform white; the appearance was disconsolate, and I found my feet chilled by the cold damp outside that covered the ground. 10

'It was about seven in the morning, and I longed to obtain food and shelter; at length I perceived a small hut, on a rising ground, which had doubtless been built for the convenience of some shepherd. This was a new sight to me; and I examined the structure; with great curiosity. Finding the door open, I entered. An old man 15 sat in it, near a fire, over which he was preparing his breakfast. He turned on hearing a noise; and perceiving me, shrieked loudly, and quitting the hut, ran across the fields with a speed of which his debilitated form hardly appeared capable. His appearance, different from any I had ever before seen, and his flight, somewhat 20 surprised me. But I was enchanted by the appearance of the hut: here the snow and rain could not penetrate; the ground was dry; and it presented to me then as exquisite and divine a retreat as Pandaemonium appeared to the daemons of hell after their sufferings in the lake of fire. I greedily devoured the remnants of 25 the shepherd's breakfast, which consisted of bread, cheese, milk, and wine; the latter, however, I did not like. Then, overcome by fatigue, I lay down among some straw, and fell asleep.

'It was noon when I awoke; and, allured by the warmth of the sun, which shone brightly on the white ground, I determined to 30 recommence my travels; and, depositing the remains of the peasant's breakfast in a wallet I found, I proceeded across the fields for several hours, until at sunset I arrived at a village. How miraculous did this appear! the huts, the neater cottages, and stately houses engaged my admiration by turns. The vegetables in the gardens, 35 the milk and cheese that I saw placed at the windows of some of

the cottages, allured my appetite. One of the best of these I entered;
but I had hardly placed my foot within the door before the children
shrieked, and one of the women fainted. The whole village was
roused; some fled, some attacked me, until, grievously bruised by
5 stones and many other kinds of missile weapons, I escaped to the
open country and fearfully took refuge in a low hovel, quite bare,
and making a wretched appearance after the palaces I had beheld
in the village. This hovel, however, joined a cottage of a neat and
pleasant appearance; but, after my late dearly bought experience,
10 I dared not enter it. My place of refuge was constructed of wood,
but so low that I could with difficulty sit upright in it. No wood,
however, was placed on the earth which formed the floor, but it
was dry; and although the wind entered it by innumerable chinks,
I found it an agreeable asylum from the snow and rain.

15 'Here then I retreated, and lay down happy to have found a
shelter, however miserable, from the inclemency of the season, and
still more from the barbarity of man.

'As soon as morning dawned, I crept from my kennel, that I
might view the adjacent cottage and discover if I could remain in
20 the habitation I had found. It was situated against the back of the
cottage and surrounded on the sides which were exposed by a
pig-sty and a clear pool of water. One part was open, and by that I
had crept in; but now I covered every crevice by which I might be
perceived with stones and wood, yet in such a manner that I might
25 move them on occasion to pass out: all the light I enjoyed came
through the sty, and that was sufficient for me.

'Having thus arranged my dwelling and carpeted it with clean
straw, I retired; for I saw the figure of a man at a distance, and I
remembered too well my treatment the night before, to trust myself
30 in his power. I had first, however, provided for my sustenance for
that day by a loaf of coarse bread, which I purloined, and a cup
with which I could drink, more conveniently than from my hand,
of the pure water which flowed by my retreat. The floor was a little
raised, so that it was kept perfectly dry, and by its vicinity to the
35 chimney of the cottage it was tolerably warm.

'Being thus provided, I resolved to reside in this hovel until something should occur which might alter my determination. It was indeed a paradise compared to the bleak forest, my former residence, the rain-dropping branches, and dank earth. I ate my breakfast with pleasure and was about to remove a plank to procure myself a little water when I heard a step, and looking through a small chink, I beheld a young creature, with a pail on her head, passing before my hovel. The girl was young and of gentle demeanour, unlike what I have since found cottagers and farm-house servants to be. Yet she was meanly dressed, a coarse blue petticoat and a linen jacket being her only grab; her fair hair was plaited, but not adorned: she looked patient, yet sad. I lost sight of her; and in about a quarter of an hour she returned bearing the pail, which was now partly filled with milk. As she walked along, seemingly incommoded by the burden, a young man met her, whose countenance expressed a deeper despondence. Uttering a few sounds with an air of melancholy, he took the pail from her head and bore it to the cottage himself. She followed, and they disappeared. Presently I saw the young man again, with some tools in his hand, cross the field behind the cottage; and the girl was also busied, sometimes in the house and sometimes in the yard.

'On examining my dwelling, I found that one of the windows of the cottage had formerly occupied a part of it, but the panes had been filled up with wood. In one of these was a small and almost imperceptible chink, through which the eye could just penetrate. Through this crevice a small room was visible, whitewashed and clean, but very bare of furniture. In one corner, near a small fire, sat an old man, leaning his head on his hands in a disconsolate attitude. The young girl was occupied in arranging the cottage; but presently she took something out of a drawer, which employed her hands, and she sat down beside the old man, who, taking up an instrument, began to play, and to produce sounds sweeter than the voice of the thrush or the nightingale. It was a lovely sight, even to me, poor wretch! who had never beheld aught beautiful before. The silver hair and benevolent countenance of the aged cottager won my reverence, while the gentle manners of the girl enticed my love. He played a sweet mournful air, which I perceived drew tears from the eyes of his amiable companion, of which the old man took no notice, until she sobbed audibly; he then pronounced a few sounds, and the fair creature, leaving her work, knelt at his feet. He raised her, and smiled with such kindness and affection that I felt sensations of a peculiar and overpowering nature: they were a mixture of pain and pleasure, such as I had never before experienced, either from hunger or cold, warmth or food; and I withdrew from the window, unable to bear these emotions.

'Soon after this the young man returned, bearing on his shoulders a load of wood. The girl met him at the door, helped to relieve him of his burden, and taking some of the fuel into the cottage, placed it on the fire; then she and the youth went apart into a nook of the cottage, and he showed her a large loaf and a piece of cheese. She seemed pleased, and went into the garden for some roots and plants, which she placed in water, and then upon the fire. She afterwards continued her work, whilst the young man went into the garden, and appeared busily employed in digging and pulling up roots. After he had been employed thus about an hour, the young woman joined him, and they entered the cottage together.

'The old man had, in the mean time, been pensive; but on the appearance of his companions he assumed a more cheerful air, and they sat down to eat. The meal was quickly despatched. The young woman was again occupied in arranging the cottage; the old man walked before the cottage in the sun for a few minutes, leaning on the arm of the youth. Nothing could exceed in beauty the contrast between these two excellent creatures. One was old, with silver hairs and a countenance beaming with benevolence and love: the younger was slight and graceful in his figure, and his features were moulded with the finest symmetry; yet his eyes and attitude expressed the utmost sadness and despondency. The old man returned to the cottage; and the youth, with tools different from those he had used in the morning, directed his steps across the fields.

'Night quickly shut in; but to my extreme wonder, I found that the cottagers had a means of prolonging light by the use of tapers, and was delighted to find that the setting of the sun did not put an end to the pleasure I experienced in watching my human neighbours. In the evening, the young girl and her companion were employed in various occupations which I did not understand; and the old man again took up the instrument which produced the divine sounds that had enchanted me in the morning. So soon as he had finished the youth began, not to play, but to utter sounds that were monotonous, and neither resembling the harmony of the old man's instrument nor the songs of the birds: I since found that he read aloud, but at that time I knew nothing of the science of words or letters.

'The family, after having been thus occupied for a short time, extinguished their lights and retired, as I conjectured, to rest.'

Chapter IV

'I lay on my straw, but I could not sleep. I thought of the occurrences of the day. What chiefly struck me was the gentle manners
of these people; and I longed to join them, but dared not. I
remembered too well the treatment I had suffered the night before
5 from the barbarous villagers, and resolved, whatever course of
conduct I might hereafter think it right to pursue, that for the
present I would remain quietly in my hovel, watching, and endeavouring to discover the motives which influenced their actions.

'The cottagers arose the next morning before the sun. The young
10 woman arranged the cottage and prepared the food; and the youth
departed after the first meal.

'This day was passed in the same routine as that which preceded
it. The young man was constantly employed out of doors, and the
girl in various laborious occupations within. The old man, whom
15 I soon perceived to be blind, employed his leisure hours on his
instrument or in contemplation. Nothing could exceed the love
and respect which the younger cottagers exhibited towards their
venerable companion. They performed towards him every little
office of affection and duty with gentleness; and he rewarded them
20 by his benevolent smiles.

'They were not entirely happy. The young man and his companion often went apart, and appeared to weep. I saw no cause for
their unhappiness; but I was deeply affected by it. If such lovely
creatures were miserable, it was less strange that I, an imperfect
25 and solitary being, should be wretched. Yet why were these gentle
beings unhappy? They possessed a delightful house (for such it
was in my eyes) and every luxury; they had a fire to warm them

when chill, and delicious viands when hungry; they were dressed in excellent clothes; and, still more, they enjoyed one another's company and speech, interchanging each day looks of affection and kindness. What did their tears imply? Did they really express pain? I was at first unable to solve these questions; but perpetual 5
attention and time explained to me many appearances which were at first enigmatic.

'A considerable period elapsed before I discovered one of the causes of the uneasiness of this amiable family: it was poverty, and they suffered that evil in a very distressing degree. Their 10
nourishment consisted entirely of the vegetables of their garden and the milk of one cow, which gave very little during the winter, when its masters could scarcely procure food to support it. They often, I believe, suffered the pangs of hunger very poignantly, especially the two younger cottagers; for several times they placed 15
food before the old man when they reserved none for themselves.

'This trait of kindness moved me sensibly. I had been accustomed, during the night, to steal a part of their store for my own consumption; but when I found that in doing this I inflicted pain on the cottagers, I abstained, and satisfied myself with berries, 20
nuts, and roots, which I gathered from a neighbouring wood.

'I discovered also another means through which I was enabled to assist their labours. I found that the youth spent a great part of each day in collecting wood for the family fire; and, during the night I often took his tools, the use of which I quickly discovered, 25
and brought home firing sufficient for the consumption of several days.

'I remember, the first time that I did this, the young woman, when she opened the door in the morning, appeared greatly astonished on seeing a great pile of wood on the outside. She uttered 30
some words in a loud voice, and the youth joined her, who also expressed surprise. I observed, with pleasure, that he did not go to the forest that day, but spent it in repairing the cottage and cultivating the garden.

'By degrees I made a discovery of still greater moment. I found 35
that these people possessed a method of communicating their

experience and feelings to one another by articulate sounds. I
perceived that the words they spoke sometimes produced pleasure
or pain, smiles or sadness, in the minds and countenances of the
hearers. This was indeed a godlike science, and I ardently desired
5 to become acquainted with it. But I was baffled in every attempt I
made for this purpose. Their pronunciation was quick; and the
words they uttered, not having any apparent connection with visible
objects, I was unable to discover any clue by which I could unravel
the mystery of their reference. By great application, however, and
10 after having remained during the space of several revolutions of
the moon in my hovel, I discovered the names that were given to
some of the most familiar objects of discourse; I learned and applied
the words, "fire", "milk", "bread", and "wood". I learned also
the names of the cottagers themselves. The youth and his com-
15 panion had each of them several names, but the old man had only
one, which was "father". The girl was called "sister", or "Agatha",
and the youth "Felix", "brother", or "son". I cannot describe the
delight I felt when I learned the ideas appropriated to each of these
sounds, and was able to pronounce them. I distinguished several
20 other words without being able as yet to understand or apply them;
such as "good", "dearest", "unhappy".

'I spent the winter in this manner. The gentle manners and
beauty of the cottagers greatly endeared them to me: when they
were unhappy, I felt depressed; when they rejoiced, I sympathised
25 in their joys. I saw few human beings besides them; and if any other
happened to enter the cottage, their harsh manners and rude gait
only enhanced to me the superior accomplishments of my friends.
The old man, I could perceive, often endeavoured to encourage
his children, as sometimes I found that he called them, to cast off
30 their melancholy. He would talk in a cheerful accent, with an
expression of goodness that bestowed pleasure even upon me.
Agatha listened with respect, her eyes sometimes filled with tears,
which she endeavoured to wipe away unperceived; but I generally
found that her countenance and tone were more cheerful after
35 having listened to the exhortations of her father. It was not thus
with Felix. He was always the saddest of the group, and, even to

my unpractised senses, he appeared to have suffered more deeply than his friends. But if his countenance was more sorrowful, his voice was more cheerful than that of his sister, especially when he addressed the old man.

'I could mention innumerable instances which, although slight, 5
marked the dispositions of these amiable cottagers. In the midst of poverty and want, Felix carried with pleasure to his sister the first little white flower that peeped out from beneath the snowy ground. Early in the morning, before she had risen, he cleared away the snow that obstructed her path to the milk-house, drew water from 10
the well, and brought the wood from the out-house, where, to his perpetual astonishment, he found his store always replenished by an invisible hand. In the day, I believe, he worked sometimes for a neighbouring farmer, because he often went forth and did not return until dinner, yet brought no wood with him. At other times 15
he worked in the garden; but as there was little to do in the frosty season, he read to the old man and Agatha.

'This reading had puzzled me extremely at first; but, by degrees, I discovered that he uttered many of the same sounds when he read, as when he talked. I conjectured, therefore, that he found on 20
the paper signs for speech which he understood, and I ardently longed to comprehend these also; but how was that possible when I did not even understand the sounds for which they stood as signs? I improved, however, sensibly in this science, but not sufficiently to follow up any kind of conversation, although I applied my whole 25
mind to the endeavour: for I easily perceived that, although I eagerly longed to discover myself to the cottagers, I ought not to make the attempt until I had first become master of their language; which knowledge might enable me to make them overlook the deformity of my figure; for with this also the contrast perpetually 30
presented to my eyes had made me acquainted.

'I had admired the perfect forms of my cottagers – their grace, beauty, and delicate complexions: but how was I terrified, when I viewed myself in a transparent pool! At first I started back, unable to believe that it was indeed I who was reflected in the mirror; and 35
when I became fully convinced that I was in reality the monster

that I am, I was filled with the bitterest sensations of despondence and mortification. Alas! I did not yet entirely know the fatal effects of this miserable deformity.

'As the sun became warmer, and the light of day longer, the
5 snow vanished, and I beheld the bare trees and the black earth. From this time Felix was more employed; and the heart-moving indications of impending famine disappeared. Their food, as I afterwards found, was coarse, but it was wholesome; and they procured a sufficiency of it. Several new kinds of plants sprang up
10 in the garden, which they dressed; and these signs of comfort increased daily as the season advanced.

'The old man, leaning on his son, walked each day at noon, when it did not rain, as I found it was called when the heavens poured forth its water. This frequently took place; but a high wind
15 quickly dried the earth, and the season became far more pleasant than it had been.

'My mode of life in my hovel was uniform. During the morning I attended the motions of the cottagers; and when they were dispersed in various occupations, I slept: the remainder of the day
20 was spent in observing my friends. When they had retired to rest, if there was any moon or the night was star-light, I went into the woods and collected my own food and fuel for the cottage. When I returned, as often as it was necessary, I cleared their path from the snow and performed those offices that I had seen done by Felix.
25 I afterwards found that these labours, performed by an invisible hand, greatly astonished them; and once or twice I heard them, on these occasions, utter the words "good spirit", "wonderful"; but I did not then understand the signification of these terms.

'My thoughts now became more active, and I longed to discover
30 the motives and feelings of these lovely creatures; I was inquisitive to know why Felix appeared so miserable and Agatha so sad. I thought (foolish wretch!) that it might be in my power to restore happiness to these deserving people. When I slept or was absent, the forms of the venerable blind father, the gentle Agatha, and the
35 excellent Felix, flitted before me. I looked upon them as superior beings, who would be the arbiters of my future destiny. I formed

in my imagination a thousand pictures of presenting myself to them, and their reception of me. I imagined that they would be disgusted, until, by my gentle demeanour and conciliating words, I should first win their favour, and afterwards their love.

'These thoughts exhilarated me and led me to apply with fresh ardour to the acquiring the art of language. My organs were indeed harsh, but supple; and although my voice was very unlike the soft music of their tones, yet I pronounced such words as I understood with tolerable ease. It was as the ass and the lapdog; yet surely the gentle ass whose intentions were affectionate, although his manners were rude, deserved better treatment than blows and execration.

'The pleasant showers and genial warmth of spring greatly altered the aspect of the earth. Men, who before this change seemed to have been hid in caves, dispersed themselves, and were employed in various arts of cultivation. The birds sang in more cheerful notes, and the leaves began to bud forth on the trees. Happy, happy earth! fit habitation for gods, which, so short a time before, was bleak, damp, and unwholesome. My spirits were elevated by the enchanting appearance of nature; the past was blotted from my memory, the present was tranquil, and the future gilded by bright rays of hope, and anticipations of joy.'

Chapter V

'I now hasten to the more moving part of my story. I shall relate
events, that impressed me with feelings which, from what I had
been, have made me what I am.

'Spring advanced rapidly; the weather became fine and the skies
5 cloudless. It surprised me, that what before was desert and gloomy
should now bloom with the most beautiful flowers and verdure.
My senses were gratified and refreshed by a thousand scents of
delight, and a thousand sights of beauty.

'It was on one of these days, when my cottagers periodically
10 rested from labour – the old man played on his guitar, and the
children listened to him – that I observed the countenance of Felix
was melancholy beyond expression; he sighed frequently; and once
his father paused in his music, and I conjectured by his manner
that he enquired the cause of his son's sorrow. Felix replied in a
15 cheerful accent, and the old man was recommencing his music
when some-one tapped at the door.

'It was a lady on horseback, accompanied by a countryman as a
guide. The lady was dressed in a dark suit, and covered with a thick
black veil. Agatha asked a question, to which the stranger only
20 replied by pronouncing, in a sweet accent, the name of Felix. Her
voice was musical but unlike that of either of my friends. On
hearing this word, Felix came up hastily to the lady, who, when
she saw him, threw up her veil, and I beheld a countenance of
angelic beauty and expression. Her hair of a shining raven black,
25 and curiously braided; her eyes were dark, but gentle, although
animated; her features of a regular proportion, and her complexion
wondrously fair, each cheek tinged with a lovely pink.

'Felix seemed ravished with delight when he saw her, every trait of sorrow vanished from his face, and it instantly expressed a degree of ecstatic jóy, of which I could hardly have believed it capable; his eyes sparkled, as his cheek flushed with pleasure; and at that moment I thought him as beautiful as the stranger. She appeared affected by different feelings; wiping a few tears from her lovely eyes, she held out her hand to Felix, who kissed it rapturously and called her, as well as I could distinguish, his sweet Arabian. She did not appear to understand him, but smiled. He assisted her to dismount, and dismissing her guide, conducted her into the cottage. Some conversation took place between him and his father; and the young stranger knelt at the old man's feet and would have kissed his hand, but he raised her, and embraced her affectionately.

'I soon perceived, that although the stranger uttered articulate sounds, and appeared to have a language of her own, she was neither understood by, nor herself understood, the cottagers. They made many signs which I did not comprehend; but I saw that her presence diffused gladness through the cottage, dispelling their sorrow as the sun dissipates the morning mists. Felix seemed peculiarly happy, and with smiles of delight welcomed his Arabian. Agatha, the ever-gentle Agatha, kissed the hands of the lovely stranger; and pointing to her brother, made signs which appeared to me to mean that he had been sorrowful until she came. Some hours passed thus, while they, by their countenances, expressed joy, the cause of which I did not comprehend. Presently I found, by the frequent recurrence of some sound which the stranger repeated after them, that she was endeavouring to learn their language; and the idea instantly occurred to me that I should make use of the same instructions to the same end. The stranger learned about twenty words at the first lesson, most of them, indeed, were those which I had before understood, but I profited by the others.

'As night came on, Agatha and the Arabian retired early. When they separated, Felix kissed the hand of the stranger and said, "Good night, sweet Safie." He sat up much longer, conversing with his father; and by the frequent repetition of her name, I conjectured that their lovely guest was the subject of their conversation. I ardently desired to understand them, and bent every faculty towards that purpose, but found it utterly impossible.

'The next morning Felix went out to his work; and, after the
5 usual occupations of Agatha were finished, the Arabian sat at the feet of the old man, and taking his guitar, played some airs so entrancingly beautiful that they at once drew tears of sorrow and delight from my eyes. She sang, and her voice flowed in a rich cadence, swelling or dying away, like a nightingale of the woods.

10 'When she had finished, she gave the guitar to Agatha, who at first declined it. She played a simple air, and her voice accompanied it in sweet accents, but unlike the wondrous strain of the stranger. The old man appeared enraptured and said some words, which Agatha endeavoured to explain to Safie, and by which he appeared
15 to wish to express that she bestowed on him the greatest delight by her music.

'The days now passed as peaceably as before, with the sole alteration that joy had taken place of sadness in the countenances of my friends. Safie was always gay and happy; she and I improved
20 rapidly in the knowledge of language, so that in two months I began to comprehend most of the words uttered by my protectors.

'In the meanwhile also the black ground was covered with herbage, and the green banks interspersed with innumerable flowers, sweet to the scent and the eyes, stars of pale radiance among the
25 moonlight woods; the sun became warmer, the nights clear and balmy; and my nocturnal rambles were an extreme pleasure to me, although they were considerably shortened by the late setting and early rising of the sun, for I never ventured abroad during daylight, fearful of meeting with the same treatment I had formerly endured
30 in the first village which I entered.

'My days were spent in close attention, that I might more speedily master the language; and I may boast that I improved more rapidly than the Arabian, who understood very little and conversed in broken accents, whilst I comprehended and could imitate almost
35 every word that was spoken.

'While I improved in speech, I also learned the science of letters as it was taught to the stranger; and this opened before me a wide field for wonder and delight.

'The book from which Felix instructed Safie was Volney's *Ruins of Empires*. I should not have understood the purport of this book had not Felix, in reading it, given very minute explanations. He 5 had chosen this work, he said, because the declamatory style was framed in imitation of the eastern authors. Through this work I obtained a cursory knowledge of history and a view of the several empires at present existing in the world; it gave me an insight into the manners, governments, and religions of the different nations 10 of the earth. I heard of the slothful Asiatics; of the stupendous genius and mental activity of the Grecians; of the wars and wonderful virtue of the early Romans – of their subsequent degenerating – of the decline of that mighty empire, of chivalry, Christianity, and kings. I heard of the discovery of the American hemisphere 15 and wept with Safie over the hapless fate of its original inhabitants.

'These wonderful narrations inspired me with strange feelings. Was man, indeed, at once so powerful, so virtuous, and magnificent, yet so vicious and base? He appeared at one time a mere scion of the evil principle, and at another as all that can be conceived as 20 noble and godlike. To be a great and virtuous man appeared the highest honour that can befall a sensitive being; to be base and vicious, as many on record have been, appeared the lowest degradation, a condition more abject than that of the blind mole or harmless worm. For a long time I could not conceive how one man 25 could go forth to murder his fellow, or even why there were laws and governments; but when I heard details of vice and bloodshed, my wonder ceased, and I turned away with disgust and loathing.

'Every conversation of the cottagers now opened new wonders to me. While I listened to the instructions which Felix bestowed 30 upon the Arabian, the strange system of human society was explained to me. I heard of the division of property, of immense wealth and squalid poverty; of rank, descent, and noble blood.

'The words induced me to turn towards myself. I learned that the possessions most esteemed by your fellow creatures were, high 35 and unsullied descent united with riches. A man might be respected

with only one of these advantages; but without either he was considered, except in very rare instances, as a vagabond and a slave, doomed to waste his powers for the profits of the chosen few! And what was I? Of my creation and creator I was absolutely
5 ignorant, but I knew that I possessed no money, no friends, no kind of property. I was, besides, endued with a figure hideously deformed and loathsome; I was not even of the same nature as man. I was more agile than they and could subsist upon coarser diet; I bore the extremes of heat and cold with less injury to my
10 frame; my stature far exceeded theirs. When I looked around I saw and heard of none like me. Was I, then, a monster, a blot upon the earth, from which all men fled and whom all men disowned?

'I cannot describe to you the agony that these reflections inflicted upon me: I tried to dispel them, but sorrow only increased with
15 knowledge. Oh, that I had forever remained in my native wood, nor known nor felt beyond the sensations of hunger, thirst and heat!

'Of what a strange nature is knowledge! It clings to the mind, when it has once seized on it, like a lichen on the rock. I wished
20 sometimes to shake off all thought and feeling; but I learned that there was but one means to overcome the sensation of pain, and that was death – a state which I feared yet did not understand. I admired virtue and good feelings and loved the gentle manners and amiable qualities of my cottagers, but I was shut out from
25 intercourse with them, except through means which I obtained by stealth, when I was unseen and unknown, and which rather increased than satisfied the desire I had of becoming one among my fellows. The gentle words of Agatha and the animated smiles of the charming Arabian, were not for me. The mild exhortations
30 of the old man, and the lively conversation of the loved Felix were not for me. Miserable, unhappy wretch!

'Other lessons were impressed upon me even more deeply. I heard of the difference of sexes; and the birth and growth of children; how the father doated on the smiles of the infant, and the
35 lively sallies of the older child; how all the life and cares of the mother were wrapped up in the precious charge; how the mind of

youth expanded and gained knowledge; of brother, sister, and all the various relationships which bind one human being to another in mutual bonds.

'But where were my friends and relations? No father had watched my infant days, no mother had blessed me with smiles and caresses; or if they had, all my past life was now a blot, a blind vacancy in which I distinguished nothing. From my earliest remembrance I had been as I then was in height and proportion. I had never yet seen a being resembling me, or who claimed any intercourse with me. What was I? The question again recurred, to be answered only with groans.

'I will soon explain to what these feelings tended; but allow me now to return to the cottagers, whose story excited in me such various feelings of indignation, delight, and wonder, but which all terminated in additional love and reverence for my protectors (for so I loved, in an innocent, half-painful self-deceit, to call them).'

Chapter VI

'Some time elapsed before I learned the history of my friends. It was one which could not fail to impress itself deeply on my mind, unfolding as it did a number of circumstances, each interesting and wonderful to one so utterly inexperienced as I was.

5 'The name of the old man was De Lacey. He was descended from a good family in France, where he had lived for many years in affluence, respected by his superiors and beloved by his equals. His son was bred in the service of his country; and Agatha had ranked with ladies of the highest distinction. A few months before
10 my arrival they had lived in a large and luxurious city called Paris, surrounded by friends and possessed of every enjoyment which virtue, refinement of intellect, or taste, accompanied by a moderate fortune, could afford.

'The father of Safie had been the cause of their ruin. He was a
15 Turkish merchant, and had inhabited Paris for many years, when, for some reason which I could not learn, he became obnoxious to the government. He was seized and cast into prison the very day that Safie arrived from Constantinople to join him. He was tried and condemned to death. The injustice of his sentence was very
20 flagrant; all Paris was indignant; and it was judged that his religion and wealth rather than the crime alleged against him had been the cause of his condemnation.

'Felix had accidentally been present at the trial; his horror and indignation were uncontrollable when he heard the decision of the
25 court. He made, at that moment, a solemn vow to deliver him and then looked around for the means. After many fruitless attempts to gain admittance to the prison, he found a strongly grated window

in an unguarded part of the building, which lighted the dungeon of the unfortunate Mahometan; who, loaded with chains, waited in despair the execution of the barbarous sentence. Felix visited the grate at night and made known to the prisoner his intentions in his favour. The Turk, amazed and delighted, endeavoured to 5 kindle the zeal of his deliverer by promises of reward and wealth. Felix rejected his offers with contempt; yet when he saw the lovely Safie, who was allowed to visit her father and who, by her gestures, expressed her lively gratitude, the youth could not help owning to his own mind that the captive possessed a treasure which would 10 fully reward his toil and hazard.

'The Turk quickly perceived the impression that his daughter had made on the heart of Felix and endeavoured to secure him more entirely in his interests by the promise of her hand in marriage, so soon as he should be conveyed to a place of safety. Felix was too 15 delicate to accept his offer; yet he looked forward to the probability of the event as to the consummation of his happiness.

'During the ensuing days, while the preparations were going forward for the escape of the merchant, the zeal of Felix was warmed by several letters that he received from this lovely girl, who 20 found means to express her thoughts in the language of her lover by the aid of an old man, a servant of her father who understood French. She thanked him in the most ardent terms for his intended services towards her parent; and at the same time she gently deplored her own fate. 25

'I have copies of these letters; for I found means, during my residence in the hovel, to procure the implements of writing; and the letters were often in the hands of Felix or Agatha. Before I depart, I will give them to you, they will prove the truth of my tale; but at present, as the sun is already far declined, I shall only have 30 time to repeat the substance of them to you.

'Safie related that her mother was a Christian Arab, seized and made a slave by the Turks; recommended by her beauty, she had won the heart of the father of Safie, who married her. The young girl spoke in high and enthusiastic terms of her mother, who, born 35 in freedom, spurned the bondage to which she was now reduced.

She instructed her daughter in the tenets of her religion and taught her to aspire to higher powers of intellect and an independence of spirit forbidden to the female followers of Mahomet. This lady died; but her lessons were indelibly impressed on the mind of Safie,
5 who sickened at the prospect of again returning to Asia and being immured within the walls of a harem, allowed only to occupy herself with infantile amusements, ill-suited to the temper of her soul, now accustomed to grand ideas and a noble emulation of virtue. The prospect of marrying a Christian and remaining in a
10 country where women were allowed to take a rank in society was enchanting to her.

'The day for the execution of the Turk was fixed; but on the night previous to it he quitted his prison, and before morning was distant many leagues from Paris. Felix had procured passports in
15 the name of his father, sister, and himself. He had previously communicated his plan to the former, who aided the deceit by quitting his house, under the pretence of a journey and concealing himself, with his daughter, in an obscure part of Paris.

'Felix conducted the fugitives through France to Lyons and
20 across Mont Cenis to Leghorn, where the merchant had decided to wait a favourable opportunity of passing into some part of the Turkish dominions.

'Safie resolved to remain with her father until the moment of his departure, before which time the Turk renewed his promise that
25 she should be united to his deliverer; and Felix remained with them in expectation of that event; and in the mean time he enjoyed the society of the Arabian, who exhibited towards him the simplest and tenderest affection. They conversed with one another through the means of an interpreter, and sometimes with the interpretation
30 of looks; and Safie sang to him the divine airs of her native country.

'The Turk allowed this intimacy to take place, and encouraged the hopes of the youthful lovers, while in his heart he had formed far other plans. He loathed the idea that his daughter should be united to a Christian; but he feared the resentment of Felix if he
35 should appear lukewarm; for he knew that he was still in the power of his deliverer if he should choose to betray him to the Italian state

which they inhabited. He revolved a thousand plans by which he should be enabled to prolong the deceit until it might be no longer necessary, and secretly to take his daughter with him when he departed. His plans were facilitated by the news which arrived from Paris.

'The government of France were greatly enraged at the escape of their victim and spared no pains to detect and punish his deliverer. The plot of Felix was quickly discovered, and De Lacey and Agatha were thrown into prison. The news reached Felix and roused him from his dream of pleasure. His blind and aged father and his gentle sister lay in a noisome dungeon while he enjoyed the free air and the society of her whom he loved. This idea was torture to him. He quickly arranged with the Turk that if the latter should find a favourable opportunity for escape before Felix could return to Italy, Safie should remain as a boarder at a convent at Leghorn; and then, quitting the lovely Arabian, he hastened to Paris, and delivered himself up to the vengeance of the law, hoping to free De Lacey and Agatha by this proceeding.

'He did not succeed. They remained confined for five months before the trial took place; the result of which deprived them of their fortune and condemned them to a perpetual exile from their native country.

'They found a miserable asylum in the cottage in Germany, where I discovered them. Felix soon learned that the treacherous Turk, for whom he and his family endured such unheard-of oppression, on discovering that his deliverer was thus reduced to poverty and ruin, became a traitor to good feeling and honour and had quitted Italy with his daughter, insultingly sending Felix a pittance of money to aid him, as he said, in some plan of future maintenance.

'Such were the events that preyed on the heart of Felix and rendered him, when I first saw him, the most miserable of his family. He could have endured poverty; and while this distress had been the meed of his virtue, he gloried in it; but the ingratitude of the Turk and the loss of his beloved Safie, were misfortunes more bitter and irreparable. The arrival of the Arabian now infused new life into his soul.

'When the news reached Leghorn that Felix was deprived of his wealth and rank, the merchant commanded his daughter to think no more of her lover, but to prepare to return to her native country. The generous nature of Safie was outraged by this command; she
5 attempted to expostulate with her father, but he left her angrily, reiterating his tyrannical mandate.

'A few days after, the Turk entered his daughter's apartment and told her hastily that he had reason to believe that his residence at Leghorn had been divulged and that he should speedily be
10 delivered up to the French government; he had, consequently, hired a vessel to convey him to Constantinople, for which city he should sail in a few hours. He intended to leave his daughter under the care of a confidential servant, to follow at her leisure with the greater part of his property, which had not yet arrived at Leghorn.

15 'When alone, Safie resolved in her own mind the plan of conduct that it would become her to pursue in this emergency. A residence in Turkey was abhorrent to her; her religion and her feelings were alike averse to it. By some papers of her father which fell into her hands she heard of the exile of her lover and learnt the name of the
20 spot where he then resided. She hesitated some time, but at length she formed her determination. Taking with her some jewels that belonged to her and a sum of money, she quitted Italy with an attendant, a native of Leghorn, but who understood the common language of Turkey, and departed for Germany.

25 'She arrived in safety at a town about twenty leagues from the cottage of De Lacey, when her attendant fell dangerously ill. Safie nursed her with the most devoted affection; but the poor girl died, and the Arabian was left alone, unacquainted with the language of the country and utterly ignorant of the customs of the world. She
30 fell, however, into good hands. The Italian had mentioned the name of the spot for which they were bound; and after her death, the woman of the house in which they had lived took care that Safie should arrive in safety at the cottage of her lover.'

Chapter VII

'Such was the history of my beloved cottagers. It impressed me deeply. I learned, from the views of social life which it developed, to admire their virtues and to deprecate the vices of mankind.

'As yet I looked upon crime as a distant evil; benevolence and generosity were ever present before me, inciting within me a desire to become an actor in the busy scene where so many admirable qualities were called forth and displayed. But in giving an account of the progress of my intellect, I must not omit a circumstance which occurred in the beginning of the month of August of the same year.

'One night, during my accustomed visit to the neighbouring wood, where I collected my own food and brought home firing for my protectors, I found on the ground a leathern portmanteau, containing several articles of dress and some books. I eagerly seized the prize, and returned with it to my hovel. Fortunately the books were written in the language, the elements of which I had acquired at the cottage; they consisted of *Paradise Lost*, a volume of Plutarch's *Lives*, and the *Sorrows of Werter*. The possession of these treasures gave me extreme delight; I now continually studied and exercised my mind upon these histories, whilst my friends were employed in their ordinary occupations.

'I can hardly describe to you the effect of these books. They produced in me an infinity of new images and feelings, that sometimes raised me to ecstasy, but more frequently sunk me into the lowest dejection. In the *Sorrows of Werter*, besides the interest of its simple and affecting story, so many opinions are canvassed, and so many lights thrown upon what had hitherto been to me obscure

subjects, that I found in it a never-ending source of speculation and astonishment. The gentle and domestic manners it described, combined with lofty sentiments and feelings, which had for their object something out of self, accorded well with my experience
5 among my protectors, and with the wants which were forever alive in my own bosom. But I thought Werter himself a more divine being than I had ever beheld or imagined; his character contained no pretension, but it sunk deep. The disquisitions upon death and suicide were calculated to fill me with wonder. I did not pretend
10 to enter into the merits of the case, yet I inclined towards the opinions of the hero, whose extinction I wept, without precisely understanding it.

'As I read, however, I applied much personally to my own feelings and condition. I found myself similar, yet at the same time
15 strangely unlike to the beings concerning whom I read, and to whose conversation I was a listener. I sympathised with and partly understood them, but I was unformed in mind; I was dependent on none, and related to none. "The path of my departure was free," and there was none to lament my annihilation. My person was
20 hideous and my stature gigantic. What did this mean? Who was I? What was I? Whence did I come? What was my destination? These questions continually recurred, but I was unable to solve them.

'The volume of Plutarch's *Lives* which I possessed, contained the histories of the first founders of the ancient republics. This
25 book had a far different effect upon me from the *Sorrows of Werter*. I learned from Werter's imaginations despondency and gloom: but Plutarch taught me high thoughts; he elevated me above the wretched sphere of my own reflections, to admire and love the heroes of past ages. Many things I read surpassed my understand-
30 ing and experience. I had a very confused knowledge of kingdoms, wide extents of country, mighty rivers, and boundless seas. But I was perfectly unacquainted with towns, and large assemblages of men. The cottage of my protectors had been the only school in which I had studied human nature; but this book developed new
35 and mightier scenes of action. I read of men concerned in public affairs, governing or massacring their species. I felt the greatest

ardour for virtue rise within me, and abhorrence for vice, as far as I understood the signification of those terms, relative as they were, as I applied them, to pleasure and pain alone. Induced by these feelings, I was of course led to admire peaceable lawgivers, Numa, Solon, and Lycurgus, in preference to Romulus and Theseus. The 5 patriarchal lives of my protectors caused these impressions to take a firm hold on my mind; perhaps, if my first introduction to humanity had been made by a young soldier, burning for glory and slaughter, I should have been imbued with different sensations.

'But *Paradise Lost* excited different and far deeper emotions. I 10 read it, as I had read the other volumes which had fallen into my hands, as a true history. It moved every feeling of wonder and awe, that the picture of an omnipotent God warring with his creatures was capable of exciting. I often referred the several situations, as their similarity struck me, to my own. Like Adam, I was apparently 15 united by no link to any other being in existence; but his state was far different from mine in every other respect. He had come forth from the hands of God a perfect creature, happy and prosperous, guarded by the especial care of his Creator; he was allowed to converse with and acquire knowledge from beings of a superior 20 nature: but I was wretched, helpless, and alone. Many times I considered Satan as the fitter emblem of my condition; for often, like him, when I viewed the bliss of my protectors, the bitter gall of envy rose within me.

'Another circumstance strengthened and confirmed these feel- 25 ings. Soon after my arrival in the hovel, I discovered some papers in the pocket of the dress which I had taken from your laboratory. At first I had neglected them; but now that I was able to decipher the characters in which they were written, I began to study them with diligence. It was your journal of the four months that preceded 30 my creation. You minutely described in these papers every step you took in the progress of your work; this history was mingled with accounts of domestic occurrences. You doubtless recollect these papers. Here they are. Every thing is related in them which bears reference to my accursed origin; the whole detail of that 35 series of disgusting circumstances which produced it is set in view;

the minutest description of my odious and loathsome person is given, in language which painted your own horrors and rendered mine indelible. I sickened as I read. "Hateful day when I received life!" I exclaimed in agony. "Accursed creator! Why did you form
5 a monster so hideous that even *you* turned from me in disgust? God, in pity, made man beautiful and alluring, after his own image; but my form is a filthy type of yours, more horrid even from the very resemblance. Satan had his companions, fellow-devils, to admire and encourage him; but I am solitary and abhorred."

10 'These were the reflections of my hours of despondency and solitude; but when I contemplated the virtues of the cottagers, their amiable and benevolent dispositions, I persuaded myself that when they should become acquainted with my admiration of their virtues, they would compassionate me and overlook my personal
15 deformity. Could they turn from their door one, however monstrous, who solicited their compassion and friendship? I resolved, at least, not to despair, but in every way to fit myself for an interview with them, which would decide my fate. I postponed this attempt for some months longer; for the importance attached to its success
20 inspired me with a dread lest I should fail. Besides, I found that my understanding improved so much with every day's experience that I was unwilling to commence this undertaking until a few more months should have added to my sagacity.

'Several changes, in the mean time, took place in the cottage.
25 The presence of Safie diffused happiness among its inhabitants; and I also found that a greater degree of plenty reigned there. Felix and Agatha spent more time in amusement and conversation, and were assisted in their labours by servants. They did not appear rich, but they were contented and happy; their feelings were serene
30 and peaceful, while mine became every day more tumultuous. Increase of knowledge only discovered to me more clearly what a wretched outcast I was. I cherished hope, it is true; but it vanished when I beheld my person reflected in water, or my shadow in the moonshine, even as that frail image and that inconstant shade.

35 'I endeavoured to crush these fears, and to fortify myself for the trial which in a few months I resolved to undergo; and sometimes

I allowed my thoughts, unchecked by reason, to ramble in the fields of Paradise, and dared to fancy amiable and lovely creatures sympathising with my feelings and cheering my gloom; their angelic countenances breathed smiles of consolation. But it was all a dream; no Eve soothed my sorrows nor shared my thoughts; I was alone. I remembered Adam's supplication to his Creator. But where was mine? He had abandoned me, and in the bitterness of my heart I cursed him.

'Autumn passed thus. I saw, with surprise and grief, the leaves decay and fall, and nature again assume the barren and bleak appearance it had worn when I first beheld the woods and the lovely moon. Yet I did not heed the bleakness of the weather; I was better fitted by my conformation for the endurance of cold than heat. But my chief delights were the sight of the flowers, the birds, and all the gay apparel of summer; when those deserted me, I turned with more attention towards the cottagers. Their happiness was not decreased by the absence of summer. They loved and sympathized with one another; and their joys, depending on each other, were not interrupted by the casualties that took place around them. The more I saw of them, the greater became my desire to claim their protection and kindness; my heart yearned to be known and loved by these amiable creatures; to see their sweet looks directed towards me with affection was the utmost limit of my ambition. I dared not think that they would turn them from me with disdain and horror. The poor that stopped at their door were never driven away. I asked, it is true, for greater treasures than a little food or rest: I required kindness and sympathy; but I did not believe myself unworthy of it.

'The winter advanced, and an entire revolution of the seasons had taken place since I awoke into life. My attention, at this time, was solely directed towards my plan of introducing myself into the cottage of my protectors. I revolved many projects; but that on which I finally fixed was, to enter the dwelling when the blind old man should be alone. I had sagacity enough to discover, that the unnatural hideousness of my person was the chief object of horror with those who had formerly beheld me. My voice, although harsh, had nothing terrible in it; I thought, therefore, that if in the absence of his children, I could gain the good-will and mediation of the old De Lacey, I might by his means be tolerated by my younger protectors.

5 'One day, when the sun shone on the red leaves that strewed the ground, and diffused cheerfulness, although it denied warmth, Safie, Agatha, and Felix departed on a long country walk, and the old man, at his own desire, was left alone in the cottage. When his children had departed, he took up his guitar, and played several
10 mournful but sweet airs, more sweet and mournful than I had ever heard him play before. At first his countenance was illuminated with pleasure, but, as he continued, thoughtfulness and sadness succeeded; at length, laying aside the instrument, he sat absorbed in reflection.

15 'My heart beat quick; this was the hour and moment of trial, which would decide my hopes, or realise my fears. The servants were gone to a neighbouring fair. All was silent in and around the cottage: it was an excellent opportunity; yet, when I proceeded to execute my plan, my limbs failed me, and I sank to the ground.
20 Again I rose; and, exerting all the firmness of which I was master, removed the planks which I had placed before my hovel to conceal my retreat. The fresh air revived me, and, with renewed determination, I approached the door of their cottage.

'I knocked. "Who is there?" said the old man – "Come in."

25 'I entered; "Pardon this intrusion", said I; "I am a traveller in want of a little rest; you would greatly oblige me if you would allow me to remain a few minutes before the fire."

' "Enter," said De Lacey, "and I will try in what manner I can to relieve your wants; but, unfortunately, my children are from
30 home, and as I am blind, I am afraid I shall find it difficult to procure food for you."

' "Do not trouble yourself, my kind host; I have food; it is warmth and rest only that I need."

'I sat down, and a silence ensued. I knew that every minute
35 was precious to me, yet I remained irresolute in what manner to commence the interview; when the old man addressed me. "By

your language, stranger, I suppose you are my countryman; – are you French?"

'"No; but I was educated by a French family, and understand that language only. I am now going to claim the protection of some friends, whom I sincerely love, and of whose favour I have some 5 hopes."

'"Are they Germans?"

'"No, they are French. But let us change the subject. I am an unfortunate and deserted creature; I look around, and I have no relation or friend upon earth. These amiable people to whom I go 10 have never seen me, and know little of me. I am full of fears, for if I fail there, I am an outcast in the world forever."

'"Do not despair. To be friendless is indeed to be unfortunate; but the hearts of men, when unprejudiced by any obvious self-interest, are full of brotherly love and charity. Rely, therefore, on 15 your hopes; and if these friends are good and amiable, do not despair."

'"They are kind – they are the most excellent creatures in the world; but unfortunately, they are prejudiced against me. I have good dispositions; my life has been hitherto harmless and in some 20 degree beneficial; but a fatal prejudice clouds their eyes, and where they ought to see a feeling and kind friend, they behold only a detestable monster."

'"That is indeed unfortunate; but if you are really blameless, cannot you undeceive them?" 25

'"I am about to undertake that task; and it is on that account that I feel so many overwhelming terrors. I tenderly love these friends; I have, unknown to them, been for many months in the habits of daily kindness towards them; but they believe that I wish to injure them, and it is that prejudice which I wish to overcome." 30

'"Where do these friends reside?"

'"Near this spot."

'The old man paused and then continued, "If you will unreservedly confide to me the particulars of your tale, I perhaps may be of use in undeceiving them. I am blind and cannot judge of your 35 countenance, but there is something in your words which persuades me that you are sincere. I am poor and an exile, but it will afford me true pleasure to be in any way serviceable to a human creature."

'"Excellent man! I thank you and accept your generous offer. You raise me from the dust by this kindness; and I trust that, by
5 your aid, I shall not be driven from the society and sympathy of your fellow-creatures."

'"Heaven forbid! Even if you were really criminal, for that can only drive you to desperation, and not instigate you to virtue. I also am unfortunate; I and my family have been condemned, although
10 innocent; judge, therefore, if I do not feel for your misfortunes."

'"How can I thank you, my best and only benefactor? From your lips first have I heard the voice of kindness directed towards me; I shall be forever grateful; and your present humanity assures me of success with those friends whom I am on the point of
15 meeting."

'"May I know the names and residence of those friends?"

'I paused. This, I thought, was the moment of decision, which was to rob me of, or bestow happiness on me forever. I struggled vainly for firmness sufficient to answer him, but the effort destroyed
20 all my remaining strength; I sank on the chair and sobbed aloud. At that moment I heard the steps of my younger protectors. I had not a moment to lose, but, seizing the hand of the old man, I cried, "Now is the time! Save and protect me! You and your family are the friends whom I seek. Do not you desert me in the hour of trial!"
25 '"Great God!" exclaimed the old man, "who are you?"

'At that instant the cottage door was opened, and Felix, Safie, and Agatha entered. Who can describe their horror and consternation on beholding me? Agatha fainted, and Safie, unable to attend to her friend, rushed out of the cottage. Felix darted forward, and with
30 supernatural force tore me from his father, to whose knees I clung: in a transport of fury, he dashed me to the ground and struck me violently with a stick. I could have torn him limb from limb, as the lion rends the antelope. But my heart sunk within me as with bitter sickness, and I refrained. I saw him on the point of repeating his
35 blow, when, overcome by pain and anguish, I quitted the cottage, and in the general tumult escaped unperceived to my hovel.'

Chapter VIII

'Cursed, cursed creator! Why did I live? Why, in that instant, did I not extinguish the spark of existence which you had so wantonly bestowed? I know not; despair had not yet taken possession of me; my feelings were those of rage and revenge. I could with pleasure have destroyed the cottage and its inhabitants, and have glutted myself with their shrieks and misery.

'When night came I quitted my retreat and wandered in the wood; and now, no longer restrained by the fear of discovery, I gave vent to my anguish in fearful howlings. I was like a wild beast that had broken the toils, destroying the objects that obstructed me and ranging through the wood with a staglike swiftness. O! what a miserable night I passed! the cold stars shone in mockery, and the bare trees waved their branches above me: now and then the sweet voice of a bird burst forth amidst the universal stillness. All, save I, were at rest or in enjoyment: I, like the arch-fiend, bore a hell within me, and finding myself unsympathised with, wished to tear up the trees, spread havoc and destruction around me, and then to have sat down and enjoyed the ruin.

'But this was a luxury of sensation that could not endure; I became fatigued with excess of bodily exertion, and sank on the damp grass in the sick impotence of despair. There was none among the myriads of men that existed who would pity or assist me; and should I feel kindness towards my enemies? No: from that moment I declared ever-lasting war against the species, and, more than all, against him who had formed me, and sent me forth to this insupportable misery.

'The sun rose; I heard the voices of men and knew that it was impossible to return to my retreat during that day. Accordingly I hid myself in some thick underwood, determining to devote the ensuing hours to reflection on my situation.

'The pleasant sunshine, and the pure air of day, restored me to
5 some degree of tranquillity; and when I considered what had passed at the cottage, I could not help believing that I had been too hasty in my conclusions. I had certainly acted imprudently. It was apparent that my conversation had interested the father in my behalf, and I was a fool in having exposed my person to the horror
10 of his children. I ought to have familiarised the old De Lacey to me, and by degrees to have discovered myself to the rest of his family, when they should have been prepared for my approach. But I did not believe my errors to be irretrievable, and after much consideration I resolved to return to the cottage, seek the old man,
15 and by my representations win him to my party.

'These thoughts calmed me, and in the afternoon I sank into a profound sleep; but the fever of my blood did not allow me to be visited by peaceful dreams. The horrible scene of the preceding day was forever acting before my eyes; the females were flying,
20 and the enraged Felix tearing me from his father's feet. I awoke exhausted; and finding that it was already night, I crept forth from my hiding-place, and went in search of food.

'When my hunger was appeased, I directed my steps towards the well-known path that conducted to the cottage. All there was
25 at peace. I crept into my hovel, and remained in silent expectation of the accustomed hour when the family arose. That hour passed, the sun mounted high in the heavens, but the cottagers did not appear. I trembled violently, apprehending some dreadful misfortune. The inside of the cottage was dark, and I heard no motion; I
30 cannot describe the agony of this suspense.

'Presently two countrymen passed by; but pausing near the cottage, they entered into conversation, using violent gesticulations; but I did not understand what they said, as they spoke the language of the country, which differed from that of my protectors.
35 Soon after, however, Felix approached with another man; I was surprised, as I knew that he had not quitted the cottage that

morning, and waited anxiously to discover, from his discourse, the meaning of these unusual appearances.

' "Do you consider," said his companion to him, "that you will be obliged to pay three months' rent and to lose the produce of your garden? I do not wish to take any unfair advantage, and I beg therefore that you will take some days to consider of your determination."

' "It is utterly useless," replied Felix; "we can never again inhabit your cottage. The life of my father is in the greatest danger, owing to the dreadful circumstance that I have related. My wife and my sister will never recover from their horror. I intreat you not to reason with me any more. Take possession of your tenement, and let me fly from this place."

'Felix trembled violently as he said this. He and his companion entered the cottage, in which they remained for a few minutes, and then departed. I never saw any of the family of De Lacey more.

'I continued for the remainder of the day in my hovel in a state of utter and stupid despair. My protectors had departed, and had broken the only link that held me to the world. For the first time the feelings of revenge and hatred filled my bosom, and I did not strive to control them; but allowing myself to be borne away by the stream, I bent my mind towards injury and death. When I thought of my friends, of the mild voice of De Lacey, the gentle eyes of Agatha, and the exquisite beauty of the Arabian, these thoughts vanished and a gush of tears somewhat soothed me. But again when I reflected that they had spurned and deserted me, anger returned, a rage of anger, and unable to injure anything human, I turned my fury towards inanimate objects. As night advanced I placed a variety of combustibles around the cottage; and, after having destroyed every vestige of cultivation in the garden, I waited with forced impatience until the moon had sunk to commence my operations.

'As the night advanced, a fierce wind arose from the woods, and quickly dispersed the clouds that had loitered in the heavens; the blast tore along like a mighty avalanche and produced a kind of insanity in my spirits, that burst all bounds of reason and reflection.

I lighted the dry branch of a tree and danced with fury around the devoted cottage, my eyes still fixed on the western horizon, the edge of which the moon nearly touched. A part of its orb was at length hid, and I waved my brand; it sank, and with a loud scream
5   I fired the straw, and heath, and bushes, which I had collected. The wind fanned the fire, and the cottage was quickly enveloped by the flames, which clung to it and licked it with their forked and destroying tongues.

'As soon as I was convinced that no assistance could save any
10 part of the habitation, I quitted the scene, and sought for refuge in the woods.

'And now, with the world before me, whither should I bend my steps? I resolved to fly far from the scene of my misfortunes; but to me, hated and despised, every country must be equally horrible.
15 At length the thought of you crossed my mind. I learned from your papers that you were my father, my creator; and to whom could I apply with more fitness than to him who had given me life? Among the lessons that Felix had bestowed upon Safie, geography had not been omitted: I had learned from these the relative situations of
20 the different countries of the earth. You had mentioned Geneva as the name of your native town; and towards this place I resolved to proceed.

'But how was I to direct myself? I knew that I must travel in a south-westerly direction to reach my destination; but the sun was
25 my only guide. I did not know the names of the towns that I was to pass through, nor could I ask information from a single human being; but I did not despair. From you only could I hope for succour, although towards you I felt no sentiment but that of hatred. Unfeeling, heartless creator! You had endowed me with
30 perceptions and passions and then cast me abroad an object for the scorn and horror of mankind. But on you only had I any claim for pity and redress, and from you I determined to seek that justice which I vainly attempted to gain from any other being that wore the human form.

35 'My travels were long, and the sufferings I endured intense. It was late in autumn when I quitted the district where I had so long

resided. I travelled only at night, fearful of encountering the visage
of a human being. Nature decayed around me, and the sun became
heatless; rain and snow poured around me; mighty rivers were
frozen; the surface of the earth was hard and chill, and bare, and I
found no shelter. Oh, earth! how often did I imprecate curses on   5
the cause of my being! The mildness of my nature had fled, and
all within me was turned to gall and bitterness. The nearer I
approached to your habitation, the more deeply did I feel the spirit
of revenge enkindled in my heart. Snow fell, and the waters were
hardened, but I rested not. A few incidents now and then directed   10
me, and I possessed a map of the country; but I often wandered
wide from my path. The agony of my feelings allowed me no
respite: no incident occurred from which my rage and misery could
not extract its food; but a circumstance that happened when I
arrived on the confines of Switzerland, when the sun had recovered   15
its warmth and the earth again began to look green, confirmed in
an especial manner the bitterness and horror of my feelings.

'I generally rested during the day, and travelled only when I was
secured by night from the view of man. One morning, however,
finding that my path lay through a deep wood, I ventured to   20
continue my journey after the sun had risen; the day, which was
one of the first of spring, cheered even me by the loveliness of its
sunshine and the balminess of the air. I felt emotions of gentleness
and pleasure, that had long appeared dead, revive within me. Half
surprised by the novelty of these sensations, I allowed myself to be   25
borne away by them, and, forgetting my solitude and deformity,
dared to be happy. Soft tears again bedewed my cheeks, and I even
raised my humid eyes with thankfulness towards the blessed sun,
which bestowed such joy upon me.

'I continued to wind among the paths of the wood, until I came   30
to its boundary, which was skirted by a deep and rapid river, into
which many of the trees bent their branches, now budding with
the fresh spring. Here I paused, not exactly knowing what path to
pursue, when I heard the sound of voices, that induced me to conceal
myself under the shade of a cypress. I was scarcely hid, when a young   35
girl came running towards the spot where I was concealed, laughing,

as if she ran from some one in sport. She continued her course along the precipitous sides of the river, when suddenly her foot slipt, and she fell into the rapid stream. I rushed from my hiding-place, and, with extreme labour from the force of the current, saved
5 her, and dragged her to shore. She was senseless; and I endeavoured, by every means in my power, to restore animation, when I was suddenly interrupted by the approach of a rustic, who was probably the person from whom she had playfully fled. On seeing me, he darted towards me, and tearing the girl from my arms, hastened towards
10 the deeper parts of the wood. I followed speedily, I hardly knew why; but when the man saw me draw near, he aimed a gun, which he carried, at my body, and fired. I sank to the ground, and my injurer, with increased swiftness, escaped into the wood.

'This was then the reward of my benevolence! I had saved a
15 human being from destruction, and as a recompense I now writhed under the miserable pain of a wound which shattered the flesh and bone. The feelings of kindness and gentleness, which I had entertained but a few moments before, gave place to hellish rage and gnashing of teeth. Inflamed by pain, I vowed eternal hatred
20 and vengeance to all mankind. But the agony of my wound overcame me; my pulses paused, and I fainted.

'For some weeks I led a miserable life in the woods, endeavouring to cure the wound which I had received. The ball had entered my shoulder, and I knew not whether it had remained there or passed
25 through; at any rate I had no means of extracting it. My sufferings were augmented also by the oppressive sense of the injustice and ingratitude of their infliction. My daily vows rose for revenge – a deep and deadly revenge, such as would alone compensate for the outrages and anguish I had endured.

30 'After some weeks my wound healed, and I continued my journey. The labours I endured were no longer to be alleviated by the bright sun or gentle breezes of spring; all joy was but a mockery which insulted my desolate state, and made me feel more painfully that I was not made for the enjoyment of pleasure.

35 'But my toils now drew near a close, and in two months from this time, I reached the environs of Geneva.

'It was evening when I arrived, and I retired to a hiding-place among the fields that surround it, to meditate in what manner I should apply to you. I was oppressed by fatigue and hunger, and far too unhappy to enjoy the gentle breezes of evening, or the prospect of the sun setting behind the stupendous mountains of   5 Jura.

'At this time a slight sleep relieved me from the pain of reflection, which was disturbed by the approach of a beautiful child, who came running into the recess I had chosen, with all the sportiveness of infancy. Suddenly, as I gazed on him, an idea seized me that this   10 little creature was unprejudiced, and had lived too short a time to have imbibed a horror of deformity. If, therefore, I could seize him and educate him as my companion and friend, I should not be so desolate in this peopled earth.

'Urged by this impulse, I seized on the boy as he passed and   15 drew him towards me. As soon as he beheld my form, he placed his hands before his eyes, and uttered a shrill scream; I drew his hand forcibly from his face and said, "Child, what is the meaning of this? I do not intend to hurt you; listen to me."

'He struggled violently. "Let me go," he cried; "monster! ugly   20 wretch! you wish to eat me and tear me to pieces – You are an ogre – Let me go, or I will tell my papa."

' "Boy, you will never see your father again; you must come with me."

' "Hideous monster! let me go. My papa is a syndic – he is M.   25 Frankenstein – he will punish you. You dare not keep me."

' "Frankenstein! you belong then to my enemy – to him towards whom I have sworn eternal revenge; you shall be my first victim."

'The child still struggled, and loaded me with epithets which carried despair to my heart; I grasped his throat to silence him, and   30 in a moment he lay dead at my feet.

'I gazed on my victim, and my heart swelled with exultation and hellish triumph; clapping my hands, I exclaimed, "I too can create desolation; my enemy is not invulnerable; this death will carry despair to him, and a thousand other miseries shall torment and   35 destroy him."

'As I fixed my eyes on the child, I saw something glittering on his breast. I took it; it was a portrait of a most lovely woman. In spite of my malignity, it softened and attracted me. For a few moments I gazed with delight on her dark eyes, fringed by deep
5 lashes, and her lovely lips; but presently my rage returned: I remembered that I was forever deprived of the delights that such beautiful creatures could bestow; and that she whose resemblance I contemplated would, in regarding me, have changed that air of divine benignity to one expressive of disgust and affright.

10 'Can you wonder that such thoughts transported me with rage? I only wonder that at that moment, instead of venting my sensations in exclamations and agony, I did not rush among mankind, and perish in the attempt to destroy them.

'While I was overcome by these feelings, I left the spot where I
15 had committed the murder, and seeking a more secluded hiding-place, I entered a barn which had appeared to me to be empty. A woman was sleeping on some straw; she was young: not indeed so beautiful as her whose portrait I held; but of an agreeable aspect and blooming in the loveliness of youth and health. Here, I thought,
20 is one of those whose joy-imparting smiles are bestowed on all but me. And then I bent over her, and whispered, "Awake, fairest, thy lover is near – he who would give his life but to obtain one look of affection from thine eyes: my beloved, awake!"

'The sleeper stirred; a thrill of terror ran through me. Should
25 she indeed awake, and see me, and curse me, and denounce the murderer? Thus would she assuredly act, if her darkened eyes opened, and she beheld me. The thought was madness; it stirred the fiend within me – not I, but she, shall suffer; the murder I have committed because I am forever robbed of all that she could give
30 me, she shall atone. The crime had its source in her: be hers the punishment! Thanks to the lessons of Felix and the sanguinary laws of man, I had learned how to work mischief. I bent over her and placed the portrait securely in one of the folds of her dress. She moved again, and I fled.

35 'For some days I haunted the spot where these scenes had taken place; sometimes wishing to see you, sometimes resolved to quit

the world and its miseries forever. At length I wandered towards
these mountains, and have ranged through their immense recesses,
consumed by a burning passion which you alone can gratify. We
may not part until you have promised to comply with my requisition. I am alone, and miserable; man will not associate with me; 5
but one as deformed and horrible as myself would not deny herself
to me. My companion must be of the same species, and have the
same defects. This being you must create.'

Chapter IX

The being finished speaking, and fixed his looks upon me in the expectation of a reply. But I was bewildered, perplexed, and unable to arrange my ideas sufficiently to understand the full extent of his proposition. He continued.

5   'You must create a female for me, with whom I can live in the interchange of those sympathies necessary for my being. This you alone can do; and I demand it of you as a right which you must not refuse to concede.'

The latter part of his tale had kindled anew in me the anger
10 that had died away while he narrated his peaceful life among the cottagers, and, as he said this, I could no longer suppress the rage that burned within me.

'I do refuse it,' I replied; 'and no torture shall ever extort a consent from me. You may render me the most miserable of men,
15 but you shall never make me base in my own eyes. Shall I create another like yourself, whose joint wickedness might desolate the world? Begone! I have answered you; you may torture me, but I will never consent.'

'You are in the wrong,' replied the fiend; 'and, instead of threat-
20 ening, I am content to reason with you. I am malicious because I am miserable. Am I not shunned and hated by all mankind? You, my creator, would tear me to pieces, and triumph; remember that, and tell me why I should pity man more than he pities me? You would not call it murder, if you could precipitate me into one of
25 those ice-rifts, and destroy my frame, the work of your own hands. Shall I respect man when he contemns me? Let him live with me in the interchange of kindness; and, instead of injury I would

bestow every benefit upon him with tears of gratitude at his accept-
ance. But that cannot be; the human senses are insurmountable
barriers to our union. Yet mine shall not be the submission of
abject slavery. I will revenge my injuries: if I cannot inspire love, I
will cause fear, and chiefly towards you my arch-enemy, because   5
my creator, do I swear inextinguishable hatred. Have a care: I will
work at your destruction, nor finish until I desolate your heart, so
that you shall curse the hour of your birth.'

A fiendish rage animated him as he said this; his face was wrinkled
into contortions too horrible for human eyes to behold; but pres-   10
ently he calmed himself and proceeded.

'I intended to reason. This passion is detrimental to me; for you
do not reflect that *you* are the cause of its excess. If any being felt
emotions of benevolence towards me, I should return them an
hundred and an hundredfold; for that one creature's sake I would   15
make peace with the whole kind! But I now indulge in dreams of
bliss that cannot be realised. What I ask of you is reasonable and
moderate; I demand a creature of another sex, but as hideous as
myself; the gratification is small, but it is all that I can receive, and
it shall content me. It is true, we shall be monsters, cut off from all   20
the world; but on that account we shall be more attached to one
another. Our lives will not be happy, but they will be harmless, and
free from the misery I now feel. Oh! my creator, make me happy;
let me feel gratitude towards you for one benefit! Let me see that I
excite the sympathy of some existing thing; do not deny me my   25
request!'

I was moved. I shuddered when I thought of the possible consequences of my consent, but I felt that there was some justice in his
argument. His tale, and the feelings he now expressed, proved him
to be a creature of fine sensations; and did I not as his maker, owe   30
him all the portion of happiness that it was in my power to bestow?
He saw my change of feeling and continued.

'If you consent, neither you nor any other human being shall
ever see us again: I will go to the vast wilds of South America.
My food is not that of man; I do not destroy the lamb and the   35
kid to glut my appetite; acorns and berries afford me sufficient

nourishment. My companion will be of the same nature as myself, and will be content with the same fare. We shall make our bed of dried leaves; the sun will shine on us as on man, and will ripen our food. The picture I present to you is peaceful and human, and you
5 must feel that you could deny it only in the wantonness of power and cruelty. Pitiless as you have been towards me, I now see compassion in your eyes; let me seize the favourable moment and persuade you to promise what I so ardently desire.'

'You propose,' replied I, 'to fly from the habitations of man, to
10 dwell in those wilds where the beasts of the field will be your only companions. How can you, who long for the love and sympathy of man, persevere in this exile? You will return, and again seek their kindness, and you will meet with their detestation; your evil passions will be renewed, and you will then have a companion to aid
15 you in the task of destruction. This may not be: cease to argue the point, for I cannot consent.'

'How inconstant are your feelings! but a moment ago you were moved by my representations, and why do you again harden yourself to my complaints? I swear to you, by the earth which I inhabit,
20 and by you that made me, that with the companion you bestow I will quit the neighbourhood of man, and dwell, as it may chance, in the most savage of places. My evil passions will have fled, for I shall meet with sympathy! my life will flow quietly away, and in my dying moments I shall not curse my maker.'

25 His words had a strange effect upon me. I compassionated him and sometimes felt a wish to console him; but when I looked upon him, when I saw the filthy mass that moved and talked, my heart sickened and my feelings were altered to those of horror and hatred. I tried to stifle these sensations; I thought, that as I could not
30 sympathise with him, I had no right to withhold from him the small portion of happiness which was yet in my power to bestow.

'You swear,' I said, 'to be harmless; but have you not already shown a degree of malice that should reasonably make me distrust you? May not even this be a feint that will increase your triumph
35 by affording a wider scope for your revenge?'

'How is this? I must not be trifled with: and I demand an answer.

If I have no ties and no affections, hatred and vice must be my portion; the love of another will destroy the cause of my crimes, and I shall become a thing of whose existence every one will be ignorant. My vices are the children of a forced solitude that I abhor; and my virtues will necessarily arise when I live in communion   5
with an equal. I shall feel the affections of a sensitive being, and become linked to the chain of existence and events, from which I am now excluded.'

I paused some time to reflect on all he had related, and the various arguments which he had employed. I thought of the promise of   10
virtues which he had displayed on the opening of his existence, and the subsequent blight of all kindly feeling by the loathing and scorn which his protectors had manifested towards him. His power and threats were not omitted to my calculations: a creature who could exist in the ice-caves of the glaciers, and hide himself from pursuit   15
among the ridges of inaccessible precipices, was a being possessing faculties it would be vain to cope with. After a long pause of reflection, I concluded that the justice due both to him and my fellow creatures demanded of me that I should comply with his request. Turning to him, therefore, I said –   20

'I consent to your demand, on your solemn oath to quit Europe forever, and every other place in the neighbourhood of man, as soon as I shall deliver into your hands a female who will accompany you in your exile.'

'I swear,' he cried, 'by the sun, and by the blue sky of Heaven,   25
and by the fire of love that burns my heart, that if you grant my prayer, while they exist you shall never behold me again. Depart to your home, and commence your labours: I shall watch their progress with unutterable anxiety; and fear not but that when you are ready I shall appear.'   30

Saying this, he suddenly quitted me, fearful, perhaps, of any change in my sentiments. I saw him descend the mountain with greater speed than the flight of an eagle, and quickly lost among the undulations of the sea of ice.

His tale had occupied the whole day, and the sun was upon the   35
verge of the horizon when he departed. I knew that I ought to hasten

my descent towards the valley, as I should soon be encompassed in darkness; but my heart was heavy, and my steps slow. The labour of winding among the little paths of the mountain and fixing my feet firmly as I advanced, perplexed me, occupied as I was by the
5 emotions which the occurrences of the day had produced. Night was far advanced when I came to the half way resting-place and seated myself beside the fountain. The stars shone at intervals, as the clouds passed from over them; the dark pines rose before me, and every here and there a broken tree lay on the ground: it was a
10 scene of wonderful solemnity and stirred strange thoughts within me. I wept bitterly; and clasping my hands in agony, I exclaimed, 'Oh! stars and clouds and winds, ye are all about to mock me: if ye really pity me, crush sensation and memory; let me become as nought; but if not, depart, depart, and leave me in darkness.'
15   These were wild and miserable thoughts; but I cannot describe to you how the eternal twinkling of the stars weighed upon me, and how I listened to every blast of wind, as if it were a dull ugly siroc on its way to consume me.

     Morning dawned before I arrived at the village of Chamounix; I
20 took no rest, but returned immediately to Geneva. Even in my own heart I could give no expression to my sensations – they weighed on me with a mountain's weight, and their excess destroyed my agony beneath them. Thus I returned home, and entering the house, presented myself to the family. My haggard and wild appear-
25 ance awoke intense alarm; but I answered no questions, scarcely did I speak. I felt as if I were placed under a ban – as if I had no right to claim their sympathies – as if never more might I enjoy companionship with them. Yet even thus I loved them to adoration; and to save them, I resolved to dedicate myself to my most abhorred
30 task. The prospect of such an occupation made every other circumstance of existence pass before me like a dream, and that thought only had to me the reality of life.

END OF VOLUME TWO

Volume Three

Chapter I

Day after day, week after week, passed away on my return to Geneva; and I could not collect the courage to recommence my work. I feared the vengeance of the disappointed fiend, yet I was unable to overcome my repugnance to the task which was enjoined me. I found that I could not compose a female without again 5 devoting several months to profound study and laborious disquisition. I had heard of some discoveries having been made by an English philosopher, the knowledge of which was material to my success, and I sometimes thought of obtaining my father's consent to visit England for this purpose; but I clung to every pretence of 10 delay, and shrank from taking the first step in an undertaking whose immediate necessity began to appear less absolute to me. A change indeed had taken place in me: my health, which had hitherto declined, was now much restored; and my spirits, when unchecked by the memory of my unhappy promise, rose proportionably. My 15 father saw this change with pleasure, and he turned his thoughts towards the best method of eradicating the remains of my melancholy, which every now and then would return by fits, and with a devouring blackness overcast the approaching sunshine. At these moments I took refuge in the most perfect solitude. I passed whole 20 days on the lake alone in a little boat, watching the clouds, and listening to the rippling of the waves, silent and listless. But the fresh air and bright sun seldom failed to restore me to some degree of composure; and, on my return, I met the salutations of my friends with a readier smile and a more cheerful heart. 25

It was after my return from one of these rambles that my father, calling me aside, thus addressed me –

'I am happy to remark, my dear son, that you have resumed your former pleasures, and seem to be returning to yourself. And yet you are still unhappy, and still avoid our society. For some time I was lost in conjecture as to the cause of this; but yesterday an idea struck me, and if it is well founded, I conjure you to avow it. Reserve on such a point would be not only useless, but draw down treble misery on us all.'

I trembled violently at his exordium, and my father continued –

'I confess, my son, that I have always looked forward to your marriage with our dear Elizabeth as the tie of our domestic comfort, and the stay of my declining years. You were attached to each other from your earliest infancy; you studied together, and appeared, in dispositions and tastes, entirely suited to one another. But so blind is the experience of man, that what I conceived to be the best assistants to my plan may have entirely destroyed it. You, perhaps, regard her as your sister, without any wish that she might become your wife. Nay, you may have met with another whom you may love; and considering yourself as bound in honour to Elizabeth, this struggle may occasion the poignant misery which you appear to feel.'

'My dear father, re-assure yourself. I love my cousin tenderly and sincerely. I never saw any woman who excited, as Elizabeth does, my warmest admiration and affection. My future hopes and prospects are entirely bound up in the expectation of our union.'

'The expression of your sentiments of this subject, my dear Victor, gives me more pleasure than I have for some time experienced. If you feel thus, we shall assuredly be happy, however present events may cast a gloom over us. But it is this gloom which appears to have taken so strong a hold of your mind, that I wish to dissipate. Tell me, therefore, whether you object to an immediate solemnisation of the marriage. We have been unfortunate, and recent events have drawn us from that every-day tranquillity befitting my years and infirmities. You are younger; yet I do not suppose, possessed as you are of a competent fortune, that an early marriage would at all interfere with any future plans of honour and utility that you may have formed. Do not suppose, however, that I wish to dictate happiness to you, or that a delay on your part would cause me any serious uneasiness. Interpret my words with candour and answer me, I conjure you, with confidence and sincerity.'   5

I listened to my father in silence, and remained for some time incapable of offering any reply. I revolved rapidly in my mind a multitude of thoughts, and endeavoured to arrive at some conclusion. Alas! to me the idea of an immediate union with my Elizabeth was one of horror and dismay. I was bound by a solemn   10 promise, which I had not yet fulfilled, and dared not break; or if I did, what manifold miseries might not impend over me and my devoted family! Could I enter into a festival with this deadly weight yet hanging round my neck, and bowing me to the ground? I must perform my engagement, and let the monster depart with his mate,   15 before I allowed myself to enjoy the delight of a union from which I expected peace.

I remembered also the necessity imposed upon me of either journeying to England, or entering into a long correspondence with those philosophers of that country, whose knowledge and   20 discoveries were of indispensable use to me in my present undertaking. The latter method of obtaining the desired intelligence was dilatory and unsatisfactory: besides, I had an insurmountable aversion to the idea of engaging myself in my loathsome task in my father's house, while in habits of familiar intercourse with those I   25 loved. I knew that a thousand fearful accidents might occur, the slightest of which would disclose a tale to thrill all connected with me with horror. I was aware also that I should often lose all self-command, all capacity of hiding the harrowing sensations that would possess me during the progress of my unearthly occupation.   30 I must absent myself from all I loved while thus employed. Once commenced, it would quickly be achieved, and I might be restored to my family in peace and happiness. My promise fulfilled, the monster would depart forever. Or (so my fond fancy imaged) some accident might meanwhile occur to destroy him, and put an end   35 to my slavery forever.

These feelings dictated my answer to my father. I expressed a
wish to visit England; but concealing the true reasons of this
request, I clothed my desires under a guise which excited no
suspicion, while I urged my desire with an earnestness that easily
5 induced my father to comply. After so long a period of an absorbing
melancholy, that resembled madness in its intensity and effects, he
was glad to find that I was capable of taking pleasure in the idea of
such a journey, and he hoped that change of scene and varied
amusement would, before my return, have restored me entirely to
10 myself.

The duration of my absence was left to my own choice; a few
months, or at most a year, was the period contemplated. One
paternal kind precaution he had taken to ensure my having a
companion. Without previously communicating with me, he had,
15 in concert with Elizabeth, arranged that Clerval should join me in
Strasburgh. This interfered with the solitude I coveted for the
prosecution of my task; yet at the commencement of my journey
the presence of my friend could in no way be an impediment, and
truly I rejoiced that thus I should be saved many hours of lonely,
20 maddening reflection. Nay, Henry might stand between me and
the intrusion of my foe. If I were alone, would he not at times force
his abhorred presence on me, to remind me of my task or to
contemplate its progress?

To England, therefore, I was bound, and it was understood that
25 my union with Elizabeth should take place immediately on my
return. My father's age rendered him extremely averse to delay.
For myself, there was one reward I promised myself from my
detested toils – one consolation for my unparalleled sufferings; it
was the prospect of that day when, enfranchised from my miserable
30 slavery, I might claim Elizabeth, and forget the past in union with
her.

I now made arrangements for my journey; but one feeling
haunted me, which filled me with fear and agitation. During my
absence I should leave my friends unconscious of the existence of
35 their enemy, and unprotected from his attacks, exasperated as he
might be by my departure. But he had promised to follow me

wherever I might go; and would he not accompany me to England?
This imagination was dreadful in itself, but soothing, inasmuch
as it supposed the safety of my friends. I was agonised with the
idea of the possibility that the reverse of this might happen. But
through the whole period during which I was the slave of my   5
creature I allowed myself to be governed by the impulses of the
moment; and my present sensations strongly intimated that the
fiend would follow me, and exempt my family from the danger of
his machinations.

It was in the latter end of September that I again quitted my   10
native country. My journey had been my own suggestion, and
Elizabeth, therefore, acquiesced; but she was filled with disquiet at
the idea of my suffering, away from her, the inroads of misery and
grief. It had been her care which provided me a companion in
Clerval – and yet a man is blind to a thousand minute circum-   15
stances, which call forth a woman's sedulous attention. She longed
to bid me hasten my return – a thousand conflicting emotions
rendered her mute, as she bade me a tearful, silent farewell.

I threw myself into the carriage that was to convey me away,
hardly knowing whither I was going, and careless of what was   20
passing around. I remembered only, and it was with a bitter anguish
that I reflected on it, to order that my chemical instruments should
be packed to go with me. Filled with dreary imaginations, I passed
through many beautiful and majestic scenes, but my eyes were
fixed and unobserving. I could only think of the bourne of my   25
travels, and the work which was to occupy me whilst they endured.

After some days spent in listless indolence, during which I traversed many leagues, I arrived at Strasburgh where I waited two days
for Clerval. He came. Alas, how great was the contrast between us!
He was alive to every new scene; joyful when he saw the beauties   30
of the setting sun, and more happy when he beheld it rise and
recommence a new day. He pointed out to me the shifting colours
of the landscape, and the appearances of the sky. 'This is what it
is to live,' he cried; 'now I enjoy existence! But you, my dear
Frankenstein, wherefore are you desponding and sorrowful?' In   35
truth, I was occupied by gloomy thoughts, and neither saw the

descent of the evening star, nor the golden sunrise reflected in the Rhine. – And you, my friend, would be far more amused with the journal of Clerval, who observed the scenery with an eye of feeling and delight, than in listening to my reflections. I, a miserable
5 wretch, haunted by a curse that shut up every avenue to enjoyment.

We had agreed to descend the Rhine in a boat from Strasburgh to Rotterdam, whence we might take shipping for London. During this voyage we passed many willowy islands, and saw several beautiful towns. We stayed a day at Mannheim, and, on the fifth from
10 our departure from Strasburgh, arrived at Mayence. The course of the Rhine below Mayence becomes much more picturesque. The river descends rapidly, and winds between hills, not high, but steep, and of beautiful forms. We saw many ruined castles standing on the edges of precipices, surrounded by black woods, high and
15 inaccessible. This part of the Rhine, indeed, presents a singularly variegated landscape. In one spot you view rugged hills, ruined castles overlooking tremendous precipices, with the dark Rhine rushing beneath; and, on the sudden turn of a promontory, flourishing vineyards with green sloping banks and a meandering
20 river and populous towns occupy the scene.

We travelled at the time of the vintage, and heard the song of the labourers, as we glided down the stream. Even I, depressed in mind, and my spirits continually agitated by gloomy feelings, even I was pleased. I lay at the bottom of the boat, and, as I gazed on
25 the cloudless blue sky, I seemed to drink in a tranquillity to which I had long been a stranger. And if these were my sensations, who can describe those of Henry? He felt as if he had been transported to Fairy-land and enjoyed a happiness seldom tasted by man. 'I have seen,' he said, 'the most beautiful scenes of my own country;
30 I have visited the lakes of Lucerne and Uri, where the snowy mountains descend almost perpendicularly to the water, casting black and impenetrable shades, which would cause a gloomy and mournful appearance were it not for the most verdant islands that relieve the eye by their gay appearance; I have seen this lake agitated
35 by a tempest, when the wind tore up whirlwinds of water and gave you an idea of what the waterspout must be on the great ocean;

and the waves dash with fury the base of the mountain, where the priest and his mistress were overwhelmed by an avalanche and where their dying voices are still said to be heard amid the pauses of the nightly wind; I have seen the mountains of La Valais, and the Pays de Vaud: but this country, Victor, pleases me more than 5 all those wonders. The mountains of Switzerland are more majestic and strange; but there is a charm in the banks of this divine river, that I never before saw equalled. Look at that castle which overhangs yon precipice; and that also on the island, almost concealed amongst the foliage of those lovely trees; and now that group 10 of labourers coming from among their vines; and that village half hid in the recess of the mountain. Oh, surely the spirit that inhabits and guards this place has a soul more in harmony with man than those who pile the glacier, or retire to the inaccessible peaks of the mountains of our own country.' 15

Clerval! beloved friend! Even now it delights me to record your words, and to dwell on the praise of which you are so eminently deserving. He was a being formed in the 'very poetry of nature'. His wild and enthusiastic imagination was chastened by the sensibility of his heart. His soul overflowed with ardent affections, and 20 his friendship was of that devoted and wondrous nature that the worldly-minded teach us to look for only in the imagination. But even human sympathies were not sufficient to satisfy his eager mind. The scenery of external nature, which others regard only with admiration, he loved with ardour:– 25

> The sounding cataract
> Haunted him like a passion: the tall rock,
> The mountain, and the deep and gloomy wood,
> Their colours and their forms, were then to him
> An appetite; a feeling, and a love, 30
> That had no need of a remoter charm,
> By thought supplied, or any interest
> Unborrow'd from the eye.[1]

1. Wordsworth's Tintern Abbey [author's footnote].

And where does he now exist? Is this gentle and lovely being lost forever? Has this mind, so replete with ideas, imaginations fanciful and magnificent, which formed a world, whose existence depended on the life of its creator – has this mind perished? Does it now only exist in my memory? No, it is not thus; your form so divinely wrought, and beaming with beauty, has decayed, but your spirit still visits and consoles your unhappy friend.

Pardon this gush of sorrow; these ineffectual words are but a slight tribute to the unexampled worth of Henry, but they soothe my heart, overflowing with the anguish which his remembrance creates. I will proceed with my tale.

Beyond Cologne we descended to the plains of Holland; and we resolved to post the remainder of our way; for the wind was contrary, and the stream of the river was too gentle to aid us.

Our journey here lost the interest arising from beautiful scenery, but we arrived in a few days at Rotterdam; whence we proceeded by sea to England. It was on a clear morning, in the latter days of December, that I first saw the white cliffs of Britain. The banks of the Thames presented a new scene; they were flat, but fertile, and almost every town was marked by the remembrance of some story. We saw Tilbury Fort, and remembered the Spanish Armada; Gravesend, Woolwich, and Greenwich – places which I had heard of even in my country.

At length we saw the numerous steeples of London, St Paul's towering above all, and the Tower, famed in English history.

Chapter II

London was our present point of rest; we determined to remain several months in this wonderful and celebrated city. Clerval desired the intercourse of the men of genius and talent who flourished at this time; but this was with me a secondary object; I was principally occupied with the means of obtaining the infor- 5 mation necessary for the completion of my promise, and quickly availed myself of the letters of introduction that I had brought with me, addressed to the most distinguished natural philosopher.

If this journey had taken place during my days of study and happiness, it would have afforded me inexpressible pleasure. But 10 a blight had come over my existence, and I only visited these people for the sake of the information they might give me on the subject in which my interest was so terribly profound. Company was irksome to me; when alone, I could fill my mind with the sights of heaven and earth; the voice of Henry soothed me, and I could thus 15 cheat myself into a transitory peace. But busy, uninteresting, joyous faces brought back despair to my heart. I saw an insurmountable barrier placed between me and my fellow-men; this barrier was sealed with the blood of William and Justine, and to reflect on the events connected with those names filled my soul with anguish. 20

But in Clerval I saw the image of my former self; he was inquisitive, and anxious to gain experience and instruction. The difference of manners which he observed was to him an inexhaustible source of instruction and amusement. He was also pursuing an object he had long had in view. His design was to visit India, in the belief 25 that he had in his knowledge of its various languages, and in the views he had taken of its society, the means of materially assisting the progress of European colonisation and trade. In Britain only could he further the execution of his plan. He was forever busy; and the only check to his enjoyments was my sorrowful and dejected mind. I tried to conceal this as much as possible, that I might not debar him from the pleasures natural to one, who was entering on a new scene of life, undisturbed by any care or bitter recollection. I often refused to accompany him, alleging another engagement, that I might remain alone. I now also began to collect the materials necessary for my new creation, and this was to me like the torture of single drops of water continually falling on the head. Every thought that was devoted to it was an extreme anguish, and every word that I spoke in allusion to it caused my lips to quiver, and my heart to palpitate.

After passing some months in London, we received a letter from a person in Scotland, who had formerly been our visitor at Geneva. He mentioned the beauties of his native country, and asked us if those were not sufficient allurements to induce us to prolong our journey as far north as Perth, where he resided. Clerval eagerly desired to accept this invitation; and I, although I abhorred society, wished to view again mountains and streams, and all the wondrous works with which Nature adorns her chosen dwelling-places.

We had arrived in England at the beginning of October, and it was now February. We accordingly determined to commence our journey towards the north at the expiration of another month. In this expedition we did not intend to follow the great road to Edinburgh, but to visit Windsor, Oxford, Matlock, and the Cumberland lakes, resolving to arrive at the completion of this tour about the end of July. I packed up my chemical instruments and the materials I had collected, resolving to finish my labours in some obscure nook in the northern highlands of Scotland.

We quitted London on the 27th of March and remained a few days at Windsor, rambling in its beautiful forest. This was a new scene to us mountaineers; the majestic oaks, the quantity of game, and the herds of stately deer, were all novelties to us.

From thence we proceeded to Oxford. As we entered this city, our minds were filled with the remembrance of the events that had been transacted there more than a century and a half before. It was here that Charles I had collected his forces. This city had remained faithful to him, after the whole nation had forsaken his cause to join the standard of parliament and liberty. The memory of that unfortunate king, and his companions, the amiable Falkland, the 5 insolent Goring, his queen and son, gave a peculiar interest to every part of the city, which they might be supposed to have inhabited. The spirit of elder days found a dwelling here, and we delighted to trace its footsteps. If these feelings had not found an imaginary gratification, the appearance of the city had yet in itself 10 sufficient beauty to obtain our admiration. The colleges are ancient and picturesque; the streets are almost magnificent; and the lovely Isis, which flows beside it through meadows of exquisite verdure, is spread forth into a placid expanse of waters, which reflects its majestic assemblage of towers, and spires, and domes, embosomed 15 among aged trees.

I enjoyed this scene; and yet my enjoyment was embittered both by the memory of the past, and the anticipation of the future. I was formed for peaceful happiness. During my youthful days discontent never visited my mind; and if I was ever overcome by *ennui*, the 20 sight of what is beautiful in nature, or the study of what is excellent and sublime in the productions of man, could always interest my heart, and communicate elasticity to my spirits. But I am a blasted tree; the bolt has entered my soul; and I felt then that I should survive to exhibit what I shall soon cease to be – a miserable 25 spectacle of wrecked humanity, pitiable to others, and intolerable to myself.

We passed a considerable period at Oxford, rambling among its environs, and endeavouring to identify every spot which might relate to the most animating epoch of English history. Our little 30 voyages of discovery were often prolonged by the successive objects that presented themselves. We visited the tomb of the illustrious Hampden, and the field on which that patriot fell. For a moment my soul was elevated from its debasing and miserable fears, to contemplate the divine ideas of liberty and self-sacrifice, of which 35 these sights were the monuments and the remembrancers. For an instant I dared to shake off my chains, and look around me with a free and lofty spirit; but the iron had eaten into my flesh, and I sank again, trembling and hopeless, into my miserable self.

We left Oxford with regret, and proceeded to Matlock, which was our next place of rest. The country in the neighbourhood of this village resembled, to a greater degree, the scenery of Switzerland; but every thing is on a lower scale, and the green hills want the crown of distant white Alps, which always attend on the piny mountains of my native country. We visited the wondrous cave, and the little cabinets of natural history, where the curiosities are disposed in the same manner as in the collections at Servox and Chamounix. The latter name made me tremble when pronounced by Henry; and I hastened to quit Matlock, with which that terrible scene was thus associated.

From Derby, still journeying northwards, we passed two months in Cumberland and Westmorland. I could now almost fancy myself among the Swiss mountains. The little patches of snow which yet lingered on the northern sides of the mountains, the lakes, and the dashing of the rocky streams, were all familiar and dear sights to me. Here also we made some acquaintances, who almost contrived to cheat me into happiness. The delight of Clerval was proportionably greater than mine; his mind expanded in the company of men of talent, and he found in his own nature greater capacities and resources than he could have imagined himself to have possessed while he associated with his inferiors. 'I could pass my life here,' said he to me; 'and among these mountains I should scarcely regret Switzerland and the Rhine.'

But he found that a traveller's life is one that includes much pain amidst its enjoyments. His feelings are forever on the stretch; and when he begins to sink into repose, he finds himself obliged to quit that on which he rests in pleasure for something new, which again engages his attention, and which also he forsakes for other novelties.

We had scarcely visited various lakes of Cumberland and Westmorland, and conceived an affection for some of the inhabitants, when the period of our appointment with our Scotch friend

approached, and we left them to travel on. For my own part I was
not sorry. I had now neglected my promise for some time, and I
feared the effects of the daemon's disappointment. He might
remain in Switzerland, and wreak his vengeance on my relatives.
This idea pursued me, and tormented me at every moment from
which I might otherwise have snatched repose and peace. I waited
for my letters with feverish impatience: if they were delayed, I was
miserable, and overcome by a thousand fears; and when they
arrived and I saw the superscription of Elizabeth or my father, I
hardly dared to read and ascertain my fate. Sometimes I thought
that the fiend followed me, and might expedite my remissness by
murdering my companion. When these thoughts possessed me, I
would not quit Henry for a moment, but followed him as his
shadow, to protect him from the fancied rage of his destroyer. I felt
as if I had committed some great crime, the consciousness of which
haunted me. I was guiltless, but I had indeed drawn down a horrible
curse upon my head, as mortal as that of crime.

I visited Edinburgh with languid eyes and mind; and yet that
city might have interested the most unfortunate being. Clerval did
not like it so well as Oxford: for the antiquity of the latter city was
more pleasing to him. But the beauty and regularity of the new
town of Edinburgh, its romantic castle and its environs, the most
delightful in the world, Arthur's Seat, St Bernard's Well, and the
Pentland Hills, compensated him for the change, and filled him
with cheerfulness and admiration. But I was impatient to arrive at
the termination of my journey.

We left Edinburgh in a week, passing through Coupar,
St Andrew's, and along the banks of the Tay, to Perth, where our
friend expected us. But I was in no mood to laugh and talk with
strangers, or enter into their feelings or plans with the good humour
expected from a guest; and accordingly I told Clerval that I wished
to make the tour of Scotland alone. 'Do you,' said I, 'enjoy yourself,
and let this be our rendezvous. I may be absent a month or two;
but do not interfere with my motions, I intreat you: leave me to
peace and solitude for a short time; and when I return, I hope it
will be with a lighter heart, more congenial to your own temper.'

Henry wished to dissuade me; but seeing me bent on this plan, ceased to remonstrate. He intreated me to write often. 'I had rather be with you,' he said, 'in your solitary rambles, than with these Scotch people, whom I do not know: hasten, then, my dear friend, to return, that I may again feel myself somewhat at home, which I cannot do in your absence.'

Having parted from my friend, I determined to visit some remote spot of Scotland, and finish my work in solitude. I did not doubt but that the monster followed me, and would discover himself to me when I should have finished, that he might receive his companion.

With this resolution I traversed the northern highlands, and fixed on one of the remotest of the Orkneys as the scene of my labours. It was a place fitted for such a work, being hardly more than a rock, whose high sides were continually beaten upon by the waves. The soil was barren, scarcely affording pasture for a few miserable cows, and oatmeal for its inhabitants, which consisted of five persons, whose gaunt and scraggy limbs gave tokens of their miserable fare. Vegetables and bread, when they indulged in such luxuries, and even fresh water, was to be procured from the mainland, which was about five miles distant.

On the whole island there were but three miserable huts, and one of these was vacant when I arrived. This I hired. It contained but two rooms, and these exhibited all the squalidness of the most miserable penury. The thatch had fallen in, the walls were unplastered, and the door was off its hinges. I ordered it to be repaired, bought some furniture, and took possession; an incident which would, doubtless, have occasioned some surprise had not all the senses of the cottagers been benumbed by want and squalid poverty. As it was, I lived ungazed at and unmolested, hardly thanked for the pittance of food and clothes which I gave; so much does suffering blunt even the coarsest sensations of men.

In this retreat I devoted the morning to labour; but in the evening, when the weather permitted, I walked on the stony beach of the sea to listen to the waves as they roared and dashed at my feet. It was a monotonous yet everchanging scene. I thought of Switzerland; it was far different from this desolate and appalling landscape. Its hills are covered with veins, and its cottages are scattered thickly in the plains. Its fair lakes reflect a blue and gentle sky; and, when troubled by the winds, their tumult is but as the play of a lively infant, when compared to the roarings of the giant ocean. 5

In this manner I distributed my occupations when I first arrived; but as I proceeded in my labour, it became every day more horrible and irksome to me. Sometimes I could not prevail on myself to enter my laboratory for several days; and at other times I toiled day and night in order to complete my work. It was, indeed, a filthy 10 process in which I was engaged. During my first experiment, a kind of enthusiastic frenzy had blinded me to the horror of my employment; my mind was intently fixed on the consummation of my labour, and my eyes shut to the horror of my proceedings. But now I went to it in cold blood, and my heart often sickened at the 15 work of my hands.

Thus situated, employed in the most detestable occupation, immersed in a solitude where nothing could for an instant call my attention from the actual scene in which I was engaged, my spirits became unequal; I grew restless and nervous. Every moment I 20 feared to meet my persecutor. Sometimes I sat with my eyes fixed on the ground, fearing to raise them, lest they should encounter the object which I so much dreaded to behold. I feared to wander from the sight of my fellow-creatures, lest when alone he should come to claim his companion. 25

In the mean time I worked on, and my labour was already considerably advanced. I looked towards its completion with a tremulous and eager hope, which I dared not trust myself to question, but which was intermixed with obscure forebodings of evil, that made my heart sicken in my bosom. 30

Chapter III

I sat one evening in my laboratory; the sun had set, and the moon was just rising from the sea; I had not sufficient light for my employment, and I remained idle, in a pause of consideration of whether I should leave my labour for the night, or hasten its
5 conclusion by an unremitting attention to it. As I sat, a train of reflection occurred to me, which led me to consider the effects of what I was now doing. Three years before I was engaged in the same manner, and had created a fiend whose unparalleled barbarity had desolated my heart, and filled it forever with the bitterest
10 remorse. I was now about to form another being, of whose dispositions I was alike ignorant; she might become ten thousand times more malignant than her mate, and delight, for its own sake, in murder and wretchedness. He had sworn to quit the neighbourhood of man, and hide himself in deserts; but she had not; and
15 she, who in all probability was to become a thinking and reasoning animal, might refuse to comply with a compact made before her creation. They might even hate each other; the creature who already lived loathed his own deformity, and might he not conceive a greater abhorrence for it when it came before his eyes in the
20 female form? She also might turn with disgust from him to the superior beauty of man; she might quit him, and he be again alone, exasperated by the fresh provocation of being deserted by one of his own species.

Even if they were to leave Europe, and inhabit the deserts of the
25 new world, yet one of the first results of those sympathies for which the daemon thirsted would be children, and a race of devils would be propagated upon the earth, who might make the very existence

of the species of man a condition precarious and full of terror. Had I a right, for my own benefit, to inflict this curse upon everlasting generations? I had before been moved by the sophisms of the being I had created; I had been struck senseless by his fiendish threats: but now, for the first time, the wickedness of my promise burst 5 upon me; I shuddered to think that future ages might curse me as their pest, whose selfishness had not hesitated to buy its own peace at the price, perhaps, of the existence of the whole human race.

I trembled, and my heart failed within me, when, on looking up, I saw, by the light of the moon, the daemon at the casement. A 10 ghastly grin wrinkled his lips as he gazed on me, where I sat fulfilling the task which he had allotted to me. Yes, he had followed me in my travels; he had loitered in forests, hid himself in caves, or taken refuge in wide and desert heaths; and he now came to mark my progress, and claim the fulfilment of my promise. 15

As I looked on him, his countenance expressed the utmost extent of malice and treachery. I thought with a sensation of madness on my promise of creating another like to him, and trembling with passion, tore to pieces the thing on which I was engaged. The wretch saw me destroy the creature on whose future existence he 20 depended for happiness, and, with a howl of devilish despair and revenge, withdrew.

I left the room, and, locking the door, made a solemn vow in my own heart never to resume my labours; and then, with trembling steps, I sought my own apartment. I was alone; none were near me 25 to dissipate the gloom, and relieve me from the sickening oppression of the most terrible reveries.

Several hours passed, and I remained near my window gazing on the sea; it was almost motionless, for the winds were hushed, and all nature reposed under the eye of the quiet moon. A few 30 fishing vessels alone specked the water, and now and then the gentle breeze wafted the sound of voices as the fishermen called to one another. I felt the silence, although I was hardly conscious of its extreme profundity, until my ear was suddenly arrested by the paddling of oars near the shore, and a person landed close to my 35 house.

In a few minutes after, I heard the creaking of my door, as if some one endeavoured to open it softly. I trembled from head to foot; I felt a presentiment of who it was, and wished to rouse one of the peasants who dwelt in a cottage not far from mine; but I was
5 overcome by the sensation of helplessness, so often felt in frightful dreams, when you in vain endeavour to fly from an impending danger, and was rooted to the spot.

Presently I heard the sound of footsteps along the passage; the door opened, and the wretch whom I dreaded appeared. Shutting
10 the door, he approached me and said in a smothered voice –

'You have destroyed the work which you began; what is it that you intend? Do you dare to break your promise? I have endured toil and misery: I left Switzerland with you; I crept along the shores of the Rhine, among its willow islands, and over the summits of its
15 hills. I have dwelt many months in the heaths of England, and among the deserts of Scotland. I have endured incalculable fatigue, and cold, and hunger, do you dare destroy my hopes?'

'Begone! I do break my promise; never will I create another like yourself, equal in deformity and wickedness.'

20 'Slave, I before reasoned with you, but you have proved yourself unworthy of my condescension. Remember that I have power; you believe yourself miserable, but I can make you so wretched that the light of day will be hateful to you. You are my creator, but I am your master – obey!'

25 'The hour of my irresolution is past, and the period of your power is arrived. Your threats cannot move me to do an act of wickedness; but they confirm me in a determination of not creating you a companion in vice. Shall I, in cool blood, set loose upon the earth a daemon, whose delight is in death and wretchedness?
30 Begone! I am firm, and your words will only exasperate my rage.'

The monster saw my determination in my face, and gnashed his teeth in the impotence of anger. 'Shall each man,' cried he, 'find a wife for his bosom, and each beast have his mate, and I be alone? I had feelings of affection, and they were requited by detestation
35 and scorn. Man! you may hate, but beware! your hours will pass in dread and misery, and soon the bolt will fall which must ravish

from you your happiness forever. Are you to be happy, while I grovel in the intensity of my wretchedness? You can blast my other passions, but revenge remains – revenge, henceforth dearer than light or food! I may die, but first you, my tyrant and tormentor, shall curse the sun that gazes on your misery. Beware; for I am ⁵ fearless, and therefore powerful. I will watch with the wiliness of a snake, that I may sting with its venom. Man, you shall repent of the injuries you inflict.'

'Devil, cease; and do not poison the air with these sounds of malice. I have declared my resolution to you, and I am no coward ¹⁰ to bend beneath words. Leave me; I am inexorable.'

'It is well. I go; but remember, I shall be with you on your wedding-night.'

I started forward, and exclaimed, 'Villain! Before you sign my death-warrant, be sure that you are yourself safe.' ¹⁵

I would have seized him; but he eluded me, and quitted the house with precipitation. In a few moments I saw him in his boat, which shot across the waters with an arrowy swiftness, and was soon lost amidst the waves.

All was again silent; but his words rang in my ears. I burned with ²⁰ rage to pursue the murderer of my peace, and precipitate him into the ocean. I walked up and down my room hastily and perturbed, while my imagination conjured up a thousand images to torment and sting me. Why had I not followed him, and closed with him in mortal strife? But I had suffered him to depart, and he had directed ²⁵ his course towards the mainland. I shuddered to think who might be the next victim sacrificed to his insatiate revenge. And then I thought again of his words – *'I will be with you on your wedding-night.'* That then was the period fixed for the fulfilment of my destiny. In that hour I should die, and at once satisfy and extinguish his malice. ³⁰ The prospect did not move me to fear; yet when I thought of my beloved Elizabeth, – of her tears and endless sorrow, when she should find her lover so barbarously snatched from her, – tears, the first I had shed for many months, streamed from my eyes, and I resolved not to fall before my enemy without a bitter struggle. ³⁵

The night passed away, and the sun rose from the ocean; my

feelings became calmer, if it may be called calmness, when the violence of rage sinks into the depths of despair. I left the house, the horrid scene of the last night's contention, and walked on the beach of the sea, which I almost regarded as an insuperable barrier
5 between me and my fellow-creatures; nay, a wish that such should prove the fact stole across me. I desired that I might pass my life on that barren rock, wearily, it is true, but uninterrupted by any sudden shock of misery. If I returned, it was to be sacrificed, or to see those whom I most loved die under the grasp of a daemon
10 whom I had myself created.

I walked about the isle like a restless spectre, separated from all it loved, and miserable in the separation. When it became noon, and the sun rose higher, I lay down on the grass, and was over-powered by a deep sleep. I had been awake the whole of the
15 preceding night, my nerves were agitated, and my eyes inflamed by watching and misery. The sleep into which I now sunk refreshed me; and when I awoke, I again felt as if I belonged to a race of human beings like myself, and I began to reflect upon what had passed with greater composure; yet still the words of the fiend rung
20 in my ears like a death-knell; they appeared like a dream, yet distinct and oppressive as a reality.

The sun had far descended, and I still sat on the shore, satisfying my appetite, which had become ravenous, with an oaten cake, when I saw a fishing-boat land close to me, and one of the men
25 brought me a packet; it contained letters from Geneva, and one from Clerval entreating me to join him. He said that he was wearing away his time fruitlessly where he was; that letters from the friends he had formed in London desired his return to complete the negoti-ation they had entered into for his Indian enterprise. He could not
30 any longer delay his departure; but as his journey to London might be followed, even sooner than he now conjectured, by his longer voyage, he entreated me to bestow as much of my society on him as I could spare. He besought me, therefore, to leave my solitary isle, and to meet him at Perth, that we might proceed southwards
35 together. This letter in a degree recalled me to life, and I determined to quit my island at the expiration of two days.

Yet, before I departed, there was a task to perform, on which I shuddered to reflect: I must pack up my chemical instruments; and for that purpose I must enter the room which had been the scene of my odious work, and I must handle those utensils, the sight of which was sickening to me. The next morning, at daybreak, I summoned sufficient courage, and unlocked the door of my laboratory. The remains of the half-finished creature, whom I had destroyed, lay scattered on the floor, and I almost felt as if I had mangled the living flesh of a human being. I paused to collect myself, and then entered the chamber. With trembling hand I conveyed the instruments out of the room; but I reflected that I ought not to leave the relics of my work to excite the horror and suspicion of the peasants; and I accordingly put them into a basket, with a great quantity of stones, and, laying them up, determined to throw them into the sea that very night; and in the mean time I sat upon the beach, employed in cleaning and arranging my chemical apparatus.

Nothing could be more complete than the alteration that had taken place in my feelings since the night of the appearance of the daemon. I had before regarded my promise with a gloomy despair, as a thing that, with whatever consequences, must be fulfilled; but I now felt as if a film had been taken from before my eyes, and that I, for the first time, saw clearly. The idea of renewing my labours did not for one instant occur to me; the threat I had heard weighed on my thoughts, but I did not reflect that a voluntary act of mine could avert it. I had resolved in my own mind, that to create another like the fiend I had first made would be an act of the basest and most atrocious selfishness; and I banished from my mind every thought that could lead to a different conclusion.

Between two and three in the morning the moon rose; and I then, putting my basket aboard a little skiff, sailed out about four miles from the shore. The scene was perfectly solitary: a few boats were returning towards land, but I sailed away from them. I felt as if I was about the commission of a dreadful crime, and avoided with shuddering anxiety any encounter with my fellow-creatures. At one time the moon, which had before been clear, was suddenly

overspread by a thick cloud, and I took advantage of the moment of darkness and cast my basket into the sea: I listened to the gurgling sound as it sunk, and then sailed away from the spot. The sky became clouded; but the air was pure, although chilled by the
5   north-east breeze that was then rising. But it refreshed me, and filled me with such agreeable sensations, that I resolved to prolong my stay on the water; and, fixing the rudder in a direct position, stretched myself at the bottom of the boat. Clouds hid the moon, every-thing was obscure, and I heard only the sound of the boat,
10 as its keel cut through the waves; the murmur lulled me, and in a short time I slept soundly.

I do not know how long I remained in this situation, but when I awoke I found that the sun had already mounted considerably. The wind was high, and the waves continually threatened the safety
15 of my little skiff. I found that the wind was north-east, and must have driven me far from the coast from which I had embarked. I endeavoured to change my course, but quickly found that if I again made the attempt, the boat would be instantly filled with water.

Thus situated, my only resource was to drive before the wind. I
20 confess that I felt a few sensations of terror. I had no compass with me, and was so slenderly acquainted with the geography of this part of the world, that the sun was of little benefit to me. I might be driven into the wide Atlantic, and feel all the tortures of star-vation, or be swallowed up in the immeasurable waters that roared
25 and buffeted around me. I had already been out many hours, and felt the torment of a burning thirst, a prelude to my other sufferings. I looked on the heavens, which were covered by clouds that flew before the wind, only to be replaced by others: I looked upon the sea, it was to be my grave. 'Fiend,' I exclaimed, 'your task is already
30 fulfilled!' I thought of Elizabeth, of my father, and of Clerval; all left behind, on whom the monster might satisfy his sanguinary and merciless passions. This idea plunged me into a reverie, so despairing and frightful, that even now, when the scene is on the point of closing before me forever, I shudder to reflect on it.

35 Some hours passed thus; but by degrees, as the sun declined towards the horizon, the wind died away into a gentle breeze, and

the sea became free from breakers. But these gave place to a heavy swell; I felt sick, and hardly able to hold the rudder, when suddenly I saw a line of high land towards the south.

Almost spent, as I was, by fatigue, and the dreadful suspense I endured for several hours, this sudden certainty of life rushed like a flood of warm joy to my heart, and tears gushed from my eyes.

How mutable are our feelings, and how strange is that clinging love we have of life even in the excess of misery! I constructed another sail with a part of my dress, and eagerly steered my course towards the land. It had a wild and rocky appearance, but, as I approached nearer, I easily perceived the traces of cultivation. I saw vessels near the shore, and found myself suddenly transported back to the neighbourhood of civilised man. I carefully traced the windings of the land, and hailed a steeple which I at length saw issuing from behind a small promontory. As I was in a state of extreme debility, I resolved to sail directly towards the town, as a place where I could most easily procure nourishment. Fortunately I had money with me. As I turned the promontory, I perceived a small neat town and a good harbour, which I entered, my heart bounding with joy at my unexpected escape.

As I was occupied in fixing the boat and arranging the sails, several people crowded towards the spot. They seemed much surprised at my appearance, but instead of offering me any assistance, whispered together with gestures that at any other time might have produced in me a slight sensation of alarm. As it was, I merely remarked that they spoke English; and I therefore addressed them in that language. 'My good friends,' said I, 'will you be so kind as to tell me the name of this town, and inform me where I am?'

'You will know that soon enough,' replied a man with a hoarse voice. 'May be you are come to a place that will not prove much to your taste; but you will not be consulted as to your quarters, I promise you.'

I was exceedingly surprised on receiving so rude an answer from a stranger; and I was also disconcerted on perceiving the frowning and angry countenances of his companions. 'Why do you answer me so roughly?' I replied; 'surely it is not the custom of Englishmen to receive strangers so inhospitably.'

'I do not know,' said the man, 'what the custom of the English may be; but it is the custom of the Irish to hate villains.'

5 While this strange dialogue continued, I perceived the crowd rapidly increase. Their faces expressed a mixture of curiosity and anger, which annoyed, and in some degree alarmed me. I enquired the way to the inn; but no one replied. I then moved forward, and a murmuring sound arose from the crowd as they followed and

10 surrounded me; when an ill-looking man approaching, tapped me on the shoulder, and said, 'Come, sir, you must follow me to Mr Kirwin's, to give an account of yourself.'

'Who is Mr Kirwin? Why am I to give an account of myself? Is not this a free country?'

15 'Ay, sir, free enough for honest folks. Mr Kirwin is a magistrate; and you are to give an account of the death of a gentleman who was found murdered here last night.'

This answer startled me; but I presently recovered myself. I was innocent; that could easily be proved: accordingly I followed my

20 conductor in silence and was led to one of the best houses in the town. I was ready to sink from fatigue and hunger; but, being surrounded by a crowd, I thought it politic to rouse all my strength, that no physical debility might be construed into apprehension or conscious guilt. Little did I then expect the calamity that was in a

25 few moments to overwhelm me, and extinguish in horror and despair all fear of ignominy or death.

I must pause here; for it requires all my fortitude to recall the memory of the frightful events which I am about to relate, in proper detail, to my recollection.

Chapter IV

I was soon introduced into the presence of the magistrate, an old benevolent man, with calm and mild manners. He looked upon me, however, with some degree of severity; and then, turning towards my conductors, he asked who appeared as witnesses on this occasion.

About half a dozen men came forward; and, one being selected by the magistrate, he deposed, that he had been out fishing the night before with his son and brother-in-law, Daniel Nugent, when, about ten o'clock, they observed a strong northerly blast rising, and they accordingly put in for port. It was a very dark night, as the moon had not yet risen; they did not land at the harbour, but, as they had been accustomed, at a creek about two miles below. He walked on first, carrying a part of the fishing tackle, and his companions followed him at some distance. As he was proceeding along the sands, he struck his foot against something, and fell at his length on the ground. His companions came up to assist him; and, by the light of their lantern, they found that he had fallen on the body of a man, who was to all appearance dead. Their first supposition was, that it was the corpse of some person who had been drowned, and was thrown on shore by the waves, but, on examination, they found that the clothes were not wet, and even that the body was not then cold. They instantly carried it to the cottage of an old woman near the spot, and endeavoured, but in vain, to restore it to life. It appeared to be a handsome young man, about five and twenty years of age. He had apparently been strangled; for there was no sign of any violence, except the black mark of fingers on his neck.

The first part of his deposition did not in the least interest me; but when the mark of the fingers was mentioned, I remembered the murder of my brother and felt myself extremely agitated; my limbs trembled, and a mist came over my eyes, which obliged me to lean on a chair for support. The magistrate observed me with a keen eye, and of course drew an unfavourable augury from my manner.

The son confirmed his father's account: but when Daniel Nugent was called, he swore positively that just before the fall of his companion, he saw a boat, with a single man in it, at a short distance from the shore; and, as far as he could judge by the light of a few stars, it was the same boat in which I had just landed.

A woman deposed, that she lived near the beach, and was standing at the door of her cottage, waiting for the return of the fishermen, about an hour before she heard of the discovery of the body, when she saw a boat with only one man in it push off from that part of the shore where the corpse was afterwards found.

Another woman confirmed the account of the fishermen having brought the body into her house; it was not cold. They put it into a bed and rubbed it; and Daniel went to the town for an apothecary, but life was quite gone.

Several other men were examined concerning my landing; and they agreed that, with the strong north wind that had arisen during the night, it was very probable that I had beaten about for many hours, and had been obliged to return nearly to the same spot from which I had departed. Besides, they observed that it appeared that I had brought the body from another place, and it was likely, that as I did not appear to know the shore, I might have put into the harbour ignorant of the distance of the town of *** from the place where I had deposited the corpse.

Mr Kirwin, on hearing this evidence, desired that I should be taken into the room where the body lay for interment, that it might be observed what effect the sight of it would produce upon me. This idea was probably suggested by the extreme agitation I had exhibited when the mode of the murder had been described. I was accordingly conducted, by the magistrate and several other persons, to the inn. I could not help being struck by the strange coincidences that had taken place during this eventful night; but, knowing that I had been conversing with several persons in the island I had inhabited about the time that the body had been found, I was perfectly tranquil as to the consequences of the affair.   5

I entered the room where the corpse lay, and was led up to the coffin. How can I describe my sensations of beholding it? I feel yet parched with horror, nor can I reflect on that terrible moment without shuddering and agony. The examination, the presence of the magistrate and witnesses, passed like a dream from my memory,   10 when I saw the lifeless form of Henry Clerval stretched before me. I gasped for breath; and throwing myself on the body, I exclaimed, 'Have my murderous machinations deprived you also, my dearest Henry, of life? Two I have already destroyed; other victims await their destiny: but you, Clerval, my friend, my benefactor –'   15

The human frame could no longer support the agonies that I endured, and I was carried out of the room in strong convulsions.

A fever succeeded to this. I lay for two months on the point of death: my ravings, as I afterwards heard, were frightful; I called myself the murderer of William, of Justine, and of Clerval. Some-   20 times I intreated my attendants to assist me in the destruction of the fiend by whom I was tormented; and at others, I felt the fingers of the monster already grasping my neck, and screamed aloud with agony and terror. Fortunately, as I spoke my native language, Mr Kirwin alone understood me; but my gestures and bitter cries were   25 sufficient to affright the other witnesses.

Why did I not die? More miserable than man ever was before, why did I not sink into forgetfulness and rest? Death snatches away many blooming children, the only hopes of their doating parents: how many brides and youthful lovers have been one day in the   30 bloom of health and hope, and the next a prey for worms and the decay of the tomb! Of what materials was I made, that I could thus resist so many shocks, which, like the turning of the wheel, continually renewed the torture?

But I was doomed to live; and in two months, found myself as   35 awaking from a dream, in a prison, stretched on a wretched bed,

surrounded by gaolers, turnkeys, bolts, and all the miserable apparatus of a dungeon. It was morning, I remember, when I thus awoke to understanding: I had forgotten the particulars of what had happened, and only felt as if some great misfortune had suddenly
5 overwhelmed me; but when I looked around, and saw the barred windows, and the squalidness of the room in which I was, all flashed across my memory, and I groaned bitterly.

This sound disturbed an old woman who was sleeping in a chair beside me. She was a hired nurse, the wife of one of the turnkeys,
10 and her countenance expressed all those bad qualities which often characterise that class. The lines of her face were hard and rude, like that of persons accustomed to see without sympathising in sights of misery. Her tone expressed her entire indifference; she addressed me in English, and the voice struck me as one that I had
15 heard during my sufferings: –

'Are you better now, sir?' said she.

I replied in the same language, with a feeble voice, 'I believe I am; but if it all be true, if indeed I did not dream, I am sorry that I am still alive to feel this misery and horror.'

20 'For that matter,' replied the old woman, 'if you mean about the gentleman you murdered, I believe that it were better for you if you were dead, for I fancy it will go hard for you! However, that's none of my business; I am sent to nurse you and get you well; I do my duty with a safe conscience; it were well if everybody did the
25 same.'

I turned with loathing from the woman who could utter so unfeeling a speech to a person just saved, on the very edge of death; but I felt languid, and unable to reflect on all that had passed. The whole series of my life appeared to me as a dream; I sometimes
30 doubted if indeed it were all true, for it never presented itself to my mind with the force of reality.

As the images that floated before me became more distinct, I grew feverish; a darkness pressed around me: no one was near me who soothed me with the gentle voice of love; no dear hand
35 supported me. The physician came and prescribed medicines, and the old woman prepared them for me; but utter carelessness was

visible in the first, and the expression of brutality was strongly marked in the visage of the second. Who could be interested in the fate of a murderer, but the hangman who would gain his fee?

These were my first reflections; but I soon learned that Mr Kirwin had shown me extreme kindness. He had caused the best room in the prison to be prepared for me (wretched indeed was the best); and it was he who had provided a physician and a nurse. It is true, he seldom came to see me, for although he ardently desired to relieve the sufferings of every human creature, he did not wish to be present at the agonies and miserable ravings of a murderer. He came, therefore, sometimes to see that I was not neglected; but his visits were short, and with long intervals.

One day, while I was gradually recovering, I was seated in a chair, my eyes half open, and my cheeks livid like those in death. I was overcome by gloom and misery, and often reflected I had better seek death than desire to remain in a world which to me was replete with wretchedness. At one time I considered whether I should not declare myself guilty, and suffer the penalty of the law, less innocent than poor Justine had been. Such were my thoughts, when the door of my apartment was opened, and Mr Kirwin entered. His countenance expressed sympathy and compassion; he drew a chair close to mine and addressed me in French –

'I fear that this place is very shocking to you; can I do anything to make you more comfortable?'

'I thank you, but all that you mention is nothing to me: on the whole earth there is no comfort which I am capable of receiving.'

'I know that the sympathy of a stranger can be but of little relief to one borne down as you are by so strange a misfortune. But you will, I hope, soon quit this melancholy abode; for, doubtless, evidence can easily be brought to free you from the criminal charge.'

'That is my least concern: I am, by a course of strange events, become the most miserable of mortals. Persecuted and tortured as I am and have been, can death be any evil to me?'

'Nothing indeed could be more unfortunate and agonising than

the strange chances that have lately occurred. You were thrown, by some surprising accident, on this shore, renowned for its hospitality; seized immediately, and charged with murder. The first sight that was presented to your eyes was the body of your friend,
5   murdered in so unaccountable a manner, and placed, as it were, by some fiend across your path.'

As Mr Kirwin said this, notwithstanding the agitation I endured on this retrospect of my sufferings, I also felt considerable surprise at the knowledge he seemed to possess concerning me. I suppose
10 some astonishment was exhibited in my countenance; for Mr Kirwin hastened to say –

'Immediately upon your being taken ill, all the papers that were on your person were brought me, and I examined them that I might discover some trace by which I could send to your relations
15 an account of your misfortune and illness. I found several letters, and, among others, one which I discovered from its commencement to be from your father. I instantly wrote to Geneva: nearly two months have elapsed since the departure of my letter: – But you are ill, even now you tremble: you are unfit for agitation of any
20 kind.'

'This suspense is a thousand times worse than the most horrible event: tell me what new scene of death has been acted, and whose I am now to lament?'

'Your family is perfectly well,' said Mr Kirwin, with gentleness:
25 'and some one, a friend, is come to visit you.'

I know not by what chain of thought, the idea presented itself, but it instantly darted into my mind that the murderer had come to mock at my misery, and taunt me with the death of Clerval, as a new incitement for me to comply with his hellish desires. I put
30 my hand before my eyes, and cried out in agony –

'Oh! Take him away! I cannot see him; for God's sake, do not let him enter!'

Mr Kirwin regarded me with a troubled countenance. He could not help regarding my exclamation as a presumption of my guilt,
35 and said, in rather a severe tone –

'I should have thought, young man, that the presence of your father would have been welcome instead of inspiring such violent repugnance.'

'My father!' cried I, while every feature and every muscle was relaxed from anguish to pleasure: 'is my father indeed come? How kind, how very kind! But where is he, why does he not hasten to me?' 5

My change of manner surprised and pleased the magistrate; perhaps he thought that my former exclamation was a momentary return of delirium, and now he instantly resumed his former benevolence. He rose, and quitted the room with my nurse, and in 10 a moment my father entered it.

Nothing, at this moment, could have given me greater pleasure than the arrival of my father. I stretched out my hand to him and cried –

'Are you, then, safe – and Elizabeth – and Ernest?' 15

My father calmed me with assurances of their welfare, and endeavoured, by dwelling on these subjects so interesting to my heart, to raise my desponding spirits; but he soon felt that a prison cannot be the abode of cheerfulness. 'What a place is this that you inhabit, my son!' said he, looking mournfully at the barred 20 windows, and wretched appearance of the room. 'You travelled to seek happiness, but a fatality seems to pursue you. And poor Clerval –'

The name of my unfortunate and murdered friend was an agitation too great to be endured in my weak state; I shed tears. 25

'Alas! yes, my father,' replied I; 'some destiny of the most horrible kind hangs over me, and I must live to fulfil it, or surely I should have died on the coffin of Henry.'

We were not allowed to converse for any length of time, for the precarious state of my health rendered every precaution necessary 30 that could ensure tranquillity. Mr Kirwin came in, and insisted that my strength should not be exhausted by too much exertion. But the appearance of my father was to me like that of my good angel, and I gradually recovered my health.

As my sickness quitted me, I was absorbed by a gloomy and 35 black melancholy, that nothing could dissipate. The image of

Clerval was forever before me, ghastly and murdered. More than once the agitation into which these reflections threw me made my friends dread a dangerous relapse. Alas! why did they preserve so miserable and detested a life? It was surely that I might fill my
5 destiny, which is now drawing to a close. Soon, oh! very soon, will death extinguish these throbbings, and relieve me from the mighty weight of anguish that bears me to the dust; and, in executing the award of justice, I shall also sink to rest. Then the appearance of death was distant, although the wish was ever present to my
10 thoughts; and I often sat for hours motionless and speechless, wishing for some mighty revolution that might bury me and my destroyer in its ruins.

The season of the assizes approached. I had already been three months in prison; and although I was still weak and in continual
15 danger of a relapse, I was obliged to travel nearly a hundred miles to the county-town, where the court was held. Mr Kirwin charged himself with every care of collecting witnesses, and arranging my defence. I was spared the disgrace of appearing publicly as a criminal, as the case was not brought before the court that decides
20 on life and death. The grand jury rejected the bill, on its being proved that I was on the Orkney Islands at the hour the body of my friend was found; and a fortnight after my removal I was liberated from prison.

My father was enraptured on finding me freed from the vexations
25 of a criminal charge, that I was again allowed to breathe the fresh atmosphere, and permitted to return to my native country. I did not participate in these feelings; for to me the walls of a dungeon or a palace were alike hateful. The cup of life was poisoned for ever; and although the sun shone upon me, as upon the happy and
30 gay of heart, I saw around me nothing but a dense and frightful darkness, penetrated by no light but the glimmer of two eyes that glared upon me. Sometimes they were the expressive eyes of Henry, languishing in death, the dark orbs nearly covered by the lids, and the long black lashes that fringed them; sometimes it was the
35 watery, clouded eyes of the monster, as I first saw them in my chamber at Ingolstadt.

My father tried to awaken in me the feelings of affection. He talked of Geneva, which I should soon visit – of Elizabeth and Ernest; but these words only drew deep groans from me. Sometimes, indeed, I felt a wish for happiness; and thought, with melancholy delight of my beloved cousin; or longed, with a devouring *maladie du pays*, to see once more the blue lake and rapid Rhone, that had been so dear to me in early childhood: but my general state of feeling was a torpor, in which a prison was as welcome a residence as the divinest scene in nature; and these fits were seldom interrupted but by paroxysms of anguish and despair. At these moments I often endeavoured to put an end to the existence I loathed; and it required unceasing attendance and vigilance to restrain me from committing some dreadful act of violence.

Yet one duty remained to me, the recollection of which finally triumphed over my selfish despair. It was necessary that I should return without delay to Geneva, there to watch over the lives of those I so fondly loved; and to lie in wait for the murderer, that if any chance led me to the place of his concealment, or if he dared again to blast me by his presence, I might, with unfailing aim, put an end to the existence of the monstrous Image which I had endued with the mockery of a soul still more monstrous. My father still desired to delay our departure, fearful that I could not sustain the fatigues of a journey: for I was a shattered wreck – the shadow of a human being. My strength was gone. I was a mere skeleton; and fever night and day preyed upon my wasted frame.

Still, as I urged our leaving Ireland with such inquietude and impatience, my father thought it best to yield. We took our passage on board a vessel bound for Havre-de-Grâce, and sailed with a fair wind from the Irish shores. It was midnight. I lay on the deck, looking at the stars, and listening to the dashing of the waves. I hailed the darkness that shut Ireland from my sight; and my pulse beat with a feverish joy when I reflected that I should soon see Geneva. The past appeared to me in the light of a frightful dream; yet the vessel in which I was, the wind that blew me from the detested shore of Ireland, and the sea which surrounded me, told me too forcibly that I was deceived by no vision, and that Clerval, my friend and dearest companion, had fallen a victim to me and the monster of my creation. I repassed, in my memory, my whole life – my quiet happiness while residing with my family in Geneva, the death of my mother, and my departure for Ingolstadt. I remembered, shuddering, the mad enthusiasm that hurried me on to the creation of my hideous enemy, and I called to mind the night in which he first lived. I was unable to pursue the train of thought; a thousand feelings pressed upon me, and I wept bitterly.

Ever since my recovery from the fever, I had been in the custom of taking every night a small quantity of laudanum; for it was by means of this drug only that I was enabled to gain the rest necessary for the preservation of life. Oppressed by the recollection of my various misfortunes, I now swallowed double my usual quantity, and soon slept profoundly. But sleep did not afford me respite from thought and misery; my dreams presented a thousand objects that scared me. Towards morning I was possessed by a kind of nightmare; I felt the fiend's grasp in my neck; and could not free myself from it; groans and cries rang in my ears. My father, who was watching over me, perceiving my restlessness, awoke me; the dashing waves were around: the cloudy sky above; the fiend was not here: a sense of security, a feeling that a truce was established between the present hour and the irresistible, disastrous future, imparted to me a kind of calm forgetfulness, of which the human mind is by its structure peculiarly susceptible.

Chapter V

The voyage came to an end. We landed, and proceeded to Paris. I
soon found that I had overtaxed my strength, and that I must
repose before I could continue my journey. My father's care and
attentions were indefatigable; but he did not know the origin of my
sufferings, and sought erroneous methods to remedy the incurable   5
ill. He wished me to seek amusement in society. I abhorred the
face of man. Oh, not abhorred! they were my brethren, my fellow
beings, and I felt attracted even to the most repulsive among them,
as to creatures of an angelic nature and celestial mechanism. But I
felt that I had no right to share their intercourse. I had unchained   10
an enemy among them, whose joy it was to shed their blood, and
to revel in their groans. How they would, each and all, abhor me,
and hunt me from the world, did they know my unhallowed acts
and the crimes which had their source in me!

My father yielded at length to my desire to avoid society, and   15
strove by various arguments to banish my despair. Sometimes he
thought that I felt deeply the degradation of being obliged to answer
a charge of murder, and he endeavoured to prove to me the futility
of pride.

'Alas! my father,' said I, 'how little do you know me. Human   20
beings, their feelings and passions, would indeed be degraded if
such a wretch as I felt pride. Justine, poor unhappy Justine, was as
innocent as I, and she suffered the same charge; she died for it;
and I am the cause of this – I murdered her. William, Justine, and
Henry – they all died by my hands.'   25

My father had often, during my imprisonment, heard me make
the same assertion; when I thus accused myself, he sometimes

seemed to desire an explanation, and at others he appeared to
consider it as the offspring of delirium, and that, during my illness,
some idea of this kind had presented itself to my imagination, the
remembrance of which I preserved in my convalescence. I avoided
5 explanation, and maintained a continual silence concerning the
wretch I had created. I had a persuasion that I should be supposed
mad; and this in itself would forever have chained my tongue. But,
besides, I could not bring myself to disclose a secret which would
fill my hearer with consternation, and make fear and unnatural
10 horror the inmates of his breast. I checked, therefore, my impatient
thirst for sympathy, and was silent when I would have given the
world to have confided that fatal secret. Yet still words like those I
have recorded would burst uncontrollably from me. I could offer
no explanation of them; but their truth in part relieved the burden
15 of my mysterious woe.

Upon this occasion my father said, with an expression of
unbounded wonder, 'My dearest Victor, what infatuation is this?
My dear son, I entreat you never to make such an assertion again.'

'I am not mad,' I cried energetically; 'the sun and the heavens,
20 who have viewed my operations, can bear witness of my truth. I
am the assassin of those most innocent victims; they died by my
machinations. A thousand times would I have shed my own blood,
drop by drop, to have saved their lives; but I could not, my father,
indeed I could not sacrifice the whole human race.'

25 The conclusion of this speech convinced my father that my
ideas were deranged, and he instantly changed the subject of our
conversation, and endeavoured to alter the course of my thoughts.
He wished as much as possible to obliterate the memory of the
scenes that had taken place in Ireland, and never alluded to them,
30 or suffered me to speak of my misfortunes.

As time passed away I became more calm; misery had her dwelling in my heart, but I no longer talked in the same incoherent
manner of my own crimes; sufficient for me was the consciousness
of them. By the utmost self-violence I curbed the imperious voice
35 of wretchedness, which sometimes desired to declare itself to the

whole world; and my manners were calmer and more composed than they had ever been since my journey to the sea of ice.

A few days before we left Paris on our way to Switzerland, I received the following letter from Elizabeth: –

MY DEAR FRIEND,   5

It gave me the greatest pleasure to receive a letter from my uncle dated at Paris; you are no longer at a formidable distance, and I may hope to see you in less than a fortnight. My poor cousin, how much you must have suffered! I expect to see you looking even more ill than when you quitted Geneva. This winter has been 10 passed more miserably, tortured as I have been by anxious suspense; yet I hope to see peace in your countenance, and to find that your heart is not totally void of comfort and tranquillity.

Yet I fear that the same feelings now exist that made you so miserable a year ago, even perhaps augmented by time. I would 15 not disturb you at this period, when so many misfortunes weigh upon you; but a conversation that I had with my uncle previous to his departure renders some explanation necessary before we meet.

Explanation! You may possibly say; what can Elizabeth have to explain? If you really say this, my questions are answered, and all 20 my doubts satisfied. But you are distant from me, and it is possible that you may dread, and yet be pleased with this explanation; and, in a probability of this being the case, I dare not any longer postpone writing what, during your absence, I have often wished to express to you, but have never had the courage to begin.   25

You well know, Victor, that our union had been the favourite plan of your parents ever since our infancy. We were told this when young, and taught to look forward to it as an event that would certainly take place. We were affectionate playfellows during childhood, and, I believe, dear and valued friends to one another as we 30 grew older. But as brother and sister often entertain a lively affection towards each other, without desiring a more intimate union, may not such also be our case? Tell me, dearest Victor, Answer me, I conjure you, by our mutual happiness, with simple truth – Do you not love another?   35

You have travelled: you have spent several years of your life at Ingolstadt; and I confess to you, my friend, that when I saw you last autumn so unhappy, flying to solitude, from the society of every creature, I could not help supposing that you might regret
5 our connection, and believe yourself bound in honour to fulfil the wishes of your parents, although they opposed themselves to your inclinations. But this is false reasoning. I confess to you, my friend, that I love you, and that in my airy dreams of futurity you have been my constant friend and companion. But it is your happiness
10 I desire as well as my own, when I declare to you that our marriage would render me eternally miserable, unless it were the dictate of your own free choice. Even now I weep to think that, borne down as you are by the cruellest misfortunes, you may stifle, by the word 'honour', all hope of that love and happiness which would alone
15 restore you to yourself. I, who have so disinterested an affection for you, may increase your miseries tenfold by being an obstacle to your wishes. Ah! Victor, be assured that your cousin and playmate has too sincere a love for you not to be made miserable by this supposition. Be happy, my friend; and if you obey me in this one
20 request, remain satisfied that nothing on earth will have the power to interrupt my tranquillity.

Do not let this letter disturb you; do not answer tomorrow, or the next day, or even until you come, if it will give you pain. My uncle will send me news of your health; and if I see but one smile
25 on your lips when we meet, occasioned by this or any other exertion of mine, I shall need no other happiness.

ELIZABETH LAVENZA
Geneva, May 18th, 17–

This letter revived in my memory what I had before forgotten,
30 the threat of the fiend – *'I will be with you on your wedding-night!'* Such was my sentence, and on that night would the daemon employ every art to destroy me, and tear me from the glimpse of happiness which promised partly to console my sufferings. On that night he had determined to consummate his crimes by my death.
35 Well, be it so; a deadly struggle would then assuredly take place,

in which if he were victorious I should be at peace, and his power over me be at an end. If he were vanquished, I should be a free man. Alas! what freedom? Such as the peasant enjoys when his family have been massacred before his eyes, his cottage burnt, his lands laid waste, and he is turned adrift, homeless, penniless, and 5 alone, but free. Such would be my liberty, except that in my Elizabeth I possessed a treasure; alas! balanced by those horrors of remorse and guilt, which would pursue me until death.

Sweet and beloved Elizabeth! I read and re-read her letter, and some softened feelings stole into my heart, and dared to whisper 10 paradisiacal dreams of love and joy; but the apple was already eaten, and the angel's arm bared to drive me from all hope. Yet I would die to make her happy. If the monster executed his threat, death was inevitable; yet, again, I considered whether my marriage would hasten my fate. My destruction might indeed arrive a few 15 months sooner; but if my torturer should suspect that I postponed it, influenced by his menaces, he would surely find other and perhaps more dreadful means of revenge. He had vowed *to be with me on my wedding-night*, yet he did not consider that threat as binding him to peace in the mean time, for as if to show me that 20 he was not yet satiated with blood, he had murdered Clerval immediately after the enunciation of his threats. I resolved, therefore, that if my immediate union with my cousin would conduce either to hers or my father's happiness, my adversary's designs against my life should not retard it a single hour. 25

In this state of mind I wrote to Elizabeth. My letter was calm and affectionate. 'I fear, my beloved girl,' I said, 'little happiness remains for us on earth; yet all that I may one day enjoy is centred in you. Chase away your idle fears; to you alone do I consecrate my life, and my endeavours for contentment. I have one secret, 30 Elizabeth, a dreadful one; when revealed to you, it will chill your frame with horror, and then, far from being surprised at my misery, you will only wonder that I survive what I have endured. I will confide this tale of misery and terror to you the day after our marriage shall take place, for, my sweet cousin, there must be 35 perfect confidence between us. But until then, I conjure you, do not mention or allude to it. This I most earnestly intreat, and I know you will comply.'

In about a week after the arrival of Elizabeth's letter, we returned to Geneva. The sweet girl welcomed me with warm affection; yet
5 tears were in her eyes; as she beheld my emaciated frame and feverish cheeks. I saw a change in her also. She was thinner, and had lost much of that heavenly vivacity that had before charmed me; but her gentleness, and soft looks of compassion, made her a more fit companion for one blasted and miserable as I was.

10 The tranquillity which I now enjoyed did not endure. Memory brought madness with it; and when I thought of what had passed, a real insanity possessed me; sometimes I was furious and burnt with rage; sometimes low and despondent. I neither spoke, nor looked at any one, but sat motionless, bewildered by the multitude
15 of miseries that overcame me.

Elizabeth alone had the power to draw me from these fits; her gentle voice would soothe me when transported by passion, and inspire me with human feelings when sunk in torpor. She wept with me, and for me. When reason returned, she would remonstrate, and
20 endeavour to inspire me with resignation. Ah! it is well for the unfortunate to be resigned, but for the guilty there is no peace. The agonies of remorse poison the luxury there is otherwise sometimes found in indulging the excess of grief.

Soon after my arrival, my father spoke of my immediate marriage
25 with Elizabeth. I remained silent.

'Have you, then, some other attachment?'

'None on earth. I love Elizabeth and look forward to our union with delight. Let the day therefore be fixed; and on it I will conse-crate myself, in life or death, to the happiness of my cousin.'

30 'My dear Victor, do not speak thus. Heavy misfortunes have befallen us, but let us only cling closer to what remains, and transfer our love for those whom we have lost to those who yet live. Our circle will be small, but bound close by the ties of affection and mutual misfortune. And when time shall have softened your
35 despair, new and dear objects of care will be born to replace those of whom we have been so cruelly deprived.'

Such were the lessons of my father. But to me the remembrance of the threat returned: nor can you wonder that, omnipotent as the fiend had yet been in his deeds of blood, I should almost regard him as invincible; and that when he had pronounced the words '*I shall be with you on your wedding-night*', I should regard the threat- 5 ened fate as unavoidable. But death was no evil to me, if the loss of Elizabeth were balanced with it; and I therefore, with a contented and even cheerful countenance, agreed with my father, that if my cousin would consent, the ceremony should take place in ten days, and thus put, as I imagined, the seal to my fate. 10

Great God! if for one instant I had thought what might be the hellish intention of my fiendish adversary, I would rather have banished myself for ever from my native country, and wandered a friendless outcast over the earth, than have consented to this miserable marriage. But, as if possessed of magic powers, the 15 monster had blinded me to his real intentions; and when I thought that I had prepared only my own death, I hastened that of a far dearer victim.

As the period fixed for our marriage drew nearer, whether from cowardice or a prophetic feeling, I felt my heart sink within me. 20 But I concealed my feelings by an appearance of hilarity, that brought smiles and joy to the countenance of my father, but hardly deceived the ever-watchful and nicer eye of Elizabeth. She looked forward to our union with placid contentment, not unmingled with a little fear, which past misfortunes had impressed, that what now 25 appeared certain and tangible happiness, might soon dissipate into an airy dream, and leave no trace but deep and everlasting regret.

Preparations were made for the event, congratulatory visits were received, and all wore a smiling appearance. I shut up, as well as I could, in my own heart the anxiety that preyed there, and entered 30 with seeming earnestness into the plans of my father, although they might only serve as the decorations of my tragedy. Through my father's exertions, a part of the inheritance of Elizabeth had been restored to her by the Austrian government. A small possession on the shores of Como belonged to her. It was agreed that, immedi- 35 ately after our union, we should proceed to Villa Lavenza, and spend our first days of happiness beside the beautiful lake near which it stood.

In the mean time I took every precaution to defend my person, in case the fiend should openly attack me. I carried pistols and a
5 dagger constantly about me, and was ever on the watch to prevent artifice; and by these means gained a greater degree of tranquillity. Indeed, as the period approached, the threat appeared more as a delusion, not to be regarded as worthy to disturb my peace, while the happiness I hoped for in my marriage wore a greater appearance
10 of certainty, as the day fixed for its solemnisation drew nearer, and I heard it continually spoken of as an occurrence which no accident could possibly prevent.

Elizabeth seemed happy; my tranquil demeanour contributed greatly to calm her mind. But on the day that was to fulfil my
15 wishes and my destiny, she was melancholy, and a presentiment of evil pervaded her; and perhaps also she thought of the dreadful secret which I had promised to reveal to her on the following day. My father was in the mean time overjoyed, and in the bustle of preparation only recognised in the melancholy of his niece the
20 diffidence of a bride.

After the ceremony was performed, a large party assembled at my father's; but it was agreed that Elizabeth and I should commence our journey by water, sleeping that night at Evian, and continuing our voyage on the following day. The day was fair, the
25 wind favourable, all smiled on our nuptial embarkation.

Those were the last moments of my life during which I enjoyed the feeling of happiness. We passed rapidly along: the sun was hot, but we were sheltered from its rays by a kind of canopy, while we enjoyed the beauty of the scene, sometimes on one side of the lake,
30 where we saw Mont Salêve, the pleasant banks of Montalègre, and at a distance, surmounting all, the beautiful Mont Blanc, and the assemblage of snowy mountains that in vain endeavour to emulate her; sometimes coasting the opposite banks, we saw the mighty Jura opposing its dark side to the ambition that would quit its native
35 country, and an almost insurmountable barrier to the invader who should wish to enslave it.

I took the hand of Elizabeth. 'You are sorrowful, my love. Ah! if you knew what I have suffered, and what I may yet endure, you would endeavour to let me taste the quiet and freedom from despair that this one day at least permits me to enjoy.'

'Be happy, my dear Victor,' replied Elizabeth; 'there is, I hope, nothing to distress you; and be assured that if a lively joy is not painted in my face, my heart is contented. Something whispers to me not to depend too much on the prospect that is opened before us, but I will not listen to such a sinister voice. Observe how fast we move along, and how the clouds, which sometimes obscure and sometimes rise above the dome of Mont Blanc, render this scene of beauty still more interesting. Look also at the innumerable fish that are swimming in the clear waters, where we can distinguish every pebble that lies at the bottom. What a divine day! how happy and serene all nature appears!'

Thus Elizabeth endeavoured to divert her thoughts and mine from all reflection upon melancholy subjects. But her temper was fluctuating; joy for a few instants shone in her eyes, but it continually gave place to distraction and reverie.

The sun sank lower in the heavens; we passed the river Drance, and observed its path through the chasms of the higher, and the glens of the lower hills. The Alps here come closer to the lake, and we approached the amphitheatre of mountains which forms its eastern boundary. The spire of Evian shone under the woods that surrounded it, and the range of mountain above mountain by which it was overhung.

The wind, which had hitherto carried us along with amazing rapidity, sunk at sunset to a light breeze; the soft air just ruffled the water, and caused a pleasant motion among the trees as we approached the shore, from which it wafted the most delightful scent of flowers and hay. The sun sunk beneath the horizon as we landed; and as I touched the shore, I felt those cares and fears revive, which soon were to clasp me, and cling to me forever.

Chapter VI

It was eight o'clock when we landed; we walked for a short time on the shore, enjoying the transitory light, and then retired to the inn, and contemplated the lovely scene of waters, woods, and mountains, obscured in darkness, yet still displaying their black
5 outlines.

The wind, which had fallen in the south, now rose with great violence in the west. The moon had reached her summit in the heavens and was beginning to descend; the clouds swept across it swifter than the flight of the vulture and dimmed her rays, while
10 the lake reflected the scene of the busy heavens, rendered still busier by the restless waves that were beginning to rise. Suddenly a heavy storm of rain descended.

I had been calm during the day; but so soon as night obscured the shapes of objects, a thousand fears arose in my mind. I was
15 anxious and watchful, while my right hand grasped a pistol which was hidden in my bosom; every sound terrified me; but I resolved that I would sell my life dearly, and not shrink from the conflict until my own life, or that of my adversary, was extinguished.

Elizabeth observed my agitation for some time in timid and
20 fearful silence, but there was something in my glance which communicated terror to her, and trembling, she asked, 'What is it that agitates you, my dear Victor? What is it you fear?'

'Oh! peace, peace, my love,' replied I; 'this night, and all will be safe: but this night is dreadful, very dreadful.'

25 I passed an hour in this state of mind, when suddenly, I reflected how fearful the combat which I momentarily expected would be to my wife, and I earnestly intreated her to retire, resolving not to

join her until I had obtained some knowledge as to the situation of my enemy.

She left me, and I continued some time walking up and down the passages of the house, and inspecting every corner that might afford a retreat to my adversary. But I discovered no trace of him, 5 and was beginning to conjecture that some fortunate chance had intervened to prevent the execution of his menaces; when suddenly I heard a shrill and dreadful scream. It came from the room into which Elizabeth had retired. As I heard it, the whole truth rushed into my mind, my arms dropped, the motion of every muscle and 10 fibre was suspended; I could feel the blood trickling in my veins, and tingling in the extremities of my limbs. This state lasted but for an instant; the scream was repeated, and I rushed into the room.

Great God! why did I not then expire! Why am I here to relate the destruction of the best hope, and the purest creature of earth? 15 She was there, lifeless and inanimate, thrown across the bed, her head hanging down, and her pale and distorted features half covered by her hair. Every where I turn I see the same figure – her bloodless arms and relaxed form flung by the murderer on its bridal bier. Could I behold this, and live? Alas! life is obstinate, and clings 20 closest where it is most hated. For a moment only did I lose recollection: I fell senseless on the ground.

When I recovered, I found myself surrounded by the people of the inn; their countenances expressed a breathless terror: but the horror of others appeared only as a mockery, a shadow of the 25 feelings that oppressed me. I escaped from them to the room where lay the body of Elizabeth, my love, my wife, so lately living, so dear, so worthy. She had been moved from the posture in which I had first beheld her; and now, as she lay, her head upon her arm, and a handkerchief thrown across her face and neck, I might have 30 supposed her asleep. I rushed towards her, and embraced her with ardour; but the deadly langour and coldness of the limbs told me, that what I now held in my arms had ceased to be the Elizabeth whom I had loved and cherished. The murderous mark of the fiend's grasp was on her neck, and the breath had ceased to issue 35 from her lips.

While I still hung over her in the agony of despair. I happened to look up. The windows of the room had before been darkened, and I felt a kind of panic on seeing the pale yellow light of the moon illuminate the chamber. The shutters had been thrown back; and,
5 with a sensation of horror not to be described. I saw at the open window a figure the most hideous and abhorred. A grin was on the face of the monster; he seemed to jeer, as with his fiendish finger he pointed towards the corpse of my wife. I rushed towards the window, and drawing a pistol from my bosom, fired: but he eluded
10 me, leaped from his station, and, running with the swiftness of lightning, plunged into the lake.

The report of the pistol brought a crowd into the room. I pointed to the spot where he had disappeared, and we followed the track with boats; nets were cast, but in vain. After passing several hours,
15 we returned hopeless, most of my companions believing it to have been a form conjured up by my fancy. After having landed, they proceeded to search the country, parties going in different directions among the woods and vines.

I attempted to accompany them, and proceeded a short distance
20 from the house; but my head whirled round, my steps were like those of a drunken man, I fell at last in a state of utter exhaustion; a film covered my eyes, and my skin was parched with the heat of fever. In this state I was carried back, and placed on a bed, hardly conscious of what had happened; my eyes wandered round the
25 room, as if to seek something that I had lost.

After an interval I arose, and, as if by instinct, crawled into the room where the corpse of my beloved lay. There were women weeping around; – I hung over it, and joined my sad tears to theirs – all this time no distinct idea presented itself to my mind; but my
30 thoughts rambled to various subjects, reflecting confusedly on my misfortunes and their cause. I was bewildered, in a cloud of wonder and horror. The death of William, the execution of Justine, the murder of Clerval, and lastly of my wife; even at that moment I knew not that my only remaining friends were safe from the malig-
35 nity of the fiend; my father even now might be writhing under his grasp, and Ernest might be dead at his feet. This idea made me

shudder, and recalled me to action. I started up, and resolved to return to Geneva with all possible speed.

There were no horses to be procured, and I must return by the lake; but the wind was unfavourable and the rain fell in torrents. However, it was hardly morning, and I might reasonably hope to arrive by night. I hired men to row and took an oar myself; for I had always experienced relief from mental torment in bodily exercise. But the overflowing misery I now felt, and the excess of agitation that I endured, rendered me incapable of any exertion. I threw down the oar; and leaning my head upon my hands, gave way to every gloomy idea that arose. If I looked up, I saw scenes which were familiar to me in my happier time, and which I had contemplated but the day before in the company of her who was now but a shadow and a recollection. Tears streamed from my eyes. The rain had ceased for a moment, and I saw the fish play in the waters as they had done a few hours before; they had then been observed by Elizabeth. Nothing is so painful to the human mind as a great and sudden change. The sun might shine, or the clouds might lower: but nothing could appear to me as it had done the day before. A fiend had snatched from me every hope of future happiness: no creature had ever been so miserable as I was; so frightful an event is single in the history of man.

But why should I dwell upon the incidents that followed this last overwhelming event? Mine has been a tale of horrors; I have reached their *acme*, and what I must now relate can but be tedious to you. Know that, one by one, my friends were snatched away; I was left desolate. My own strength is exhausted; and I must tell, in a few words, what remains of my hideous narration.

I arrived at Geneva. My father and Ernest yet lived; but the former sunk under the tidings that I bore. I see him now, excellent and venerable old man! his eyes wandered in vacancy, for they had lost their charm and their delight – his Elizabeth, his more than daughter, whom he doated on with all that affection which a man feels, who in the decline of life, having few affections, clings more earnestly to those that remain. Cursed, cursed be the fiend that brought misery on his grey hairs, and doomed him to waste in wretchedness! He could not live under the horrors that were accumulated around him; the springs of existence suddenly gave way: he was unable to rise from his bed, and in a few days he died in my arms.

5 What then became of me? I know not; I lost sensation and chains and darkness were the only objects that pressed upon me. Sometimes, indeed, I dreamt that I wandered in flowery meadows and pleasant vales with the friends of my youth, but I awoke, and found myself in a dungeon. Melancholy followed, but by degrees
10 I gained a clear conception of my miseries and situation, and was then released from my prison. For they had called me mad; and during many months, as I understood, a solitary cell had been my habitation.

Liberty, however, had been an useless gift to me, had I not, as I
15 awakened to reason, at the same time awakened to revenge. As the memory of past misfortunes pressed upon me, I began to reflect on their cause – the monster whom I had created, the miserable daemon whom I had sent abroad into the world for my destruction. I was possessed by a maddening rage when I thought of him, and
20 desired and ardently prayed that I might have him within my grasp to wreak a great and signal revenge on his cursed head.

Nor did my hate long confine itself to useless wishes; I began to reflect on the best means of securing him; and for this purpose, about a month after my release, I repaired to a criminal judge in
25 the town, and told him that I had an accusation to make; that I knew the destroyer of my family; and that I required him to exert his whole authority for the apprehension of the murderer.

The magistrate listened to me with attention and kindness: – 'Be assured sir,' said he, 'no pains or exertions on my part shall be
30 spared to discover the villain.'

'I thank you,' replied I; 'listen, therefore, to the deposition that I have to make. It is indeed a tale so strange, that I should fear you would not credit it were there not something in truth which, however wonderful, forces conviction. The story is too connected
35 to be mistaken for a dream, and I have no motive for falsehood.' My manner, as I thus addressed him, was impressive, but calm; I

had formed in my own heart a resolution to pursue my destroyer
to death; and this purpose quieted my agony, and for an interval
reconciled me to life. I now related my history, briefly, but with
firmness and precision, marking the dates with accuracy, and never
deviating into invective or exclamation.   5

The magistrate appeared at first perfectly incredulous, but as I
continued he became more attentive and interested; I saw him
sometimes shudder with horror; at others a lively surprise,
unmingled with disbelief, was painted on his countenance.

When I had concluded my narration I said, 'This is the being   10
whom I accuse, and for whose seizure and punishment I call upon
you to exert your whole power. It is your duty as a magistrate, and
I believe and hope that your feelings as a man will not revolt from
the execution of those functions on this occasion.'

This address caused a considerable change in the physiognomy   15
of my own auditor. He had heard my story with that half kind of
belief that is given to a tale of spirits and supernatural events; but
when he was called upon to act officially in consequence, the whole
tide of his incredulity returned. He, however, answered mildly, 'I
would willingly afford you every aid in your pursuit; but the creature 20
of whom you speak appears to have powers which would put all
my exertions to defiance. Who can follow an animal which can
traverse the sea of ice, and inhabit caves and dens where no man
would venture to intrude? Besides, some months have elapsed
since the commission of his crimes, and no one can conjecture to   25
what place he has wandered, or what region he may now inhabit.'

'I do not doubt that he hovers near the spot which I inhabit; and
if he has indeed taken refuge in the Alps, he may be hunted like
the chamois, and destroyed as a beast of prey. But I perceive your
thoughts: you do not credit my narrative, and do not intend to   30
pursue my enemy with the punishment which is his desert.'

As I spoke, rage sparkled in my eyes; the magistrate was intimi-
dated: – 'You are mistaken,' said he. 'I will exert myself; and if it
is in my power to seize the monster, be assured that he shall suffer
punishment proportionate to his crimes. But I fear, from what you   35
have yourself described to be his properties, that this will prove

impracticable; and thus, while every proper measure is pursued, you should make up your mind to disappointment.'

'That cannot be; but all that I can say will be of little avail. My revenge is of no moment to you; yet, while I allow it to be a vice, I
5 confess that it is the devouring and only passion of my soul. My rage is unspeakable, when I reflect that the murderer, whom I have turned loose upon society, still exists. You refuse my just demand: I have but one resource; and I devote myself, either in my life or death, to his destruction.'

10 I trembled with excess of agitation as I said this; there was a frenzy in my manner, and something, I doubt not, of that haughty fierceness which the martyrs of old are said to have possessed. But to a Genevan magistrate, whose mind was occupied by far other ideas than those of devotion and heroism, this elevation of mind
15 had much the appearance of madness. He endeavoured to soothe me as a nurse does a child, and reverted to my tale as the effects of delirium.

'Man,' I cried, 'how ignorant art thou in thy pride of wisdom! Cease; you know not what it is you say.'

20 I broke from the house angry and disturbed, and retired to meditate on some other mode of action.

Chapter VII

My present situation was one in which all voluntary thought was swallowed up and lost. I was hurried away by fury; revenge alone endowed me with strength and composure; it moulded my feelings, and allowed me to be calculating and calm, at periods when otherwise delirium or death would have been my portion. 5

My first resolution was to quit Geneva forever; my country, which, when I was happy and beloved, was dear to me, now, in my adversity, became hateful. I provided myself with a sum of money, together with a few jewels which had belonged to my mother, and departed. 10

And now my wanderings began, which are to cease but with life. I have traversed a vast portion of the earth, and have endured all the hardships which travellers, in deserts and barbarous countries, are wont to meet. How I have lived I hardly know; many times have I stretched my failing limbs upon the sandy plain, and prayed 15 for death. But revenge kept me alive; I dared not die, and leave my adversary in being.

When I quitted Geneva, my first labour was to gain some clue by which I might trace the steps of my fiendish enemy. But my plan was unsettled; and I wandered many hours round the confines 20 of the town, uncertain what path I should pursue. As night approached, I found myself at the entrance of the cemetery where William, Elizabeth, and my father reposed. I entered it, and approached the tomb which marked their graves. Every thing was silent, except the leaves of the trees, which were gently agitated by 25 the wind; the night was nearly dark; and the scene would have been solemn and affecting even to an uninterested observer. The spirits of the departed seemed to flit around, and to cast a shadow, which was felt but not seen, around the head of the mourner.

The deep grief which this scene had at first excited quickly gave way to rage and despair. They were dead, and I lived; their murderer also lived, and to destroy him I must drag out my weary existence. I knelt on the grass, and kissed the earth, and with quivering lips exclaimed, 'By the sacred earth on which I kneel, by the shades that wander near me, by the deep and eternal grief that I feel, I swear; and by thee, O Night, and the spirits that preside over thee, to pursue the daemon, who caused this misery, until he or I shall perish in mortal conflict. For this purpose I will preserve my life: to execute this dear revenge will I again behold the sun, and tread the green herbage of earth, which otherwise should vanish from my eyes forever. And I call on you, spirits of the dead; and on you, wandering ministers of vengeance, to aid and conduct me in my work. Let the cursed and hellish monster drink deep of agony; let him feel the despair that now torments me.'

I had begun my adjuration with solemnity, and an awe which almost assured me that the shades of my murdered friends heard and approved my devotion; but the furies possessed me as I concluded, and rage choked my utterance.

I was answered through the stillness of night by a loud and fiendish laugh. It rang on my ears long and heavily; the mountains re-echoed it, and I felt as if all hell surrounded me with mockery and laughter. Surely in that moment I should have been possessed by frenzy, and have destroyed my miserable existence, but that my vow was heard, and that I was reserved for vengeance. The laughter died away; when a well-known and abhorred voice, apparently close to my ear, addressed me in an audible whisper, 'I am satisfied: miserable wretch! you have determined to live, and I am satisfied.'

I darted towards the spot from which the sound proceeded; but the devil eluded my grasp. Suddenly the broad disk of the moon arose, and shone full upon his ghastly and distorted shape, as he fled with more than mortal speed.

I pursued him; and for many months this has been my task. Guided by a slight clue, I followed the windings of the Rhone, but vainly. The blue Mediterranean appeared; and; by a strange chance, I saw the fiend enter by night, and hide himself in a vessel bound for the Black Sea. I took my passage in the same ship; but he escaped, I know not how.

Amidst the wilds of Tartary and Russia, although he still evaded   5
me, I have ever followed in his track. Sometimes the peasants, scared by this horrid apparition, informed me of his path; sometimes he himself, who feared that if I lost all trace of him, I should despair and die, left some mark to guide me. The snows descended on my head, and I saw the print of his huge step on the white plain.   10
To you first entering on life, to whom care is new, and agony unknown, how can you understand what I have felt and still feel? Cold, want, and fatigue, were the least pains which I was destined to endure; I was cursed by some devil, and carried about with me my eternal hell; yet still a spirit of good followed and directed my   15
steps and, when I most murmured, would suddenly extricate me from seemingly insurmountable difficulties. Sometimes, when nature, overcome by hunger, sunk under the exhaustion, a repast was prepared for me in the desert, that restored and inspirited me. The fare was, indeed, coarse, such as the peasants of the country   20
ate; but I will not doubt that it was set there by the spirits that I had invoked to aid me. Often, when all was dry, the heavens cloudless, and I was parched by thirst, a slight cloud would bedim the sky, shed the few drops that revived me, and vanish.

I followed, when I could, the courses of the rivers; but the   25
daemon generally avoided these, as it was here that the population of the country chiefly collected. In other places human beings were seldom seen; and I generally subsisted on the wild animals that crossed my path. I had money with me, and gained the friendship of the villagers by distributing it; or I brought with me some food   30
that I had killed, which, after taking a small part, I always presented to those who had provided me with fire and utensils for cooking.

My life, as it passed thus, was indeed hateful to me, and it was during sleep alone that I could taste joy. O blessed sleep! often, when most miserable, I sank to repose, and my dreams lulled me   35
even to rapture. The spirits that guarded me had provided these

moments, or rather hours, of happiness that I might retain strength
to fulfil my pilgrimage. Deprived of this respite, I should have sunk
under my hardships. During the day I was sustained and inspirited
by the hope of night: for in sleep I saw my friends, my wife, and
5 my beloved country; again I saw the benevolent countenance of
my father, heard the silver tones of my Elizabeth's voice, and
beheld Clerval enjoying health and youth. Often, when wearied by
a toilsome march, I persuaded myself that I was dreaming until
night should come, and that I should then enjoy reality in the arms
10 of my dearest friends. What agonising fondness did I feel for them!
how did I cling to their dear forms, as sometimes they haunted
even my waking hours, and persuade myself that they still lived! At
such moments vengeance, that burned within me, died in my heart,
and I pursued my path towards the destruction of the daemon,
15 more as a task enjoined by heaven, as the mechanical impulse of
some power of which I was unconscious, than as the ardent desire
of my soul.

What his feelings were whom I pursued I cannot know. Sometimes, indeed, he left marks in writing on the barks of the trees, or
20 cut in stone, that guided me, and instigated my fury. 'My reign is
not yet over' – these words were legible in one of these inscriptions
– 'you live, and my power is complete. Follow me; I seek the
everlasting ices of the north, where you will feel the misery of cold
and frost, to which I am impassive. You will find near this place, if
25 you follow not too tardily, a dead hare; eat and be refreshed. Come
on, my enemy; we have yet to wrestle for our lives, but many hard
and miserable hours must you endure until that period shall arrive.'

Scoffing devil! Again do I vow vengeance; again do I devote thee,
miserable fiend, to torture and death. Never will I give up my
30 search, until he or I perish; and then with what ecstasy shall I join
my Elizabeth and my departed friends, who even now prepare for
me the reward of my tedious toil and horrible pilgrimage!

As I still pursued my journey to the northward, the snows
thickened, and the cold increased in a degree almost too severe to
35 support. The peasants were shut up in their hovels, and only a
few of the most hardy ventured forth to seize the animals whom

starvation had forced from their hiding-places to seek for prey. The rivers were covered with ice, and no fish could be procured; and thus I was cut off from my chief article of maintenance.

The triumph of my enemy increased with the difficulty of my labours. One inscription that he left was in these words: – 'Prepare! your toils only begin; wrap yourself in furs, and provide food, for we shall soon enter upon a journey where your sufferings will satisfy my everlasting hatred.'

My courage and perseverance were invigorated by these scoffing words; I resolved not to fail in my purpose; and, calling on Heaven to support me, I continued with unabated fervour to traverse immense deserts, until the ocean appeared at a distance, and formed the utmost boundary of the horizon. Oh! how unlike it was to the blue seasons of the south! Covered with ice, it was only to be distinguished from land by its superior wildness and ruggedness. The Greeks wept for joy when they beheld the Mediterranean from the hills of Asia, and hailed with rapture the boundary of their toils. I did not weep, but I knelt down, and, with a full heart, thanked my guiding spirit for conducting me in safety to the place where I hoped, notwithstanding my adversary's gibe, to meet and grapple with him.

Some weeks before this period I had procured a sledge and dogs, and thus traversed the snows with inconceivable speed. I know not whether the fiend possessed the same advantages; but I found that, as before I had daily lost ground in the pursuit, I now gained on him, so much so that when I first saw the ocean he was but one day's journey in advance, and I hoped to intercept him before he should reach the beach. With new courage, therefore, I pressed on, and in two days arrived at a wretched hamlet on the sea-shore. I enquired of the inhabitants concerning the fiend, and gained accurate information. A gigantic monster, they said, had arrived the night before, armed with a gun and many pistols; putting to flight the inhabitants of a solitary cottage, through fear of his terrific appearance. He had carried off their store of winter food, and, placing it in a sledge, to draw which he had seized on a numerous drove of trained dogs, he had harnessed them, and the same night, to the joy of the horror-struck villagers, had pursued his journey across the sea in a direction that led to no land; and they conjectured that he must speedily be destroyed by the breaking of the ice, or frozen by the eternal frosts.

5 On hearing this information, I suffered a temporary access of despair. He had escaped me; and I must commence a destructive and almost endless journey across the mountainous ices of the ocean, – amidst cold that few of the inhabitants could long endure and which I, the native of a genial and sunny climate, could not 10 hope to survive. Yet at the idea that the fiend should live and be triumphant, my rage and vengeance returned, and, like a mighty tide, overwhelmed every other feeling. After a slight repose, during which the spirits of the dead hovered round, and instigated me to toil and revenge, I prepared for my journey.

15 I exchanged my land-sledge for one fashioned for the inequalities of the Frozen Ocean; and purchasing a plentiful stock of provisions, I departed from land.

I cannot guess how many days have passed since then; but I have endured misery, which nothing but the eternal sentiment of a just 20 retribution burning within my heart could have enabled me to support. Immense and rugged mountains of ice often barred up my passage, and I often heard the thunder of the ground sea, which threatened my destruction. But again the frost came, and made the paths of the sea secure.

25 By the quantity of provision which I had consumed, I should guess that I had passed three weeks in this journey; and the continual protraction of hope, returning back upon the heart, often wrung bitter drops of despondency and grief from my eyes. Despair had indeed almost secured her prey, and I should soon have sunk 30 beneath this misery. Once, after the poor animals that conveyed me had with incredible toil gained the summit of a sloping ice-mountain, and one, sinking under his fatigue, died, I viewed the expanse before me with anguish, when suddenly my eye caught a dark speck upon the dusky plain. I strained my sight to discover 35 what it could be, and uttered a wild cry of ecstasy when I distinguished a sledge, and the distorted proportions of a well-known

form within. Oh! with what a burning gush did hope revisit my heart! warm tears filled my eyes, which I hastily wiped away, that they might not intercept the view I had of the daemon; but still my sight was dimmed by the burning drops, until, giving way to the emotions that oppressed me, I wept aloud.   5

But this was not the time for delay: I disencumbered the dogs of their dead companion, gave them a plentiful portion of food; and, after an hour's rest, which was absolutely necessary, and yet which was bitterly irksome to me, I continued my route. The sledge was still visible; nor did I again lose sight of it, except at the moments   10 when for a short time some ice-rock concealed it with its intervening crags. I indeed perceptibly gained on it; and when, after nearly two days' journey, I beheld my enemy at no more than a mile distant, my heart bounded within me.

But now, when I appeared almost within grasp of my foe, my   15 hopes were suddenly extinguished, and I lost all trace of him more utterly than I had ever done before. A ground sea was heard; the thunder of its progress, as the waters rolled and swelled beneath me, became every moment more ominous and terrific. I pressed on, but in vain. The wind arose; the sea roared; and, as with   20 the mighty shock of an earthquake, it split, and cracked with a tremendous and overwhelming sound. The work was soon finished: in a few minutes a tumultuous sea rolled between me and my enemy, and I was left drifting on a scattered piece of ice, that was continually lessening, and thus preparing for me a hideous   25 death.

In this manner many appalling hours passed; several of my dogs died; and I myself was about to sink under the accumulation of distress when I saw your vessel riding at anchor, and holding forth to me hopes of succour and life. I had no conception that vessels   30 ever came so far north, and was astounded at the sight. I quickly destroyed part of my sledge to construct oars; and by these means was enabled, with infinite fatigue, to move my ice-raft in the direction of your ship. I had determined, if you were going south-wards, still to trust myself to the mercy of the seas rather than   35 abandon my purpose. I hoped to induce you to grant me a boat with which I could pursue my enemy. But your direction was northward. You took me on board when my vigour was exhausted, and I should soon have sunk under my multiplied hardships into a death which I still dread – for my task is unfulfilled.

5   Oh! when will my guiding spirit, in conducting me to the dae-mon, allow me the rest I so much desire; or must I die, and he yet live? If I do, swear to me, Walton, that he shall not escape; that you will seek him, and satisfy my vengeance in his death. And do I dare to ask of you to undertake my pilgrimage, to endure the

10 hardships that I have undergone? No; I am not so selfish. Yet, when I am dead, if he should appear; if the ministers of vengeance should conduct him to you, swear that he shall not live – swear that he shall not triumph over my accumulated woes and survive to add to the list of his dark crimes. He is eloquent and persuasive;

15 and once his words had even power over my heart: but trust him not. His soul is as hellish as his form, full of treachery and fiendlike malice. Hear him not; call on the manes of William, Justine, Clerval, Elizabeth, my father, and of the wretched Victor, and thrust your sword into his heart. I will hover near, and direct the

20 steel aright.

WALTON, in continuation

August 26th, 17–

You have read this strange and terrific story, Margaret; and do you not feel your blood congeal with horror, like that which even

25 now curdles mine? Sometimes, seized with sudden agony, he could not continue his tale; at others, his voice broken, yet piercing, uttered with difficulty the words so replete with anguish. His fine and lovely eyes were now lighted up with indignation, now subdued to downcast sorrow, and quenched in infinite wretchedness. Some-

30 times he commanded his countenance and tones, and related the most horrible incidents with a tranquil voice, suppressing every mark of agitation; then, like a volcano bursting forth, his face would suddenly change to an expression of the wildest rage, as he shrieked out imprecations on his persecutor.

35   His tale is connected, and told with an appearance of the simplest

truth; yet I own to you that the letters of Felix and Safie, which he showed me, and the apparition of the monster seen from our ship, brought to me a greater conviction of the truth of his narrative than his asseverations, however earnest and connected. Such a monster has, then, real existence! I cannot doubt it; yet I am lost in surprise ⁣5 and admiration. Sometimes I endeavoured to gain from Frankenstein the particulars of his creature's formation: but on this point he was impenetrable.

'Are you mad, my friend?' said he; 'or whither does your senseless curiosity lead you? Would you also create for yourself and the ⁣10 world a demoniacal enemy? Peace, peace! learn my miseries, and do not seek to increase your own.'

Frankenstein discovered that I made notes concerning his history: he asked to see them, and then himself corrected and augmented them in many places; but principally in giving the life and ⁣15 spirit to the conversations he held with his enemy. 'Since you have preserved my narration,' said he, 'I would not that a mutilated one should go down to posterity.'

Thus has a week passed away, while I have listened to the strangest tale that ever imagination formed. My thoughts, and ⁣20 every feeling of my soul, have been drunk up by the interest for my guest, which this tale, and his own elevated and gentle manners, have created. I wish to soothe him; yet can I counsel one so infinitely miserable, so destitute of every hope of consolation, to live? Oh, no! the only joy that he can now know will be when he composes ⁣25 his shattered spirit to peace and death. Yet he enjoys one comfort, the offspring of solitude and delirium: he believes, that when in dreams he holds converse with his friends, and derives from that communion consolation for his miseries, or excitements to his vengeance, that they are not the creations of his fancy, but the ⁣30 beings themselves who visit him from the regions of a remote world. This faith gives a solemnity to his reveries that render them to me almost as imposing and interesting as truth.

Our conversations are not always confined to his own history and misfortunes. On every point of general literature he displays ⁣35 unbounded knowledge, and a quick and piercing apprehension.

His eloquence is forcible and touching; nor can I hear him, when he relates a pathetic incident, or endeavours to move the passions of pity or love, without tears. What a glorious creature must he have been in the days of his prosperity, when he is thus noble and godlike in ruin! He seems to feel his own worth, and the greatness of his fall.

'When younger,' said he, 'I believed myself destined for some great enterprise. My feelings are profound; but I possessed a coolness of judgment that fitted me for illustrious achievements. This sentiment of the worth of my nature supported me, when others would have been oppressed; for I deemed it criminal to throw away in useless grief those talents that might be useful to my fellow-creatures. When I reflected on the work I had completed, no less a one than the creation of a sensitive and rational animal, I could not rank myself with the herd of common projectors. But this thought, which supported me in the commencement of my career, now serves only to plunge me lower in the dust. All my speculations and hopes are as nothing; and, like the archangel who aspired to omnipotence, I am chained in an eternal hell. My imagination was vivid, yet my powers of analysis and application were intense; by the union of these qualities I conceived the idea, and executed the creation of a man. Even now I cannot recollect, without passion, my reveries while the work was incomplete. I trod heaven in my thoughts, now exulting in my powers, now burning with the idea of their effects. From my infancy I was imbued with high hopes and a lofty ambition; but how am I sunk! Oh! my friend, if you had known me as I once was, you would not recognise me in this state of degradation. Despondency rarely visited my heart; a high destiny seemed to bear me on, until I fell, never, never again to rise.'

Must I then lose this admirable being! I have longed for a friend; I have sought one who would sympathise with and love me. Behold, on these desert seas I have found such a one; but, I fear, I have gained him only to know his value, and lose him. I would reconcile him to life, but he repulses the idea.

'I thank you, Walton,' he said, 'for your kind intentions towards so miserable a wretch; but when you speak of new ties, and fresh affections, think you that any can replace those who are gone? Can any man be to me as Clerval was; or any woman another Elizabeth? Even where the affections are not strongly moved by any superior excellence, the companions of our childhood always possess a certain power over our minds, which hardly any later friend can obtain. They know our infantine dispositions, which, however they may be afterwards modified, are never eradicated; and they can judge of our actions with more certain conclusions as to the integrity of our motives. A sister or a brother can never, unless indeed such symptoms have been shown early, suspect the other of fraud or false dealing, when another friend, however strongly he may be attached, may, in spite of himself, be contemplated with suspicion. But I enjoyed friends, dear not only through habit and association, but from their own merits; and wherever I am, the soothing voice of my Elizabeth, and the conversation of Clerval, will be ever whispered in my ear. They are dead; and but one feeling in such a solitude can persuade me to preserve my life. If I were engaged in any high undertaking or design, fraught with extensive utility to my fellow-creatures, then could I live to fulfil it. But such is not my destiny; I must pursue and destroy the being to whom I gave existence; then my lot on earth will be fulfilled, and I may die.'

September 2nd

MY BELOVED SISTER,   I write to you, encompassed by peril, and ignorant whether I am ever doomed to see again dear England, and the dearer friends that inhabit it. I am surrounded by mountains of ice, which admit of no escape, and threaten every moment to crush my vessel. The brave fellows, whom I have persuaded to be my companions, look towards me for aid; but I have none to bestow. There is something terribly appalling in our situation, yet my courage and hopes do not desert me. Yet it is terrible to reflect that the lives of all these men are endangered through me. If we are lost, my mad schemes are the cause.

And what, Margaret, will be the state of your mind? You will not hear of my destruction, and you will anxiously await my return.

Years will pass, and you will have visitings of despair, and yet be tortured by hope. Oh! my beloved sister, the sickening failing of your heart-felt expectations is, in prospect, more terrible to me than my own death. But you have a husband, and lovely children; you may be happy: Heaven bless you, and make you so!

My unfortunate guest regards me with the tenderest compassion. He endeavours to fill me with hope; and talks as if life were a possession which he valued. He reminds me how often the same accidents have happened to other navigators, who have attempted this sea, and in spite of myself, he fills me with cheerful auguries. Even the sailors feel the power of his eloquence; when he speaks, they no longer despair; he rouses their energies, and, while they hear his voice, they believe these vast mountains of ice are molehills, which will vanish before the resolutions of man. These feelings are transitory; each day of expectation delayed fills them with fear, and I almost dread a mutiny caused by this despair.

September 5th

A scene has just passed of such uncommon interest, that although it is highly probable that these papers may never reach you, yet I cannot forbear recording it.

We are still surrounded by mountains of ice, still in imminent danger of being crushed in their conflict. The cold is excessive, and many of my unfortunate comrades have already found a grave amidst this scene of desolation. Frankenstein has daily declined in health: a feverish fire still glimmers in his eyes; but he is exhausted, and when suddenly roused to any exertion, he speedily sinks again into apparent lifelessness.

I mentioned in my last letter the fears I entertained of a mutiny. This morning, as I sat watching the wan countenance of my friend – his eyes half closed, and his limbs hanging listlessly – I was roused by half a dozen of the sailors, who demanded admission into the cabin. They entered, and their leader addressed me. He told me that he and his companions had been chosen by the other sailors to come in deputation to me, to make me a requisition, which, in justice, I could not refuse. We were immured in ice, and should probably never escape; but they feared that if, as was possible, the ice should dissipate and a free passage be opened, I should be rash enough to continue my voyage, and lead them into fresh dangers, after they might happily have surmounted this. They insisted, therefore, that I should engage with a solemn promise, that if 5 the vessel should be freed I would instantly direct my course southwards.

This speech troubled me. I had not despaired; nor had I yet conceived the idea of returning, if set free. Yet could I, in justice, or even in possibility, refuse this demand? I hesitated before I 10 answered; when Frankenstein, who had at first been silent, and, indeed, appeared hardly to have force enough to attend, now roused himself; his eyes sparkled, and his cheeks flushed with momentary vigour. Turning towards the men, he said –

'What do you mean? What do you demand of your captain? Are 15 you then so easily turned from your design? Did you not call this a glorious expedition? And wherefore was it glorious? Not because the way was smooth and placid as a southern sea, but because it was full of dangers and terror; because, at every new incident, your fortitude was to be called forth, and your courage exhibited; 20 because danger and death surrounded it, and these you were to brave and overcome. For this was it a glorious, for this was it an honourable undertaking. You were hereafter to be hailed as the benefactors of your species; your names adored, as belonging to brave men who encountered death for honour, and the benefit of 25 mankind. And now, behold, with the first imagination of danger, or, if you will, the first mighty and terrific trial of your courage, you shrink away, and are content to be handed down as men who had not strength enough to endure cold and peril; and so, poor souls, they were chilly and returned to their warm firesides. Why, that 30 requires not this preparation; ye need not have come thus far, and dragged your captain to the shame of a defeat, merely to prove yourselves cowards. Oh! be men, or be more than men. Be steady to your purposes, and firm as a rock. This ice is not made of such stuff as your hearts may be; it is mutable, and cannot withstand 35 you, if you say that it shall not. Do not return to your families with the stigma of disgrace marked on your brows. Return as heroes who have fought and conquered, and who know not what it is to turn their backs on the foe.'

He spoke this with a voice so modulated to the different feelings expressed in his speech, with an eye so full of lofty design and heroism, that can you wonder that these men were moved? They looked at one another, and were unable to reply. I spoke; I told them to retire, and consider of what had been said: that I would not lead them farther north if they strenuously desired the contrary; but that I hoped that, with reflection, their courage would return.

They retired, and I turned towards my friend, but he was sunk in languor, and almost deprived of life.

How all this will terminate, I know not; but I had rather die than return shamefully – my purpose unfulfilled. Yet I fear such will be my fate; the men, unsupported by ideas of glory and honour, can never willingly continue to endure their present hardships.

September 7th

The die is cast; I have consented to return, if we are not destroyed. Thus are my hopes blasted by cowardice and indecision: I come back ignorant and disappointed. It requires more philosophy than I possess, to bear this injustice with patience.

September 12th

It is past; I am returning to England. I have lost my hopes of utility and glory; – I have lost my friend. But I will endeavour to detail these bitter circumstances to you, my dear sister; and, while I am wafted towards England, and towards you, I will not despond.

September 9th, the ice began to move, and roarings like thunder were heard at a distance, as the islands split and cracked in every direction. We were in the most imminent peril; but, as we could only remain passive, my chief attention was occupied by my unfortunate guest, whose illness increased in such a degree that he was entirely confined to his bed. The ice cracked behind us, and was driven with force towards the north; a breeze sprung from the west, and on the 11th the passage towards the south became perfectly free. When the sailors saw this, and that their return to their native country was apparently assured, a shout of tumultuous joy broke from them, loud and long-continued. Frankenstein, who was dozing, awoke and asked the cause of the tumult. 'They shout,' I said, 'because they will soon return to England.'

'Do you then really return?'

'Alas! yes; I cannot withstand their demands. I cannot lead them unwillingly to danger, and I must return.'

'Do so, if you will; but I will not. You may give up your purpose, but mine is assigned to me by Heaven, and I dare not. I am weak; but surely the spirits who assist my vengeance will endow me with sufficient strength.' Saying this, he endeavoured to spring from the bed, but the exertion was too great for him; he fell back and fainted.

It was long before he was restored; and I often thought that life was entirely extinct. At length he opened his eyes; he breathed with difficulty, and was unable to speak. The surgeon gave him a composing draught, and ordered us to leave him undisturbed. In the mean time he told me, that my friend had certainly not many hours to live.

His sentence was pronounced; and I could only grieve, and be patient. I sat by his bed, watching him; his eyes were closed, and I thought he slept; but presently he called to me in a feeble voice, and bidding me come near, said –

'Alas! the strength I relied on is gone; I feel that I shall soon die, and he, my enemy and persecutor, may still be in being. Think not, Walton, that in the last moments of my existence I feel that burning hatred, and ardent desire of revenge, I once expressed; but I feel myself justified in desiring the death of my adversary. During these last days I have been occupied in examining my past conduct; nor do I find it blameable. In a fit of enthusiastic madness I created a rational creature, and was bound towards him, to assure, as far as was in my power, his happiness and well-being. This was my duty; but there was another still paramount to that. My duties towards the beings of my own species had greater claims to my attention, because they included a greater proportion of happiness or misery. Urged by this view, I refused, and I did right in refusing,

to create a companion for the first creature. He showed unparalleled malignity and selfishness, in evil; he destroyed my friends; he
devoted to destruction beings who possessed exquisite sensations,
happiness, and wisdom; nor do I know where this thirst for vengeance may end. Miserable himself, that he may render no other
wretched, he ought to die. The task of his destruction was mine,
but I have failed. When actuated by selfish and vicious motives, I
asked you to undertake my unfinished work; and I renew this
request now, when I am only induced by reason and virtue.

'Yet I cannot ask you to renounce your country and friends, to
fulfil this task; and now that you are returning to England, you will
have little chance of meeting with him. But the consideration of
these points, and the well balancing of what you may esteem your
duties, I leave to you; my judgment and ideas are already disturbed
by the near approach of death. I dare not ask you to do what I think
right, for I may still be misled by passion.

'That he should live to be an instrument of mischief disturbs
me; in other respects, this hour, when I momentarily expect my
release, is the only happy one which I have enjoyed for several
years. The forms of the beloved dead flit before me, and I hasten
to their arms. Farewell, Walton! Seek happiness in tranquillity,
and avoid ambition, even if it be only the apparently innocent one
of distinguishing yourself in science and discoveries. Yet why do I
say this? I have myself been blasted in these hopes, yet another
may succeed.'

His voice became faint as he spoke; and at length, exhausted by
his effort, he sunk into silence. About half an hour afterwards he
attempted again to speak, but was unable; he pressed my hand
feebly, and his eyes closed forever, while the irradiation of a gentle
smile passed away from his lips.

Margaret, what comment can I make on the untimely extinction
of this glorious spirit? What can I say, that will enable you to
understand the depth of my sorrow? All that I should express would
be inadequate and feeble. My tears flow; my mind is overshadowed
by a cloud of disappointment. But I journey towards England, and
I may there find consolation.

I am interrupted. What do these sounds portend? It is midnight; the breeze blows fairly, and the watch on deck scarcely stir. Again there is a sound as of a human voice; but hoarser; it comes from the cabin where the remains of Frankenstein still lie. I must arise, and examine. Good night, my sister.

Great God! what a scene has just taken place! I am yet dizzy with the remembrance of it. I hardly know whether I shall have the power to detail it; yet the tale which I have recorded would be incomplete without this final and wonderful catastrophe.

I entered the cabin where lay the remains of my ill-fated and admirable friend. Over him hung a form which I cannot find words to describe: – gigantic in stature, yet uncouth and distorted in its proportions. As he hung over the coffin, his face was concealed by long locks of ragged hair; but one vast hand was extended, in colour and apparent texture like that of a mummy. When he heard the sound of my approach, he ceased to utter exclamations of grief and horror, and sprung towards the window. Never did I behold a vision so horrible as his face, of such loathsome, yet appalling hideousness. I shut my eyes, involuntarily, and endeavoured to recollect what were my duties with regard to this destroyer. I called on him to stay.

He paused, looking on me with wonder; and, again turning towards the lifeless form of his creator, he seemed to forget my presence, and every feature and gesture seemed instigated by the wildest rage of some uncontrollable passion.

'That is also my victim!'.he exclaimed: 'in his murder my crimes are consummated; the miserable series of my being is wound to its close! Oh, Frankenstein! generous and self-devoted being! what does it avail that I now ask thee to pardon me? I, who irretrievably destroyed thee by destroying all thou lovedst. Alas! he is cold, he cannot answer me.'

His voice seemed suffocated; and my first impulses, which had suggested to me the duty of obeying the dying request of my friend, in destroying his enemy, were now suspended by a mixture of curiosity and compassion. I approached this tremendous being; I dared not again raise my eyes to his face, there was something so

scaring and unearthly in his ugliness. I attempted to speak, but the
words died away on my lips. The monster continued to utter wild
and incoherent self-reproaches. At length I gathered resolution
to address him in a pause of the tempest of his passion: 'Your
5 repentance,' I said, 'is now superfluous. If you had listened to the
voice of conscience, and heeded the stings of remorse, before you
had urged your diabolical vengeance to this extremity, Frankenstein would yet have lived.'

'And do you dream?' said the daemon; 'do you think that I was
10 then dead to agony and remorse? – He,' he continued, pointing to
the corpse, 'he suffered not in the consummation of the deed – oh!
not the ten-thousandth portion of the anguish that was mine during
the lingering detail of its execution. A frightful selfishness hurried
me on, while my heart was poisoned with remorse. Think you that
15 the groans of Clerval were music to my ears? My heart was fashioned
to be susceptible of love and sympathy; and when wrenched by misery to vice and hatred, it did not endure the violence of the change,
without torture such as you cannot even imagine.

'After the murder of Clerval, I returned to Switzerland, heart-
20 broken and overcome. I pitied Frankenstein; my pity amounted to
horror: I abhorred myself. But when I discovered that he, the
author at once of my existence and of its unspeakable torments,
dared to hope for happiness; that while he accumulated wretchedness and despair upon me, he sought his own enjoyment in feelings
25 and passions from the indulgence of which I was forever barred,
then impotent envy and bitter indignation filled me with an
insatiable thirst for vengeance. I recollected my threat, and resolved
that it should be accomplished. I knew that I was preparing for
myself a deadly torture; but I was the slave, not the master, of an
30 impulse, which I detested, yet could not disobey. Yet when she
died! – nay, then I was not miserable. I had cast off all feeling,
subdued all anguish, to riot in the excess of my despair. Evil
thenceforth became my good. Urged thus far, I had no choice but
to adapt my nature to an element which I had willingly chosen.
35 The completion of my demoniacal design became an insatiable
passion. And now it is ended; there is my last victim!'

I was at first touched by the expressions of his misery; yet, when I called to mind what Frankenstein had said of his powers of eloquence and persuasion, and when I again cast my eyes on the lifeless form of my friend, indignation was rekindled within me. 'Wretch!' I said, 'it is well that you come here to whine over the desolation that you have made. You throw a torch into a pile of buildings; and when they are consumed, you sit among the ruins, and lament the fall. Hypocritical fiend! if he whom you mourn still lived, still would he be the object, again would he become the prey, of your accursed vengeance. It is not pity that you feel; you lament only because the victim of your malignity is withdrawn from your power.'

'Oh, it is not thus – not thus,' interrupted the being; 'yet such must be the impression conveyed to you by what appears to be the purport of my actions. Yet I seek not a fellow-feeling in my misery. No sympathy may I ever find. When I first sought it, it was the love of virtue, the feelings of happiness and affection with which my whole being overflowed, that I wished to be participated. But now, that virtue has become to me a shadow, and that happiness and affection are turned into bitter and loathing despair, in what should I seek for sympathy? I am content to suffer alone, while my sufferings shall endure; when I die, I am well satisfied that abhorrence and opprobrium should load my memory. Once my fancy was soothed with dreams of virtue, of fame, and of enjoyment. Once I falsely hoped to meet with beings who, pardoning my outward form, would love me for the excellent qualities which I was capable of unfolding. I was nourished with high thoughts of honour and devotion. But now crime has degraded me beneath the meanest animal. No guilt, no mischief, no malignity, no misery, can be found comparable to mine. When I run over the frightful catalogue of my sins, I cannot believe that I am the same creature whose thoughts were once filled with sublime and transcendent visions of the beauty and the majesty of goodness. But it is even so; the fallen angel becomes a malignant devil. Yet even that enemy of God and man had friends and associates in his desolation; I am alone.

'You, who call Frankenstein your friend, seem to have a

knowledge of my crimes and his misfortunes. But, in the detail which he gave you of them, he could not sum up the hours and months of misery which I endured, wasting in impotent passions. For while I destroyed his hopes, I did not satisfy my own desires.
5 They were forever ardent and craving; still I desired love and fellowship, and I was still spurned. Was there no injustice in this? Am I to be thought the only criminal, when all human kind sinned against me? Why do you not hate Felix, who drove his friend from the door with contumely? Why do you not execrate the rustic who
10 sought to destroy the saviour of his child? Nay, these are virtuous and immaculate beings! I, the miserable and the abandoned, am an abortion, to be spurned at, and kicked, and trampled on. Even now my blood boils at the recollection of this injustice.

'But it is true that I am a wretch. I have murdered the lovely and
15 the helpless; I have strangled the innocent as they slept, and grasped to death his throat who never injured me or any other living thing. I have devoted my creator, the select specimen of all that is worthy of love and admiration among men, to misery; I have pursued him even to that irremediable ruin. There he lies, white and cold in
20 death. You hate me; but your abhorrence cannot equal that with which I regard myself. I look on the hands which executed the deed; I think on the heart in which the imagination of it was conceived, and long for the moment when these hands will meet my eyes, when that imagination will haunt my thoughts no more.

25 'Fear not that I shall be the instrument of future mischief. My work is nearly complete. Neither yours nor any man's death is needed to consummate the series of my being, and accomplish that which must be done; but it requires my own. Do not think that I shall be slow to perform this sacrifice. I shall quit your vessel on
30 the ice-raft which brought me thither, and shall seek the most northern extremity of the globe; I shall collect my funeral pile, and consume to ashes this miserable frame, that its remains may afford no light to any curious and unhallowed wretch, who would create such another as I have been. I shall die. I shall no longer feel
35 the agonies which now consume me, or be the prey of feelings unsatisfied, yet unquenched. He is dead who called me into being;

and when I shall be no more, the very remembrance of us both will speedily vanish. I shall no longer see the sun or stars, or feel the winds play on my cheeks. Light, feeling, and sense will pass away; and in this condition must I find my happiness. Some years ago, when the images which this world affords first opened upon me, when I felt the cheering warmth of summer and heard the rustling of the leaves and the warbling of the birds, and these were all to me, I should have wept to die; now it is my only consolation. Polluted by crimes, and torn by the bitterest remorse, where can I find rest but in death?

'Farewell! I leave you, and in you the last of human-kind whom these eyes will ever behold. Farewell, Frankenstein! If thou wert yet alive and yet cherished a desire of revenge against me, it would be better satiated in my life than in my destruction. But it was not so; thou didst seek my extinction, that I might not cause greater wretchedness; and if yet, in some mode unknown to me, thou hadst not ceased to think and feel, thou wouldst not desire against me a vengeance greater than that which I feel. Blasted as thou wert, my agony was still superior to thine; for the bitter sting of remorse will not cease to rankle in my wounds until death shall close them for ever.

'But soon,' he cried, with sad and solemn enthusiasm, 'I shall die, and what I now feel be no longer felt. Soon these burning miseries will be extinct. I shall ascend my funeral pile triumphantly, and exult in the agony of the torturing flames. The light of that conflagration will fade away; my ashes will be swept into the sea by the winds. My spirit will sleep in peace; or if it thinks, it will not surely think thus. Farewell.'

He sprung from the cabin window, as he said this, upon the ice-raft which lay close to the vessel. He was soon borne away by the waves, and lost in darkness and distance.

THE END

Language Notes and Activities

AUTHOR'S INTRODUCTION (1831) AND P. B. SHELLEY'S PREFACE (1817)

Focus

The original preface was written by P. B. Shelley, Mary's husband, giving the impression that he had written the novel himself. Mary's own introduction came much later. They both try to explain how the novel came about. Think about the differences between the two approaches. Which do you find more interesting?

Follow-up

Why do you think they are so different? What do they add to your understanding of the novel? What would be lacking if they were not added to the text of the novel itself?

Frankenstein; or the modern Prometheus (1.00): in Greek mythology Prometheus, having usurped the powers of the higher gods by creating man, is alienated forever from men and gods by being chained to the frozen top of the Caucasus. The Shelleys were reading Aeschylus's play *Prometheus Bound* in 1816, and P. B. Shelley's poem *Prometheus Unbound* (1819) was on a similar theme.

'Did I request thee' (1.00): quotation from Milton's *Paradise Lost* (1667). Milton's Satan, like Prometheus, defied God and suffered.

William Godwin (3.00): Mary Shelley's father. The books mentioned were considered radical and dangerous. There are echoes of both in *Frankenstein*.

Standard Novels (5.00): later edition of 1831, in which Mary Shelley made some significant changes in line with the growing conservatism of the 1830s (for example she changed Elizabeth from a cousin to an adopted sister).

a young girl (5.5): she was eighteen.

two persons of distinguished literary celebrity (5.12): William Godwin and Mary Wollstonecraft (author of *Vindication of the Rights of Woman*). Mary Shelley was always acutely aware of her literary heritage.

my childhood's companion and friend (5.23): her half sister, Fanny Imlay.

in the country (5.26): Somerstown, on the outskirts of London, now hard to imagine as ever being countryside.

Scotland (5.27): Mary was sent to stay with the Baxters, friends of Godwin, in 1812.

eyry (6.4): usually spelt eyrie. The nest of the eagle, built high up in rocks or trees. By association, a safe place, high up.

My husband (6.17): Percy Bysshe Shelley.

Travelling, and the cares of a family (6.25): the couple had travelled to the Continent in 1814 and again in 1816. She gave birth to a daughter in 1815, who died very young, and a son, William, in 1816.

study (6.26): Mary Shelley always read and studied, and kept records in her diary.

1816 . . . Byron (6.29): Byron had met Claire Clairmont in London, and she bore his child, Allegra, in 1817. He claimed she had pursued him.

Childe Harold (6.32): Byron's first book, published 1812.

we will each write a ghost story (7.21): the famous scene also referred to in Shelley's Preface.

Tom of Coventry (7.32): The original 'Peeping Tom', who was allegedly struck blind, or dead, as a result of watching Lady Godiva ride naked through Coventry.

Capulets (7.33): Juliet's family in *Romeo and Juliet*.

Sanchean phrase (8.12): a quote from Sancho Panza in Cervantes's *Don Quixote*, which both Mary and Percy were reading in 1816.

Columbus and his egg (8.21): story related by Washington Irving in *Christopher Columbus* (1828), in which the explorer demonstrated how he would find the way to the Indies, by smashing the end of an egg and so making it stand up.

nearly silent listener (8.26): she gives herself a passive role.

Darwin (8.30): Erasmus Darwin, grandfather of Charles Darwin, author of *The Botanic Garden* (1789) and other books on evolution and the growth of plants.

galvanism (8.36): after Luigi Galvini, who first discovered 'animal electricity'.

witching hour (9.3): midnight.

my imagination . . . I saw (9.5): by describing the creation of her novel as given to her in this way Mary absolves all responsibility for it.

unhallowed arts (9.9): against religion.

phantasm (9.10): unreal being.

parquet (9.29): wooden floors where blocks of wood were set in patterns and varnished, then found more commonly on the continent than in England.

It was on . . . (10.4): see also 57.1.

I certainly did not (10.8): she denies that her husband gave her the idea for the story, though she credits him with encouraging her.

hideous progeny (10.14): she compares herself to Frankenstein, and his creation to hers. She compares her novel to a child.

my companion (10.19): Shelley.

I (11.5): P. B. Shelley gives the impression that he is the author, and gives a much more active account of its creation than Mary does.

enervating effects (12.4): novels at the time were commonly accused of weakening the morals or judgement of the reader, but P. B. Shelley claims that *Frankenstein* has high moral standards.

majestic region (12.13): Switzerland, near Geneva, where the Shelleys stayed in the summer of 1816, and where Byron and Polidori were the other story writers.

the only one (12.26): not strictly true, see Polidori's *The Vampyre* (1819).

VOLUME ONE

Focus
This section opens with a series of four letters from Robert Walton to his sister Margaret Saville. What sort of person is he? Why is he going to the North Pole? What do you think his sister feels about his expedition?

The letters introduce some of what will become major themes of the novel. See what you can find about ambition, scientific discovery, and the role of family and home.

Follow-up
What tensions/contrasts do these letters set up? Think about known/unknown; masculine/feminine; heat/cold; natural/unnatural; home/travel.

Walton has rejected an easy life at home for an adventure and a quest for knowledge. Are you sympathetic to his ambitions? Why? Or why not? He alternates between revealing a desire for personal glory and a desire to benefit mankind. Which do you think is stronger?

How does Walton describe the stranger he takes on ship? Can you find any similarities between the two men? What kind of story do you think he has to tell?

If you know Coleridge's poem *The Ancient Mariner*, how many similarities can you find? If you don't know the poem, you might like to check it out, to see how many shared themes you can find.

St Petersburgh (13.2): the city in Russia.
forebodings (13.5): his sister clearly does not approve of his trip.
climes (13.13): region.

pole (13.14): North Pole.

without example (13.23): he doesn't know what to expect because no one has ever been there but he is convinced it will be beautiful and calm.

heavenly bodies (13.24): stars or planets beyond the solar system.

country of eternal light (14.1): description is close to death/heaven.

needle (14.2): magnetic North.

celestial observations (14.3): readings/theories from the stars.

enticements (14.7): this is what encourages me.

passage near the pole (14.14): there were theories that such a passage was possible. It would help trade routes to the North Pacific Ocean.

a steady purpose (14.21): Walton compares his ambition to magnetism.

dying injunction (14.31): deathbed promise.

niche . . . temple (15.1): recognition as a poet.

bent (15.6): ambition.

inuring (15.9): getting used to.

whale-fishers (15.10): whale fishing boats used to leave from Dundee.

under-mate (15.16): sailor.

second dignity (15.18): second in command.

Archangel (16.2): Russian port on the White Sea.

a friend (17.15): Frankenstein of course has a friend, Clerval, who tries to do what Walton wants, but he fails to control Frankenstein.

execution (17.19): action.

keeping (18.7): proportion.

regulate my mind (18.9): help him exercise self-control.

dross (18.12): the useless parts.

rugged bosoms (18.13): rough people.

fosterage (18.27): care.

groundwork (18.27): basic nature.

romantic (18.33): here she uses the term to mean related to love.

inexorable (19.14): unwilling to change his mind.

uneducated (19.17): like Walton himself.

as silent as a Turk (19.17): a contemporary phrase.

the land of mist and snow . . . albatross . . . 'Ancient mariner' (19.35): cf. Coleridge's poem of 1798.

There is something at work in my soul (20.5): he now says he is going on his journey because of the effect of this poem.

the marvellous (20.8): what cannot be explained by reason. Cf. 29.14, where Frankenstein uses the word to draw Walton into his story.

renovating (21.12): refreshing.

testimonies (22.1): written proof.

untamed yet obedient (22.2): he believes there will be no threat, that nature is controllable.

lay to (23.8): stopped moving.

ground sea (24.3): the sea moving under the ice.

savage . . . European (24.15): he contrasts the monster with Frankenstein.

capitulated (24.30): gave up (his search by coming on to the ship).

daemon (25.31): monster.

elemental foes (27.17): weather, coldness, ice.

slave of passion (27.32): being unable to control his emotions.

unfashioned creatures (28.4): incomplete.

I once had a friend (28.7): Henry Clerval.

divine wanderer (28.23): possibly a reference to the myth of the Wandering Jew. See also *Melmoth The Wanderer* by C. R. Maturin (1820). The same story lies behind Wagner's 'The Flying Dutchman'.

immeasurably above any other person (28.29): as if his suffering has made him superior.

memory of these evils (29.4): i.e. his story.

serpent (29.7): snake. Frankenstein fulfilled his ambition and has suffered. He hopes that Walton will not suffer for his.

wild and mysterious regions (29.17): see also the Romantic setting for his tale, the mountains of Switzerland.

internal evidence (29.20): scientific truth.

manuscript (30.3): Mary Shelley's device for being able to re-tell the story.

storm . . . vessel . . . wrecked (30.11): she describes Frankenstein's life as a boat (it is hard not to think forward to the death by drowning of P. B. Shelley in 1822).

CHAPTERS 1–8

Focus

This is the beginning of Frankenstein's story. It is re-told by Walton in letters to his sister, but the narrative voice now passes to Frankenstein. How does he describe his childhood, his parents, his adopted sister, and his education?

Why does he become fascinated by magic and alchemy? What do his father and teachers think about his fascination?

How does he describe his obsession with creating life?

What does he feel when he succeeds?

Follow-up

Think about the themes introduced here: family, education, landscape, imagination, science, love, friendship.

How and why does Mary Shelley introduce the binaries of masculine/feminine; science/art; unnatural/natural?

Which of these are positive and which negative?

I (31.1): this is the start of Frankenstein's story.
Genevese (31.1): native of Geneva.
syndics (31.3): government magistrates.
Lucerne (31.18): the story moves to Switzerland.
a fair exotic (33.6): a delicate plant.
Italy (33.17): Frankenstein travels in Italy as a child much as Mary Shelley's children did.
innocent and helpless (33.25): reference to Rousseau's view of innocent childhood in *Emile* (1762).
guided by a silken cord (33.33): reference to the Greek myth of

Theseus, Ariadne and the Minotaur. Theseus was only able to find his way out of the labyrinth after killing the Minotaur by following the silken cord he had taken in with him to mark the route.

cot (34.8): cottage.

had died on giving her birth (34.27): similar to Mary Wollstonecraft, who died in childbirth.

schiavi ognor frementi (34.32): one of those who fought to free Italy from Austrian rule.

aerial creations of poets (36.8): poetry.

campagne (36.23): a country cottage or house.

Roncesvalles (37.9): reference to the French epic poem the *Song of Roland*.

tyrants . . . agents (37.14): reference to Rousseau's *Emile*.

secrets of heaven and hell (37.24): cf. Goethe's *Faust*.

reflections upon self (38.15): self-blame.

my after tale (38.17): what happened later.

passion (38.18): obsession.

Natural philosophy (38.22): the old term for physics.

Cornelius Agrippa (38.28): magician and philosopher (1486–1535).

Paracelsus and Albertus Magnus (39.13): Paracelsus (1493–1541) was a Swiss alchemist and physician. He thought human beings could be produced without parents through alchemy. Albertus Magnus (1193–1280) was a Dominican theologian who thought magic essential to the pursuit of knowledge. He made a brazen head that could answer questions.

philosopher's stone . . . elixir of life (40.7): alchemists thought one would turn base metal into gold and the other would confer eternal life.

blasted stump (40.31): the tree has been destroyed by lightning. This shows Frankenstein the power of electricity.

Ingolstadt (42.2): a German university.

chaise (44.20): light carriage.

'old familiar faces' (44.28): reference to the Charles Lamb poem 'The Old Familiar Faces', 1798.

chimeras (46.17): fantasies.

panegyric (47.4): praise.

Language Notes and Activities

no supernatural horrors (51.32): Frankenstein is scientific and rational.

I succeeded (52.20): he doesn't tell the reader how exactly but later suggests that he applies a spark of electricity (56).

like the Arabian (52.35): reference to a story in *One Thousand and One Arabian Nights*.

eight feet in height (53.35): thus he explains why he made the creature bigger than a normal man.

No father (54.8): Frankenstein imagines that he will feel like a father, and the creature like a son.

the great object (55.22): his ambition.

It was on a dreary night (57.1): this was the beginning of Mary Shelley's first draft of the story.

Unable to endure . . . (57.26): he is horrified by what he has created, and rejects it.

I thought I saw Elizabeth . . . dead mother (58.5): Frankenstein's terrible dream prefigures Elizabeth's death but also reveals his deep fears and guilt about himself and his relationships with his family.

Dante (58.31): reference to the circles of Hell in *The Inferno* where the guilty are punished forever.

Like one . . . (59.extract): reference to the Ancient Mariner, who feels similarly guilty, and haunted by his crime of shooting the albatross.

The Vicar of Wakefield (60.16): Goldsmith's novel of 1766.

Ernest (64.24): Frankenstein's brother.

Justine Moritz (65.14): similar story to Elizabeth's, i.e. she was an orphan taken in.

Ariosto . . . Angelica (65.35): reference to Ariosto's *Orlando Furioso* 1532.

William (67.2): Frankenstein's second brother.

the palaces of nature (75.15): from Byron's *Childe Harold's Pilgrimage* 1812.

storm (76.11): Here critics have pointed out how Frankenstein would not have been able to see the monster from such a distance, though it is a suitably dramatic scene.

230

my own vampire (77.29): Frankenstein starts to see the creature as part of himself. Polidori's story *The Vampyre* was published in 1819. Stoker's novel *Dracula* was published in 1897.

trial (82.1): see also the trial scene in Godwin's *Caleb Williams* and other Jacobin novels of the day such as Robert Bage's *Hermsprong* (1796), the sub-title of which is 'Man as he is not'.

did not credit it (88.25): he did not believe it.

a hell within (89.3): reference to Milton's Lucifer.

thrice-accursed hands (89.25): perhaps because he has committed three crimes: the creation of the monster, and the murders of William and Justine as a consequence of the first.

unhallowed arts (90.3): unholy, wicked, accursed.

VOLUME TWO

Focus
On the glacier Frankenstein meets the monster and hears his story and his request for a mate. How important is the setting of this scene?

The monster claims that he was created innocent but he describes how circumstances have corrupted him. Do you agree with him?

Think about how he educated himself. What kind of things has he had to learn? What things does the monster consider most important?

Follow-up
Think about the relationship between Frankenstein and the monster. What do they want from each other? What do they get from each other?

Why does the monster kill William and Justine? Who do you think is responsible?

Do you feel sorry for the monster? Or for Frankenstein? Who do you feel most sympathy for?

Language Notes and Activities

Why does Frankenstein agree to make a mate for the monster?

grief (92.7): Mary Shelley may be remembering what her father
   told her when she lost her first baby in 1815.
thoughtlessly bestowed (93.11): i.e. the creative process should be
   taken seriously. Frankenstein did not think about the consequences of his act.
the true murderer (94.19): because he created the monster.
brake (95.3): bushes.
a type (95.4): symbol or emblem.
access (95.8): a sudden outburst.
Omnipotence (95.25): god-like power.
guise (95.28): manner.
aiguilles . . . dôme (96.10): peaks and summit (French).
presence-chamber (97.7): usually a reception room in a palace.
brawling (97.8): noisy.
necessary beings (98.33): cf. Godwin's 'Doctrine of Necessity',
   which said that 'In the life of every human being there is a chain
   of events . . . in consequence of which it was impossible for him
   to act in any instance otherwise than he has acted' (*Political
   Justice*, Book IV, Chapter VIII).
We rest . . . (99.1): the last part of Shelley's *Mutability* (1816).
superhuman speed (99.29): the monster is not only bigger than
   normal, but also moves far faster.
Do your duty towards me (100.20): as a father and as a creator.
glut the maw of death (100.23): commit more murders.
the spark (100.27): refers to the electric spark.
thy Adam (101.8): like a God, Frankenstein has created the monster.
begone (101.13): go away.
I was benevolent (101.18): full of kindness.
Listen to my tale (101.34): like the Ancient Mariner.
author (102.9): creator, cause.
the original era (104.1): the monster discovers all the basic facts of
   life: light, dark, movement, fire, birdsong and so on.
dress my food (106.29): prepare, cook.
Pandaemonium (107.24): Lucifer's great hall in *Paradise Lost*.

wallet (107.32): bag.

grab (109.10); meaning 'garb', clothes, outfit.

godlike science (114.4): speech.

to discover myself (115.27): to reveal myself.

uniform (116.17): the same routine every day.

ass and the lapdog (117.9): story from La Fontaine's 'The Ass and the Lap-dog' in *Fables* IV, 5. When the ass sees his master petting the dog, he tries to behave like the dog but gets beaten instead.

frequent recurrence of some sound (119.27): repetition of words.

herbage (120.22): plants.

Volney's Ruins (121.3): *Les Ruines, ou Méditations sur les révolutions des empires* (1791) by the Comte de Volney.

high and unsullied descent (121.35): noble birth without inter-breeding or 'marrying out'.

a blot (122.11): a dark patch or a disgrace.

grated (124.27): barred.

Mahometan (125.2): Muslim.

noisome (127.11): bad-smelling, unhealthy.

meed (127.33): reward, or consequence.

As yet I looked upon crime (129.4): he was still innocent, good.

leathern portmanteau (129.13): leather case or trunk.

Paradise Lost (129.17): Milton's poem is based on the Bible, *Plutarch's Lives* portrays the heroes of the ancient world, and the sentimental hero of Goethe's the *Sorrows of Young Werther* (1772) commits suicide. The idea is that these three books teach the basics of society.

The path . . . free (130.18): from Shelley's *Mutability*.

as a true history (131.12): as the truth.

your journal (131.30): he refers to the document that forms pp. 31–103 of this book.

solitary (132.9): alone, isolated.

an outcast in the world forever (135.12): rejected, friendless.

undeceive (135.25): explain the truth.

Why did I live? (137.1): why was I alive?

arch-fiend (137.15): Lucifer in *Paradise Lost*. He goes on to declare war on Frankenstein as Lucifer does on God.

my father (140.16): he feels bonded like a son to his father, and so goes to find him. He also criticises Frankenstein's irresponsible fathering.

revenge (142.27): reference to Lucifer. From this point the novel becomes a revenge tragedy.

a beautiful child (143.8): William.

the fiend within me (144.28): he has been corrupted by the way people have treated him.

requisition (145.4): the monster's request to have a mate.

I am malicious because I am miserable (146.20): this was Godwin's explanation for wrongdoing; not original sin but the effects of society.

ice-rifts (146.25): fissures in the glacier.

my arch-enemy (147.5): my worst enemy.

feint (148.34): a pretence.

siroc (150.18): sirocco. A strong, hot wind that blows from North Africa to parts of southern Europe.

VOLUME THREE

Focus
The narrative now returns to Frankenstein, who has promised to make the monster a mate. Why does he start to do this but then changes his mind? And what are the consequences?

As you read this volume think about how the author balances the viewpoints of Frankenstein and the monster. They are becoming increasingly like each other. How many similarities can you find?

Follow-up
Compare Frankenstein's trial with Justine's. Does this change your view about justice and right and wrong in the novel?

Why does Frankenstein call the monster his shadow? Think about how Frankenstein and the monster begin to merge roles.

Why is the end of the novel set at the North Pole? How does this add to the tension?

What effect is created when the narrative returns to Robert Walton? Do you think his viewpoint changes anything?

enjoined me (151.4): which I had promised to do.

disquisition (151.6): investigation, research.

horror and dismay (153.10): he implies that this is not just because of the task ahead of him. He is unable to desire any normal human relationships.

engagement (153.15): promise.

machinations (155.9): planning, plotting.

bourne (155.25): end.

picturesque (156.11): a favourite term in the eighteenth century and often contrasted by the Romantics with the grand scenery they preferred. Clerval prefers the picturesque and Frankenstein the grand.

vintage (156.21): grape harvest.

the priest and his mistress (157.2): one of the local legends.

'very poetry of nature' (157.18): quotation from Leigh Hunt's 'The Story of Rimini' (1813).

'The sounding cataract . . .' (157.26): from Wordsworth's 'Tintern Abbey' (1798).

the image of . . . (159.21): here Mary Shelley makes more explicit the fact that Henry Clerval and Frankenstein are also doubles, as well as the monster and Frankenstein. The *doppelgänger* was a popular Romantic metaphor. Stevenson's *Dr Jekyll and Mr Hyde* (1886) is perhaps the most famous example. Wilde's *Picture of Dorian Gray* (1890) is another, later example.

colonisation (160.1): the empire.

Falkland (161.5): Lucius Cary, second Viscount Falkland (1610?–43). The character Falkland in Godwin's novel *Caleb Williams* (1794) is partly based on him.

Goring (161.6): Lord George Goring (1608–57).

Isis (161.13): name of the Thames in Oxford.

ennui (161.20): boredom.

blasted tree (161.23): dead tree hit by lightning.

Hampden (161.33): John Hampden (1594–1643); one of the leaders of the Parliamentary opposition to Charles I.

cave (162.9): possibly High Tor Grotto near Matlock.

cheat me (162.21): help me forget my misery.

on the stretch (162.29): the traveller can never relax.

superscription (163.9): handwriting.

as his shadow (163.13): see the note on 159.21. It is as if Clerval were part of himself, his double.

mortal (163.17): bringing the death penalty.

Orkneys (164.13): islands off the north coast of Scotland. From the description Mary Shelley gives it seems unlikely she ever visited them.

laboratory (165.9): given the previous description of the run-down cottage, the word laboratory sounds odd. Nor does he explain where he gets all the bits and pieces from that he had needed in Ingolstadt to create the monster.

she had not (166.14): Frankenstein is assuming that a female monster will be equally free-thinking, and may well refuse to obey her mate.

sophisms (167.3): deceiving persuasion.

pest (167.7): curse or plague.

casement (167.10): window.

Slave (168.20): their roles have been reversed. The monster considers himself the master.

snake (169.7): reminder of how Lucifer hid himself in the garden of Eden.

inexorable (169.11): unpersuadable, determined.

wedding-night (169.13): critics have noted the sexual undertones . . .

with precipitation (169.17): quickly.

I almost felt as if (171.8): Frankenstein is almost becoming the monster.

skiff (171.31): small boat.

dress (173.10): clothes.

Irish (174.4): possible destination but a long way from Orkney, and he had left Clerval in Perth.

deposed (175.7): stated, explained.

my murderous machinations (177.13): Frankenstein and the monster become closer: he dreams he is both murderer and victim.

turnkeys (178.1): prison guards.

livid like those in death (179.14): possibly a reference to the figure of death in *The Ancient Mariner*.

borne down (179.29): struck down.

destiny (182.5): fate.

assizes (182.13): sessions held periodically for the purpose of administering justice.

maladie du pays (183.6): homesickness (French).

Image (183.20): created form or shape; here meaning also symbol.

Havre-de-Grâce (183.28): the original name for Le Havre.

laudanum (184.10): alcoholic tincture of opium; common medicine at the time used for pain relief and as a sleeping pill. Its overuse caused visions.

another (187.35): someone else.

consummate (188.34): to conclude, to bring to a conclusion. Here in the context of the wedding night it has a sexual undertone.

apple was already eaten (189.11): cf. Adam and Eve in *Paradise Lost*.

I would die to make her happy (189.12): the irony is that he is wrong.

this tale (189.34): again, emphasis on narrative and the telling of the truth.

nicer (191.23): more careful, more discriminative.

decorations (191.32): scenery on stage.

artifice (192.6): trickery.

this night . . . dreadful (194.24): he means that after the night all will be well, but the night itself, their wedding night, will be dreadful.

expire (195.14): die.

bridal bier (195.19): a bier is where a corpse is laid out before burial. The usual phrase would be 'bridal bed'.

grin (196.6): draws a parallel with the monster looking through the window in Orkney when Frankenstein destroyed the female monster.

acme (197.25): culmination or highest point.

revenge (198.15): now Frankenstein declares revenge on the monster and pursues him: their roles are reversed.

The magistrate (198.28): the magistrate is the first person to hear Frankenstein's story. He points out that such a monster will not be easy to catch. Frankenstein accepts that he alone will have to find him.

wanderings (201.11): see note to 28.23.

shades (202.8): ghosts, spirits.

Scoffing (204.28): mocking.

The Greeks (205.16): Xenophon (431–*c.* 350 BC) records this in the *Anabasis* when he describes leading the Greek soldiers out of Asia in 400 BC.

inequalities (206.15): rough ground.

ground sea (206.22): sea under the ice.

manes (208.17): spirits of the dead.

asseverations (209.4): assertions.

particulars (209.7): details.

mutilated (209.17): inaccurate.

noble and godlike (210.4): see Milton's Lucifer.

projectors (210.15): schemers, people with plans.

archangel (210.18): see Milton's Lucifer.

encompassed (211.24): surrounded.

The die is cast (214.18): the decision has been made.

mummy (217.15): Egyptian mummy.

consummated (217.27): this is the last, and worst, of my crimes.

self-devoted (217.28): meaning he was devoted to the needs of others.

Evil thenceforth (218.32): cf. Milton, *Paradise Lost*, 4,l.110, 'Evil be thou my Good.'

that I wished to be participated (219.18): that in which I wished to share.

crime (219.28): murder.

contumely (220.9): abuse.

funeral pile (220.31): he plans to burn himself to death. It may be a parody of Walton's dream of finding a tropical paradise at the pole.

Further Activities and Study Questions

How far do you think Frankenstein is a Romantic hero?

Do you think *Frankenstein* is a purely Gothic novel?

How important is it to understand the literary references?

Think about how Mary Shelley uses intertextuality with reference to either *Paradise Lost* or *The Ancient Mariner*.

Discuss the structure of the novel. How would you draw it in a diagram?

Is there a hero? If so, who is it?

The author was a woman, yet none of the main characters is female. Do you think it is a feminist novel?

It has been claimed that *Frankenstein* was the first science fiction novel. Do you agree?

Who do you feel most sympathy for in the novel? Frankenstein or the monster?

Character Notes

Victor Frankenstein

Robert Walton believes that Frankenstein is a 'glorious spirit' and describes the benevolence and sweetness in his face. Yet the story Frankenstein tells reveals him as driven by ambition. He cuts himself off from his loving family and friends in order to pursue his obsessions. He knows that this is wrong but he cannot stop himself. When the monster comes alive he is not prepared to be responsible for it. When Justine dies he keeps quiet although he knows she is innocent. He feels sorry enough to try to make a mate for the monster, but then changes his mind. He assumes it will be him that the monster kills, and so fails to protect Elizabeth.

Is he a Romantic hero? He certainly suffers, but so does everyone else. Like the monster he too is alienated from the pleasures of normal life, but in his case it is a kind of rebellion against all normal ties to responsibility. Mary Shelley calls him the New Prometheus, the seeker after knowledge, but it is not clear whether his sin is to try to usurp God by creating life, or to refuse to take any responsibility for what he creates.

The Monster

The monster is described as a new Adam or a Noble Savage. Created benevolent, innocent and free from prejudice, he represents the possibility of a new start. His education describes how he moves from nature to culture, and from innocence to experience; and how he learns about society and his role in it. He wants love but he is rejected because he is different. When the De Lacey family reject him we sympathise with him. It is only after he murders William that we start to waver, and see him as Satan rather than Adam.

He is very eloquent. Having read the right kind of books the monster is able to persuade Frankenstein to create a mate for him. At the same time he is Frankenstein's double, killing off those whom Frankenstein has already rejected in his search for the secret of life. The monster represents Frankenstein's own aggressive instincts, his fears of family, women, and sexuality.

Robert Walton

Walton is another double for Frankenstein. He rebels against his father and goes to sea, much as Frankenstein rebels against his father's dismissal of his scientific interests. Each son pursues the forbidden. Like Frankenstein, Walton is obsessed with his quest. He knows his sister disapproves but he keeps trying to convince her. He too alternates between a selfish explanation and a more altruistic one.

But there are differences. Walton is not so alienated. He longs for an intimate friend. And unlike Frankenstein he depends on his sailors, rather than working alone. When they insist on returning home, he is forced to fulfil his responsibilities towards them, whereas Frankenstein never does this.

Alphonse and Caroline Frankenstein

Caroline Frankenstein serves to establish an ideal of femininity. She is a passive dependent, and later dies saving Elizabeth. Alphonse Frankenstein becomes a husband and father late in life and then retires from the world, thus emphasising the dichotomy between private and public life in the novel. As parents they perhaps do not allow Frankenstein enough independence as a child. Only when he leaves home can he act as an individual, and he cannot prevent himself from taking this to extremes.

Elizabeth Lavenza

Elizabeth is initially noticed because of her beauty and this remains important. In the original 1818 text she is Frankenstein's cousin, but in 1831 she becomes an adopted sister, which loosens the blood tie. Her role is as an ideal, spiritual figure, set apart rather like the monster. She is treated as a possession by Frankenstein, and yet he loses her. In character she is the complete opposite of Frankenstein, and while important in the home, she is totally ineffectual in the outside world, failing to save Justine, for example.

Justine

The servant Justine is also adopted by the family. Like Elizabeth she is impossibly good and helpless when it comes to saving herself. Her role in the novel is to be the monster's second victim, and her death prefigures Elizabeth's.

Safie and the De Laceys

A different kind of femininity is found in Safie. She has plenty of initiative and is independent in spirit. Although the De Laceys are moral, honest people, from their story we see that they cannot fight against more unscrupulous characters. On the other hand, however good they are, they reject the monster out of hand. They are the only people he loves.

Henry Clerval

Henry Clerval is a balanced character, and a loyal friend to Frankenstein. He likes literature and languages, and prefers softer landscapes than Frankenstein does – the picturesque rather than the sublime and grand. He brings out the best in Frankenstein but even so he is unable to save him.

Text Summary

VOLUME ONE

Frankenstein is an account of the life of Victor Frankenstein, as
related by him to the British sailor, Robert Walton, who in turn
re-tells the story in a series of letters to his sister at home. Walton
is on an expedition to the North Pole. From the ship the sailors see
a giant racing over the ice on a sledge, and chasing after him is
Frankenstein. They bring him on board and he tells his story.

Frankenstein describes his childhood, his parents, and Elizabeth,
his adopted 'more than sister'. He also describes his friend Henry
Clerval, who however does not share his passion for science.
Frankenstein goes to university in Ingolstadt, where he becomes
increasingly isolated from his family and friends. He becomes
obsessed with trying to discover the secret of the life force. One
November evening he finally succeeds in bringing to life a body
made from dead tissue.

As soon as he sees the body come alive he is horrified and rushes
out of the house. When he comes back, the monster has gone
and he is relieved. Clerval notices that Frankenstein is behaving
strangely but believes him when he says it is because he has been
studying too hard. Frankenstein then falls ill.

When he recovers a letter comes from his father to tell him that
his little brother William has been murdered, and that their servant
Justine has been arrested. Frankenstein rushes home full of fore-
boding. On the way he glimpses the monster, and feels that it must
be connected to the tragedy. He realises what must have happened,
but says nothing and Justine is found guilty and is executed.

VOLUME TWO

The family is distraught and Frankenstein is tormented by guilt. He goes climbing in the Alps to try to find some peace but he meets the monster, who insists on telling him his story. The monster explains how, despite his ugly appearance, he was not originally evil in intention. He claims that Frankenstein has made him evil because he rejected him, as has everyone else who has seen him. He explains how he learnt about the facts of life, first the basics of fire and food by experience, and then later about language and politics, by living in a hovel adjoining the cottage of the De Lacey family and overhearing them. He becomes well educated and benevolent, but at the same time discovers that he is lonely and different from everyone else. Although he loves the De Lacey family they are terrified when they see him.

So he has decided there is no justice in life, and he blames Frankenstein for creating him and then abandoning him. He has sworn vengeance on him, and he killed William because he was related. He also planted the evidence on Justine, because she represented the life from which he was excluded. He now demands that Frankenstein create a mate for him, and promises to emigrate to South America with her and live peacefully.

VOLUME THREE

Reluctantly Frankenstein agrees. He decides to delay his marriage to Elizabeth until after he has fulfilled his promise, but he can't do it at home. He travels to Scotland with Clerval, where he leaves his friend in Perth and goes to the Orkneys. When the female monster is almost complete, Frankenstein changes his mind, and destroys his work. In return the monster promises to be with him on his wedding night.

Frankenstein sets off in a small boat, but is blown off course to Ireland. There he is arrested for the murder of Clerval, whose body has just been found. After spending some time ill and in prison,

Frankenstein is released and his father takes him home. He marries Elizabeth and the monster murders her on their wedding night. Frankenstein swears to pursue and destroy him, and follows him as far as the Arctic, where he is picked up by Walton.

Walton concludes the story by describing Frankenstein's death. The monster then re-appears to express his sorrow at what he has done, and disappears over the ice to die.

Critical Responses

Frankenstein is Mary Shelley's most famous work. Few people bother to read her other, later fiction, her travel writing or the biographical essays, or consult her edition of Shelley's poems (1839). However, although *Frankenstein* was immediately successful, it was not considered worthy of serious academic and critical attention until the 1970s.

Today Mary Shelley is ranked among the best, most talented writers of her generation, and *Frankenstein* can be approached fruitfully from a multitude of different interpretative angles inspired by the reading practices of critical schools as different as feminism, psychoanalysis, Marxism, cultural criticism, even post-colonialism. There seem to be no limits. Why is this?

Berthold Schoene-Harwood suggests that the enduring appeal of *Frankenstein* is 'its textual "monstrosity"'.[1] The novel succeeds in including 'a range of apparently irreconcilable opposites, for example, old and new, life and death, masculinity and femininity, horror and enthusiasm, and fantasy and real life'.[2] Mary Shelley herself presents her own ambiguity when she talks about her 'hideous progeny'. We know that her personal experience may have caused this ambiguity: her first baby was born prematurely and died, and she always felt guilty about causing her own mother's death. But she is also talking as a writer, and about the responsibility of the writer.

Contemporary reviews focused on this issue of responsibility. Early critics fell into two camps: those that felt moral outrage and disapproval, and those that were intrigued and admiring. The political situation is important because Britain was going through a time of the Luddite riots and the introduction of cautious reform. There was suspicion of the more radical views of the eighteenth century that had brought about the French Revolution, and both Mary's parents, Godwin and Wollstonecraft, were considered dangerously radical. Her husband, Percy, was also considered atheistical and politically radical, and some of the contemporary criticism was undoubtedly caused by the fact that the novel was dedicated to Godwin, and written, many assumed, by P. B. Shelley.

The more conservative critics were even more shocked when they realised that a teenage girl was the author. These early reviews analysed the morality of the book. And as Schoene-Harwood points out, well into the twentieth century critics have found fault with *Frankenstein*. They disliked either the theme or the style, and most of them blamed the shortcomings of the book on the sex of the author.

The early critics found it impossible to consider Mary Shelley except in comparison with her husband. In 1970 Sylvia Norman was still comparing Mary's creative imagination to her husband's and finding it clichéd and unsophisticated: 'She lacked the inner life.'[3] Even in 1988 Muriel Spark tried to argue that the great achievement of *Frankenstein* was due to the author's naivety and total lack of experience.

The current academic reappraisal of Mary Shelley's literary achievement was set in motion by the publication of *The Endurance of Frankenstein*, a collection of essays edited by George Levine and U. C. Knoepflmacher in 1979. The aim of this volume was to re-introduce *Frankenstein* to its readers as 'the most important minor novel in English'.[4] This book has inspired a wide spectrum of critical works that share a common interest in re-reading. In fact it sometimes seems as if Mary Shelley's novel has become an obsession with critics and theorists. So why is it such a popular text, and what do the different theories add to our understanding of *Frankenstein*?

FEMINISM

The re-discovery of Mary Shelley was part of the late 1970s re-discovery of many forgotten women writers and particularly of the Female Gothic. As a result for the first time she was valued in her own right; and there are now many more books and biographies on Mary Shelley than on her husband. *Frankenstein* is firmly part of the feminist canon. It has also been called the missing link between the novels of the eighteenth and nineteenth centuries, because it combines Gothic elements with realism.

This re-discovery began with Ellen Moers's book *Literary Women* in 1977, and in particular her chapter on 'Female Gothic' (which was later reprinted in *The Endurance of Frankenstein*[5]). For Moers the fact that Mary Shelley was a woman is the key thing, for '*Frankenstein* is a birth myth.' Mary Jacobus in the early 1980s counters this because she felt it limited the book's power; to see *Frankenstein* as a birth myth 'may tell us about women's lives, but it reduces the text itself to a monstrous symptom'.[6]

The second most important reading is the chapter in Gilbert and Gubar's *The Madwoman in the Attic*.[7] They read *Frankenstein* as a daughterly, that is both obedient and mutinous, rewrite of *Paradise Lost*, with Frankenstein as Eve. Another classic feminist view is that of Barbara Johnson in her essay 'My Monster/My Self.'[8] She points out that although all the main characters are male, everyone suffers under patriarchy.

Burton Hatlen argued in 1983 that Mary Shelley was strongly influenced by the radical egalitarianism of the French Revolution as reflected in her parents' work, as well as that of her fellow Romantics. But whereas the male Romantics identify with Milton's Satan, Mary Shelley gives this a feminist perspective: 'Like Percy Shelley in *Prometheus Unbound*, Mary Shelley has set out to rewrite *Paradise Lost* – not as a tragedy but rather as a nightmare, perhaps even as a farce.'[9]

Bette London in 1993 saw *Frankenstein* as a novel about 'man-making', but it is also 'the autobiography of a woman'.[10] Her feminist perspective foregrounds what Schoene-Harwood summarises as the 'masculine quandary that leaves the individual male divided between an impossible ideal and its inevitably self-annihilative realisations'.[11]

PSYCHOANALYSIS

In Mary Shelley's 1831 Introduction she denies all responsibility for the novel, saying that it came from 'far beyond the usual bounds of reverie' (9.7). And this is still the key question for criticism: did Mary Shelley know what she was doing? Or is the book an outpouring from her subconscious? Jungian interpretations of the novel have dwelt on the dreams, and the enduring power of *Frankenstein* itself is seen as evidence of the power of Archetypes over us all, whereas Freudian critics have examined the image of the blasted tree, and the effects of the death of Frankenstein's mother. It has been suggested that he tries to re-create his mother by creating the monster, and the fact that he is revolted by the act reveals that he knew he was committing a crime: 'the filth is also the maternal presence he is assembling from phantasmal body parts and buried wishes'.[12] When the monster comes to life he is unable to act as a father to it, just as he is unable to be a good son. He is terrified of sexuality too: thoughts of marriage fill him with horror, and of course he tries to reproduce without using a woman, a highly unnatural act.

Many critics have explored the psychoanalytic possibilities of *Frankenstein*. The danger, as Fred Botting points out,[13] is that these possibilities are almost infinite, and they move further and further away from the text. The most helpful critics try to answer the key questions in the historical context. For example, Devon Hodges explains that the unusual narrative form and disturbing imagery of *Frankenstein* must be seen as 'illustrations of the woman writer's dream to explode the patriarchal order from within by experimenting with hitherto unemployed, new techniques and devices of female representation.'[14]

INTERTEXTUALITY

The novel repeatedly draws attention to its own intertextuality. The sub-title is 'The New Prometheus', it is dedicated to Godwin, it is full of literary references, and we are given the details of the monster's own reading programme: *Paradise Lost, Plutarch's Lives* and the *Sorrows Of Young Werther*. These fall into three main groups of texts: those by Mary Shelley's parents that she read and re-read (Elisabeth Bronfen, for example, shows 'how the Shelleys – both husband and wife – were locked in a prolific, yet problematically incestuous intertextual relationship with the Godwins'[15]); those by her husband that they discussed together; and those on her extensive reading programme that she recorded in her diaries and letters. She also drew on her husband's teenage reading of Paracelsus and Albertus Magnus. Mary Poovey therefore sees Mary Shelley as a woman writing under enormous patriarchal pressure.[16] But all the time she was re-evaluating, re-reading and re-writing what she read.

James O'Rourke[17] interprets *Frankenstein* specifically as a critique of William Godwin and P. B. Shelley, but Mary Shelley was also extremely critical of Rousseau, for example, because he did not practise what he preached: his own children were abandoned in orphanages. In fact paternal neglect is a major theme in the novel. She is equally questioning of her two main texts: *Paradise Lost* and *Prometheus Bound*.

Theodore Ziolkowski suggests that it was Mary Shelley's questioning of these two representational myths, and her 'inability to reconcile the conflict inherent in her two sources', that was her strength.[18] It was her almost scientific approach to these key texts that made *Frankenstein* such a modern novel.

MARXISM

Fred Botting has pointed out that 'in times of crisis images of monstrosity remind people of the precarious instability and ultimately unmanageable diversity of the society in which they live'.[19]

It was no coincidence that the Gothic novel became popular at the time of the French Revolution. While sharing many of the characteristics of the Gothic novels, however, *Frankenstein* was written after the Reign of Terror. It was, therefore, a more serious analysis of the issues of revolutionary fervour and social freedom.

In the character of Victor Frankenstein we can see parallels with the political views of both Godwin and P. B. Shelley. Paul O'Flinn has pointed out that it was written at the time of the second wave of the Luddite riots, and has to be seen in the context of deep changes in the nature of British society.[20] Both Byron and P. B. Shelley had responded publicly and politically to the Luddite crisis. Mary Shelley shared their radicalism, but although she dedicated her novel to Godwin, the text shows that she feared the effects of both anarchy and oppression. The main political message repeated through the novel is that 'for people together, problems can be solved: for the man alone, they can overwhelm him'.[21]

The monster, who has worked for the De Lacey family, turns on them when they reject him, and burns their house down. For Victorians like Elizabeth Gaskell, 'The actions of the uneducated seem to me typified in those of Frankenstein, that monster of many human qualities, ungifted with a soul, a knowledge of the difference between good and evil'.[22] Interestingly, Mrs Gaskell also confuses the creator with the monster, and does not realise that the monster knows good from evil. As Paul O'Flinn observes, she has absorbed the 'dominant political reading of the text, the sense that the middle classes are threatened by a monster of their own making'.[23] The Frankenstein metaphor can be, and has been, applied to any period of political scare.

POST-COLONIALISM

Gayatri Chakravorty Spivak has shown that post-colonial re-readings are also possible. She points out that Walton is exploring new routes to the Pole. Clerval wants to learn Indian languages so that he can work for the British Empire. The Arab/Turkish Safie cannot live safely in Turkey. On a deeper level the monster is a kind of Caliban, a natural savage, who is corrupted by his experience in society as an outsider. Although the novel is ostensibly about the origin and evolution of man in society, it describes a peculiarly English cultural identity. Spivak reads *Wide Sargasso Sea* as *Jane Eyre*'s reinscription and *Frankenstein* as an analysis – even a deconstruction – of a 'worlding' such as *Jane Eyre*'s.[24] She also notes, with satisfaction, that the monster disappears into the darkness at the end of the novel. The post-colonial subject is not defeated by the text. This area of study is growing and bringing new insights.

CONCLUSION

Mary Shelley urged her novel to go forth and multiply, and it shows no sign of stopping doing just that. There is already a multitude of re-writings, cultural, social, cinematic, feminist, Marxist, post-colonial, and no doubt there will be many more. The myth of *Frankenstein* continues to reverberate with meanings because each generation finds in it echoes of its own fears.

Notes

1. *Mary Shelley, Frankenstein, A readers' guide to essential criticism*, ed. Berthold Schoene-Harwood (Cambridge, Icon, 2000).
2. Ibid., p. 8.
3. Sylvia Norman in Schoene-Harwood (ed.), *op. cit.*, p. 27.
4. George Levine and U. C. Knoepflmacher, in Schoene-Harwood (ed.), *op. cit.*, p. 28.
5. *The Endurance of Frankenstein*, eds. Levine and Knoepflmacher (Berkeley, University of California Press, 1979), pp. 77–87.
6. Mary Jacobs in Schoene-Harwood (ed.), *op. cit.*, p. 89.
7. *The Madwoman in the Attic*, Sandra M. Gilbert and Susan Gubar (New Haven, Yale University Press, 1979).

8. *Mary Shelley's Frankenstein*, Harold Bloom (New York and Philadelphia, Chelsea House, 1987), pp. 55–66.

9. Burton Hatlen in Schoene-Harwood (ed.), *op. cit.*, p. 110.

10. Bette London in Schoene-Harwood (ed.), *op. cit.*, p. 122.

11. Bette London and Colleen Hobbs in Schoene-Harwood (ed.), *op. cit.*, p. 130.

12. Paul Sherwin in Schoene-Harwood (ed.), *op. cit.*, p. 68.

13. *Frankenstein and Mary Shelley, New Casebooks*, ed. Fred Botting (London, Macmillan, 1995).

14. Devon Hodges in Schoene-Harwood (ed.), *op. cit.*, p. 86.

15. Elisabeth Bronfen in Schoene-Harwood (ed.), *op. cit.*, p. 31.

16. Mary Poovey in Schoene-Harwood (ed.), *op. cit.*, p. 39.

17. James O'Rourke in Schoene-Harwood (ed.), *op. cit.*, p. 48.

18. Theodore Ziolkowski in Schoene-Harwood (ed.), *op. cit.*, p. 63.

19. Fred Botting (ed.), *op. cit.*, p. 131.

20. Paul O'Flinn in 'Production and Reproduction: The case of *Frankenstein*', reprinted in *Frankenstein and Mary Shelley, New Casebooks*, ed. Fred Botting (London, Macmillan, 1995), pp. 21–47.

21. Fred Botting, *op. cit.*, p. 28.

22. *Op. cit.*, p. 30.

23. *Op. cit.*, p. 31.

24. *Op. cit.*, p. 236.

Suggestions for Further Reading

If you want to read more on *Frankenstein*

Fred Botting (ed.), *Frankenstein and Mary Shelley, New Casebooks* (London, Macmillan, 1995). A selection of essays on all the key readings.

Maurice Hindle, *Mary Shelley, Frankenstein* (London, Penguin, 1994). A useful volume in the series of Penguin Critical Studies, which analyses the text in detail.

Berthold Schoene-Harwood (ed.), *Mary Shelley, Frankenstein, A reader's guide to essential criticism* (Cambridge, Icon, 2000). A useful summary of key critical works with quotations.

If you want to read more about Mary Shelley's other books

E. J. Clery, *Writers and Their Work, Women's Gothic From Clara Reeve to Mary Shelley* (Tavistock, Northcote House, 2000). An interesting book that puts Mary Shelley into the context of other contemporary women writing Gothic fiction.

Jane Blumberg, *Mary Shelley's Early Novels* (London, Macmillan, 1993). A study of *Frankenstein*, *Valperga*, *Matilda* and *The Last Man*.

Anne K. Mellor, *Mary Shelley, Her Life, Her Fiction, Her Monsters* (London, Routledge, 1988). A detailed study of Mary Shelley's life and work.

Two biographies

Miranda Seymour, *Mary Shelley* (London, John Murray, 2000). The most recent biography.
Richard Holmes, *Shelley: The Pursuit* (London, Weidenfeld & Nicolson, 1974). A wonderfully readable biography of P. B. Shelley.

List of Films

There have been numerous films inspired by *Frankenstein*. Here are some of the most well known. For more information try the web site *http://meinseite.i-one.at/frankenstein/frankenstein-start.htm*

1930s (Universal Studies)

Frankenstein
Bride of Frankenstein
Son of Frankenstein

1950s–1970s (Hammer Studios)

Curse of Frankenstein
Revenge of Frankenstein
The Evil of Frankenstein
Frankenstein Created Woman
Frankenstein Must Be Destroyed
Frankenstein and the Monster From Hell

1970s–1990s

Young Frankenstein
The Rocky Horror Picture Show
Frankenstein Unbound

Mary Shelley's Frankenstein
Blade Runner
Robocop
Re-Animator
Star Trek: Next Generation
The 6th Day

Audio Extracts 🎧

Total = approx. 74 minutes

READ MORE IN PENGUIN

In every corner of the world, on every subject under the sun, Penguin represents quality and variety – the very best in publishing today.

For complete information about books available from Penguin – including Puffins, Penguin Classics and Arkana – and how to order them, write to us at the appropriate address below. Please note that for copyright reasons the selection of books varies from country to country.

In the United Kingdom: Please write to *Dept. EP, Penguin Books Ltd, Bath Road, Harmondsworth, West Drayton, Middlesex UB7 0DA*

In the United States: Please write to *Consumer Services, Penguin Putnam Inc., 405 Murray Hill Parkway, East Rutherford, New Jersey 07073-2136*. VISA and MasterCard holders call 1-800-631-8571 to order Penguin titles

In Canada: Please write to *Penguin Books Canada Ltd, 10 Alcorn Avenue, Suite 300, Toronto, Ontario M4V 3B2*

In Australia: Please write to *Penguin Books Australia Ltd, 487 Maroondah Highway, Ringwood, Victoria 3134*

In New Zealand: Please write to *Penguin Books (NZ) Ltd, Private Bag 102902, North Shore Mail Centre, Auckland 10*

In India: Please write to *Penguin Books India Pvt Ltd, 11 Community Centre, Panchsheel Park, New Delhi 110017*

In the Netherlands: Please write to *Penguin Books Netherlands bv, Postbus 3507, NL-1001 AH Amsterdam*

In Germany: Please write to *Penguin Books Deutschland GmbH, Metzlerstrasse 26, 60594 Frankfurt am Main*

In Spain: Please write to *Penguin Books S. A., Bravo Murillo 19, 1°B, 28015 Madrid*

In Italy: Please write to *Penguin Italia s.r.l., Via Vittorio Emanuele 45/a, 20094 Corsico, Milano*

In France: Please write to *Penguin France, 12, Rue Prosper Ferradou, 31700 Blagnac*

In Japan: Please write to *Penguin Books Japan Ltd, Iidabashi KM-Bldg, 2-23-9 Koraku, Bunkyo-Ku, Tokyo 112-0004*

In South Africa: Please write to *Penguin Books South Africa (Pty) Ltd, P.O. Box 751093, Gardenview, 2047 Johannesburg*

READ MORE IN PENGUIN

A CHOICE OF CLASSICS

Matthew Arnold	**Selected Prose**
Jane Austen	**Emma**
	Lady Susan/The Watsons/Sanditon
	Mansfield Park
	Northanger Abbey
	Persuasion
	Pride and Prejudice
	Sense and Sensibility
William Barnes	**Selected Poems**
Mary Braddon	**Lady Audley's Secret**
Anne Brontë	**Agnes Grey**
	The Tenant of Wildfell Hall
Charlotte Brontë	**Jane Eyre**
	Juvenilia: 1829–35
	The Professor
	Shirley
	Villette
Emily Brontë	**Complete Poems**
	Wuthering Heights
Samuel Butler	**Erewhon**
	The Way of All Flesh
Lord Byron	**Don Juan**
	Selected Poems
Lewis Carroll	**Alice's Adventures in Wonderland**
	The Hunting of the Snark
Thomas Carlyle	**Selected Writings**
Arthur Hugh Clough	**Selected Poems**
Wilkie Collins	**Armadale**
	The Law and the Lady
	The Moonstone
	No Name
	The Woman in White
Charles Darwin	**The Origin of Species**
	Voyage of the Beagle
Benjamin Disraeli	**Coningsby**
	Sybil

READ MORE IN PENGUIN

A CHOICE OF CLASSICS

Charles Dickens	**American Notes for General Circulation**
	Barnaby Rudge
	Bleak House
	The Christmas Books (in two volumes)
	David Copperfield
	Dombey and Son
	Great Expectations
	Hard Times
	Little Dorrit
	Martin Chuzzlewit
	The Mystery of Edwin Drood
	Nicholas Nickleby
	The Old Curiosity Shop
	Oliver Twist
	Our Mutual Friend
	The Pickwick Papers
	Pictures from Italy
	Selected Journalism 1850–1870
	Selected Short Fiction
	Sketches by Boz
	A Tale of Two Cities
George Eliot	**Adam Bede**
	Daniel Deronda
	Felix Holt
	Middlemarch
	The Mill on the Floss
	Romola
	Scenes of Clerical Life
	Silas Marner
Fanny Fern	**Ruth Hall**
Elizabeth Gaskell	**Cranford/Cousin Phillis**
	The Life of Charlotte Brontë
	Mary Barton
	North and South
	Ruth
	Sylvia's Lovers
	Wives and Daughters

READ MORE IN PENGUIN

A CHOICE OF CLASSICS

Edward Gibbon	**The Decline and Fall of the Roman Empire** (in three volumes)
	Memoirs of My Life
George Gissing	**New Grub Street**
	The Odd Women
William Godwin	**Caleb Williams**
	Concerning Political Justice
Thomas Hardy	**Desperate Remedies**
	The Distracted Preacher and Other Tales
	Far from the Madding Crowd
	Jude the Obscure
	The Hand of Ethelberta
	A Laodicean
	The Mayor of Casterbridge
	A Pair of Blue Eyes
	The Return of the Native
	Selected Poems
	Tess of the d'Urbervilles
	The Trumpet-Major
	Two on a Tower
	Under the Greenwood Tree
	The Well-Beloved
	The Woodlanders
George Lyell	**Principles of Geology**
Lord Macaulay	**The History of England**
Henry Mayhew	**London Labour and the London Poor**
George Meredith	**The Egoist**
	The Ordeal of Richard Feverel
John Stuart Mill	**The Autobiography**
	On Liberty
	Principles of Political Economy
William Morris	**News from Nowhere and Other Writings**
John Henry Newman	**Apologia Pro Vita Sua**
Margaret Oliphant	**Miss Marjoribanks**
Robert Owen	**A New View of Society and Other Writings**
Walter Pater	**Marius the Epicurean**
John Ruskin	**Unto This Last and Other Writings**

READ MORE IN PENGUIN

A CHOICE OF CLASSICS

Walter Scott	**The Antiquary**
	Heart of Mid-Lothian
	Ivanhoe
	Kenilworth
	The Tale of Old Mortality
	Rob Roy
	Waverley
Robert Louis Stevenson	**Kidnapped**
	Dr Jekyll and Mr Hyde and Other Stories
	In the South Seas
	The Master of Ballantrae
	Selected Poems
	Weir of Hermiston
William Makepeace Thackeray	**The History of Henry Esmond**
	The History of Pendennis
	The Newcomes
	Vanity Fair
Anthony Trollope	**Barchester Towers**
	Can You Forgive Her?
	Doctor Thorne
	The Eustace Diamonds
	Framley Parsonage
	He Knew He Was Right
	The Last Chronicle of Barset
	Phineas Finn
	The Prime Minister
	The Small House at Allington
	The Warden
	The Way We Live Now
Oscar Wilde	**Complete Short Fiction**
Mary Wollstonecraft	**A Vindication of the Rights of Woman**
	Mary and **Maria** (includes Mary Shelley's **Matilda**)
Dorothy and William Wordsworth	**Home at Grasmere**

PENGUIN STUDENT EDITIONS

Series Editors: Ronald Carter and John McRae

Penguin Student Editions have been specifically designed for readers
who are studying a text in detail. They include a helpful introduction
and explanatory notes, character sketches, a text summary, a chrono-
logy, language notes, a selection of questions and topics for discussion
and analysis, as well as suggestions for further reading.

Also published: